MINTA in SPITE of HERSELF

BOOK THREE
THE ELLSWORTH ASSORTMENT

CHRISTINA DUDLEY

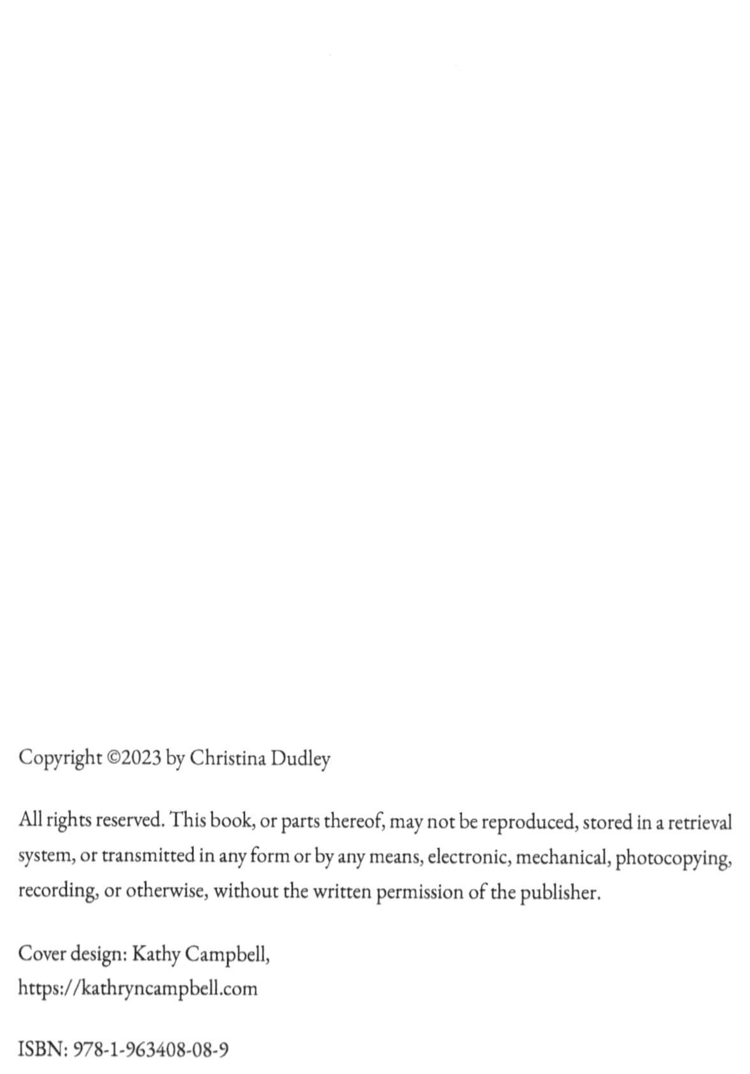

Cover design: Kathy Campbell,
https://kathryncampbell.com

ISBN: 978-1-963408-08-9

WILLIAM ELLSWORTH = (1) HENRIETTA BALDRIC   CHARLES ELLSWORTH = JEANNE MARTINEAU
= (2) CATHERINE CATCHWAY
= (3) ANNE FIELDING
= (4) MIRANDA GREGORY

BENJAMIN   AUSTIN

(1) FLORENCE = ROBERT FAIRCHILD

(1) LILY = SIMON KENNER

(2) TYRONE

(2) ARAMINTA

(3) BEATRICE

(4) WILLIAM

THE
Ellsworth Assortment

PROLOGUE

July 1801

This is Christian Charity indeed,
to become ones Brother's Keeper.
— Edward Pelling, ***A practical discourse upon charity***
***in its several branches* (1693)**

The culmination of the school year for pupils of Mrs. Turcotte's Seminary for Young Ladies was undoubtedly their attendance at the Winchester College Domum Ball. For it was at this ball, held in St. John's rooms in the Causeway, that the students of Mrs. Turcotte's displayed for the College alumni the graces, skills, manners, and deportment they acquired under her exacting eye. Every young lady who reached the age of fifteen was allowed to participate, and all lessons in the last days of June preceding the ball were given over entirely to dance and etiquette.

"No girl of mine will discredit this seminary through clumsiness, inattention or improper conduct," intoned Mrs. Turcotte, her spine straight as steel and her eyes sharp and tiny behind the thick lenses of her spectacles. Surveying the two lines of girls, the headmistress' scrutiny lingered on the end pair: Miss Araminta Ellsworth and Miss Agatha Weeks. Had those two not hailed from the wealthiest families in town, Mrs. Turcotte would long ago have recommended they be educated at home, for their tomboyish tendencies were her despair. Miss Agatha would not have been so bad if not for Miss Araminta, for Miss Agatha was a follower at heart. But she and Miss Araminta had been inseparable since they entered school at the age of eight. On that fateful day, some older girls—boarders—teased Aggie for her flyaway white-blonde hair, calling her "ghost" and "dandelion," only to have Araminta fly at them and kick them in the shins. Miss Horrocks, the teacher of the youngest children, was too panic-stricken to pull little Araminta off the bigger girls, and it had been the first—but not the last—time Mrs. Turcotte herself was summoned to deal with the matter. *I should have known from that moment*, the headmistress told herself a thousand times over the ensuing years. *But I thought she would grow out of it.*

Now here they were, big girls of fifteen, and Miss Araminta had not grown out of it at all. And if *she* still preferred sports to sewing, imprudence to Italian, and wildness to watercolors, there was never going to be any hope of Miss Agatha leading the way to demure young ladyhood.

Only look at them this morning! Miss Araminta's blonde hair would have been her boast, were it ever brushed and dressed properly, but what good was pretty hair when the girl was everlastingly rumpled from the sports she played, and when she always spoke with such unladylike confidence? In vain had Mrs. Turcotte reminded her of Cordelia, whose voice "was ever soft, gentle, and low—an excellent thing in woman." At least Miss Araminta's regular features were not marred this important week by any gashes such as she had suffered when her bowstring snapped in her face, or bruises, such as when Miss Aggie hit a cricket ball and Miss Araminta tripped and caught it with her eye, rather than with her hands. But what had happened to Miss Aggie's face—what *was* that red scrape on her cheek? And the lace hanging loose from her hem? Had the girl fallen down the stairs?

From long practice, Mrs. Turcotte shut her eyes and hardened her heart against these affronts and turned back to the accompanist. "All right, Miss Blinker. Let us have it once more from the beginning..."

Minta and Aggie were late for the Domum Ball.

It was not intentional, though they had spent that afternoon shooting turnips off the garden wall with Minta's bow and arrow (and just as often hitting the wall instead). Because neither girl boarded at the seminary, they had Mrs. Turcotte's permission to make their own way to St. John's assembly rooms in the evening, which meant they were excused from joining the orderly lines behind the headmistress and marching behind her up Southgate Street and along the High Street to the Causeway.

However, if Minta's older sister Miss Lily Ellsworth had not fortunately called them in, the pair might have missed the ball altogether.

"Heavens, you two! What are you still doing out here? Minta, didn't you tell Papa you needed the carriage at eight this evening? It's past six now, and you can hardly go to the Domum Ball looking like that."

"Looking like what?" demanded Minta.

"Looking like you always do," retorted Lily. "Like someone tied you to the back of the post coach and dragged you a good half-mile. Now come—if Monk is to do anything with your hair, she will need all the time she can get."

"It's easy for Lily to talk," grumbled Minta, while she and Aggie submitted to the maid's ministrations and the disapproving clicks of her tongue. "Lily is no good for anything but sitting indoors and sewing and being looked at. So *of course* she never gets rumpled or tears her dress or sits in anything that leaves a stain. She's just cross because she never went to a Domum Ball."

"Why didn't she?" asked Aggie, fiddling with the hairpin that was poking into her scalp. Monk slapped her hand away.

"Oh, a hundred reasons. Firstly, my older sisters never went to Turcotte's. They had governesses, you know."

"You mean the second and third Mrs. Ellsworths?"

Araminta grimaced at her friend. "Yes, you goose. My mama was their first governess and first stepmother, and my sister Beatrice's mama was their second governess and second stepmother. Bea's mama was always ill, so she could never chaperone Florence or Lily when they were at the age for it, and then she went and died, and we all had to don mourning for months. Now that it's finally all past and Papa has married again, Lily is itching to go to a ball."

"Perhaps she can attend the Domum Ball when your brother is Superannuate," suggested Aggie, referring to Araminta's twin Tyrone, who was in his fourth year at Winchester.

"In three years? I doubt it. Lily intends on going *now* to every last ball and assembly she can, beginning with the Race Ball. But the Race Ball is in a week and the Domum Ball is today, so it is very good fun to beat her to it."

Being driven in the carriage down the High Street by the chief Hollowgate groom Greaves in his livery was also very good fun, though Araminta insisted on having the hood down, which meant the hair which Monk had so carefully arranged was somewhat wind-blown by the time they drew up before St. John's rooms.

"How late do you think we are?" asked Aggie. "I don't see the other girls or old Turcotte anywhere."

Indeed, the only people to be seen in the Causeway were gentlemen of various ages, who naturally turned to inspect these new arrivals.

"Ooh," muttered Aggie, shrinking back. "I don't like it."

But Araminta returned stare for stare and wished she had a monocle like that one old fellow, or an ivory-tipped cane like that other—were all the gentlemen here going to be creaking old codgers? She knew that Election Week at Winchester College drew alumni from near and far, but some of these Wykehamists might have been 14th-century contemporaries of the revered bishop himself.

"I'm to fetch you both at eleven o'clock, miss," Greaves reminded her, as he opened the barouche door and lowered the step.

"Oh, Greaves," she protested, "can't we say midnight? Aggie and I don't want to be the first to leave."

"Miss Lily said you would try to get around me," the groom mourned. "And I was to say that she intends to come with me at eleven to drag you out herself."

With a roll of her eyes, Minta resigned herself to the early departure. The only thing more humiliating than being the first to leave would be being hunted down by her older sister. Thrusting her gloved hand in Greaves', she let him assist her to the pavement, followed by Aggie, and then the girls clasped each other's hands and Araminta lifted her chin and marched them through the loitering gentlemen toward the arched doorway.

The ballroom was on the first floor, but before they started up the stairs, a young man standing beside an alcove advanced toward them. "May I take your wraps?"

It was his very deep voice that made Araminta look at him. In fact, his voice was not the only extreme thing about him. His hair and eyes, for instance, were very dark and his skin very pale. And while Araminta was a strong and tall girl who often found herself looking gentlemen directly in the eyes, this young man was a deal taller. She did not have to tilt her head to look at him, to be sure, but she did have to adjust her gaze upward. If Araminta had been the sort of young lady who thought very much about whether young men were handsome or not, she might have noticed that he wasn't handsome so much as *arresting*. It might have been the intentness of his dark eyes. Or that he looked like he had more than a dash of foreignness in him. Or that his nose was quite long and a little crooked and his eyebrows arched, and he had unusually long lashes. In any event, Araminta was *not* that sort of young lady, and she hardly gave him a second glance. Until—

"Thank you," she said, untying her light cape while she looked up and down and all around at the stairs and the pink walls and white plasterwork and paintings of various noblemen and benefactors. But because she was looking everywhere but at what she was doing, when she whisked her cape off, it caught on her stepmother's pearl brooch, jerking it from her bodice (with a tearing sound) to soar through the air—

—Into the open palm of the young man.

"I say!" Araminta grinned. "Good catch."

He grinned back, holding the brooch out to her. "The result, I'm afraid, of countless days and years I spent as a junior in the blistering sun, forced to be long-stop to a fast bowler."

"Ah! I know exactly what you refer to. My brother Tyrone complained about all that watching out at cricket, his first few years. But he never got any good at fielding, I'm afraid."

"Tyrone? Are you Tyrone Ellsworth's sister, then?"

"I am. I'm Minta." She gave a bounce of a curtsey. "—Miss Araminta Ellsworth, and this is my friend Aggie—that is, Miss Agatha

Weeks. But if old Turcotte performs introductions upstairs, pretend like you've never seen us before because she'd be in a lather if she knew we'd gone and introduced ourselves."

"Silent as the grave," he promised.

"Don't go silent as the grave quite yet—because you didn't say your name. I want to tell Tyrone I met you."

The young man made a neat bow. "Nicholas Carlisle. As Ellsworth's sister, it probably wouldn't surprise you to learn that your brother made a few pence off me this year helping me get my Latin grammar right, now that he's Fifth Book."

"It doesn't surprise me one bit. Tyrone is an expert at anything found between the covers of a book. It's all he's good for, isn't it, Aggie?"

Her friend gave an anxious nod, glancing up the staircase again, in case Mrs. Turcotte came in search of them.

"Why have they got you taking wraps, then?" Araminta asked the young man. "I thought all the graduating boys were stewards at the supper."

"We will be. But this keeps me out of trouble."

"Speaking of trouble, Minta..." Aggie ventured, poking her friend.

"Oh, all right," Araminta sighed. She threw the young man a rueful look. "If old Turcotte doesn't lay eyes on us soon, she'll have the constabulary out for us."

"Can't have that," said Carlisle. "Farewell, then."

"Good-bye," she answered. "And mind you don't spill anything on us when you're serving the food."

"Only if you promise to stop flinging your jewelry at people. You could put someone's eye out."

When they appeared at the top of the stairs, Mrs. Turcotte did indeed swoop down upon them. "Where have you two been? Horrocks was waiting for you these twenty minutes until I finally told her I would find you. After all that I have told you about courtesy and punctuality—and what on earth have you already done to your gown, Miss Araminta?"

The reproaches must be borne with, and Minta was glad the public setting ensured Mrs. Turcotte must make them brief and deliver them behind a tight smile. But soon enough it was over, and then the poor headmistress must drag them around, introducing them to the various gentlemen whom the other pupils had already met. And though Araminta and Aggie were young and comparatively awkward, they found some dance partners among the prefects and seniors, if not the alumni.

"You know it's only because they know your brother that they ask you," said Head Girl Miss Caraway, one Minta would be most delighted to see gone after the end of the school year. "Otherwise they would not waste their time with fifteen-year-olds."

If scornful remarks and ostracism were the too-common weapons at a girls' school, Araminta had never proven a very satisfactory target, and she shrugged this arrow off in her usual manner. "I like to meet some of the boys I've heard my brother talk about."

"At least Miss Araminta does not shame us with her dancing," tittered Miss Caraway's primary sycophant Miss Emmeline Price. "It might be the only thing she has managed to learn."

"I do love to dance," agreed Minta. "It's almost as good as sport."

But Miss Caraway and Miss Emmeline had already lost interest in her, sailing off on the arms of their partners. Minta did think she would like to dance with Mr. Nicholas Carlisle, but she did not see him again until they were trooping into the coffee room for the supper, and then he was assigned a table in the opposite corner and was too occupied with carrying and serving food to be bothered, even if she could get up from her seat.

Mrs. Turcotte's pupils were all placed at adjacent tables, with Mrs. Turcotte and the teachers anchoring the ends, and somehow Minta and Aggie were stuck beside the tiresome Miss Caraway and her court.

"I hope Mr. Francis Taplin serves us!" hissed Miss Emmeline, making excited little fists when she saw the young man heading their way, his arms bearing a loaded silver tray.

Miss Caraway sat up straighter and inspected her reflection in the back of her spoon, but Miss Geraldine asked, "Who?"

"Mr. Francis Taplin," drawled Miss Caraway. "Did you not get to dance with him?"

"I didn't," admitted Miss Geraldine, abashed. She turned, craning her neck to have a look at the fellow.

"He asked Isabella first," Miss Emmeline informed her, indicating Miss Caraway. "And me second."

"And me never," sighed Miss Geraldine. "He's terribly handsome. But I think he won't be our steward." This, as he veered away from them to muted groans of disappointment.

It might have been her relative plainness or her precarious position in the group, but Minta thought Geraldine Farney the least tiresome of the Caraway clique. Therefore, if Geraldine sighed after a handsome gentleman, Minta was curious enough to inspect him herself.

She saw a tall and elegant young man with fair light brown hair and excellent tailoring. Agile, too, as he maneuvered between fellow stewards, chairs, and tables. The Caraway clique, as befitted the cream of Mrs. Turcotte's Seminary for Young Ladies, behaved admirably as Mr. Taplin served the luckier table. They neither giggled nor whispered to each other nor turned their heads, though those fortunate enough to be on the right side of the table observed him beneath their lashes. Thus it was that Minta, who had the effrontery to turn not only her head but her entire *person* to scrutinize him, stood forth in sharp contrast and caught the young man's eye.

He had a long, loose mouth which twisted in a knowing grin at her, and then one eyelid dropped in a wink.

Not the least bit embarrassed but entirely indignant, Minta's hand itched for something she might hurl at him, only to have that same hand pinched by Miss Caraway.

"It isn't polite to stare," the head girl reminded her coolly.

"That may be, but it wasn't polite of him to wink, either."

"He wouldn't have winked if he didn't think you were ill-mannered because you were *staring*."

Minta's mouth opened to retort, but Aggie kicked her under the table and shook her head. True enough—there was nothing to be gained by squabbling with Caraway.

When the food was served (the steward at their table being a round-faced, chubby senior whom Minta had danced with and whose name she had forgotten) and the distracting Winchester stewards gone away to enjoy their own meal, the Caraway clique settled down to serious gossip.

"I asked Mr. Taplin if he got a New College fellowship, and he said New College was for bores like his stepbrother, so he is going to Balliol as a commoner."

"Who's his stepbrother, then?"

"Mr. Nicholas Carlisle. Over there. That one."

Minta didn't turn around and stare this time, but she did sit up a little straighter and raise her eyebrows at Aggie.

"Oh! Him? How...foreign he looks. And he's not *nearly* as handsome."

"Oh, I don't know. You just don't like dark gentlemen. There's something...distinctive about him."

"Well, don't be getting ideas, Violet, because Mr. Carlisle hasn't any prospects. It seems Mr. Taplin's father married Mr. Carlisle's mother after she was widowed. She died shortly afterward, and Mr. Carlisle has been on the Taplins' hands ever since."

"Hadn't he anyone else to take him in?"

"Apparently not in Winchester! So it's a fortunate thing for Mr. Carlisle that he did succeed in getting a New College fellowship because he'll have to find a profession, having nothing to inherit."

"The Taplins' estate—Beaumond—it shares a boundary with ours," Aggie volunteered unexpectedly.

The eyes of the Caraway clique turned on the pale girl with her whitish hair. It was well known that the Weeks family had made its fortune in silk manufacturing and that Mr. Weeks had "aspirations." Not only had he purchased The Acres, but he built a fine modern home on the grounds beside the remnants of the abbey, keeping the ruin for its picturesque quality. What money could not do he hoped to accomplish through his three daughters, Miss Weeks, Miss Frederica, and Miss Agatha, all educated at Mrs. Turcotte's, all well-portioned, and all expected to marry into the more established county families. At least, Miss Weeks and Miss Frederica were expected to. No one knew really what to expect of white-haired, sport-mad Aggie, forever getting into scrapes with Araminta Ellsworth.

"Beaumond borders The Acres?" Miss Caraway asked with seeming indifference.

"It does."

"Then have you ever seen Mr. Taplin when you were at home?" pressed Miss Emmeline, too curious to follow Miss Caraway's disdainful lead.

"I haven't," admitted Aggie. But when the older girls lost interest and shrugged she added, "But my papa has met with the senior Mr. Taplin before. To talk business or something."

This vague boast met with the scorn it deserved, and no more attention was given to the two younger girls. Nor did Miss Caraway's court discuss Mr. Francis Taplin again, but instead traded observations on some of the alumni they had met and danced with, to Minta's and Aggie's boredom.

By the time the Winchester prefects and seniors returned to clear away the dishes and cutlery and serve the tea, Minta was fidgeting with impatience. "It's nearly eleven! We won't get to dance again, just like I feared."

"Do you think Lily meant her threat?" Aggie asked. "If we don't come down, will she come after us?"

"Probably. But I wish it were permissible for girls to ask young men to dance. If it were, I'd go and ask that Mr. Brigg before we left. Tyrone said he was the worst prefect, always beating and bullying."

"Then whyever would you want to dance with him?"

"To step on his feet, of course! Maybe even kick him in the shins, if I could pass it off as a dance step. I kept looking his way to hint that he should come and ask me to partner him, but he never did."

"Oh, Minta, you probably alarmed him. If you wanted him to come over, you should have done like Caraway and her clique do. I was watching them tonight, and they do a lot of ducking their heads and fluttering their lashes and grinning like fools behind their fans, and the men come right over."

"Pah! In that case, I don't think even kicking Brigg would compensate for acting so silly. Not that it matters—look at the clock. If they don't wind this supper up, Lily will be up the stairs to drag us out by our ears!"

Araminta wasn't far wrong. By the time the ball guests were rising from their seats, she and Aggie had to waste their remaining seven minutes waiting for Mrs. Turcotte to finish whatever she was saying to the college warden so they could take their leave of her.

"Wasn't she delighted to see us go!" Minta laughed as they descended the stairs once more. "That was the happiest she looked all evening."

"And other than arriving a little late, we were so well-behaved," Aggie agreed. "It really isn't fair that now she just *expects* us to make trouble."

They slid to a halt before the alcove, glancing around for Mr. Nicholas Carlisle to fetch them their wraps, but there was no sign of him.

"I'll get them," said Minta. "He's probably up dancing, since he didn't get to before." Hoisting herself onto the table, she spun on her bottom, swinging her legs over, and skipped into the room which had been curtained off as a closet.

"Oof!" It was dark behind the curtain, and she unexpectedly ran into an obstacle. An obstacle which felt remarkably like two people embracing.

There was a low, silky laugh. "One of your friends, my dear? Well—the more, the merrier."

And then, before Minta could register this turn of events, she felt an arm slip about her waist and a hand run down her backside!

"Let go of me!"

She didn't think—she simply punched. Instantly she was released, as whoever it was that had grabbed her gave a *whoof* and fell back far enough for Minta to deliver the kick to the shins she had intended for Mr. Briggs.

"Minta!" cried Aggie, scrambling over the table herself and whipping the curtain aside. Light flooded in, Aggie gawping at the sight that met her eyes. For there was Minta, eyes blazing and arms akimbo, glowering at none other than Mr. Francis Taplin, who was hopping on one foot and clutching his injured limb to him, while a serving maid looked from one to the other in amazement.

"Are you all right, Minta?" Aggie gasped.

"Is *she* all right?" hissed Mr. Taplin.

"*You* are no gentleman!" declared Araminta, her breast still heaving with outrage. She spied her cape over his shoulder but dreaded further contact with him. "Stand aside, sir, and don't think to touch me again!"

"I never thought to touch you in the first place," he growled.

"Then you oughtn't to have done it without thinking," she retorted.

"Good Lord, Francis—what's amiss?" came a very deep voice that Minta remembered.

"Nothing, nothing," sighed Mr. Taplin. "Nothing that need concern you, Nick. I apologize to you, Miss—Miss—" but as Minta had no intention of telling him her name, he was forced to continue. "Well—I beg your pardon. An honest mistake. And now, my fair companion and I will continue our—assignation—elsewhere. Pardon us."

He made a smart little bow and took the maid by the hand to lead her out of the closet, Araminta noting with satisfaction that he limped slightly. With any luck he would get a deep bruise that went every shade of blue, black, green, and purple.

"I'm afraid to ask," said Nicholas Carlisle when his brother was gone.

But Minta snatched up her cape and Aggie's. And this time, instead of climbing over the table, she shoved it aside.

"Then don't."

Three Years Later

July 1804

Chapter One

If we do meet again, why, we shall smile.
— Shakespeare, *Julius Caesar* V.i.2470 (1599)

The ball came out of nowhere and struck him in the calf. Even through the layers of his old robe and his trousers it stung, eliciting from Carlisle an involuntary curse.

"Oop! My apologies, sir," a cheerful voice accosted him, and he turned with a frown to see not a young Winchester junior as he expected, but rather a young lady with mussed hair and wrinkly gown and the unmistakable glow of perspiration. She scooped up the ball, planted her feet and threw a perfect *bullet* some distance across the Meads, to be caught by an equally unlikely feminine partner, whose white-blonde hair was nearly all tumbled down her back.

"Hold on a moment," Carlisle muttered, half to himself, memory stirring. "I *know* you."

"I doubt it," said the girl, not even glancing at him as she held up her hands to receive the next throw. But as the ball sailed through the warm July air, Carlisle's hand flashed out, and he snatched it an instant before it reached her.

"You give that back," she ordered, turning on him smartly. "Though I'll admit it was a nice catch."

"The brooch," he said, still holding the ball above her head. "You were the young lady with the brooch."

She stared at him some moments, and then her face lit with delight. "Ah! Your voice! You do know me! And I know you—you were the young man who caught my brooch when it ripped from my bodice at the Domum Ball, oh—a hundred years ago or so."

"Has it been that long already?" he asked dryly.

"It seems that long. You see, Aggie and I—you remember Miss Agatha Weeks, don't you?" (Pointing, and then beckoning her friend over.) "Aggie and I were *not encouraged* by old Turcotte to attend another Domum Ball since that one when we were fifteen, but we're going to this year's because my twin brother Tyrone passed his examinations and made the Roll for New College."

Carlisle gave a bow. "I congratulate him. And I suspect, if you are twins, I should congratulate you as well on passing out of school...?"

This made her laugh. "Yes, but the one you really ought to congratulate is old Turcotte. She won't be sorry to see the back of me, I imagine, nor Aggie. Aggie—" calling to her approaching friend "—you remember this fellow? We met him forever and ever ago at our first and penultimate Domum Ball."

"Nicholas Carlisle," he prompted.

Miss Agatha smiled politely. "Minta and I were debarred from attending thereafter because we turned up late."

"No, no," put in Minta. "Turcotte might have got over that, except for the row in the closet with that rogue of a young man—" she broke off abruptly, even as Carlisle said, "You mean my stepbrother?"

Araminta clapped a palm to her forehead. "The dickens!—I forgot that part. Yes. Your stepbrother it was. Pardon me, Mr. Carlisle. It was all years ago, at any rate."

"A century, I believe you said it was."

"—Too long ago to be worth going on about, is what I mean. Let's change the subject. Do you come back every year to the school for Election Week festivities?"

He couldn't help grinning at her forthrightness and lack of subtlety, but he answered, "In truth, this is the first time I have."

"Really? Your first time back for Election Week or your first time back to Winchester at all?"

"Both. My first time back to the school *and* the city. I've been at New College myself, you know."

"But what about the vacations?"

A shadow crossed his face. "I spent them in London. Visiting an uncle."

"Ooh. I wish I had an uncle in London. But mine lives nowhere more exciting than St. Thomas Street. You remember him—Charles Ellsworth—an assistant master at College in mathematics."

"Of course I do. A great favorite with all the Wykehamists."

"Yes, he is, and I will tell him you said so. Where does your uncle live in London, then?"

"Cornhill."

Now neither Araminta nor Aggie had much idea of the geography of the capital, so Carlisle need not have feared any snobbery on their part. In fact, Araminta was on the point of asking whether they grew corn in Cornhill, when she found herself clutched around the knees by a pair of pudgy arms.

"Ah, Willsie." Bending down, she hoisted the tow-headed toddling boy up, giving him an intermediary swing which made him chortle with joy. "My baby brother, whom my baby sister was supposed to be watching over."

"And I am watching over him," declared a younger girl with light brown hair, hustling over to them. She was as neat as her older sister was disheveled. "But you know how Willie can run."

"Mr. Carlisle, allow me to introduce my sister Miss Beatrice Ellsworth and my little brother Mr. William Ellsworth, Junior. Or Willsie." She took the little boy's plump arm and made him wave.

Carlisle made another bow. It had been a long time, but anyone who hailed from Winchester or its environs knew of the Ellsworths of Hollowgate: of wealthy Mr. William Ellsworth, his four successive wives, and his five—now *six*—children by those women. The details were hazy (impossible that they shouldn't be), but he knew the Miss Ellsworth he addressed now was not the oldest. The children, despite their different mothers, were all close, and Carlisle wondered with a pang what that must be like. In his own family, matters were quite different.

"So, if this is the first time you've returned," resumed Araminta, still joggling her little brother to keep him entertained, "do you find it much changed?"

He shook his head. "There are more soldiers, perhaps, now that the peace has ended."

"Yes!" A martial and unladylike fire lit her eyes. "Is that why you've come back? You've purchased a commission?"

A sore subject at Beaumond, where Carlisle's stepfather and stepbrother lived, but Miss Ellsworth would have no notion of that. She and her friend Miss Agatha seemed to be sharing a secret joke, and Carlisle supposed they were at the age to find men in uniform appealing.

He replied merely, "No. Quite the opposite. I'm here to learn to be a doctor. Mr. Beckford has agreed to take me on. Do you know him?"

"Of course we do!" she cried. "It was Mr. Beckford who brought each one of us into the world, from my oldest sister Florence down to little Willsie here. And didn't he assist your mother as well, Aggie?"

"He did. He delivered all three of us. My sisters and me, that is."

"I love Mr. Beckford," spoke up young Miss Beatrice solemnly. She did indeed and had, ever since she and their older sister Lily had been accosted in Cock Lane years earlier, and the doctor had come to their aid along with Lily's now husband.

While Carlisle could not guess the reason for Miss Beatrice's earnestness, he appreciated these encomiums to his future mentor, having not received much encouragement at Beaumond.

"How convenient for you, Mr. Carlisle," Miss Ellsworth rejoined, "to find a doctor to learn from so near to your home. I don't suppose Beaumond is more than a ten-minute walk, if you took the footpath from Weeke."

"That's right. I imagine I will become very familiar with the footpath from Weeke."

"Minta! Minta!" a voice called, and the group turned to see a tall, pale, dark-haired young woman beckoning as she strode over, her own young son in tow. "Gracious—hadn't you and Aggie better prepare for the Domum Ball? It will take some doing, it appears."

"Oh, Flossie—in a little while," coaxed Miss Ellsworth. "I was just about to ask Mr. Carlisle here if he wanted to play at catch-ball with Aggie and me. This is Mr. Carlisle." She pointed. "Mr. Carlisle, this is my oldest sister Mrs. Robert Fairchild, and my nephew Peter." So saying, she set Willie down. "Go on, Wills—play with your nephew Peter for a minute."

"How do you do, Mr. Carlisle." But Florence was not to be deterred. "I beg you will excuse them, sir—but, Minta, did you or did you not give Mrs. Turcotte your solemn oath that, in return for her allowing you and Aggie to attend the ball again, you would be on your best behavior?"

"I did not give any 'solemn oath,'" protested her sister, "and I don't care about that silly old ball any more than I ever did."

"Well, I care that this is my first time chaperoning you, and I won't have my Robert embarrassed in front of the other Wykehamists by his harum-scarum sister-in-law, who looks like she just crawled from under a haystack."

Araminta swelled in preparation of making an indignant reply, but Carlisle hastily interjected. "I would have to refuse your kind offer at catch-ball in any event, Miss Ellsworth. You see how everyone is adjourning to the Chamber quadrangle for more singing of the Domum. But perhaps you and Miss Agatha would be kind enough to save me a dance this evening?"

"*More* singing?" repeated Minta in disgust, not to be distracted by his polite invitation. "Everyone is practically hoarse from singing that silly song over and over at the top of their lungs, just so they can be heard over the military band."

"You not being an old Wykehamist yourself, Miss Ellsworth, you cannot imagine how the Domum tugs at the heart-strings."

"No, I don't suppose I can." But Aggie was pinching her arm, and Florence was pressing her lips together, and Beatrice looked somewhat knocked up by the heat, so Minta submitted with poor grace. "Very well. Home to Hollowgate, that I may not shame my brother-in-law. We will speak with you later, Mr. Carlisle—if you have any voice left after all those Domums."

Carlisle watched the little party go, feeling unexpectedly heartened, before turning to look for his stepbrother. Francis being nowhere in sight, however, he joined a clutch of former fellow pupils to make his way back to the Chamber quad.

His homecoming at the beginning of the week had not held any surprises. It had disappointed him, in fact, by its predictability. No one met the coach from London, and Carlisle was left to shoulder his satchel and walk to Beaumond, after leaving instructions for his trunk to be retrieved later from the George. While Beaumond was neither as grand as Hollowgate nor as modern as The Acres, it had ever been a well-tended, respectable estate, its square and unexceptionable house set amidst a park and trailing the usual appurtenances of dower house, lodge, stables, gardens, and tenant farms. He and his mother had come there when he was four, but, in all the years since, and especially after his mother's death, he had never felt he belonged. His stepfather was kind—fond, even—but Carlisle was too aware of his position as the stepson, the interloper. The one who had no real place there except out of charity.

"Mr. Carlisle! The sight of you is good for sore eyes," declared the butler Hemings, and his opinion was echoed by the housekeeper, several footmen, and a maid or two. "But where is your baggage? Should I dispatch a pair of grooms for the trunk?"

"Let it rest at the George for now," Carlisle answered. "Where are my stepfather and Mr. Francis?"

"Oh—both in Mr. Taplin's study, sir, along with Mr. West." Hemings leaned closer to add, "Begging your pardon, but I believe Mr. Francis is—er—*in the suds* again."

Carlisle grimaced but managed to keep back, *Well, what else is new?* "I'll announce myself then," he said.

Squaring his shoulders, he knocked at the study door. If Mr. West the family attorney was there, Francis' trouble must be serious.

"Nicholas." His stepfather John Taplin half rose from behind his desk, resting his not inconsiderable weight on his knuckles. "My boy. You've come back at last." The wheeziness and effort of his speech made Carlisle frown. Could the man truly have aged so much in three years? But he stepped forward to shake his stepfather's hand before bowing to the attorney Mr. West and nodding toward Francis, who lounged in an armchair by the window, one leg hooked over the armrest, booted foot swinging.

"You find us mid-sermon," drawled Francis. "Or is it no longer considered a sermon if it is delivered by two speakers?"

"Should I return another time?" asked Carlisle.

"Yes," said his stepbrother.

"No, no," said his stepfather. He sighed and gestured at the unoccupied armchair beside Francis. "Nicholas had better hear this too."

"Why?" demanded Francis, unhooking his leg and sitting forward. "What would Nick care about Beaumond mortgages? He has no inheritance in the place. He's going to be a *doctor*, God help us! Thrown in his lot with his Cheapside-living, ointment-peddling apothecary of an uncle."

"And if Nicholas has had to seek a profession, whose fault is that?" countered his father, now rapping those same knuckles on the desk.

"Well, why can't you be don, Nick? Or a cleric? Or—or—a lawyer, if you must—" (This with a curt nod at Mr. West, who merely raised an eyebrow in response.) "Why must you insist on a profession so low and grubbing and ungentlemanlike?"

"Mr. Beckford is a gentleman," replied Carlisle, his chest tightening as it always did when his stepbrother goaded him.

Taplin made a scoffing sound. "Not one worthy of calling at Beaumond, unless someone has taken ill. If you had to insist on becoming a doctor, why could you not stay in London, instead of coming to haunt us in Winchester?"

"As I have explained, London is a great deal more expensive, and my allowance will stretch further in Winchester."

"You might have lived with the ointment peddler at very little expense."

"My *uncle* Mr. Blair did indeed offer," returned Carlisle, "but having spent my vacations in London the past few years, I have learned to prefer a quieter setting. Moreover, I have many fond memories of Winchester, both town and gown."

"And I have fond memories of *you*," sighed his stepfather. "You are more than welcome at Beaumond again."

"Thank you, Father. But, as I have said, I know my choice of profession is—a step down—in the world, and I don't wish to...cast any shadows on Beaumond or the Taplins as I make my way."

"As if you living with Beckford, concocting potions and compounding medicines in his back room, not a mile from Beaumond, will not cast any shadow upon us," protested Francis.

"In that respect I do regret Mr. Beckford is so near," Carlisle conceded. "But I had few other connections to draw upon, in requesting that someone take me under his wing."

"Don't listen to your brother," his stepfather rejoined. "You will live at Beaumond again. It is ridiculous for you to think of boarding with the doctor. You have lived all these years as a gentleman's son, and you may continue to claim the privileges of one, as far as I am concerned. Call for the carriage, host suppers at Beaumond, accompany me or your brother to various appropriate activities and entertainments." The senior Taplin shook his head in regret. "I meant you to have some independence, Nicholas. Beaumond for

Francis and an independence for you, but circumstances have not allowed—"

"Oh, say it, Father," Taplin interrupted. "Had I not been so extravagant—had I not lived like the gentleman I am, like any young man in my position is expected to—some stipend could have been spared for Nick."

"Son, if you do not change your ways, Nicholas' independence will not be the only thing gone by the wayside!"

"And...we pick up with the sermon again." He gave his stepbrother a droll wink. "You'll see I may not know how to make medicine, Nick, but I can swallow my dose with the best of them. Let us have it all said, Father. I am at leisure."

"Do you not ask why I have summoned Mr. West?"

"I suppose to deal with money matters."

"Yes. We must mortgage another portion of the estate, and if we are not careful—if *you* do not take measures, my son—soon Beaumond will belong more to our neighbor than to the Taplins."

"I don't see why Weeks should be so greedy," complained Taplin. "He already has The Acres, so what does he want with Beaumond? But I suppose buying us out would be a feather in his cap. Silk manufacturer, wasn't he?"

"May it never come to 'buying us out,' whatever Weeks' reasons," John Taplin said darkly. "My son, whether Beaumond continues in the Taplin family or whether we are ruined all depends now on what you choose to do."

"Yes, yes, and I do not think you justified in glowering at me, when I consider all I have already done at your behest. I *hear* you, sir. My racehorse and my hunter are gone—"

"Because you lost them gambling!"

"They are gone, in any event, and I will hold off on replacing them. And since I am to spend the next six months at least confined to home, I have given my *chère amie* an emerald necklace and her *nunc dimittis*. Quite a sacrifice on my part, for her beauty was such that she has already been snapped up by a marquess, and I don't know whether to be insulted by her recovery or flattered to have preceded a peer of the realm. Yes, sir, I don't know what more you would have of me. You still refuse to purchase me an officer's commission, I assume."

"I *do* refuse. I think you far more likely to find yourself in debt again if you are not under my eye, even if we could afford the commission at present."

"Then these measures I have taken will have to do," shrugged Taplin.

"Certainly your...efforts will help stanch the flow," murmured Mr. West in his peculiar hissy voice.

"But they will not refill the coffers, Francis, my boy." The older man folded his hands together, his gaze drifting to the window.

"Pardon me, but how can they not, sir? Is that not how it works? I spend less; we continue to collect rents; the situation improves."

"But given how much of the estate is now mortgaged, and how many of those rents no longer come to us, those measures are not enough. We must pay Weeks his interest, moreover, and we cannot reduce our expenses to *nothing*."

"How long would it take to be out of debt?" Taplin turned on the attorney. "If I mind my p's and q's?"

Mr. West shook his head slowly. "If no more of Beaumond was mortgaged, perhaps a generation."

Both young men stared, Carlisle dismayed and Taplin outraged.

"A generation!"

"Mr. West tells me we must have an influx of money," resumed his father, "if we hope to be free sooner."

"And where will this influx come from?"

"Isn't it plain?" His father gave a heavy sigh. "You must marry, Francis. And marry well. That is to say, you must marry money."

Taplin's handsome face distorted with disgust. "Marry?"

"It was my understanding you were fond enough of women," said John Taplin dryly. "And of money, for that matter. Or at least the spending of it."

"But a wife!" There was a long silence. Taplin swung his leg over the armrest again, scowling and picking at the brocade upholstery.

"A wealthy wife might not only save Beaumond, but also restore that town life you so enjoyed."

Restlessly, the handsome young man sprang up and paced the study. "So she might." He favored his father with a bitter smile. "I hadn't really thought of getting shackled so soon, but now I am to hurl myself at the nearest creature with a generous portion? Might it not wait until next season in London then? More heiresses to be found there, you know."

His father's eyes narrowed, and he took another heavy breath. "You did not seem eager when in town to spend your time in the best company."

"Well, a man must sow his oats."

"As Mr. Carlisle observed, London is an expensive place for rich and humble alike," suggested the attorney Mr. West. "There are indeed more heiresses to be found in London, but the initial outlay for yourself would be higher as well: a townhouse rental or a hotel; club dues; subscriptions...additional temptations of city life."

"Which you already discovered," his father muttered.

Taplin raised a hand. "Let me forestall this portion of the lecture, at least, for I see where it tends. I do not deny I did not live as *cheaply* as Nick in town—"

"Nor did you at Oxford." John Taplin laid a flat palm atop the blue bag his attorney had brought. "I have it all here. All the correspondence and accounts of your last several years."

"—Yes, please also spare me the bit on how I should have got a New College fellowship, had I worked as hard at Winchester as dear Nick. Sterling Nick. Faultless Nick. If only Nick had been your true son, sir, and not your stepson. If only Nick had been the heir to Beaumond, how glorious would the future be."

"Excuse me," said Carlisle, rising.

"No, do stay. Don't be so modest when you hear praise of yourself," Taplin mocked.

"This has nothing to do with your brother," roared his father, losing his temper at last and slamming his hand down on that same blue bag. "And it is time you take responsibility for your own actions.

You alone have endangered the family seat and your own future, and you alone can remedy it. You need to marry money and to do it as quickly and as inexpensively as possible. Winchester is full of suitable women under the age of five-and-thirty, and may God grant that one of them of sufficient fortune will be willing, for the sake of an ancient name and a fair property, to burden herself with a charming, handsome spendthrift."

"Five-and-thirty?" gasped Taplin.

His father fixed him with a beady eye. "Beggars should be no choosers. A woman of forty even, if she be fool enough."

Taplin slumped in his seat. "Sir! If this paragon were forty, you might do well to woo her yourself."

"Watch yourself, young man, or I just might."

Chapter Two

"A lovely sight. Lovely," pronounced Mr. William Ellsworth, beaming upon them in the entrance hall of Hollowgate. His wife, his eldest daughter Florence, and the maid Monk were applying the finishing touches to Araminta, who resignedly kept her mouth shut as they fiddled and fussed, while Beatrice and Willie perched on the staircase watching.

"It's too bad Lily can't see you before you step out the door," Florence teased, "for the effect is sure to be spoiled before we reach St. John's rooms." But their sister Lily was expecting her first child and wasn't venturing far from the Kenners' home in the cathedral close these days.

Minta wore white—a new dress, which she likely would not be able to wear more than this once, as she was certain to spill tea on it or tread on the hem as she danced. Her blonde hair was dressed and curled and wound with one of Lily's blue ribbons, and Florence had brought her new gloves because every other one of Minta's was stained or had a hole in the first finger or was missing its match. Not many beside her father might call her "lovely," for Araminta Ellsworth was neither delicate like Florence, nor pleasantly rounded and beautiful like Lily, but she was healthy and strapping—if one was not daunted by such things—with pleasing, regular features.

"I'll make Tyrone dance with me twice," said Minta, "so that takes care of two of them."

"And Robert will dance with you twice," Florence offered up her husband. Robert Fairchild had not attended the Domum Ball since he himself was Superannuate, but for Minta's sake the Fairchilds would go as chaperones. "So that's four of them settled."

"Oh! And that Mr. Carlisle I saw again in Meads asked to partner Aggie and me, so that's one more, if he remembers. Then the rest of the time I will stand around and talk to Aggie, I suppose, along with weathering old Turcotte's frowns for the last time."

"Just don't *move* when you're not dancing," Beatrice piped up, "and Turcotte'll have nothing to frown about."

This made Minta roll her eyes, but Florence laughed. "That reminds me—Lily did tell me to remind you not to shout or brag or tell any of your partners that you could do something better than he could."

"Or even that you could do it at *all*, depending on what it is," added Beatrice.

But this was too much for Minta. "Great guns! The way you all carry on, you would think I cared a straw for what any of the gentlemen think. And as for all this advice—Lily is hardly one to talk—she may not have shouted or bragged, but she was always thinking herself cleverer than everyone else. And as for you, Bea, a ten-year-old would do better to spare her breath to cool her porridge."

St. John's rooms were much as Minta remembered from years earlier. There was the same collection of older alumni scattered outside (or at least they looked the same, to her young eyes), and from the windows and arched door the same light spilling out and hum of voices and sound of musicians tuning. This time she had her brother-in-law's arm to place her hand on, and she noted with a curl of her lip that Robert Fairchild's presence forestalled the scrutiny she and Aggie had drawn when they were fifteen. But because Fairchild was himself an old Wykehamist, it took the party a few minutes to get in the door because of the several times he was hailed and must stop to make introductions. Everyone she met asked both her and Florence for dances, no matter his age, which solved *that* problem, and she supposed with a smothered sigh that old partners were better than no partners at all.

But where were Aggie and Tyrone?

The latter was found soon enough, he having been assigned the task of taking the guests' wraps and cloaks as Nicholas Carlisle had done three years earlier, but after working out in which dances he would do his duty by his sisters, they passed onward up the staircase.

The assembly room was a goodly size, some sixty feet in length, and, if not for Aggie's white-blonde hair, Araminta would think later, she might never have recognized her dearest friend.

It was Aggie's oldest sister Mrs. King whom Araminta spied first, standing beside the balding, bespectacled fellow of the college she had married. Aggie's mother having accompanied an aged, asthmatic aunt to the seaside in June, it was Aggie's sisters who must take up chaperoning duties of their youngest sibling. The former Miss Weeks had distinctive dark-gold hair and a tendency to reveal her prominent two front teeth when she smiled or laughed (as she was doing at that moment). And there on Mrs. King's far side was the person who must be Aggie but who looked more like—well—like a princess!

Princess might be an exaggeration, but Minta stared nonetheless. For Aggie's hair was curled and shining and glossy and tidy and piled atop her head, with nary a stray wisp, much less any strand plastered to her forehead or neck with perspiration. Her dress and gloves, like Minta's, were white and probably equally new, and Minta couldn't help but think, *Great guns! Where did Aggie get that bosom? Has she had it all along?*

But what made Aggie most unrecognizable of all was the expression on her face, one Minta had never before seen there and could hardly put a name to. Was it...spellbound? Blank? Fatuous? *Besotted?*

Even as the Fairchilds and Minta made their slow and decorous way across the rose ballroom under the eye of Lely's Charles II, and even as they paused again to greet others and make introductions, Minta's mind was turning over this puzzle. She kept waiting for Aggie to look over and drop her silly look and come to meet them, but Aggie did not, and finally Minta followed her friend's vacant gaze by triangulation as it drifted hither and thither, from group to group in the assembly room, only to discover the one common element.

Mr. Francis Taplin.

At least, Minta was fairly certain it was Mr. Francis Taplin. Some memories and faces might fade with time, but she was not likely to forget her encounter with Mr. Taplin at the previous Domum Ball and his hand on her backside! Whatever was Aggie watching him for?

"Hm," murmured her brother-in-law a minute later. "Taplin."

"Ah," said Florence. "Mr. Taplin."

From their subdued tones Minta understood that the man had been a topic of discussion between them at some point.

"Will he expect you to greet him?" Florence asked.

"If he falls in our way naturally," answered her husband. "I've been introduced to him, of course, but he's West's client."

Minta shuddered, having not the least desire to be around if Mr. Taplin fell in their way naturally. "I'm going to talk to Aggie," she told her sister.

"All right, dearest. Though I hardly recognize her this evening, she looks so nice and tidy." There was a mirthful gleam in Flossie's grey eyes when she added, "I suspect she might say the same of you."

She might, Minta thought with a grimace, if she ever managed to tear her eyes away from Mr. Taplin.

"Flossie says you look nice and tidy," Minta reported when she reached her friend.

Aggie appeared to be waking from a dream. "Did she really?" she asked hopefully. "Phronsie lent me her maid, and I am forbidden to drink anything but water all evening, lest I spill on my new dress."

"It might be better if you didn't eat, either," Mrs. King giggled, showing her two front teeth. "And it wouldn't hurt if you and Miss Ellsworth kept your distance from each other. This is no time for scrapes, Aggie. Just try to hold still until Mr. King can lead you safely into the first dance."

Aggie sighed. "Yes, Phronsie."

"Have *you* got a partner for the first dance, Miss Ellsworth?" Mrs. King asked.

"Mr. Fairchild, my own brother-in-law."

"Perfect. Ah! And don't look now, but I see Mr. Francis Taplin making his way over."

This observation met with two rather different responses. Aggie went positively scarlet, her breath going shallow as she wrung her gloved hands. The blood rushed to Minta's face as well, and sparks fairly flew from her ordinarily mild eyes. She too clenched her hands—but into fists.

"I don't want to meet that person again," she hissed to Aggie. "Let's run off and get some lemonade."

But Aggie stood stock still and didn't seem to have heard her.

Fine.

Whatever was occupying her friend, Minta did not intend to wait around. Spinning about, she intended to march right back to Florence and Robert, but instead marched straight into Mr. Francis Taplin.

"*Whoof,*" Mr. Taplin huffed, for the second time in as many meetings with Miss Araminta Ellsworth. Her clenched fist had caught him emphatically in the midsection.

"Oh, dear me!" gasped Mrs. King, her eyes wide and her front teeth appearing in a nervous giggle. "Miss Ellsworth, do be cautious."

Wincing, Mr. Taplin straightened, an it's-no-matter smile pasted unsuccessfully on his handsome face. "Mr. King," he wheezed. Flushing, he cleared his throat and tried again. "Mr. King. I came this direction in hopes of being introduced to your family."

"Taplin," bowed the Winchester College fellow. He pushed up his spectacles. "A pleasure to see you again this Election Week. May I present to you my wife Mrs. King and her youngest sister Miss Agatha Weeks, as well as Miss Agatha's dear friend Miss Ellsworth."

"Sorry about the fist in the gut," muttered Minta, with what sincerity she could muster. There did not seem to be any glint of recognition or awareness in Mr. Taplin's eye, which somehow added to her annoyance. Did he run his hands over so many young ladies' backsides that they blurred in his mind? Well, this was one young lady who remembered *him* and who had no desire to be in his presence a moment longer than necessary. With punishing coolness, she made a curt curtsey, but the effect was entirely ruined when she unfortunately managed to step on her hem, so that in springing back up there was a fatal ripping sound. Pretending not to hear it, Minta masked it with a cough. Then she added something unintelligible about rejoining the Fairchilds and took herself off as speedily as she could.

Before she was halfway back across the room, however, Minta was abruptly jerked to a halt and—just as abruptly—set free, albeit with another, longer, even dreadfuller tearing noise.

"Blast!" came a familiar deep voice. "I beg your pardon."

Slowly, still twitching as she pictured what Florence was going to say about the damage to her new dress, Minta turned to see Mr. Carlisle bending to retrieve what looked like a banner of lace and muslin. When he stood again, holding up the material in dismay, a snort escaped her. "Are you hanging out a white flag? There is no call for surrender, sir. It appears you won the battle."

"It appears I did," he answered, making his bow and smiling. "I'm glad it was you, Miss Ellsworth. Other young ladies here might not joke with me if they were the ones to suffer from my heedlessness. There is one surrender I do owe you, however—that of your...train?...to your custody." He passed it to her with a rueful smile. "I'm sorry. I didn't see it trailing behind you. I'm afraid I'm something of a dunce at ladies' fashions."

That made Minta laugh. "You *are* a dunce if you think my dress had a train. This is St. John's assembly room, not the court of St. James. You only managed to rip the part of my skirt which was already dragging on the floor because I tore it myself in a fit of clumsiness. When I was making my curtsey to your brother, as a matter of fact. But I will happily blame it all on you because my sister Flossie will not be pleased when she sees the state I'm in!"

"Mrs. Fairchild appears a gentle enough person."

"Oh, she is," replied Minta cheerfully. "She'll cluck at me some while she sews me up, and she won't even look daggers at *you* for your part in it, but it'll be a nuisance all the same. Now, if it had been my sister Lily...Why then, I might have tried to repair it myself, to avoid the rough side of her tongue."

He was grinning at her now, and she noticed his mouth was slightly crooked beneath his long nose, which was itself slightly crooked, but it all seemed to balance out in a way she found quite pleasing.

"You'll likely miss the first dance. Who was your promised partner, Miss Ellsworth?"

"Oh, Flossie's husband Robert, so it's no calamity."

"Suppose it takes longer than one dance to fix things?"

"Well, then I might miss my chance to stand up with the other old buffers I have lined up. Mr. Fairchild is an attorney, you know, in addition to being an old Wykehamist like yourself. But he's an *older* old Wykehamist—maybe even as old as thirty now—so everyone who stopped us on the way inside was at least eight-and-twenty but far more likely to be eight-and-seventy!"

He gave a low whistle. "Any eight-and-seventy-year-old who still has the agility to trip it as he goes 'on the light fantastick toe' deserves your respect, Miss Ellsworth, not your derision."

This drew another laugh, which made those nearby glance over. "Very well, very well," she conceded. "I have a habit of exaggerating, as my family will tell you. Perhaps the oldest of my proposed partners is closer to eight-and-*forty*. Old enough to be a father or an uncle, but probably not a grandfather or great uncle. And I shouldn't make fun because it was very polite of them to ask me. I can dance just fine, but my sisters do tell me I'm a madcap."

Mr. Carlisle considered her musingly. (Minta was by this point winding her torn remnant in and out between the fingers of one hand.) He suspected the gentlemen she complained of were motivated by more than mere courtesy because she was, despite the depredations to her dress, looking remarkably well.

"I hope in granting these dances right and left, Miss Ellsworth, you haven't forgotten I claimed one from you and one from Miss Agatha."

The light in Minta's face faded, and she glanced back toward her friend. "I haven't forgotten." Stupid Mr. Taplin was still speaking with the Kings, and Aggie was still gawping at him! What on earth was happening? Did Aggie not remember what they had caught that Mr. Taplin doing, three years ago? Did she not remember his insult to her *dearest friend*?

"Yes, please do come and claim your dance, Mr. Carlisle," sighed Minta. "But I had better go now. There is a decided draft about my ankles."

Florence was indeed dismayed by the damage Minta had done to her dress before the dancing had even properly begun, and she insisted on repairing it herself as they retreated to one of the alcoves. "I find it helps if I give a little sweep with my slipper as I curtsey," she advised, "to keep my skirts clear."

"Yes, yes, I know, Flossie. It's just that I had much on my mind, and I didn't like the person I was being introduced to, and he didn't even remember me, that I could tell, after how he had conducted himself!" Minta recounted the incident from three years prior, while her sister stitched and clucked, just as Minta had predicted.

"I will say two things about it," Florence replied. "Firstly, young men do grow up, and Mr. Taplin may have improved in those three years; and secondly, even if he has not improved, the Taplins are prominent folk in the area, and you know how important it is to remain on good terms with our neighbors. You need not like him, Minta, but neither should you go out of your way to make your dislike plain. Common courtesy is always due."

"Ye-e-es, Flossie," repeated Minta absently. She was peering out at the dancers. Aggie was partnered respectably by her brother-in-law Mr. King, while Mr. Taplin was dancing with a young lady Minta didn't know. All fine and good, but Minta saw how Aggie still kept darting glances toward the young man. It seemed impossible, but Araminta could draw no other conclusion: Aggie was smitten!

"Smitten," she whispered.

It defied belief. The two of them had never shown symptoms of the silliness which infected so many seminarians at Turcotte's as they grew. Unlike them, Araminta and Aggie had never spent hours analyzing every young man encountered: his appearance, his situation in life, what he said or did on any and every occasion, what he might have been thinking while he said or did what he said or did. In fact, they made fun of girls who spent their mental efforts thus. After all, there was time enough for such things in the distant future, but the present held far too much interest to waste it thinking about young men. The present held sport and adventure and scrapes and jests and—oh! *everything* that made life amusing and worthwhile! How could Aggie now forget all that, so unexpectedly and so suddenly? And how could she do so for so unpromising an object?

I need to talk to her. Perhaps she just needs a good shake.

"There," pronounced Florence, snapping off the thread and standing. She replaced her little housewife in her reticule and accepted Minta's grateful kiss. "All better, if one doesn't look too closely. You have missed the first dance, but Robert will take a later one, I daresay. Do you have someone to stand up with for the next?"

"Tyrone. And here he comes."

If not for her unease over Aggie, Araminta would have admitted a ball was greater fun than she thought. She had always liked dancing, to be sure, since it required energy and skill, and even if her partners were her brother and brother-in-law, followed by a succession of old men, the existence of those same gentlemen ensured that Minta did not have to fret herself over being partnerless. She soon decided to ignore Mr. Taplin's presence as much as possible, unabashedly guiding her partners to places in the set at the greatest distance from him. She also made an inward vow that she would not watch Aggie make a cake of herself because it would only ruin her evening. Tomorrow would be soon enough to let Aggie know Minta thought she was out of her mind.

But her forbearance was tested when Mr. Carlisle reappeared to claim his dance. The supper dance, no less. Not that she minded Mr. Carlisle—no, not at all. She rather liked him. But when Minta placed her hand on his arm and tried by pressure to direct him as far away from his stepbrother as she could, he was surprised enough to say, "Miss Ellsworth, may I ask why you are *dragging* me to the bottom of the room?"

Rarely embarrassed, she found herself coloring now. "I'm used to leading."

"I wasn't questioning your lead, but rather the course you set," he replied. "Wouldn't you prefer to be near your friend Miss Agatha?"

"Er—"

It so happened that Mr. Taplin was leading Aggie to the floor at that very moment.

"Er—we are close but not inseparable."

"Aren't you? I confess I have to this point always thought of you both as a pair."

"All the more reason for us to dance down here. One can't always be a pair."

This last she said with a painful gulp which did not escape his notice, and it was compassion rather than impertinent curiosity which compelled him to ask, "You haven't had a falling out, have you?"

"No," said Minta reluctantly, shaking her head. "Of course not. Aggie and I never fight." Or had never before fought.

"Is it my brother, then?" Mr. Carlisle persisted, even as he told himself it was not his business to ask. "That you object to?"

Her hazel eyes met his dark ones. He was trustworthy, was he not? Even though Mr. Taplin was his own brother? She was a good reader of people in general, and seeing nothing treacherous in his gaze, she took the plunge. "It—is Mr. Taplin I would—avoid at present," said Minta carefully. "So, if you don't mind, let them take the top of the room."

Mr. Carlisle inclined his head and, without another word, allowed Minta to tug him where she pleased.

Perhaps it was because she had to defer confronting Aggie that she found herself confiding in Mr. Carlisle as they danced. Or perhaps it was because he did not press her to.

"I was introduced to Mr. Taplin again earlier," she began, as they armed left and right. "Because I was standing by the Kings, Aggie's sister and her husband. Mr. Taplin did not appear to remember me."

"Indeed? That seems unlikely."

"You remembered me because of the brooch," she continued, "but I don't know if you also remember what happened later that evening, when I went to fetch my cloak? I stumbled upon Mr. Taplin and—"

"I remember," he interrupted.

"Thank you," Minta said simply. "I was surprised Mr. Taplin did not. But then I thought it *was* three years ago, and perhaps he is in the habit of fondling a great many young ladies."

Carlisle did not have to ponder this idea more than an instant to know Miss Ellsworth was probably right in her assumption, but nor was he in the habit of speaking ill of his own brother. What would it serve?

He compromised with, "Francis has always been popular with young ladies, in any event. And I believe you have grown a little taller in those three years. Taller, and more—er—" A tiny line appeared between his brows as he tried to come up with another character-istic, preferably a complimentary one. To call her more elegant or more polished wouldn't be true—in those respects she was about the same. Her face and person had lost the childish roundness of earlier youth, to be sure, but what young lady liked to hear she was not so plump as of yore? Although Carlisle was not the favorite with women his brother was, he knew enough to keep clear of *that* pit.

"—More amenable to instruction," he finished. "You must be. Otherwise I would not have credited the transformation from the young lady I saw playing catch-ball in Meads a few hours ago to my present partner in the ballroom."

"Hmm...you think?" Despite being at the end of the line of dancers, Minta leaned to peer around the couples at Aggie. "I'm not the only one. If I hadn't known Aggie for years and seen her nearly every day of that whole time, I might have said her transformation tonight was even greater."

"Do you mean anything in particular by that, or is it just that her hair, too, is dressed?" He gave her his funny, crooked-balanced grin again. "Or is her transformation greater because she managed to keep her hem intact?"

Much as Minta might find herself liking Mr. Carlisle, she was not about to tell him she thought her dearest friend was smitten by his brother. He might make what observations he liked, but Araminta would say nothing until she spoke to Aggie herself.

Therefore she gave a little shrug and resolved to dismiss the whole matter again. "Who can say? Perhaps it's only that, when one sees a person appear and behave one way, every single day of one's life or thereabouts, any change from routine can seem jarring. And then one doesn't know—is the change permanent or just an…anomaly? An aberration in the pattern?"

"That makes sense," he nodded. "And then one wonders further, is the change superficial or *fundamental*? Can the old be recovered again?"

Her eyes rose to his again, and he saw her relief at being understood. "Yes. Yes, Mr. Carlisle. That is it exactly. You know precisely what I mean. What a pleasure it is, not to have to explain oneself. Aggie and I have been, if not *inseparable*, at least *not often separated*. Not in anything—proximity or what we liked to do or how we looked at things."

"Consequently, she surprised you this evening."

"Yes. She surprised me."

"Is it that she is enjoying the dancing, and you are not, Miss Ellsworth?"

"Who says I'm not enjoying it? A lot of the enjoyment in dancing depends on the partner," she answered frankly, "but I like you."

Her older sisters might have winced to hear this artless admission, but Carlisle found himself oddly moved. How often, after all, is one told for no reason at all and with nothing to be gained by it, that one is liked?

He could not, for his own part, remember it happening before. Not to *him*. Therefore his answer was quiet.

"The feeling, Miss Ellsworth, is mutual."

And in this perfect accord, they finished their dance.

Chapter Three

Love is merely a madness; and, I tell you, deserves as well a dark house and a whip as madmen do.
— Shakespeare, *As You Like It*, III.ii.1476 (1599)

With the Fairchilds as chaperones, Araminta had been allowed to remain at the Domum Ball until the early hours, but she was nevertheless out of bed before ten on the following morning, long habit and anxiety to see Aggie driving her.

One corner of the Weeks' estate met a flank of the Hollowgate acreage where a brook fell over a little fall before bending to the southwest, and it was there that Minta and Aggie were often wont to meet because it did not require walking alone along the Romsey Road. And it was there that Minta repaired, as soon as she stuffed down toast and tea.

There was no sign of Aggie.

Of course, Aggie might still be sleeping, despite being a fellow early bird, and Minta skipped from stone to stone across the stream and took off at a run. The girls had been in and out of each other's houses for ten years and more, and none of the Weekses would blink at Araminta appearing at the house or even bursting into Aggie's own room, which was what she did, some ten minutes later.

Aggie was still in bed, but she sat up abruptly, her hair a white aureole about her head because she had not braided it and one strand pasted to her cheek where she had slept on it. "Minta!"

"Good morning, Sleepyhead." Rocking back and forth to build momentum, Minta launched herself across the room and onto Aggie's four-poster bed.

"Ooh!" complained Aggie. "You crushed my foot. What time is it, anyway?"

"Half-eleven," answered her unrepentant friend. "Long past time to be up. I have three dozen things to say to you, none of which I had any chance to say last night, so they must all be said *right this instant.*"

Collapsing back across her pillows, Aggie dragged an arm across her eyes. "What, then? I don't see why it couldn't wait for the afternoon. I couldn't fall asleep till nearly *four*, I was so excited."

Minta rolled onto her front to fix Aggie with suspicious eyes. "*Why* were you so excited? Because you enjoyed the ball?"

There was a pause, and then Aggie rolled in her turn to meet her friend's gaze. Color washed over her small, fine features. "That, yes. But something else. Something more. Promise you won't tell anyone?"

A great, big ball of heaviness formed in the pit of Minta's stomach. *Oh, no. Oh,* no! She wasn't even going to try to deny it?

"You know I won't," Minta whispered.

Aggie giggled. Giggled! There was no other word for it. The weight in Minta's stomach added another stone.

"Very well, then. It's this." Aggie drew in a long breath and held it a moment before saying in a rush, "I think Mr. Francis Taplin is the most admirable, most delightful, most handsome, most *marvelous* man in all the world."

"Mr. Francis Taplin!" screeched Araminta, crushed beneath the blow. Hearing her fears confirmed was ghastlier by far than imagining them herself.

"Hush!" Aggie cried, slapping at her. "Shhh! You're worse than a brass hunting-horn!"

"Mr. Francis Taplin!" Araminta repeated in a whisper which was still shrill as a piper. "Him? Whatever can you be thinking, Agatha Weeks? What is the least bit admirable or marvelous about him?"

Aggie scowled. Throwing off the coverlet, she sat up and tucked her legs and muslin nightdress beneath her. "I knew you wouldn't be pleased. But you're just being silly because he offended you three years ago. *Three* years ago, Minta. It's ridiculous to bear a grudge so long. Ridiculous and unchristian."

Her own ire rising, Minta struggled to a sitting position herself. "Even if I am ridiculous to remember it, I hardly see how such conduct can be a point in his favor!"

"I'm not saying it's a point in his favor—I'm saying, only imagine if someone went to old Turcotte for a testimonial on us, after all we've done at that school!"

"Well, *I* am not old Turcotte, full of fussy opinions!" retorted Minta. "Nor can any of our mischief at school be compared to Mr. Taplin *groping* me at St. John's rooms, not to mention embracing that serving maid behind the curtains. Where Turcotte's objections to us are mere trifles, Mr. Taplin's conduct would be condemned by any lady or gentleman."

Aggie's scowl deepened and her lower lip protruded. "It's long in the past, at any rate. And even gentlemen do silly things when they're young. You ought to forgive him and forget about it, Minta. I'm sure Mr. Hepple would say the same."

Mr. Hepple was the harassed curate of St. Eadburh's who had replaced Araminta's brother-in-law after Simon Kenner became a prebendary of the cathedral. Although the rector Mr. Gregory paid an adequate salary for the size of the congregation and the required duties, Mr. Hepple had married imprudently young, and his stipend must stretch to support an equally harassed wife and four disheveled children. Truth be told, neither Araminta nor Aggie paid great heed to Mr. Hepple, except to think it would be better never to marry at all than to marry too young on too little money.

"Mr. Hepple might recommend forgiveness," admitted Araminta, "but I am certain he would also caution me against being in the company of such a person."

"Then you may tell him you *weren't* in the company of such a person," Aggie rejoined, "because Mr. Taplin didn't ask you to dance, did he?"

Minta stared at her. "Are you saying I take you to task out of jealousy? Agatha Weeks, I would never have believed it of you."

In fairness to Aggie, she retreated from this stance, but her expression remained sullen. "Very well. I retract that. But I must say, it's most unfriendly of you not even to ask me a single question or to show the least bit of excitement for me."

How can I show any excitement that you should lose your head for such a person? Minta choked on the words, but with a struggle succeeded in swallowing them down to join the lump in her stomach. She wasn't a girl given to tears—out of all the so-called Ellsworth Assortment Beatrice held that crown—but she felt them pricking now. Not tears of anguish, but ones of anger and frustration.

But Aggie was her oldest friend. Her dearest friend. Even if Aggie had lost her mind she was still so, and Minta loved her. And perhaps—perhaps what she and Mr. Carlisle had discussed might be the case. Perhaps this particular change, this infatuation with Mr. Taplin, might be an aberration. A superficial, passing fancy. In which case squabbling about it was certainly not worth the loss of Aggie's friendship.

She swallowed again. And when she spoke, her voice was calmer, gentler. Mrs. Turcotte would have been proud. "I am sorry, Aggie. You're—right. I haven't asked a single question. But I will now. Tell me what Mr. Taplin is like—now—and why you...admire him."

Aggie bit her own trembling lip, and both girls reached at the same time to clutch each other's hands. But when Minta gave a squeeze, Aggie broke into a tentative smile. "Do you really want to know?"

"Yes, please," answered Minta humbly. That is, she wanted to know for Aggie's sake, and not because she wanted to hear nonsense about marvelous young men.

"Well, then!" Aggie's smile became a delighted, besotted grin, and she gave a little wriggle of enthusiasm. "Even you must have noticed, Minta, how handsome he is. Remember Caraway and her court talking about him? I didn't notice at the time, but they were right. He is terribly, terribly, dreadfully, awfully handsome. He has such a fine, upright person and such lovely clothing. And his forelock has this cunning little wave to it, and he has this habit of tossing it back when he laughs! Oh—everywhere he went the young ladies watched, and when he asked me to dance I thought I would die of joy and bliss!"

Joy and bliss had always struck Araminta as interchangeable, but she kept this to herself.

"And he's so very charming," Aggie went on, releasing Minta's hands so she could clasp her own to her chest and shut her eyes. "When we were dancing—and he's a very graceful partner and didn't step on my feet once like Mr. King did—I of course couldn't think of a single thing to say, but it didn't matter at all because he was so good at asking questions and suggesting answers for me if my tongue got too tied."

"What did he ask?"

"Oh…I don't know. Many things. I was distracted because he has eyes like an angel. Or what I imagine an angel's eyes would be like—bright and intense. But I think he asked about my favorite dances and if I had always lived in Winchester—"

"How could he not know you have always lived in Winchester, if Beaumond borders The Acres?"

Aggie frowned again. "I don't know. Maybe because of attending Turcotte's Seminary. Not all the girls hail from Winchester, you know. He asked about my sisters, too—how long Phronsie had been married and if Frederica had a sweetheart." She ducked her chin and gave a smug little smile with lashes lowered that appalled Araminta. "I think he was hinting at whether or not *I* had a sweetheart."

If Minta hadn't thought it would earn her a savage pinch, she would have asked if Mr. Taplin also quizzed Aggie about Mr. Weeks' account books and each daughter's corresponding marriage portion. Because there was no denying the Weekses were very wealthy. It was not that the Miss Weekses were not attractive in and of themselves, but no prudent person would deny the effectiveness of a healthy portion as an improving cosmetic.

"Do you suppose he will call today?" Minta asked, instead. "So many of Lily's beaux would, the day after a ball or assembly."

Aggie's eyes flew wide. "He might, then! He might. Do you think he might? Oh! Where is Banniker?" Struggling free of the bed-clothes, she clambered up and stumbled to the door to thrust her head out and holler for the maid.

Banniker, a raw young girl all arms and legs and not a day older than her mistress, came sliding and scrambling at this unusual urgency, expecting at least to find Miss Agatha on fire or held hostage by brigands.

"Banniker, you must get me ready—instantly!" Aggie commanded. "Look at my hair—and fetch me my striped muslin. Minta, do you think my striped muslin suits me best?"

"You tore your striped muslin climbing over the stile, you did," panted Banniker. "And I stitched it up, but—but it's not as pretty as before."

"Oh, drat. What about my blue, then? The pale one?"

"That one has the stain on the bodice because you and Miss Ellsworth were throwing apricots at each other." Her eyes slid toward Minta at this, in case Miss Ellsworth took umbrage. "Digweed put it twice in the boiler and used milk on it, but there's still a spot right here." She pointed to her own chest.

"What will I do?" wailed Aggie, turning desperate eyes on her friend. Minta's own dress boasted two separate stains and fraying lace, though it was laundered and pressed.

"Wear your shawl over the blue," suggested Minta. "One little apricot stain is nothing, and he shouldn't be staring at your bosom anyway."

"Yes, yes, all right." Aggie and Banniker tripped over each other in their haste and confusion, but soon enough Aggie had her dress on and her shawl pinned and the nest on her head restored to smoothness, and the girls were descending the staircase.

The Weeks' home at The Acres was unlike the Ellsworths' Hollowgate in being some 150 years newer, uniform, modern, and elegant. A fashionably picturesque park surrounded it, complete with folly and lake and grotto, but the crown jewel of the setting was undoubtedly the ruined abbey. When Minta and Aggie first became friends, there had been a long period where Minta was always to be found at The Acres, exploring and playing where nuns had lived and walked, but eventually even magnificent ruins pall through familiarity. As the girls took up archery and ball sports, moreover, Hollowgate's grounds proved more amenable because of the vast lawn and because there was no lake there to swallow up arrows or balls. As for the interior of the great house, Minta had spent little enough time there. Indeed, she spent little enough time within the walls of her own Hollowgate, so it was to be expected that she paid little attention to other people's houses.

"Where should I await him—if he comes?" asked Aggie anxiously, brushing crumbs off her lap after she bolted dry toast.

"It's such a beautiful day. Why don't we find your mallets and play a little pall-mall in front of the house? Then we would at least have something to do if Mr. Taplin does not come." Minta was not ordinarily wild for pall-mall (knocking a ball through a hoop—*bah!*), but she would prefer that to sitting within doors doing nothing.

"Oh, no—we had better not. It would be just my misfortune if you hit the ball too hard and knocked one of my teeth out."

"How could I possibly knock one of your teeth out, unless you were lying on the ground?" protested Minta. "I promise I can be careful."

Aggie raised a skeptical brow. "Even if I believed you, if he really does call, I don't want to be standing out front as if I were waiting for him. And I don't want to be sweaty! I think it would be better to sit in the morning room. Frederica will be there—she always is—and that would look more...genteel."

"If it's genteel you want, perhaps you'd rather I went home," Minta frowned. She didn't *want* to go home. She thought Aggie needed a bulldog present, if Taplin did come, and Miss Weeks wouldn't be any use.

"Of course I don't want you to go. And if he doesn't come in the next hour, we'll play pall-mall. Come on." Aggie took her hand and gave a jerk, and the next minute they were sitting in the sunlit morning room, with its scrolled wallpaper and walnut Hepplewhite furniture. Miss Frederica Weeks was indeed there, seated at the desk writing notes, and when she saw them she gave her funny laugh—*hm-hmm-hm.* "Am I to be graced with your presence today?"

"For a little while," replied her sister vaguely.

The only problem was that there was nothing for them to do indoors. Aggie had a workbasket in name only—she was as wretched a seamstress as Araminta—but she pulled it to her nevertheless, retrieving some wrinkled piece of something that she had probably last touched the Christmas before. Stifling a guffaw, Minta reached for a volume on the side table, only to recoil when she discovered it was Mrs. More's *Strictures on the Modern System of Female Education.*

"Can't we play draughts?" Minta whispered. "You do have a board, don't you?"

Nodding, Aggie tossed her sewing back in her basket. But before she could retrieve the necessary articles, one of the footmen appeared. "Mr. Francis Taplin of Beaumond, if you please."

The elder Miss Weeks stared even as she hurried to rise, hissing, "Mr. Taplin? But I don't even know the man!"

There was no time for Aggie to reply, and she was too flustered to do so in any event, but when Mr. Taplin entered, he found the three young ladies serene and demure, all standing exactly as they had learned at Mrs. Turcotte's and all then dropping curtseys to the exact depth the good headmistress decreed.

"Ah, Miss Agatha. I hope you are not too fatigued after the ball."

"N-no," said Aggie.

"Would you do me the kindness of introducing me to your sisters?"

As if I *were a* Weeks! grumbled Minta inwardly. The more times the stupid man did not remember ever encountering her, the more vexed she grew with him.

"They're not both my sisters," said Aggie, while Miss Weeks *hm-hmm-hm*ed in the background. She pointed in a most un-Turcotte-approved manner at Frederica. "*She* is, though. Freddy, this is Mr. Taplin. Mr. Taplin, this is my second sister Miss Weeks. My oldest sister Mrs. Philip King you met at the ball. And *she*—" swinging her finger around like a signpost to level it at Minta "is Miss Ellsworth of Hollowgate."

Miss Ellsworth of Hollowgate, however, glowered at him, and Taplin didn't spare her more than a glance, choosing to bestow his attention on more grateful objects.

"Ah. I understand. *Two* of the fabled Miss Weekses. What a pleasure."

"Won't you sit down?" asked Miss Weeks, when she saw her younger sister at a loss what to do next. Miss Weeks swept around the desk to take a seat on the sofa and patted it significantly until Aggie dropped down beside her. Of course Mr. Taplin could not sit while Miss Ellsworth remained standing, and though his handsome face betrayed neither discomfiture nor impatience, Miss Weeks was compelled to add querulously, "My dear Miss Ellsworth, which chair would *you* like?"

Flumping onto the nearest, Minta folded her hands in her lap.

"How is it that *you* were not at the Domum Ball, Miss Weeks?" Mr. Taplin asked.

Lowering her lashes and giving her characteristic *hmm*, she replied, "Oh, I'm afraid I had no call to be there, sir. It has been a few years since I was a pupil at Mrs. Turcotte's seminary, and I have no affiliation with Winchester College as my sister Mrs. King does. But I plan on attending other balls and assemblies, beginning with the Race Ball."

He bowed in acknowledgement. "Then I hope to have the honor of dancing with *both* Miss Weekses on that occasion."

Now, Minta had no desire to dance with the man, but she thought it rude of him not to ask her as well, since she was *sitting there*, for heaven's sake. He did not ask, however, and neither Miss Weeks seemed to notice his omission.

"Will you be going to the races?" ventured Aggie. She went pink as he turned to her.

"I have a confession to make," he answered, ducking his chin with a rueful smile. "I've promised my father that I won't. At the races it's a little too tempting to visit the betting post, if you know what I mean."

"I don't," said Aggie, sighing. "We've never been to the races. Though Minta has."

The three looked at her. "It was a few years ago. With my father and siblings. I liked it very much. But we didn't bet, of course."

"Then you were very wise," said Mr. Taplin graciously. "I daresay young ladies grow wiser sooner than young men, but, having now sown my wild oats, I am determined to recover lost ground."

Minta's twin Tyrone would have frowned over Mr. Taplin's muddled metaphors, but Minta was more concerned with measuring the man's sincerity. *Was* she being unjust, to judge him by his actions from three years earlier? It was certainly true that no other respected man of her acquaintance had fondled a series of young women at *any* age that she knew of, but that didn't mean it hadn't happened. Such things were hardly appropriate topics of conversation in polite company.

Yes, all right—never mind the fondling for now, and never mind Mr. Taplin's poor memory in not remembering her—perhaps he was absent-minded and not as quick as his stepbrother Mr. Carlisle. The more pressing matter was determining if he showed any indication of sharing Aggie's infatuation. If he didn't, none of the other matters mattered!

"How do you like being in Winchester again, after your time in Oxford and London?" Aggie's sister asked. "It must seem rather dull."

"By no means!" he assured her. "There is nothing like time away to make one appreciate the charms of home. Balliol would have been utopia, if not for the studies required—" (an appreciative *hm-hmm-hm* here from Miss Weeks) "—never my strong suit, I'm afraid. And I defy London to produce anything of value or amusement which may not also be found here. Winchester too has its theatres and circulating libraries, its shops and coffee houses, its concerts and balls and festivals. No, indeed—I won't hear Winchester maligned."

Both Miss Weekses swelled with Wintonian pride, and Minta would have thought such talk mere pleasantry, except that he then added, "But in one regard, Winchester far surpasses anywhere else in the kingdom."

When both Weeks sisters begged him to enlarge upon this declaration, he inclined his head and said boldly, "Nowhere else have I met such charming young ladies as yourselves."

Minta's revolted expression would have drawn a reprimand from Mrs. Turcotte, had the good woman been at hand, but both Aggie and Frederica swallowed this nonsense whole, and Miss Weeks' *hm-hmm-hm* was joined in chorus by a sound Minta had never heard Aggie make in the entire ten years of their friendship: a titter that began high and almost piercing, before sinking down, down, down to a murmur. *HEE-EEe-Eee-eee-ee-mm.*

What on God's dear earth was *that*?

After such an assault Araminta was too stunned and disheartened to register much of what followed, and she was only roused from this state by his eventual leave-taking. He said a few more foolish things;

the Weekses blushed and made their awful sounds in chorus again; and then he was gone.

"Oh!" cried Aggie, springing up when the door shut behind him and a safe interval passed. "Oh!" She spun in a circle on the Axminster carpet before throwing herself across the sofa. "Isn't he divine?"

"Quite a handsome and respectable and respectful young man," agreed her sister, scarcely less excited. "If I weren't already nearly engaged to Mr. Chester I would quite envy you his attentions. As it is, I will be quite pleased to introduce him to Mr. Chester." (Mr. Linus Chester being a wealthy widower with a house in Mayfair, only two children, and an earl for a great-grandfather, Miss Weeks' generosity in assigning her share of Mr. Taplin's potential affections to her younger sister requires no further explanation.) Rising, Miss Weeks returned to her place at the writing desk. "In fact, I have only one *tiny* concern about Mr. Taplin."

Aggie sat up abruptly. "What? Tell me, Frederica!"

"Well..." Miss Weeks drew the feather of her quill along her jawline, pursing her lips. "My tiny concern is that I detected a lapse in courtesy on Mr. Taplin's part, I'm afraid. You see, while he asked both you and me for dances at the Race Ball, Aggie, he neglected to ask Miss Ellsworth."

Aggie's mouth popped open as she absorbed this. "He—didn't! Of course, Minta didn't say she would even be at the ball—"

"But there again," said Miss Weeks, "he didn't ask her that, either."

"Oh, Minta!" breathed her friend, distressed for her sake. "I wish I had said something! I don't know what, but *something*—"

"It seems unfair that a young man should have to ask someone he doesn't want to ask, merely because she happens to be sitting in the room with those he does want to ask," Araminta lied, hiding another flare of annoyance. "I assure you, I am not offended. And if he had happened to ask me, I don't know that I could have accepted because I never thought of going to the Race Ball."

"But you will, won't you?" urged Aggie. "It won't be like the Domum Ball, where all the Winchester boys are expected to ask all the Turcotte girls to dance. Mr. Taplin might be my only partner! Say you will come, Minta—please. Then we will each have someone to talk to."

There was a moment's silence, and then Minta answered slowly, "I will come."

Aggie shrieked with delight and threw herself at her friend, while Minta tried her best to look happy about her decision. Because she didn't care especially if she went to another ball in her life. But if she didn't go to this one, what might become of Aggie? And who would watch out for Aggie, if she did not?

CHAPTER FOUR

**From friendship's source the balsam flows.
— Robert Lloyd, *Poetical Works,* "To G. Colman" (a.
1764)**

It was a glum Araminta who returned to Hollowgate, without Aggie for once, and without any plans to spend the afternoon together because Miss Weeks had said, "Aggie, let me try a new way to put up your hair," and Aggie had *leapt* at the suggestion. Actually *leapt*!

Snapping a switch from a rowan tree she passed, Minta waved and slashed absently at every bush and rock and fence post and stile. For what had come over Aggie? Why was she being so silly over such a person as this Mr. Taplin? And what did *he* want with *her*?

It was not that Minta thought Aggie unattractive—she never thought much about anyone's looks, to be honest, but she would have said, if asked, that Aggie looked well enough and that, far more importantly, Aggie was game and fun and loyal and a first-rater, out and out. But did Mr. Taplin value the same qualities in Aggie as Minta did? Did he also seek an accomplice in life's adventures? If he did, he could hardly do better than Agatha Weeks, Minta thought. But it could not be simply that. It could not be only mischief and high spirits he sought, or he might have noticed her as well, Araminta Ellsworth.

No. There was more to it.

She thought back to the serving maid she had caught him embracing at the Domum Ball years earlier. The details were blurred, but she could not remember any resemblance between the maid and Aggie. The maid had brown curls spilling from under a mob cap, and everyone knew Aggie was fair as fair could be. And the maid had been plump, where Aggie was slender. But the maid—yes—the maid had had a decidedly prominent bosom. A bosom...such as Aggie now boasted!

Unconsciously Minta's pace slowed.

Could it be Aggie's bosom that drew Mr. Taplin? It would help explain why Mr. Taplin favored Agatha Weeks over Araminta Ellsworth, for Minta had very little bosom to speak of. Yes—it might not be the only reason, but it was likely *a* reason.

Oh, wretchedness! How horrible—how utterly miserable it was to grow up. To leave behind the gambols of youth and hang one's happiness on whether or not some flattering, bosom-loving gentleman paid one any attention.

A drop of moisture fell upon her hand as it swung the switch, and Minta glanced with surprise into the cloudless blue sky. But the sky was not the culprit.

In wonder and amazement, she put a finger to her own face, whence the drop had come. She was...crying? She could not remember the last time she had cried. It might have been when Aggie dropped the elm branch on her foot as they helped the Hollowgate groundskeepers build a bonfire. But even that had been a response to the pain of a broken toe, not *grief*.

Grief?

Yes. Growing up was very, very disagreeable.

Injury was soon added to insult because, when Minta reached the brook separating the two estates again, she took the stones across the water at a run, unaware that one of them had become slick and wet. Her boot sliding straight off the other end of it, up flew her legs from under her, and she landed with a crash and a splash in the stream, her rowan switch capping the moment by slicing a gash of several inches along her forearm.

Groaning, it was a moment before Araminta could struggle up, mud and water streaming from her and her cut beginning to bleed freely. But this was not her first encounter with disaster, so she soon rose, shaking herself off and wringing out what she could. She would have torn a strip from her ruined dress to stanch her wound, but she suspected the soiled material would do as much harm as good. With a sigh and a shrug, she went her way, this time more carefully.

Thinking to avoid as many questions as possible, Minta stole around to the door leading from the kitchen to the kitchen garden and outbuildings. Wilcomb the cook would likely have the necessary items to clean her up before she dashed up to her room for fresh clothing.

Slipping inside, however, the first thing she heard was "—You would recommend another poultice then, later in the evening?" And then— "Good gracious, Araminta!"

Sheepishly, Minta turned to face her stepmother. And not just her stepmother. For the kitchen at Hollowgate was likely the most occupied room in the house just then. Mrs. Ellsworth was there, consulting with Mr. Beckford the doctor. Mr. Carlisle was there, looking on over his mentor's shoulder. Beatrice was there because she tended to follow Mrs. Ellsworth around. Wilcomb and the kitchen maid Clement were there, mixing the seed meal and mustard for the poultice. Everyone and everything stopped when they saw her; mouths fell open; Beatrice gasped; the jug of water in Wilcomb's hands thumped down on the table; the maid gave a muted shriek.

"Is someone sick?" asked Minta.

"Someone sick?" echoed her stepmother helplessly. "It's—it's Willie. He has a summer cold. But—you—"

"Minta, you look like you were drowned and then murdered," Beatrice breathed.

"Oh, it's nothing," growled Minta crossly, even as blood and water dripped onto the flagstones and Wilcomb recovered enough to give a disapproving cluck. "If you must know, I fell crossing the stream between Hollowgate and The Acres." Holding up her arm, she showed them the gash. "This is what's doing all the bleeding. The rest is just mud and mortification."

"Then you had better run up and put on a clean frock," said her stepmother, uncomfortably aware of how Minta's wet clothing was plastered to her form and outlining her legs.

"Wouldn't it make sense to bandage her wound first?" spoke up Mr. Carlisle. "Or she will just bleed on the clean frock as well, Mrs. Ellsworth."

"Yes, true." Mrs. Ellsworth bit her lip, but she fetched one of Wilcomb's starched aprons and enveloped her stepdaughter in it, eliciting another disapproving cluck from the cook and a sigh from Minta.

Frowning at her injured arm, Mr. Beckford said, "We had better clean that before we bind it. Carlisle, why don't you do the honors?"

The young man stepped forward, only to have Minta snatch her arm away. "Oh, I could do it myself by this point—I've watched my sister Flossie dress my wounds often enough."

"I'm sure you have learned much," answered Mr. Carlisle, sounding amused, "but tying one's own bandage can be a tricky business."

Wilcomb as well had seen her share of wound-dressing in her time at Hollowgate, for she pushed over the jug of water and fetched clean rags from a drawer while Clement carried over a wooden stool for Araminta to perch on.

With a sigh, she did so and lay her arm across the table. Although there was no novelty to be found in Minta injuring herself (or others), everyone crowded around nevertheless from the novelty of observing Mr. Carlisle's attempt at wound-dressing. Mrs. Ellsworth wondered if she ought to object to Mr. Carlisle "practicing" on her stepdaughter, but she need not have feared, for the young man was conscientious and careful.

When he took her arm in his hands to turn it this way and that for inspection, however, Minta stiffened.

"I'm sorry." His dark eyes were solicitous. "Did I hurt you?"

"N-no." On the contrary, it had been the warmth and gentleness of his hands that startled her, but she kept this to herself. Moreover, there was all at once a funny, unfamiliar tremble in her stomach that she could not account for. Was it because he was a stranger to her in this capacity? Certainly neither Florence's ministrations nor Mr. Beckford's had ever caused a stir of this sort.

He dampened the rag and deftly cleaned the area while she held her breath and stared past his shoulder.

"Minta has lost quarts and quarts of blood over the years," put in Beatrice. "And so has Aggie."

"How fortunate then, that she makes such good, strong, healthy blood," he replied.

"Copious, too," Mrs. Ellsworth added dryly.

"Before you bind it, Carlisle, would you recommend that antiseptic balsam of your uncle's?" Mr. Beckford smiled at Mrs. Ellsworth deprecatingly. "He has been singing its praises since he arrived."

"Is a balsam a tree?" asked Beatrice, and Minta was glad she did because she didn't know what it was either.

"It's a medicinal preparation," Carlisle explained. "My uncle in London develops medicines of various sorts."

"Carlisle has been encouraging me to compound my own medicines. These young people with their ideas," chuckled Mr. Beckford. "I've told him I'm too old to learn such tricks, but I am happy to try some of his uncle's preparations, some of them finding wide use in London, he tells me."

Minta guessed from the old doctor's tone that he placed no great trust in any newfangled medicines, but neither did he think them harmful. Mr. Carlisle, in the meantime, had unlocked Mr. Beckford's medicine chest and withdrawn a little stoneware pot labeled *Blair's Balsam*.

"What does it contain?" she asked. "Will I smell like rotten eggs?"

He grinned. "There's no sulfur, no. It's my uncle's trade secret, but if you sniff it, you can guess at least some of its ingredients." Removing the lid, he waved it beneath Minta's nose.

"Licorice! And—and thyme?"

"Yes, and some oil, and plenty other things I can't identify. But he advertises it for wounds and all manner of skin conditions. Will you allow me?"

Warily, she nodded. With one hand he took hold of her wrist. "Your pulse is jumping."

"Yours would as well, if someone were going to smear mystery ointment on you," replied Minta tartly. She didn't care about the experiment, in truth—it was that ongoing tremble in her stomach which alarmed her.

He only chuckled. "Only the exact ingredients are a mystery. As I told Mr. Beckford, it has proven singularly effective on my uncle's customers. They swear by it." He dipped two fingertips in the little pot to take up the amber-colored salve and then, still holding her wrist lightly, smoothed the balsam along her golden skin.

Minta sucked in her breath.

Carlisle raised a questioning brow. "It doesn't sting, does it?"

"No. It's just that it's—it's—it surprised me," she finished lamely. It was better than saying, *It's just that your fingers are warm and my insides are not behaving, for whatever reason.* Had she caught Aggie's affliction? Was she going to start being awkward and odd around gentlemen?

She was *not*, she promised herself.

Because she had never been, in all her life, and now was no time to begin. *Someone* had to keep her head about her, if Aggie was going to lose hers.

"Poultice is ready," said Wilcomb.

"Then let us apply it," answered Mr. Beckford. "Mrs. Ellsworth, if you will lead the way."

"Of course. And I hope you and Mr. Carlisle have time for sandwiches and small beer before you go. Wilcomb can make them while we see to Willie."

"Thank you. Carlisle, I suppose you will be capable of bandaging Miss Ellsworth…?"

Mr. Carlisle bowed his acknowledgment, and then the good doctor and Beatrice and Mrs. Ellsworth hurried away.

As the cook scraped the worktable clean, Clement fetched bread and greens and pork for the meal.

Mr. Carlisle wiped the remaining salve from his fingers and took up the bandages, while Araminta resolutely fixed her eyes upon the copper hearth kettle. Though the servants were present, the silence between them seemed to ring in its loudness. Or did it only seem so to her? Whatever the case, she could think of nothing to say while he worked and did her best to confine her thoughts to the most uninteresting and commonplace subjects she could devise. Embroidery patterns. Different varieties of cheese. The hole in her stocking she was even now wiggling her toe through.

Her wayward gaze drifted to him against her will, however. There was a line between his dark brows as he frowned, absorbed in his task. He wound the bandage about her forearm as if she were made of glass, his touch firm yet light.

"There we go," he said when her injury was wrapped and tidy. He stood back, his countenance smoothing. Araminta felt her own tension ease as well, to have a little distance between them and his hands no longer on her.

"You had better leave that alone for a few days," he advised. "And I'm afraid sports may be difficult."

She didn't protest this, though he had expected her to. But Minta was thinking dully that there was little use in sports if Aggie would not join her.

"Very well," she murmured.

"Do you have any questions about caring for it?"

"What? Oh—no." She stared at the bandage.

"My uncle has found that any scarring is minimized by the balsam and should fade altogether after a few months," Carlisle added.

"That's good."

His forehead furrowed in bemusement. Well, if it wasn't the sports and it wasn't the fear of scarring, what was causing her uncharacteristic constraint?

"Are you in pain, Miss Ellsworth?"

That made her look up. "No. Why do you ask?"

"Your silence concerns me. You have been so cheerful and easy the other times I met you."

"Oh—was I?"

"You were."

She could think of no response to this, but after a second he lit on another possibility. "Was all well with your friend Miss Agatha? You came from The Acres, I believe you said."

At that she blanched, her eyes widening. Had he read her mind?

"Ah," he said lightly. "Then it *is* Miss Agatha."

"It is," whispered Minta. And suddenly—was it because he had surprised her with his perception?—or was it the compassion in his dark eyes?—it all threatened to come spilling out, just as it had at the ball.

"You remember I mentioned a-a change in her at the Domum Ball? I noticed how she wasn't herself there. She—she—was different."

"I remember. So you called on her this morning to see if she was—recovered?" When she gave a sorrowful nod he hardly needed to add, "And you found her still—as she had been?"

"Yes! Not herself! That is, while she is perfectly well—in body—in her mind—" Her face crumpled in distress. "I can't explain. Aggie and I have always been great friends and always thought alike—but now—"

When she didn't seem able to continue, he prompted softly, "But now you do not?"

Slowly, sadly, she shook her head.

"It can be a sad part of growing older, Miss Ellsworth—how one can grow different."

"Yes." There was a pressure behind her eyes, and Minta had the dire feeling that tears threatened again. Tears! For the second time in one day?

"Did you speak to her of it, since you have been friends so long?"

"I—tried." She had not tried very hard, she knew, but she had seen it would not be well received.

The urge to make a confidant of him grew. "You see, Mr. Carlisle—I don't even know if I ought to be saying this to you, so can you please pretend you don't know any of the people of whom I speak? I know that's impossible—of course it's impossible—but I think Aggie might—like young men now. Might—like—a particular young man."

With an effort Carlisle hid a smile. Poor girl. What—her tomboyish companion was abandoning her, to join the well-traveled paths of the rest of their sex? Ah, well—it likely would happen to Miss Ellsworth soon enough, and when it did, *then* he might be permitted to tease her about it. But not now. It would be unkind to tease her about it *now*.

"So I went this morning to The Acres," Minta went on hurriedly, "to speak with her about it—about whether she liked this particular person, and I didn't even need to ask it before she confessed. She admitted it—straight out—in the most ridiculous, empty-headed manner." Her hands rose to cover her face, but the movement made her wince, and she lowered them again.

"Miss Ellsworth, I know you will draw little comfort from this, but—the change in Miss Agatha—is not uncommon. Is, in fact, the way of the world. One day you yourself might even...think of marrying."

He half expected a round denial, but she surprised him. "I know it. I know I might—one day. Sometime hence. But it isn't simply that I didn't expect it so soon from Aggie—it isn't even just that I didn't expect her to change first. I mean—it is, but it isn't, you know?"

Appealingly, she looked at him, and he noticed that the hazel of her eyes was a shifting blend of browns and greens.

When he didn't reply, she sighed, lowering her gaze. "No, I expect you don't. I'm the one being ridiculous and empty-headed."

"It may all come to nothing, Miss Ellsworth. These things often do."

She nodded. "Yes. It might. I would feel more optimistic, however, if Mr. Tap—" Her mouth snapped shut, and her hand flew to cover it—pain or no pain.

But this was shutting the stable door after the steed was stolen.

Mr. Carlisle's head turned sharply and his dark eyes raked her, now wary and alert. "What about Mr. Taplin?"

Minta gulped. How would she feel, if Mr. Carlisle had come complaining to her about any of her siblings? *Great guns—now I've done it! No, no—she hadn't said anything bad about Mr. Taplin. She had only complained about Aggie liking a "particular young man." She had* not *said she found the young man objectionable, in and of himself.*

"What...about Mr. Taplin?" he repeated ominously.

"Er—I thought Aggie might take encouragement in her silliness because—Mr. Taplin called at The Acres. That's all. Nothing about Mr. Taplin specifically. She...thinks him handsome. Which he is. Handsome."

To Minta's great relief, there was a clatter and a crash, and then Wilcomb began berating Clement for her clumsiness, something about "listening to others too hard to mind what she was about," but Minta sprang down from her stool to help pick up the scattered items. The next thing she knew, Mr. Carlisle was bending beside her, his face set and stern, even as he retrieved slices of bread and onions and pork.

"Oh, please, sir, don't, sir," pleaded Clement, snatching the food from him and imagining what the cook would have to say about letting the gentleman scrabble for sandwich scraps that had been intended for his lunch.

But Carlisle didn't even notice the maid's distress. When the floor was clean again, he wiped his hands carefully and then folded the rag in a neat square. Then he replaced the balsam taken from Mr. Beckford's medicine chest and locked it again.

Then he looked at Araminta.

"My brother called at The Acres?"

"Y-yes." For the life of her she couldn't understand why he was so struck by it. She had run over their entire conversation once more in her head while they retrieved sandwich bits from the flagstones, and she was still certain she had not maligned Mr. Francis Taplin.

Could Mr. Carlisle possibly object to Aggie, when it came to his brother? It made no sense at all, since Minta didn't want Aggie to like Mr. Taplin, but she felt indignation rise at the thought that Mr. Carlisle might not want his brother to like *Aggie*. Why, Aggie was worth fifteen of Mr. Taplin! Aggie was worth fifteen of *anybody*!

"Do you not like the idea of him calling there?" she prompted, danger in her tone.

He hesitated.

"You have an objection of some sort to the Weekses?" Her voice was rising. "Or to Aggie in particular?"

"I'm sure the Weekses are a fine family and Miss Agatha a fine young lady," he answered at last.

"Then why are you—perturbed—about it?"

Lamely, he said, "Miss Agatha is not the usual sort my brother pursues." But even that was too much to say, he realized. For Francis to have a "sort" implied that he had pursued enough young women for a pattern to become discernable. It implied that Francis was a rakish young man. True enough, but Carlisle hadn't meant to say it. But it was at least better than coming out and saying his brother was also now a fortune hunter.

A fortune hunter who appeared to have lit upon Miss Agatha Weeks as a promising solution to his problems.

Minta was thinking hard, however. And whatever he had said or not said, she had reached her own conclusions.

"If Aggie isn't Mr. Taplin's usual sort," she meditated, "either he has had some change of heart, as she has, or he has other reasons for making up to her. If he is, indeed, making up to her. I suppose it's possible that he will spend the day calling on all the young ladies he danced with at the Domum Ball."

"He may."

It might have been the lack of conviction in his voice, but it was Minta's turn to give the sharp look. "You don't think so, though."

"He may," Carlisle said again, attempting to throw some fervor into it.

"Mr. Carlisle. If Aggie is not the sort of young lady Mr. Taplin generally favors, and if you think it unlikely that he will be calling on all of his dance partners today, then may I ask what you think motivated him?"

Feeling perspiration break out on his scalp, he made another effort at evasion. "I know my father was encouraging him to…think about marriage. Therefore, it might be irrelevant what Francis usually favors in a young lady because—some young men might have different criteria for a wife than for a—for a—"

"For a mistress?" Minta supplied.

"Miss Araminta!" declared Wilcomb, a sign of her extreme disapproval, for she never involved herself in correcting the children's conduct unless it impinged on how she ran her kitchen.

Of all the Ellsworths, Minta had probably been reprimanded the most by the cook, but that was always for accidentally kicking over baskets of fruit or breaking the china or spilling things, so the uniqueness of this reproof distracted her. "I beg your pardon, Wilcomb," she said, "but surely when something so nearly concerns Aggie you can't object to me speaking very baldly."

"I can object, but I don't guess it will make any difference," muttered the cook. Thankfully, she caught just then the murmur of voices and footsteps returning along the passage. That would be Mrs. Ellsworth and the rest, and Miss Araminta's brass would be her stepmother's to deal with.

But Minta heard the same sounds, and she reached urgently for Mr. Carlisle's sleeve. "Please, sir—Aggie said she would be at the Race Ball, and your brother asked her to dance. I wasn't planning on going, but now I must, and you must too, don't you see? You must come and observe and tell me what is happening. Please, Mr. Carlisle! *Please.*"

The door opened and she released him. But as the room filled again—Mrs. Ellsworth giving further instructions about the poultices and Beatrice telling Mr. Beckford about how old and sleepy the terrier Snap had become and Wilcomb apologizing for the sandwich tray being not quite ready—Carlisle could see that Miss Ellsworth nearly vibrated with intensity, the beseeching glances she continued to throw him piercing him like so many arrows. Who could withstand such an onslaught?

Certainly not he.

He waited for the others to be diverted by the setting of the table and serving of the food and drink and then gave one sole tap on her bandaged arm.

"I will be there."

When her face lit like a sunrise, Carlisle thought for a second that she might kiss him in her gratitude. She did not, of course, but when he and Mr. Beckford had eaten their sandwiches and were returning down Hollowgate's gravel drive along the avenue of limes, he found himself remembering the look.

Miss Araminta Ellsworth seemed to be the sort of girl who could look very ordinary or very pretty, depending on her mood and circumstances. And his willingness to help her, awkward thought it might prove for him, appeared to be exactly one of those favorable circumstances.

CHAPTER FIVE

**They that have many Irons in the fire, some must burne.
— Capt. John Smith, *The generall historie of Virginia,
New-England and the Summer Isles* (1624)**

"What's this? The humble practitioner of physic dreams of capturing a princess all his own?"

Carlisle regarded his reflection impassively in the pier glass as the footman doing duty as a valet brushed his coat.

"Is that what happens at the Race Ball, Francis? Princesses are wooed and won?"

His brother sauntered into his chamber, handsome and impeccably clad in black and buff, his boots and pomaded hair gleaming. "That's my aim, in any event. Or I should say, that is the quest I have been burdened with. Win a princess. But *you*, my dear, free brother, are under no similar obligation. *You* are not required to attend balls.

In fact, I thought you pulled a face when my father suggested you maintain pretensions to gentlemanhood."

Carlisle gritted his teeth. "I may not have the means to pass myself off long as one, nor the means to marry, but I do like to dance."

Taplin gave a bark of a laugh and leaned his elbow on the mantel. "What has money to do with being a gentleman or with marrying? You ought to do as I do. My father tells me we haven't a ha'penny, so I am to dress myself on credit and replenish the family coffers by winning a bride through charm alone."

"You do have your name to back you," Carlisle pointed out. "As well as Beaumond."

"Exactly," agreed his brother. "And those are part and parcel of my charm. Though, if I don't act quickly, Beaumond might cease to be part of my parcel."

"Have you a princess in mind, then?" Carlisle knew it would be self-defeating to ask straight out what Francis' intentions toward Miss Agatha Weeks might be. He must approach by indirection.

"I intend to collect more than one, to be safe." Taplin waved a vague, manicured hand. "We will see. And while I don't expect to find everlasting bliss in the marriage state, I would still prefer a bride who does not actively repulse me—there's the getting of an heir, you know. Though perhaps you would be glad, Nick, if, as my father advised, I took a woman as old as five-and-thirty. Because then she might never bear children, and I might name you as the heir to Beaumond—when my ancient cousin Rupert Taplin dies, that is."

Carlisle shrugged as much as his form-fitting coat would allow. "Far too many possible slips 'twixt cup and lip for me there, Francis.

I had better just persevere with learning my profession and earning my own bread."

"And dancing at balls with your betters," Taplin drawled, in the cool, cutting way he had. For someone who had so many more worldly blessings than he (mortgaged estate notwithstanding), Carlisle could never fathom why his brother still felt the need to take him down a peg or two.

"If your father doesn't object to me maintaining my pretensions to gentility, Francis, why should you?" he asked quietly. Lord. If he hadn't promised Miss Ellsworth that he would be at the Race Ball, it would be all too tempting to back out—after telling his brother exactly where he could put his superiorities.

"Well, it's not from any fear you could steal one of my chosen princesses," retorted Taplin. "Have you ever asked yourself, Nick, why my father urged you to keep up appearances? I thought not. It's perfectly plain that he's ashamed of your chosen profession and anxious lest you damage my prospect of marrying well. Though I suppose Father and I must congratulate ourselves that you did not choose to become a grubbing apothecary like your Blair uncle—we were very afraid of it, for a time, as you kept spending your long vacations in town."

"I did consider it," said Carlisle in the same low voice. He held up a hand so the footman would leave off fussing over him. "Because I discovered I *liked* my uncle's little laboratory. I *liked* the chemicals and botanicals and exotic materia medica shipped from every corner of the globe. But it was out of respect for my stepfather, and precisely because I did not want to saddle the Taplins with a 'grubbing apothecary' for a connection, that I chose the practice of medicine instead."

"How can we thank you enough?" Taplin chuckled dryly. "A country doctor is indeed to be preferred to some Clerkenwell quack fiddling with roots and minerals. Well, cheer up. As a country doctor you may afford to marry in twenty years, whereas I believe you said your uncle has never been able to?"

"He never has married, at any rate. Business was always too uncertain."

"Alas." Taplin pushed off of the mantel. "All too *common* a story, I'm afraid. May you have a happier ending, dear brother. In fact, should I succeed in landing my princess coated in gold dust, I may persuade her to part with an additional ten thousand pounds, after she has paid off the Taplin debts." His white, straight teeth flashed in a grin. "It could be like a marriage portion for you, Nick. Or do men not have marriage portions?"

Carlisle didn't deign to answer, but he knew he would sooner die a bachelor like his Blair uncle than take a penny from Francis' condescending hands. Or rather, from Francis' bride's hands. If he disdained becoming a fortune hunter, neither would he be one by proxy.

While there was considerable overlapping in attenders between the Domum Ball and the Race Ball, the latter included a wider share of the community, as well as many race spectators from out of town. As a result, the rose-colored room was already full and warm, chandeliers ablaze and window sashes propped up.

Carlisle entered on his brother's heels, intent on observing where Francis directed his attentions. He had spoken of "princesses," and Carlisle was eager to reassure Miss Ellsworth that her dear friend was but one of several and certainly not the chief.

But no sooner had they passed the tuning musicians than he heard Francis give a soft, "Ahh." Following his gaze, Carlisle spied Miss Agatha Weeks herself across the room, standing awkwardly between her older sisters Mrs. King and Miss Weeks. At least Miss Agatha was adjusting her glove and did not witness Francis' entrance. Someone else had, however. As Carlisle watched, Miss Ellsworth flew to Miss Agatha's side, seizing her by the upper arms and spinning her to look at the portrait of Colonel Brydges suspended above them, conveniently in a direction opposite to where he and Francis stood. It was not very subtly or gracefully done, but Carlisle found himself grinning. Moreover, Miss Ellsworth had succeeded in delaying the inevitable, for Francis shrugged and glanced around, his eyes lighting next on a young lady standing beside a much older woman who looked familiar.

Even as Taplin and Carlisle racked their brains trying to place the old woman, some cleric approached her, bowing and saying in a melodious voice, "Mrs. Fellowes—what a pleasure. I hope you and the dean are well."

"Thank you, Mr. Gillery. Have you met my granddaughter Miss Wright of Meadowsweep? Anna, this is Mr. Gillery, a precentor of the cathedral."

"Gillery...Gillery," muttered Taplin. "Didn't he have a brother a few years ahead of us? Pompous ass—præfect of chapel, was he not?"

"Yes," replied Carlisle. "A good singer, though, the younger Gillery. Apparently music runs in the family."

"Mm." Taplin shrugged this off. "Well, if that young lady is granddaughter of the dean, I imagine she falls in the category of Generously-Portioned—in fortune, if not in figure." He sighed. "I prefer the fair, buxom shepherdess sort myself, but, if wishes were horses..." He trailed off, his languor sharpening suddenly. "I say—there's young Gillery now. Fare you well, brother. I'm off to be introduced."

Having neither the ambition nor the wherewithal to court a dean's granddaughter, Carlisle made his way across the ballroom to Miss Ellsworth and Miss Agatha. They had finished their impulsive study of Brydges' portrait and were once more facing the company, an uneasy crease to Miss Agatha's brow as she rose to her tiptoes. He realized he was obstructing her view of something—ah—her view of Francis, most likely. Oh, dear. His brother might be still considering the full panoply of heiresses available, but this particular heiress seemed to have made up her mind.

"Good evening, Miss Ellsworth, Miss Agatha, Miss Weeks, Mrs. King." Miss Agatha's older sisters returned his bow with polite curt-seys before returning to their conversation, but Miss Ellsworth and Miss Agatha's smiles were genuine.

"How is your arm doing, Miss Ellsworth? One might never know you had been injured."

"The wonder and convenience of long gloves," replied Araminta, holding out the limb in question. "Though it's awfully hot with so many layers on it, and it's starting to itch."

"Oh, Miss Ellsworth!" tittered Mrs. King, overhearing. Her two front teeth emerged in a tight smile. "Please don't say 'itch' in company."

Araminta gave a tight smile in return. "Pardon me." Then she edged around so that her back was to Aggie's sisters. "You don't happen to have anything for you-know-what, have you?" she hissed. "I mean for the condition I'm not supposed to mention."

With difficulty he stifled a laugh. "I'm afraid nothing *on* my person, Miss Ellsworth."

"Then I will just have to keep slapping it," she said, doing just that. "When something stings, it doesn't itch—I mean it doesn't do *that thing*. The problem is, I can hardly slap it hard enough through the bandages and the glove to make it sting."

"The problem is, you look demented when you slap your own arm," put in Aggie.

"Miss Agatha's objection aside," he rejoined, "slapping it might reopen your scab."

"I said that too, Mr. Carlisle," said Aggie. "And imagine if Minta were to do that and bleed through all those layers at the Race Ball! We would never live it down."

Araminta took great comfort in Aggie's "we." So much so that she promised, "I won't slap it any more, then, Aggie. But you must distract me from thinking of it."

"Perhaps I might be of assistance there," Carlisle spoke up again. "I came this way in hope that I might have the honor of a dance with each of you."

While Miss Agatha smiled and nodded at him, Miss Ellsworth clapped her gloved hands and bounced on her toes. "Ooh! Yes, please." She tilted her head two degrees toward her friend and pointed with her eyes, expressing as clearly as she could without words, *Aggie first.*

Obediently, Carlisle inclined toward the fair-haired Miss Agatha, but before he could lift a hand toward her the threesome heard, "Thinking you'd steal a march on me, Nick? I've outflanked you there, because I asked Miss Agatha for my dance a few days ago."

It was Francis, of course. Handsome, eyes hooded, a lounging air. "Have you already forgotten me and accepted my sneaking brother, Miss Agatha, for this first dance?"

"N-no." Flaxen Aggie went red as a poppy and then pale as her hair. Her smile wobbled between joy and timidity.

"Well, then." He extended an arm. She placed her hand on it, and they sailed off, leaving Araminta to slap her itching arm in vexation.

"Would you look at that? That's the *third* time! *Why* does he behave as if I don't exist?"

Carlisle regarded her evenly. "Do you want him particularly to notice you, Miss Ellsworth?"

She flashed indignant hazel eyes at him. "Not for my own sake, no. For my own sake, he might ignore me till kingdom come. But it does irk me when I am right beside Aggie, and he will not even show me common courtesy. Shouldn't he make up to me as well, if I am Aggie's friend, in order to secure my good opinion?"

"Perhaps he thinks it will please her more if he does not divide his attention between you," Carlisle mused. "I remember but a short time ago, you were happy to get as far from him as possible. But now... Would you like to dance, in any event? Near to him or far from him, as you wish."

"I would like to dance, but not this set, if you don't mind," she answered frankly. "For this one, I want to watch them."

They did just that as the lines of happy partners formed. It was not until the music began that she spoke again. "If you please, Mr. Carlisle, could you explain why Aggie would mind, if Mr. Taplin were merely to speak with me as he would any other person?"

He took a slow breath, choosing his words carefully. "Miss Ellsworth, possibly this will make no sense to you, but I can only say that it is something I understand in my bones. You see, you're a confident, jolly girl—a leader. Miss Agatha is a jolly girl as well, and not without confidence of her own, but she is in the habit of deferring to you. She's more like a lieutenant who follows your lead. And I'm sure that, if she had ever given it a thought, she would have declared it only natural that a gentleman like my brother would prefer *you* to her. Therefore, how can it be otherwise than flattering to find it not the case, especially if she...seems to like him?"

Her eyes still on Aggie and Mr. Taplin, Minta's shoulders drooped, and she absently smacked her itchy arm a couple more times. She didn't even want or like Mr. Taplin, so why should it matter if he didn't care if she were alive or dead? Was she, in fact, jealous of Aggie? Did she say to herself that she was prettier or richer or more desirable and should therefore be noticed before Aggie? If she did, she ought to have her head chopped off! Nor did she believe it—truly. Truly, she didn't. For starters, the Weekses were most likely wealthier than the Ellsworths. Not by much, but by a little. And for seconds, Aggie had that bosom. And for thirds, Mrs. Turcotte had told Araminta a hundred times if she told her once, that gentlemen did not like having young ladies lord it over them, and hadn't Mr. Carlisle just said Araminta was a "leader," to whom Aggie had been wont to bow the knee? "Leader" and "lieutenant" sounded less dreadful than calling Minta a tyrant and Aggie her slave, but Mr. Carlisle only used kinder words because he was a kind man.

Minta gave herself a shake, scowling. This would never do.

Tearing her gaze from the couple, she fixed it on her companion. "Thank you for helping me understand, Mr. Carlisle. It's not that I don't wish Aggie everything that is good—of course I do. I just don't know if Mr. Taplin falls in that bucket, begging your pardon."

Carlisle was fairly certain Francis did not in this instance, but he forbore to say so.

After another moment she went on. "You will not say whether you think your brother good or not. At least in regards to Aggie. I understand. It isn't fair of me to ask. If you asked me such a question about any of my siblings, I would resent it and likely sock you for it."

Still he said nothing, though he flushed because his silence was itself incriminating.

She was not slow to understand, and a little sigh escaped her. "Mr. Carlisle—and I beg you not to sock me for this question either—you began to say at Hollowgate that Aggie was not Mr. Taplin's usual sort of sweetheart. Would it be too much to ask what you meant by that?"

This was safer ground because his brother's "usual sort" did not take into account characteristics required by the more serious business of marriage.

"By his own admission, Miss Ellsworth, Francis generally prefers the fair and buxom shepherdess sort of young lady."

Her eyes widened, and she stared at Mr. Taplin making his figure-eight in the set. "There is no denying Aggie is 'fair.' It would be hard to find someone fairer, her hair is so light."

Carlisle cleared his throat. "Er—'fair' might also mean 'pretty.' Not that Miss Agatha isn't well enough."

"And she is buxom, I believe," Minta added without a blush. (She didn't expect Mr. Carlisle to say anything in response to *that*, and indeed he did not.) "But what do you suppose he meant by the 'shepherdess' bit?"

His mouth twisted wryly. He knew exactly what Francis meant: a fresh, unrefined girl who would give much while demanding little. And one who would not be overparticular about her virtue. Therefore, *not* Miss Agatha—or indeed any gentlewoman—there.

He compromised by saying, "One without pretensions to gentility," only to have the innocent Miss Ellsworth reply, "Well, that's Aggie all over. No wonder he likes her." Her eyes narrowed thoughtfully. "Mr. Carlisle, do you think he likes her best yet? He doesn't know her very well."

"I think...he has not seen anything yet to *dis*like," he answered.

She considered this. Taplin bent his head toward Aggie and whatever he said to her evoked a timid smile. Aggie was not the only one flattered and admiring. Minta saw the eyes of other young ladies drawn in Taplin's direction. Were any of them fairer? Buxomer? More shepherdessish than Aggie?

"Mr. Carlisle," she said again abruptly, returning her candid gaze to him, "do you think your brother is simply amusing himself at present? Not just with Aggie, but in general. Or do you think he intends anything more serious? Serious, like marriage."

Carlisle ran a hand along the back of his head, disarranging his dark hair. "I—er—believe he is, in fact, thinking of marrying if he—finds someone he likes."

"I suppose that makes sense," she sighed. "A rich, handsome, landed gentleman such as he is."

Carlisle coughed. "My brother has been very fortunate."

She was silent a minute, giving him hope she would turn the subject, but she soon began again. "Good old Mrs. Turcotte would faint dead away if she heard me ask this, sir—" she leaned closer, conspiratorially "—but do you suppose the Taplins are anywhere near as wealthy as the Weekses?"

He inhaled sharply. What to say? He could not outright *lie*, and his tongue was not smooth enough to evade a question so bald. Francis would have been able to turn Miss Ellsworth away with a teasing reply, but Carlisle for the life of him could only manage a stiff "No—not as wealthy."

"But wealthy enough?" she pressed. "I mean, I am trying to see the good in this, Mr. Carlisle. You know I am not overly—fond—of your brother, and I am sorry to hurt you by saying so. Aggie tells me I am unreasonable to hold a grudge for the incident at that Domum Ball years ago and that I must work to overcome it. But if

I cannot—yet—love Mr. Taplin's character, I may at least trust that he is worthy of Aggie in other respects. Say, because of his—good family name and eligible situation?"

Carlisle marveled that his conversations with Miss Ellsworth led so often to the sensation of standing too close to a fire. Indeed, he felt perspiration breaking out, but this time the joke did come. "Miss Ellsworth—what a shame you were born a young English lady. You would have made an excellent Inquisitor."

"Meaning, I make you feel uncomfortable, even if you have no cause to be." Her laugh was rueful. "I beg your pardon. Turcotte would have been right to reprove me: it was a dreadful and crass question. And, of course, I imagine the Taplins are tremendously wealthy, when not being compared to Aggie's family."

And then she would have dropped the subject, but Carlisle's conscious smote him. Truly—if he did not say something now and penniless Francis wooed and won Miss Agatha, would Miss Ellsworth not be justified in thinking that he had lied to her? That he had allowed her to believe something patently untrue?

It should not matter. People of their class frequently pretended to have more money than they could actually call their own. Francis was not alone in living on credit, nor in aspiring to support his extravagance by marrying well.

But, for whatever reason, he could not lie to Miss Ellsworth. He could not repay her frankness and honesty with evasion and omission.

"Miss Ellsworth," he said, his voice pitched even lower than usual. It was hardly more than a rumble, but she heard him and gave him a questioning look. And when he saw those candid eyes, warm and trusting, he knew he was doing the right thing.

"Miss Ellsworth—I need to tell you—in confidence—that money matters are not so well at Beaumond as they have been in times past."

She said nothing, her eyes whipping back to the dancers, but he could tell by the utter stillness in which she held herself that she was struck and listening.

"And I have to tell you that, however fair and…buxom and—er—ingenuous your friend might be, it is likely that her fortune holds—equal attraction. In my brother's defense, however, I will also add that other measures have been advised, and will be attempted, to repair the family fortunes, in addition to making a prudent match. It's just that—well—the prudent match would be the quickest and most efficacious."

Still she did not answer, but he saw her gloved hands clench.

The dance was ending. Taplin and Aggie bowed to each other, and then he took her by the hand to lead her back to her sisters.

"Oh, no," whispered Araminta feverishly. "Oh, no. Oh, dear. What shall I do? What can be done? If he must marry money—if this is the case—he can have any other heiress he likes, but I won't let him have Aggie. I won't. *I can't.*"

"Miss Ellsworth—"

"Mr. Carlisle, I won't tell a word of what you have told me to anybody, but *please*—I can't let a fortune hunter prey on my dearest friend! Mr. Taplin must choose someone else. You must advise me. You must help me. You must advise him. Can't you push him toward someone else?"

"Miss Ellsworth, Francis is not much in the habit of coming to me for counsel." *Or to anyone*, he added inwardly.

"Then *I* must do something. I must warn Aggie." Araminta wrung her hands, not even noticing the twinge of protest from her scabbed arm. "But look at her face!"

He did look and could not deny that Miss Agatha threw downright besotted glances at his brother as they talked. Thank God Francis was not eager to thrust his head into the noose so quickly, or Carlisle suspected he could have had Miss Agatha's hand at a word. Another couple hailed his brother then, and he and Miss Agatha paused to converse with them.

"She won't listen to me if I criticize him," Minta agonized. "She will only be angry. Oh, why can't he go away? Why can't he prefer somebody else?" Her eyes swept the ballroom, as if she might nominate another candidate on the spot. "Or perhaps—I could even pay someone to—to impersonate his ideal. A fair, buxom shepherdess sort of girl. There must be a thousand such in Hampshire."

"Miss Ellsworth, should you find even one such impersonator, he might like her well enough, but she will not divert him from his purpose unless she has a fortune herself."

"Oh—true. Too true." She groaned. "And a rich young lady would not be swayed by an offer of money from me! I would just have to hope she decided to like him on her own."

"Yes."

"But that is too passive, Mr. Carlisle! Too dependent on chance. No, I must do something myself."

He stared at her, wondering, his mouth curling into that crooked grin of his, and she was amazed to feel that funny tremble in her midsection again, as if she wasn't beside herself with distress. As if he had reached out and touched her.

"What exactly do you propose, Miss Ellsworth? Will you kidnap Francis? Break your word to me and publish my brother's infamy in the *Chronicle*?"

"No. Nothing like that." She pressed a hand to her middle to stifle the inexplicable flutter.

"What, then?"

Taking a deep breath, she faced him directly. "I had better—yes—I will win him myself."

"You?" he exclaimed with unflattering astonishment.

"Yes. I. I will win him myself, somehow. I am blonde, at least."

"You are blonde, to be sure," he agreed, the doubt still obvious in his voice.

"The rest will be a little more trouble." She gave her itchy arm an absent slap. "The buxom bit and the shepherdess bit."

Indeed, he thought those two items might prove well nigh insurmountable.

If Miss Ellsworth shared his pessimism, however, it did not show. And whatever she had in mind to win his brother, Carlisle himself was not to get off scot free. For the last thing she murmured to him before Francis and Miss Agatha rejoined them was, "And, Mr.

Carlisle—if you feel any friendship for me or pity for Aggie—I pray you will—no—more than that. I *beg*—that you will help me."

CHAPTER SIX

**Criticism the Muses Handmaid prov'd, To dress her Charms, and make her more belov'd.
— Alexander Pope, *An essay on criticism* (1711)**

"Why the rush, my dear?" asked Mrs. Ellsworth at breakfast the following day, noting with concern how her stepdaughter took enormous bites of her toast and washed them down with gulps of tea.

"—Have to get to The Acres," mumbled Araminta behind her hand. She made a face as she forced down the giant lump. "Before anyone calls." If she planted herself at Aggie's until the hours for calling were passed, any courting Mr. Taplin meant to carry out would have to be done with Minta there, watching his every move.

"Well, take it gently—I imagine the Miss Weekses are still abed," replied her stepmother.

"And if you gobble like that, you'll likely choke," observed her brother Tyrone, turning the page of his book.

"If she does, may we send for Mr. Beckford?" asked Beatrice.

Araminta considered. Mrs. Ellsworth was probably right (as was Tyrone). There was no use choking or spilling tea on herself in her hurry. With an effort she slowed her movements, even taking a second piece of toast and beginning to butter it. "Speaking of Mr. Beckford, how is Willsie Wills today, Mama?" she asked. "Any better?"

"His fever is gone, but now he is coughing and sounds heavy. I will ask Mr. Beckford to come by, just to examine him. Listen to his lungs."

"I am sure little Willie will be up and running about again in no time," pronounced her husband with his invincible cheer.

"All the same, I would like to hear the doctor say so."

A feeble growl from the aging family terrier emerged from under the table, signaling the approach of Bobbins the footman with the morning post. There was the usual stack of letters for Mr. Ellsworth, one for Mrs. Ellsworth—and a note for Minta.

"Aggie must be awake after all!" But it was not Aggie's hand. No, this one was dark, bold, minute. She had to told the paper to the light to peer at it.

Beaumond

13 July 1804

Miss E—
Have no fear of F calling on A this morning. He is
indisposed.

—N. C.

She gave a little gasp, which no one noticed, and then folded the
note precisely into a tiny square and tucked it away. Mr. Taplin
indisposed! What a boon. It would give her the entire day, then, to
take the first steps in her plan.

"Papa—Mama—what would you say to me having some new
dresses made?" Minta blurted. "I thought several dresses, perhaps,
as I am now of age to attend balls and such. I cannot wear the same
thing every time."

If she had suggested that she would be going on a journey to the
moon, her family might have looked less surprised.

Her brother was the first to recover. "Even if you wear the same
dress every time, it always looks different," he pointed out, "as you
invariably tear or stain it and it has to be repaired."

"That's true," she agreed, "but it would be nice to have more
than one, especially if that one became more and more ribboned and
patched and stained each day."

"But Minta," Beatrice puzzled, "—you hate everything about
new clothing. Being measured, choosing patterns and material, being fitted."

"Can't a person change?" she retorted. "Can't a girl grow up?"
Turning to her stepmother, she said, "I know you haven't time to
sew me a new wardrobe, Mama, and it would be a lot to ask of Monk.

And, as for wearing anything I tried to sew myself, it would be better to go about in rags! So I thought I could call on Aunt Jeanne, and she could accompany me to the modiste."

"Oh—indeed." Mrs. Ellsworth looked about helplessly. "I suppose that would serve. What do you say to it, William?"

"Splendid, splendid. So my Araminta has decided she will no longer hide her beauty under a bushel."

"Something like that." Flicking the toast crumbs from her fingertips, she pushed back her chair. "I'll go right away, then, if Monk is free. And I'll take a few of my gowns that aren't in too sorry shape because perhaps those can be made presentable sooner than altogether-new dresses." With a glance at the clock she added, "Aunt Jeanne won't mind how early I call."

"But suppose Mrs. Charles Ellsworth already has plans for the day?" Mrs. William Ellsworth said.

"If she does, she won't have them long," returned Araminta. "Aunt Jeanne can't resist a trip to the dressmaker."

"*Mais bien sûr, cherie!*" cried Jeanne Ellsworth, throwing her arms around her niece in delight, her black eyes sparkling. "I would love nothing more than to see you properly dressed. But who would have expected this pleasure? I thought my Araminta would never love anything but *le sport*. How glad I am to mistake myself. You must tell me with whom you are so soon in love."

"I'm not in love with anyone, Aunt Jeanne," explained Minta patiently. "I knew you would think I was, but I must disappoint you. It isn't love that drives me to the dressmaker—it's that I must rescue my dear friend Aggie."

"Miss Agatha Weeks?"

"Yes. She has a fortune hunter after her. And, worse, she likes him! She'll be completely taken in, if I don't do something."

Her aunt raised a skeptical brow. "And what do you propose to do that involves new dresses?"

"I'm going to win him myself," Minta declared stoutly. "Not to marry, of course. I don't want to hand over Papa's fortune any more than I want Aggie to hand over Mr. Weeks'. But I need to lure Mr. Taplin away from Aggie until her eyes are opened and the danger is past. I don't know if it will work, but I must try. And I've asked Mr. Taplin's brother Mr. Carlisle what sort of girl Mr. Taplin prefers, and he tells me 'fair, buxom, and like a shepherdess.'"

Jeanne Ellsworth stared and then burst out with her tinkling laugh. "What is this? What is this? I know 'fair,' and you are fair, Minta—though not as fair as Miss Agatha—her hair is almost white! And I know what is a *bergère*, but I do not understand what this 'buxom' is or why this man wants to marry someone who keeps the sheep."

"Buxom is—buxom is—" But here the French lessons from Mrs. Turcotte's Seminary for Young Ladies failed her. There had been no instruction on such words. Araminta blew out a breath and then held her open hands up in front of her chest. "Buxom is *this*. You know, Aunt Jeanne—big up here. And I discovered Aggie has become *buxom*!"

"Ahhh...*plantureuse, tu veux dire*." Mrs. Charles Ellsworth shook her head, clicking her tongue in dismay over her niece's decidedly modest bosom.

"I know, I know," said Minta. "This is a perfectly good chest for sport, but not such a good one for catching Mr. Taplin. What would you suggest?"

"I would suggest a very talented modiste," replied her aunt dryly. "One very skilled at sewing the little ruffles in the bodice and at attracting the eye elsewhere. But it can be done. Men have been fooled before. *Et voilà*—that is the 'fair' and that is the 'buxom.' What about the sheep?"

Minta pulled a face. "I don't know exactly about the sheep. Mr. Carlisle said he meant shepherdess-like qualities: innocence, modesty—not too refined. I don't know—maybe peaceful? Are shepherdesses peaceful?"

"I think the ones in the paintings are. Peaceful and clean and quiet and feminine." She looked at Minta, and Minta looked at her, and then they both began to laugh.

"Well," Araminta gasped, when she had enough breath, "At least that doesn't sound very much like Aggie, either, so I will just have to do my best. Mr. Carlisle promises to help me."

"Again this Mr. Carlisle," observed her aunt, tapping her lips thoughtfully.

Minta sighed. "Oh, Aunt Jeanne, don't look at me like that. Not everything is a love story."

But her aunt shook her head, her silver-streaked dark curls bouncing. "That only means you have not read to the end."

As Minta had placed herself in Jeanne Ellsworth's capable hands for this portion of her plan, she made no objection to visiting the modiste of her aunt's choosing ("I have never been able to buy anything from this person, but I very much admire the window"), just at the top of St. Thomas Street, a stone's throw from the Guildhall. Therein she stood for the inordinate amount of time it took to take every measurement and then spent the rest of the visit tossing a ball of yarn while her aunt, the modiste and the Hollowgate maid Monk conferred over fabrics and patterns and trims and Minta's unpromising bosom.

"Her posture is good," declared the modiste, an *emigrée* with whom Mrs. Ellsworth frequently lapsed into rapid French, "but her shoulders quite broad."

"Too broad," pronounced Jeanne. "You must make her figure look *plus mignonne. Plus délicate*." More on this subject followed, in which Minta caught the words "*bergère*" and "*plantureuse*," but she shrugged and didn't bother to ask for translations.

When at last the details were hammered out and the substantial order placed, they returned to the Ellsworths' cottage in St. Thomas Street so that Jeanne could trim and repair and modify the old gowns her niece had brought, even while she made suggestions to Monk on dressing Araminta's hair. "She has beautiful waves and curls. You must neither scrape it all back nor let it fall in every direction."

"Madam," Monk answered with some asperity, "I have only scraped it back because Miss Araminta herself requested it—"

"Otherwise it gets in my way when I am doing things," Minta spoke up. Both ignored her.

"—And as for 'falling in every direction,'" the maid went on, "she *will* be careless about hairpins and will rarely have a ribbon or a band in it."

"Hairpins poke awfully, and a ribbon would only fall out," ventured Minta.

Aunt Jeanne jabbed a peremptory finger at her. "You want to distract this Mr. Taplin, or don't you? You are fair. We are helping the buxom. But there is no shepherdess in a painting who looks like someone held her under the bridge until she drowned and then let her hair dry in a hundred directions."

Minta sighed and said no more, sitting like a wigmaker's dummy while the two women criticized and plotted and Monk curled and pomaded and ribboned her.

What enabled her to bear all with patience was the certainty that, tedious as it was, this was all in service of rescuing Aggie.

There was no denying that Mr. Carlisle had met her idea with incredulity at the Race Ball, but, over the course of the evening, as they had snatched further opportunities of speech, Araminta flattered herself that she had won him over. Well—perhaps not *won him over*, but she had persuaded him that the situation called for urgent and desperate effort.

"Miss Ellsworth, while I admire your devotion to Miss Agatha," he said, when their dance called him to lead her in promenade up the room, "I feel obligated to tell you again that winning—or even distracting---my brother from his pursuits may prove no easy task for you."

"If it were easy, it would hardly require the attempt," countered Minta, not at all daunted. "Look here—I'm no belle like my sister Lily was, but I have yellow hair like Mr. Taplin prefers, and I too have a generous portion, so I am halfway there. There must be something that can be done about my bos—er—my person. I will ask my aunt Jeanne. She used to be in the theatre back in France, it so happens, so she knows all about altering one's appearance with costume and paint. Not that I will wear paint, naturally."

"Naturally." He could not help smiling. The figures of the dance separated them, but when they came back together, he said, "Very well. Your aunt will aid you in...making the most of your exterior, but—"

"But it's my interior which gives you pause?" asked Minta with a laugh. "What sorts of interiors would you say Mr. Taplin prefers?" When he didn't answer right away, she frowned thoughtfully. "If I think how Aggie has been since she developed her *tendre* for him, I would guess he likes...quiet—even tongue-tied—and adoring. Perhaps even...timid?"

He did not deny it.

"I understand those qualities might be difficult for you to assume, Miss Ellsworth."

She didn't know if they would be or not. She had never before *tried* to be different than how she was. "I don't talk excessively," Araminta answered. "At least, my family has never complained of it. But I will have to practice pretending that I am quiet out of timidity."

"And I'm afraid that, when you do talk, you had better refrain from speaking your mind straight out with your customary frankness," he suggested.

"Oh, dear. That's harder. More demure, then?"

"More demure in words. But you may always *look* your admiration for him, I suppose."

"Oh, dear," said Minta again. "If I can manage it. I'm not sure I know how to look admiring."

"Ah, but you do," he corrected. "I've seen it twice: once, when I caught your brooch, and again, when I caught your ball. The look you gave me on each occasion was your admiring look. A wide smile and a light in your eyes that made me feel quite proud of myself. Simply pretend Francis has performed feats that take your breath away."

"Mm." She pondered this as she took hands with the gentleman on her diagonal and then exchanged places with the lady to her left. That brought her back to Mr. Carlisle. "*Is* Mr. Taplin good at sport? Or has he other worthy talents or characteristics that would help me to admire him?"

One of his eyebrows lifted in amusement. "I daresay most young ladies find him very handsome. Dashing, too."

Minta blew out a resigned breath. "Aggie does, at least. So I will try to imagine it. I like your looks better, myself."

"You *do*?" he uttered, surprised into the question. Hastily, he tried to play off his artless astonishment. "That is—very kind of you to say so, Miss Ellsworth—"

"I like how kind and friendly you look," she went on musingly, oblivious to his discomfiture. "And I like how your smile reaches your eyes. And you're taller than I am—not every gentleman is, you know. Taller, without being awkward and gangling."

In such a crowded and noisy place as the Race Ball, encased in gloves and with her mind on the Aggie problem, it was easy for Araminta to say such things and to forget all about the peculiar tremor she had felt when Mr. Carlisle bandaged her bare arm. But even as she congratulated herself on this, the odd little tremor returned. With a gloating vengeance.

It might have been because her partner's dark eyes were all at once fixed on her, studying her most intently. Or it might have been that his color was high, and his grip on her hand when he took it in his was rather tighter than it had been.

For whatever reason, Minta dropped her own gaze in confusion, stumbling over her own slippers and bumbling into the young lady beside her.

"Do be careful," said that young lady crossly as Minta begged her pardon and Mr. Carlisle caught her by the elbow.

His grip was still firm, but she was relieved to see his unsettling look was gone as if she had dreamed it, replaced by his uneven grin that was somehow perfectly perfect.

"Yes, Miss Ellsworth, I had better warn you as you plot and intrigue. Your machinations may lead to unintended consequences. Therefore I pray you—*do* be careful."

Chapter Seven

Assume a virtue, if you have it not.
— Shakespeare, *Hamlet,* III.iv.2560 (c.1599)

Mr. Beckford and Mr. Carlisle were just leaving Hollowgate when Araminta returned with her maid. And while Mr. Carlisle's eyes widened at the sight of her, it was left to the doctor to say, "Why, bless me, Miss Ellsworth, if there isn't something different about you today."

"It's my hair," replied Minta simply, whipping off her bonnet to reveal the neatness and precision of her curls. "Monk here did it, with help from my aunt. You're used to seeing it untidy, I suppose." She gave Carlisle a bright glance, to which he bowed his head in the slightest nod. *Yes, he saw the difference.*

"How is Willsie, Mr. Beckford?" she asked. "Any better?"

"Progressing well. I expect his cough will linger, but I have left instructions for Mrs. Ellsworth." Mr. Beckford touched the brim of his hat. "If you will excuse me—Carlisle, I will get on to the Hamblys, and you might meet me there?"

"Yes, sir."

The doctor headed down the front steps to the drive, while Monk dropped a curtsey before disappearing down the screens passage. Seeing the question on Miss Ellsworth's lips, Carlisle said, "I'm staying back because I told Beckford I had something which might make your scab less bothersome."

"Surely we might say the word 'itchy' here, in the privacy of the entry hall," she whispered teasingly. "But I thank you all the same. Is it another ointment of your uncle's?"

"Not this one. I mixed it myself, based on something I found in the College of Physicians' *Pharmacopoeia and Dispensatory*." Reaching in his pocket, he withdrew a tiny pewter container. But when he made to take her arm, Minta hastily retreated, on pretense of hanging up her bonnet. Just the thought of him rubbing whatever concoction he had made into her skin again made her heart give an alarming little flip that she did not want to think too hard about.

"Heavens, what a title for a book! I thank you for your recipe, Mr. Carlisle, but I had better apply the stuff myself later, before I go to bed. I'm turning over a new leaf, you recall, so I can't be getting stains on my sleeves. And Monk just wrapped my arm again this morning."

"Very well." He placed the salve on the marquetry cabinet by the door.

She thought he might go then, even though she did not want him to, but he lingered. "I hope—you are recovered from the ball?"

"I'm perfectly well. And you?"

"Well, as well."

"But your brother Mr. Taplin is indisposed, your note said."

Carlisle gave a humorless laugh. "He is."

"Nothing too dreadful, I hope?"

"No. Nothing too dreadful. A young man's ailment: headache, a dislike of light, thirst. He'll be better shortly."

The innocent Araminta blinked in puzzlement—it sounded quite serious to her—but she deferred to his greater medical knowledge. "Do you suppose he will recover enough, from such symptoms, to call at The Acres on Monday?"

"Most certainly."

"All right, then. Because I will be waiting for him."

His grin appeared. "That sounds ominous. What plans do you have for Francis, Miss Ellsworth, besides your newly tidy hair?"

Her hazel eyes glowed up at him with eagerness. "Oh, so much! He will not recognize me."

"And here I thought your complaint was that he has already failed to do so three times."

Laughing, Minta gave him a playful shove before she knew what she was about. Then she lifted a horrified hand to her mouth. "Great guns! I beg your pardon." Another gasp followed this blunder. "And I had better stop saying that. Old Turcotte would rap my knuckles with her ruler if she were here."

"If that was her practice, I'm amazed you have any knuckles left," Carlisle returned. "But consider your knuckles rapped in spirit, then, and go back to telling me what weapons you will wield, to conquer Francis' heart."

"Well, I've ordered new dresses today, although I don't think any of them will be ready so soon as Monday. But my aunt Jeanne did what she could for some of my old ones, so there's that…And then I plan to stick like a burr to Aggie, forcing him to acknowledge me sooner or later. I will sit right beside her, with my arm about her waist, if I have to. And then I'll do my best to seem quiet and adoring and timid, just like we discussed."

Perching on the cabinet, Carlisle crossed his arms over his chest, his free leg swinging. "Let's see it, then."

"See what?"

"See this quietness and adoration and timidity. Your planned performance. Pretend I'm Francis, calling on Miss Agatha." Popping up again, he made an elaborate bow. "Good morning, Miss Agatha. Oh, and good morning to you, Miss Whatsyourname. I didn't see you there at first. I thought you were a spot on the carpet."

Minta gave a mock-indignant gasp but then sank into a curtsey worthy of St. James. "Mr. Taplin. I can—I can hardly find words to express my surpassing pleasure that you have finally deigned to acknowledge me."

"Oh—I'm sorry—were you speaking to me? I heard a buzzing in my ear."

She laughed and went to shove him again, only to retract her hand just in time.

Carlisle clicked his tongue, shaking his head. "I'll pretend I didn't see that. But come, come. That laugh will never do. Far too loud and hearty. Try again."

Pulling a face, Minta tried to give a more genteel titter.

"And that one's too mocking. Again."

She let out a frustrated breath but then shut her eyes, trying to remember how Miss Caraway and her toadies sounded, years earlier. Light, demure, muted. Old Turcotte had always looked on them with approval in the etiquette lessons. "A young lady's laugh should never draw attention to itself. It must hardly cause a ripple on the surface of the conversation. Nor must a young lady be *carried away* by her amusement. She must not bray like a donkey, nor *double over* in mirth, Miss Ellsworth, Miss Weeks. No. The carriage must remain upright—thus—and no more than the upper teeth be seen—at the most. So."

How she and Aggie had elbowed each other and snickered at such instructions! Alas, those days were gone, possibly never to return.

With a sigh, Minta braced herself and then tentatively produced the foreign sound.

Carlisle's brow lifted. "Well! That's more like it. You show promise, Miss Ellsworth. Shall we continue?" His chest swelling, he straightened and adopted his brother's expression of lazy charm, his eyes hooded. "How did you enjoy the ball, Miss Ellsworth?"

Araminta recoiled. "Oh, dear me—how do you do that?"

"Do what?"

"Look like that! You don't look a thing like Mr. Taplin, and yet that was very much Mr. Taplin."

"Was it?" The look vanished the next instant, and Carlisle held up conciliatory palms. "I...apologize? You must steel yourself, however. If you can't stand me mimicking Francis, how will you manage Francis himself?"

"It's not the same thing," she protested. "It's a matter of expectations. I expect *you* to be—I don't know—kind and modest and honest and friendly—and when you suddenly did not appear so—when you looked...subtle and rather sly, it took me aback. That's all."

His countenance darkened. "Oh? You were startled to discover I could have a less amiable side? But doesn't everyone?"

"I suppose," she agreed unwillingly, her brow knit. And then, more strongly: "Of course everyone does—have a less amiable side. I don't mean to say anyone is perfect. And I suppose it's lucky that one person's notion of 'sly and subtle' is another person's notion of charming and polished." At least, she and Aggie now seemed to view young men through different lenses.

She repressed another sigh at this thought but then raised her chin, resolved anew on her plan. She mustn't be squeamish about this. Mr. Carlisle was right—she must steel herself for the work.

But then—"Mm." He shook his head. "That look will never do."

"What look?" she protested. "I haven't even begun to look."

"That look like you were preparing to bully me into submission."

"That wasn't part of it!" Minta complained, hammering her hand on the cabinet. "That was just me preparing myself for the exercise."

"Heavens. I recommend you do your preparations in private then, and don't let Francis see them. Shall I count to three, then?" he asked. "Thus: one…two…three—*Miss Ellsworth, how did you enjoy the ball?*"

She pasted a silly smile on her face, showing no more than the acceptable amount of teeth. "It was lovely."

"I hope you did not suffer from the exertions and the warmth of the room."

"I—no—that is, I—didn't?"

"I am glad to hear it. A young lady of your delicacy and grace."

"Oh—er—thank you. H-how did *you* like it, Mr.—Taplin?"

"In your company it could not be otherwise than pleasurable."

Araminta was conscious of her face heating, but it was half in embarrassment and half in indignation. The latter won out.

"You must stop it, Mr. Carlisle! I don't like you saying such things. Such oily, flattering things."

"Oily!" he laughed, his assumed façade falling away again. "Miss Ellsworth, however can you hope to succeed, when you cannot sustain this act for more than a few sentences at a time?"

"It will be easier when I am with Mr. Taplin," she retorted, crossing her arms over her chest. "Because I will not have to reconcile such nonsensical words with *your* face and *your* voice. The real Mr. Taplin might say whatever he pleases and make whatever faces he likes. I am prepared for it. But from *you*—!"

Carlisle shook his head in resignation, hardly knowing whether to be delighted that Miss Ellsworth's opinion of him was so indestructibly good—or chagrined that this scheme of hers stood not the slightest chance of prospering. How could her plan to impersonate Francis' ideal ever succeed? Would not the real, the genuine,

Miss Araminta Ellsworth come leaking through every crack, if not altogether bursting free?

"I had better leave off provoking you, then, and be on my way," he said after a time, straightening and taking up his hat. "Or Beckford will think I fell down a well."

"Oh, Mr. Carlisle," said Minta, "don't think I don't appreciate your help! On the contrary. I do. Very, very much. Thank you for *attempting* to tutor me. I hope to bring you a good report, when I do see your—brother." She had nearly said "your dreadful brother" but managed to catch herself in time.

How fortunate she was, to have the *good* brother's assistance, in winning the reprehensible one. And how fortunate she herself was—though she had never thought about it before—that her own siblings' characters needed no apology. To think that it was Mr. Francis Taplin the girls were so silly for! It was Mr. Taplin's handsome person and ancient name and estate which so outshone the brother who was worth ten of him. Nay—twenty of him!

She regarded Carlisle steadily as her mind worked through these things, her candid gaze sharpening into an awareness that made him suddenly draw back.

"What?"

"Mr. Carlisle—at the Race Ball you remember we were talking about how Aggie might find it flattering how Mr. Taplin ignores me."

"Yes...?"

"And you said this was something you 'understood in your bones.' What did you mean by that?"

Heavens. Had he said that? It was curious, really, the conversations he had with Miss Ellsworth. They were like no other. Probably because *she* was like no other. He could not think of another young lady of his acquaintance who asked the bald questions she did or rapped back with her own bald answers.

He answered her. Not that her clear gaze gave him any alternative.

"I meant, Miss Ellsworth, that I...understand what it is like to live in someone's shadow."

She nodded, continuing to study him.

Had anyone been there to notice, they would have chided Minta for letting a guest remain standing so long in the entry hall, instead of offering him a chair in the parlor and something to drink, but neither she nor Carlisle thought of it.

"It must be very hard," she said at last, "to have no parent living. I lost my mother years ago—I hardly remember her—but I still have my father, and, apart from little Willsie, my siblings and I are all in the same boat. That is, we have all lost our mothers but still have our father. It certainly must be easier for us because of our shared circumstances."

Carlisle was uncomfortably aware of a tightness in his throat. He was unused to sympathy—it made him feel exposed somehow. But Miss Ellsworth's sympathy did not shade into pity, thank God. Her eyes continued open and frank and musing.

When he could speak, he took refuge in following her train of thought. "Yes. My acquaintance with your family has not been long or particularly deep, but I confess I have already admired how well you and your siblings all get on, despite being of such—miscellaneous—origin."

She grinned. "We do our share of wrangling, I assure you, Mr. Carlisle. But on the whole we do rub along. I suppose Papa's money helps. He gives all us daughters the same—generous—marriage portion and Tyrone his equal lump. My oldest sister Florence will get Hollowgate in the end, but since it originally came from her mother's family the Baldrics, no one begrudges her it. My mother was just one of the governesses, you know. As was Beatrice's. But supposing Papa left everything to Flossie and nothing to the rest of us—why then there might be some jealousy! Only, Flossie is so tender-hearted that she would probably just dole it out to each of us in any event."

"That would indeed be tender-hearted." He hesitated, debating what should or should not be said, but the urge to defend his stepfather was too strong. "I would not have you think, Miss Ellsworth, that my stepfather Mr. Taplin is any less generous than Mr. William Ellsworth. Beaumond belongs to the Taplins, of course, and must go to Francis, but my stepfather has supplied me with a home while he lives and an allowance adequate to my station in life. My decision to become a doctor and to spend time with my humble apothecary of an uncle in London was mine alone."

"You mean you did not choose it because you learned of the Taplins' strait circumstances?"

"I did not. I was not aware of how—lean—things at Beaumond had become until I returned a few weeks ago. It makes it all the more urgent that I support myself, eventually. Although my allowance is not extravagant, I don't doubt my stepfather would find it a relief to be free of it."

"Ah." She shook her head, her mouth rueful. "What a world it is! You choose to work, to improve your situation, while your brother—he hopes to marry his way out of it. And yet it is your brother the world smiles upon."

But this was drawing too close to the pity Carlisle did not want, and he waved it off, saying with jesting servility, "I don't care a straw for the world's smiles, Miss Ellsworth, so long as I reign supreme in your esteem."

"My goodness, that's charming," she replied bluntly. "I suppose you would be as bad as your brother, given the chance."

"That's what I've been trying to tell you."

"Then I, for one, thank heaven you were spared all the blessings showered upon Mr. Taplin," Minta grinned. "For look what it's done to him, and even the one of you is trouble enough."

CHAPTER EIGHT

**That trot became a gallop soon,
In spite of curb and rein.
— William Cowper, "The diverting history of John
Gilpin" (1782)**

From the time Mr. Carlisle left her, Araminta practiced. She minced her way around the house and to church on Sunday. She spoke (whenever she remembered) in a soft, gentle and low Cordelian voice that would have made Mrs. Turcotte weep. She choked her loud guffaws down to gentle titters. She threw not one ball nor launched one arrow nor turned one somersault. She even spent a (cumulative) half-hour sewing.

"Do you feel quite well, Araminta?" asked her stepmother, when the family gathered in the drawing room on Sunday evening. Little Willie was up and about for the first time in days, and he whizzed from chair to sofa to pianoforte, Mrs. Ellsworth not having the heart to send him early to bed.

Beatrice at the instrument paused in her playing. "I was going to ask the same thing, Mama."

"Of course I'm well," answered Minta in her Cordelia voice, scowling at the two layers of fabric she had inadvertently stitched together. "Why would I not be well?"

"You might have caught Willie's cold," said Beatrice. "Your throat is scratchy."

"No, it's not."

"Something is wrong with it," muttered Tyrone from where he stretched on a sofa, reading. "For you sound like the ghost of Hamlet's father."

"That's all you know," retorted Minta. "I *sound* like Cordelia in *King Lear*."

"If Cordelia sounded like the ghost of Hamlet's father."

"Minta sew," put in her youngest brother, removing his finger from his mouth to jab it at her work.

"See?" said Beatrice. "Even Willsie knows something is amiss with you."

"Don't suck your fingers, dearest," murmured Mrs. Ellsworth to her little boy.

Minta ventured her new feminine titter, which only made matters worse, for they all exchanged glances and even her placid father stared. Then she huffed with impatience, her voice rising out of Cordelian ranges into its normal register. "Well, never mind. All of you. I'm perfectly fine. Tyrone, why don't you accompany Bea on your fiddle? It's been ages since you played."

Monday could not come soon enough, in Araminta's opinion, but it came at last and found her just as she had promised Mr. Carlisle—glued to Aggie's side in the morning room at The Acres. She wore a dress that used to be white but upon which she had spilled tea and which Monk had then had to dye all over with more tea, but the effect was good, and her thick hair was again curled and dressed and banded with a brown ribbon. Even Aggie's sister Frederica had blinked at the sight of her and said, "I declare, you and Agatha will yet surprise me." For Minta was not the only one fresh and presentable. Aggie, too, was a vision of neatness in light blue.

They did not have to wait long, which was fortunate because Aggie's sewing grew more lumpy and uneven the longer she worked at it, and Minta kept catching herself whistling after reading the same page of Mrs. Meeke's *Which Is the Man?* over and over.

"Mr. Francis Taplin," announced the bewigged footman.

Instantly electricity filled the room. They were on their feet, skirts smoothed and—in imitation of Miss Weeks—cheeks pinched for color, when Mr. Taplin entered, spotless, handsome and smiling.

"Ah, Miss Weeks. Miss Agatha. Miss—Effingham."

"Ellsworth," murmured Minta, her Cordelian tones hampered by gritted teeth. She kept her eyes lowered, lest she glare her annoyance.

But Mr. Taplin, though repeating her name correctly, took no notice of her mood. He was already chattering and asking questions of the Weekses about their time at the Race Ball, to which Miss Weeks responded readily and Aggie with besotted timidness.

It was indeed effective for Minta to sit as close beside Aggie on the sofa as possible, for each smile Mr. Taplin bestowed on her dear friend must perforce be shared with her, and she took care to imitate both him and his auditors. When he smiled, she smiled back demurely. When he nodded, she nodded. When he made anything approaching a joke or witticism, her mild titter sounded in chorus with Aggie's and Miss Weeks'. And, triumph of triumphs, after ten or so minutes of this, he tossed a remark at her, like he might a table scrap to a beseeching dog.

"Miss Eff—Ellsworth, rather. It was kind of you to dance with my brother at the ball. He has been attending with Mr. Beckford at Hollowgate, he tells me."

She ducked her chin and gave a miniature titter, not without noting his little jab at Mr. Carlisle. Why should it be a kindness to dance with Mr. Carlisle? "Yes," she replied.

With an apologetic look at the Miss Weekses, Taplin added, "My father and I shake our heads at Nick's choice of profession, but he has always been interested in dirtying his hands trying to figure out how things work, whether they be chemical or organical or medical."

"Imagine!" said Miss Weeks with a shudder.

"My," said Aggie.

"Ah," said Minta. She tried not to say anything more.

Not one word more.

But Mr. Taplin looked so *insufferable*, sitting there with one leg crossed over the other, his polished boots gleaming, his hair gleaming, his eyes gleaming, his teeth gleaming.

Briefly she wrestled with herself, and herself won—or lost.

"I find admirable both Mr. Carlisle's curiosity and his industry," she blurted.

Miss Weeks and Aggie gave little starts, but Mr. Taplin only opened his eyes very wide in innocent surprise. "You don't say."

"I do say, or I wouldn't have said it," she rapped back, even as the first trickle of dismay ran down her spine. *Shut up, Minta! Shut* up!

Another bout of internal wrestling—and this time the shrewder half of her managed to pin the frank half. Thus, she gave one of those infernal titters, this one with a modest hand raised to cover her teeth. "Oh, heavens. I mean to say, you gentlemen do think of such grand things."

Other than wanting to punch herself in the face for uttering such an inanity, Minta was relieved to see Miss Weeks relax and Mr. Taplin chuckle. Only Aggie turned to favor her with a suspicious frown, which Minta bore as blankly as she could. Why should Aggie be the only one allowed to behave like a ninny?

"What a beautiful day it is," declared Miss Weeks, decisively changing the subject.

"So it is!" agreed Mr. Taplin. "As a matter of fact, I came to The Acres today with no other thought in my head but that I would like to invite—er—all of you for a drive. Though I'm afraid I only have the phaeton today, which sadly fits three at the most."

Araminta slipped her arm around Aggie's waist, having no intention of being left behind, but Miss Weeks said with grace enough, "I will have to decline your kind invitation, I'm afraid, Mr. Taplin, for I have promised Mr. Linus Chester I would be at home when he called today." She simpered and *hmm-hm-hmm*ed as she delivered this news, and Mr. Taplin obligingly bowed and expressed his regrets that she could not accompany them.

Minta could feel the tremble of excitement in Aggie's slim form. Or maybe it was in her own form. Or in both of them. Somehow it felt twice as dangerous that Frederica would not be with them. The two of them would be crushed in the phaeton with Mr. Taplin (Who would sit beside him? Minta wondered. Could she possibly manage to thrust herself between him and Aggie?) and driven who-knew-where with no one at hand to watch over them or make things smooth.

It was Mr. Taplin who arranged things. The two girls were standing on the front steps, clutching each other's hands as the phaeton was brought around, Mr. Taplin slightly apart but on Araminta's side. But upon stepping forward to say a word to the groom, when he stepped back he was on Aggie's side, and to her he extended his hand. "May I assist you, Miss Agatha?"

She squeaked out a response but placed her hand in his, and up she went. Then that same hand was offered to Minta, and she had to remind herself to look abashed and grateful. Then around he went to climb in. With a chuck to the matched horses, they were off.

I might as well not exist, Araminta thought, some twenty minutes later. It was not that Mr. Taplin excluded her—it would be hard to exclude someone wedged into such a snug space as the three of them were—it was that he made no effort to single her out. Whereas he did single out Aggie.

"What a glorious day, is it not? Do you drive often, Miss Agatha?"

"Miss Agatha, look over there. I believe that fence marks the boundary between The Acres and Beaumond."

"Miss Agatha, would you like to hold the reins? There is nothing to fear. These bays are not only the handsomest in Hampshire, but they're also the most tractable and sensitive. I never need to use the whip on them, just soft words and a light hand. In fact, I don't know what they'd do if you were rough with them—probably run to Land's End. But your little hands will be just right."

"Run to Land's End?" gasped Aggie. "I hope not. How fortunate you understand them so well."

Now, Minta knew and Aggie knew that neither one of them had been trusted to drive anything since the age of eleven, when they stole into a visitor's gig at The Acres and took it on a rollicking jaunt across the grounds. (They hadn't intended to drive it across the grounds, but that was the direction the horse took when the whip was cracked several times in succession by an enthusiastic Minta. Although the whip hadn't touched him, the sound was enough to spur him to a panic, and only the girls' combined dragging on the reins and the action by several grooms to head them off brought the jolting adventure to an end. It had been a long enough spree, however, to destroy three prize flower-borders, get the girls nearly beheaded by low branches, and provoke Mr. Weeks into a fine fury.)

"I don't—think I'd better drive," said Aggie. A more experienced girl than Miss Agatha Weeks would have delighted in telling Mr. Taplin of the long-ago adventure and would have won laughter and admiration from him for it, but Aggie only sat stiff as a board, turning colors.

"Nonsense," returned Mr. Taplin. "Silkie and Clarion are perfect lambs."

"I don't know..."

"I'll do it!" declared Minta, leaning past her friend.

Aggie whirled around (as much as she could whirl around in such cramped conditions) to fix Minta with a Significant Look. At which Minta, aware that her face could be seen by Mr. Taplin if he cared to look, blinked vacantly.

"But Minta—I thought you did not like to drive."

"I am willing to do it," she replied in a low voice—even lower than Cordelia, in the hope Mr. Taplin wouldn't overhear. "I am willing to do something I would not do otherwise, that you might be spared."

"'Spared,' indeed! Why do you use a word like that? It's only driving," Aggie added contrarily, at full volume. "And Mr. Taplin says the horses are perfect lambs."

"Some things...can be more *dangerous* than they appear," hissed Minta. "Even things Mr. Taplin believes harmless. It's not that I want to drive, Aggie—it's that I *don't want you injured*. Don't you see? I'm looking out for you."

But Minta saw by the mutinous set of Aggie's mouth that Aggie did not see. Or she refused to see. And she certainly refused to acknowledge any subtler shades or hidden meanings in her friend's words.

And then Mr. Taplin deserved a hearty blow on the head for interceding the next moment. "Now, now, Miss Agatha, don't let your more cautious friend frighten you. Would I suggest anything that would endanger you? And, I might point out, if any of the three of us *were* to overset the carriage, you would not be the only one threatened by injury. But never mind that because I won't let it happen. Here—take these reins. I will put my hands right over yours, thus, but I will not intervene unless I think necessary."

Swallowing a lump of fury, Araminta sat back with a jerk, staring off in the opposite direction so Mr. Taplin would not glimpse the murder in her eyes. He only wanted to grab at Aggie! For, while Silkie and Clarion might be lambs, it was the Wolf who would have hold of her dearest friend for the next half hour.

Never had there been a longer ride. Aggie squeaking and gasping and giggling. Mr. Taplin whooping and laughing and insisting on righting the reins (and squeezing Aggie's hands) with unnecessary frequency.

It required all of ten minutes for Araminta to take herself in hand and realize there was nothing to be gained by silent pouting. Mr. Taplin already barely noticed her, and now he thought her an interfering killjoy. It was too frustrating. The morning had only resulted in her appearing *less* winning to him, rather than more. She had only succeeded in thrusting Aggie closer to Mr. Taplin, rather than drawing her away. Moreover, she had put Aggie's back up and made her less likely to heed good counsel. Drat. Drat drat drat.

Mr. Taplin's brother Mr. Carlisle would not be impressed by her progress when she reported it.

But thinking of Mr. Carlisle helped calm her.

Come now.

She could do this. She was doing better already. Why, Mr. Taplin had spoken to her more than once. (Not that he could help doing so without openly cutting her, but still—)

Fair, buxom, and shepherdess-like. Fair, buxom, and shepherdess-like, she chanted to herself. The assistance to her bust would have to wait another day or two, but she could get back to the rest.

Gradually, she began to insert herself again. When Mr. Taplin whooped, Araminta clapped her hands. When he laughed, she tittered. When he praised Aggie, Minta said, "Yes!" and "Yes, indeed!" (She dared not say more, for Aggie would already have been suspicious, were she not so intent on the driving.) When at last they pulled up before the entrance to The Acres again, and Mr. Taplin assisted her to descend, Minta threw a shy hitch in her voice and murmured, "You were right, Mr. Taplin. It was a lovely drive, and I was foolish to be afraid. How well you managed everything."

"I am flattered to hear you say so, Miss Ellsworth."

It wasn't much, and he then released her hand to reach for Aggie's, but it was a beginning.

Further rewards were in store for Minta, however, for Mr. Taplin took his leave afterward and—better still—told Aggie with regret that he would be gone a few days at a friend's invitation but certainly hoped he might see her again when he returned. "There will be more assemblies, you know. And the theatre and concerts and plenty more amusement to be had, Miss Agatha, so don't forget me while I'm gone."

Aggie blushed and wished him a good journey.

When he took himself off at last, she turned with a sigh to Minta. "I am not entirely sorry he will be absent a little while."

"You're not?" asked Minta, hope welling up.

"No. Because I'm getting some new dresses made. I'm hardly fit to be seen in the ones I have."

"Oh." Minta thought about mentioning her own new wardrobe but decided against it. To do so would only trumpet her own plans. And if they had this little reprieve from the man's company, perhaps the old Aggie might be persuaded to show her face again…?

"Well," she began, "since this old light blue of yours is destined for your maid Banniker—"

"Banniker says my cast-offs aren't fit for a beggar to wear."

"Then, since this old light blue of yours is destined for the rag basket, why don't we climb the abbey ruins one last time and then play some catch-ball or shoot some fruit off the trees?"

She could see Aggie waver before the refusal rose to her lips, but before it could be uttered, Minta hastily threw in a sop: "If we're away from the house and everyone else, we can talk about Mr. Taplin. What you like about him. For it's plain he likes you."

That did the trick. And, though she might have had to listen to more of Mr. Taplin's nonexistent perfections than she would have liked, Araminta got the old Aggie to herself for another golden afternoon.

Chapter Nine

"Basingstoke!" exclaimed Mr. John Taplin. "Whatever will you be doing there?" He sat at table with his son and stepson, the late afternoon sun filtering through the velvet window draperies.

"Old Rellert invited me, sir. Nick—you remember Rellert from Oxford."

Carlisle did indeed, as such a boisterous, unwise fellow was not easily forgotten. He gave a short nod.

"Why should he invite you to Basingstoke?" persisted his father. "Does he hail from there?"

"No, no. He's a Somerset man himself. But I'll be frank with you, sir—he's taken rooms at the Crown there, both to attend the Stockbridge races and the festivities afterward, and I thought it would be good fun to make one of his party."

His father heaved a long sigh, signaling with a lift of his fingers that the footmen should leave the room, which they did after carrying away some of the empty dishes and refilling Taplin's glass when he tapped it.

"I thought, son—nay, you gave me your word, did you not?—that you would leave off the expensive frivolities which have already imperiled your future. Has your resolve given way so soon?"

Taplin grimaced. "Can a stay in shared rooms at a country inn be called expensive, sir?"

"It can if that stay involves visits to the betting post."

"I give you my word of honor: I'll venture no more than...say, twenty pounds, all told. And, if I should win, I may even come home richer than when I left."

"It was my understanding, Francis, that you were to leave off gambling and the wild life altogether and put your shoulder to a wholly different wheel now."

"You mean the wheel of finding a wife, sir."

"Yes."

"Yes," repeated Taplin. "And not just any old wife, but a wealthy one, a girl filled to overflowing with deeds, ducats and dowries. Believe me: I have not forgotten my task. Indeed, a just man would say I have earned myself this little holiday, after the hard work I have put in and the success I have met with."

His father's head lifted, and Carlisle's eyes likewise turned to him.

"Have you met with success already, Francis?"

"I have, if I can be excused the immodest boast. While I am not yet engaged, I would say I have made remarkable progress in so short a time and, with continued exertion along the same lines, might bag two heiresses if I wished, or if it were allowed. Imagine having *two* fortunes at my disposal!"

Mr. John Taplin availed himself of a slow, steadying sip of wine, but Carlisle could see his hand tremble. Carlisle felt rather unstable himself. Was it already too late for Miss Agatha, then? And—worse—were Miss Ellsworth's plans doomed even before they could rightly be implemented?

"Who are these promising ladies, if I might ask?" pressed their father.

"You might as well say promising *young* ladies, Father," grinned Taplin, "because I find I will not need to gather any withered, crapey woman of five-and-thirty to my heart. I believe Miss Wright to be but seventeen and Miss...Agatha Weeks perhaps nineteen."

"Miss Agatha of The Acres?"

"The same. And Miss Wright of Meadowsweep, outside Romsey. Granddaughter to Dean Fellowes, if it interests you. But I see it does not. Your preference lies already with Miss Agatha, I suppose." Nonchalantly, Taplin sawed another bite of his roast and popped it in his mouth.

"I am sure they are both...pleasing young ladies," breathed his father. "If I think first of Miss Agatha, it is only because of the mortgages her father holds."

"Exactly," said Taplin, chewing. "Miss Wright is rather prettier, but Miss Agatha has the mortgages. They both like me, as far as I can tell. I've called on both, danced with both. I took Miss Agatha driving today, and I'll invite Miss Wright to something when I come back."

"Do *you* have a preference, Francis?" his father asked weakly, half ashamed of the question. If his son must make such a mercenary match, it felt false to pretend it might aspire to anything else. But still he thought what a boon it would be, if Francis' heart followed where needs led!

The young man shrugged at the question. "Come, Father. I'll do your bidding and my duty, but you mustn't expect my heart to be involved. Either young lady will do for our purposes." He turned then to his stepbrother, shaking his head in mock chagrin. "Ah, Nick, you don't know how lucky you are, to be nameless and landless. You may marry whom you please."

"Thank you," Carlisle answered dryly. "You well know I cannot afford to marry, even if I did please."

"Oh, that's right." Taplin sighed. "We each have our cross to bear, I suppose." Taking another sip of his wine, he swished it around in his mouth before swallowing it with a choked chuckle. "But why should my scheme not also work for you, Nick? You have no heavily-mortgaged estate to redeem, but surely you would appreciate a little more small change in your pocket? Supposing you were to attract a wealthy bride of your own?"

"Thank you for thinking of me," Carlisle replied, "but even if I weren't determined to make my own way, I am not blessed with heiresses falling at my feet as you are."

"In fact," continued his brother, ignoring him and raising his wineglass like a sceptre, "Nicholas Carlisle, I do hereby bequeath to you either Miss Anna Wright or Miss Agatha Weeks for your marital and financial purposes, with all the rights and privileges thereto appertaining, depending on whichever one is left over after I choose."

"That's enough, my boy," interposed his grieved father. "These are respectable young ladies from respectable families, and they do not deserve to have their names bandied about because we were foolish. I am glad of your news—I cannot help but be. But let us change the subject."

They did accordingly, talking doggedly of the July haymaking and of what one of the tenants proposed to do with some of his acreage; they made observations on the weather and the crops, but no one's mind was much upon the conversation. By the following morning, Taplin made an early start for Basingstoke, and Carlisle set off down the Weeke footpath to Mr. Beckford's.

The good doctor was not in, however, and his housekeeper Mrs. Ecton informed him, "He got called out early this morning, sir. Mrs. Purrock's baby is come, and about time. Each one gets later and later, it seems to me, as if the poor things didn't want to come into the world or were ashamed of being the fourteenth or fifteenth Purrock, or however many there are now. But Mr. Beckford says as you're to step out to the booksellers in College Street and pick up those new textbooks he ordered, if you please. Here's the list."

As a former student of Winchester College, Carlisle had frequented the book shops in College Street, including Drubbands', which carried volumes of a scientific and medical nature. But he had never before in his visits to the dusty, musty, close little shop found a young lady within. There was one today, however, in a tidy muslin dress and chip bonnet, by the bookcase in the back, paging through a copy of Buchan's *Domestic Medicine*.

Carlisle would have ignored her, except that, in turning a leaf of Buchan, a visible puff of dust escaped, and the young lady succumbed to a sneezing fit. One made up not of dainty, squeaky, miniature sneezes, but rather a series of distinct, loud explosions, escalating in violence until she cried, "Great guns!"

"Miss Ellsworth," said Carlisle, "can that be you?"

A pair of startled hazel eyes appeared above the handkerchief the young lady was using to dab her face. "Mr. Carlisle!"

To his amazement, she blushed and slammed Buchan shut, replacing it hastily on the shelf, only to have to pull it off again because it had caught the corner of her pocket-cloth.

"H-how do you do?" she fumbled.

He didn't mean to embarrass her, but his curiosity spurred him. With a nod toward the book she now had her back to, he asked, "Was there something you did not want to ask Mr. Beckford?"

"Oh—no—nothing. Nothing important. Just curious. What—brings you here?"

He held up the notepaper with the doctor's list. "A few books for Mr. Beckford." Turning to place this note on Mr. Drubbands' desk, he realized, with belated embarrassment of his own, that she might have been consulting Buchan in reference to women's problems.

By this point Araminta was recovering, and she said airily, "What is that saying on great minds often thinking alike? We—my brother Tyrone and my sister Beatrice and I—are in College Street because Tyrone ordered some books as well. The circulating library beside the White Hart can't keep up with him, you know."

"Does Mr. Tyrone Ellsworth share your medical curiosity?"

"No, no. He and Bea are next door. They'll be along in a few minutes. Or I will go and meet them."

Simultaneously it occurred to both of them that this was a lucky meeting wherein they might share their news, and they unconsciously drew closer together.

"Mr. Carlisle," hissed Minta, "while I have this moment—"

"Miss Ellsworth," murmured Carlisle, "I think it best to tell you—"

They both paused, laughing ruefully and throwing a glance toward the bookseller Mr. Drubbands, who was moving books on the shelves behind him, rummaging for the required volumes. Carlisle nodded for Araminta to proceed.

"Thank you. Mr. Carlisle, I feel obliged to tell you that I seem to be failing with your brother. I know I have not had many opportunities and that I don't have my new dresses yet—I ordered new dresses—but nevertheless it is discouraging. Yesterday he came to take Aggie driving, and he had to take me as well because I was sitting there, but he still had little to say to me, even though I tried my best to be silly and timid and admiring and everything we talked about. And I'm terribly afraid Aggie likes him better each day. I haven't given up hope altogether because—well—my new gowns will—er—flatter me, the modiste tells me, but I do confess to being quite anxious."

He absently took up a volume of Lavoisier's *Elements of Chemistry*, running a finger up and down the spine. He hated to tell her that his brother had all but settled on Miss Agatha as the solution to the Taplin problems, but there was nothing to be gained by keeping her in the dark, and the appeal in her eyes tugged at him.

His mouth twisted a little at the corner, and Minta drew another step nearer without being aware of it.

"Miss Ellsworth, I fear you may be right," he said in his low voice, "that your scheme is in danger of failing. I am sorry to tell you so, but Francis himself expressed yesterday his...satisfaction with Miss Agatha."

"No!" she mouthed, her face crumpling. "Who did he say this to? To you? To others?"

"To my father and me as we sat at dinner."

"Ah." She clutched herself around the middle, her breathing rapid. "But he can't decide so soon! I need more time! My new dresses..."

In spite of himself, he smiled. "These really must be some extraordinary dresses."

Drawing herself up with rather touching dignity, she said, "They are meant to make me look better."

"No modiste can do that, I don't imagine."

He meant it as a compliment, thinking to himself that she was like a ray of light in musty, dusty, fusty Drubbands'. From her fair hair and open face to the column of her person, always taut with energy. But Minta understood him to mean precisely the opposite. She shrunk visibly, a shadow darkening her features.

"I meant only that my aunt Jeanne and the modiste tell me there are—flaws of the figure—which proper clothing can attempt to—to disguise or correct," she rejoined quietly. "That's all. I didn't mean to imply that—"

Horrified, he cut her off. "Miss Ellsworth! Surely you don't think I was saying there was anything wrong or—or unpleasing in your looks? No! I meant no dress could have any effect on you, however nicely it's made. Because you're—you're splendid, and don't let anyone or anything tell you otherwise. Not even my brother's inexplicable neglect."

Minta's mouth dropped open, and there was no one to tell her to shut it again. She was distantly aware of a rushing and thumping in her ears, and it took her some moments to realize it was the sound of her own blood and heart, seemingly knocking about within her. Was this how her sister Lily felt, whenever someone remarked on her beauty? Breathless—astonished—unsteady? It could hardly be possible, or Lily would not be able to go about her daily life! Maybe if one received compliments of this nature all the time, one got accustomed to it. Maybe Lily yawned behind her hand, to be told for the thousandth time that she was lovely. But for Araminta, who could not recall ever in her life being told she was "splendid" (not that she had fretted much about it, until Mr. Taplin appeared), she did not think a day would be enough time in which to recover. She had the unbelievable and mortifying desire to throw herself into Mr. Carlisle's arms and to kiss him for saying such words; and at the same time, she wanted to flee home to study herself in a mirror and see if it was really true. Was she, in fact, splendid?

"Thank you," she croaked inadequately.

She was in no state to notice he had flushed himself. He did not know what had possessed him to declare such a thing—not that he didn't mean what he said, but he had never said such a thing to any woman in his life, and the answering blaze and wonder in her eyes quite unmastered him. His grip on Lavoisier tightened until old Mr. Drubbands asked, "Will you be wanting that one, too?"

Carlisle almost tossed it at him and then took hold of Miss Ellsworth's elbow to guide her to a farther corner.

"Miss Ellsworth, when Francis was telling us that he would likely continue to...see Miss Agatha, I did think of one more possible thing you—we—might try."

She gulped, thankful he couldn't feel her flying pulse. If he had taken her by the wrist he might have thought she was having some kind of fit. He released her then, in any case, and she managed to say, "What—thing—did you think of?"

His smile was doleful. "Miss Ellsworth, your siblings and you seem to get along so harmoniously that what I say perhaps won't make any sense to you. But Francis and I...you know we were at school and university together, though I am a year older in age. Only when I was in London staying with my uncle have I spent any amount of time without my brother about. What I mean to say is, between Francis and me there has always been—there is no other word for it—competition. There shouldn't be, but there is. It seems unlikely because—well—Francis has...everything. My father's name and blood. Beaumond to inherit. His handsomeness and charm. *Everything.* Whereas I—" he broke off, but there was no need for him to finish. She understood. He was the stepson, without the name and without the family and without the estate. Without Mr. Taplin's odious golden handsomeness.

"In any event," resumed Carlisle, "there is this competition. For whatever reason, Francis pits us against each other, no matter if he 'wins' every time. I can hardly account for it, but it has always been so."

"I'm sorry for it," she mumbled. She wanted to tell him she had an inkling where the issue lay—that it had something to do with Mr. Carlisle's kindness and intelligence. And something also to do with his resolve—he accepted what life dealt him but had interest and initiative enough to pursue a profession, rather than dwell on what he had not been given. How could Mr. Taplin not be jealous of such qualities, idle and useless as he himself was?

Much as Minta would have liked to tell Mr. Carlisle again that she thought him infinitely to be preferred to his brother, somehow she couldn't summon her usual forthrightness. Not when her insides were demonstrating a will of their own and not when he was standing so close.

Moreover, an idea pierced her in a most unpleasant and unexpected fashion. She nearly gasped—"Are you saying, Mr. Carlisle, that you think *you* should court Aggie?"

"What? No. That's not it at all."

"Oh," she said. Thank heavens, for she did not think she could greet such a plan with convincing enthusiasm.

"I mean to suggest, Miss Ellsworth, that I should pretend to court *you*."

If the notion of Mr. Carlisle courting Aggie caused Minta a pang, that did not render the same notion applied to *herself* any more welcome. Why that should be, she could not yet explain, but nor could she stop the thought before it streaked through her head: *of course he would have to pretend.*

She was silent, struggling, but she did not need to think of what to say because he hurried on.

"If you and I had a...counterfeit courtship, nothing would so quickly bring you to my brother's attention, I'm afraid. Francis would notice you then because he notices anything I have or want to have. And then, in order to keep me in my place, I don't doubt Francis would transfer his preference to *you*. Miss Agatha would be saved."

"Saved," she whispered.

He watched the parade of expressions fleet across her open countenance—dismay, embarrassment, worry. Being as modest in his view of himself as Araminta believed, it did not occur to him she would object out of hurt. That she would mind because he did not pursue her in earnest.

"If you were willing to deceive my brother as to your own true nature and your lack of interest in him," he reminded her gently, "I do not think you will find my plan so different."

"No," she replied, hardly audible. "You're right all around. It *isn't* any different."

"Nor do I think we would have to pretend very long," he went on, "if that concerns you. Francis is not slow in these things."

"Mm-hm." She swallowed. "But—Mr. Carlisle—suppose you wanted to court someone else in earnest? Only think what damage it might do your cause, if she sees you paying me attentions."

He chuckled at this. "Have no fear there, Miss Ellsworth—though it is very kind of you to mention it. I cannot afford to marry for years and years. By the time I got around to paying some good woman my 'attentions,' the tale of my brief and doomed courtship of you would be 'compounded with the forgotten dust.' We are quite safe there."

"I see." She chewed her lip thoughtfully. Yes, it likely would work. The combination of her new dresses, with their bosom-enhancing promise, added to Mr. Taplin's natural sense of competition, might succeed where her own efforts had thus far failed. (Efforts which included that morning's fruitless search for a bosom-enhancing elixir or ointment in Buchan's *Domestic Medicines*.)

This was Aggie's fate in her hands.

There was no alternative. Of course they must try it.

Misinterpreting her continued silence, Carlisle heard himself say, "I understand if *you* began to have...feelings for someone else, Miss Ellsworth, you would not like to appear...changeable."

That snapped her from her reverie. "What? Oh, nonsense. If this fictional gentleman you postulate could stomach me running after your brother and behaving like the veriest mooncalf, I imagine he would be relieved to find me preferring a man of sense."

Warmed by her matter-of-fact praise, his lopsided grin appeared. "Then we are in agreement? We will be sham sweethearts and rescue Miss Agatha for her own good?"

"We will, sir."

"Let us shake on it, then."

They did so, unconsciously gripping each other a touch harder and a moment longer than the compact required, and then he must get back to purchasing Mr. Beckford's books, and she must rejoin her siblings.

The little bell attached to the door of Drubbands' rang as Minta pushed her way out. A jolly, tinkling sound, but it nevertheless struck her as the faintest warning.

For though Mr. Carlisle might deem his plan "quite safe," Minta could not help but feel that pretending a liking for him, and he for her, would be anything but.

Chapter Ten

A little Rakishness becomes Youth, Madam.
— John Hewitt, *A Tutor for the Beaus: or Love in a Labyrinth* (1737)

Mr. Taplin's absence provided a welcome respite from Minta's trials. For one thing, Aggie reappeared at Hollowgate, and the girls resorted to their favorite activities out of doors, lawn bowling and archery and running about. Their bonnets went missing, their old clothing suffered a few tears and stains, their persons likewise sustained scrapes, and their hair reverted to dishevelment.

But even with all these joys, something was changed.

"Ah," sighed Aggie, rolling over onto her stomach in the grass and nibbling on a piece of hay. "I do wonder when Mr. Taplin will return."

Minta was lying on her back, an arm across her eyes to block out the late July sun. "Soon enough, I imagine."

"But my new gowns are finished, and I can't wait to wear them."

This most un-Aggie-like sentiment caused Minta a little pang before she decided she may as well make use of it. She had given much thought to how her counterfeit courtship with Mr. Carlisle might work, and Aggie's remark gave her a place to begin.

Flinging off her arm, Minta sat up. "Aggie. I had new dresses made too."

"You did?" Aggie scrambled to a sitting position as well, her expression somewhere between eager and uneasy. "I thought you didn't care for such things."

"What? Me?"

"Yes. You. Here I was thinking you have thought me silly of late, because I've begun to take more trouble with my appearance."

"I see that," grinned Minta, pointing at the streamer of lace dangling from her friend's sleeve. Aggie had snagged it on a hedgerow they forced their way through, to avoid walking all the way to the gap.

"You know what I mean," said Aggie, winding the lace around two fingers and tucking it up. "When Mr. Taplin is around. *Then* I care about my appearance. And I thought you thought I was being silly because of that."

Minta decided on a half-truth. "I did," she answered slowly, "until I began to understand your feelings better. That is, why you acted the way you did."

Aggie swallowed audibly, and the unease in her look deepened. "Do you mean, you began to understand why I...like Mr. Taplin so well?"

"Yes..."

"Because—you have begun to like him too?"

"Oh, no!" cried Minta, to Aggie's surpassing relief. "Not because I like Mr. Taplin too, but because I—I think I might be beginning to like somebody else. So therefore, I too would like to look my best and perhaps behave in ways I haven't before."

"Oh!" breathed Aggie. "Oh, that's marvelous. I'm so glad for you, Minta. And for me, too. Because, isn't it funny? We never cared about such things before, and now—we do! That means we can help each other in this. Do it together, as we always have. Won't you—tell me who it is you admire?"

"Certainly. It's Mr. Nicholas Carlisle," declared Minta. "I like Mr. Nicholas Carlisle."

Aggie gave a squeal of delight, clapping her hands. Her lace came untucked again and unrolled like a carpet. "Hurrah! He's very agreeable, Mr. Carlisle is. Kind, courteous. And Mr. Taplin's stepbrother! Maybe one day you and I will be sisters."

Despite the summer sunshine, Minta could not repress the shiver that vision provoked, but the smile she produced must have been convincing because Aggie gave a happy purr and took Minta's hands in her own. "Do you think Mr. Carlisle likes you back? Do you think he guesses you like him?"

"Possibly. And possibly," she replied vaguely. "I hope so!"

"How fun it will be to go to balls and such now! Oh, Minta, who knew young gentlemen were so—so wonderful?"

"Mm," said Minta.

Aggie's brow clouded. Pleased as she was to have her bosom friend struck as well by Cupid's arrow (however glancingly), she puzzled over Araminta's restraint. Shouldn't this be a time for dreams and exultation and reckless avowals? Being in love at the same time would not be nearly as fun if Araminta was going to be uncharacteristically cautious. It was true that Mr. Carlisle was no Mr. Taplin, but still—

Ah—it must be that. Araminta must be anxious over Mr. Carlisle's disadvantages.

With sympathy, Aggie squeezed her friend's hands. "Oh, Minta—it's too bad Mr. Carlisle is so poor."

"Poor?" echoed Minta, surprised. "Yes. Too bad." She had not honestly thought one way or another about Mr. Carlisle's financial prospects. But, yes, she supposed it was too bad he was poor. More pressingly, it was too bad Aggie's Mr. Taplin was scarcely better off.

"For Mr. Carlisle can't possibly marry, can he?" persisted Aggie. "He couldn't afford to."

"He could marry a rich girl."

Aggie's eyes grew round. "You mean you would consider marrying a poor man, Minta? A poor *doctor*?"

"At least he hasn't any debts that I know of," Minta couldn't forbear saying, "and he works hard. Not that I have any intention of marrying him."

Aggie had been about to question her friend's tone—was there some hidden jab at Mr. Taplin in it?—but this last statement distracted her. "How do you already know you won't marry him? You just said you liked him, Minta."

"And so I do."

"Then how can you already be so certain?"

"Because—I'm not thinking of marrying *anyone* at present. Are *you*, Aggie? If Mr. Taplin asked you, would you say yes to him?"

Aggie's chin jutted out and she jabbed at the torn lace again. "I—I don't see why not. I could go farther and fare worse. And he is the handsomest, most charming person I've ever met. And think! Beaumond borders The Acres!"

"What about—his wild oats he mentioned?" ventured Minta, crossing her fingers beneath the folds of her dress. Thank heavens for her plan, and please God that it would work, for Aggie was far, far gone.

Now Aggie turned on her friend with a scowl. "What about them? Every young man with spirit has done things he—grows out of. Perhaps Mr. Taplin—used to be—heedless with money or—or given to rakishness, but everyone knows a rake can reform. You're as bad as my papa. When Frederica told him that Mr. Taplin had called at The Acres, Papa grumbled something about how he hadn't made his fortune 'just to be handing it over to some handsome scapegrace.' As if Mr. Taplin were some nameless fortune hunter!"

With difficulty Minta managed not to whoop—what a trump Mr. Weeks was!—but the attempt to school her features into sympathy with Aggie's indignation only resulted in what looked like a dyspeptic grimace.

"Still—a father's opinion…" she replied, when she could disguise the amusement in her voice. "What would you do if your papa didn't approve the match, Aggie?"

Aggie frowned over this possibility, ripping up handfuls of the Hollowgate lawn as she did so. "Of course, it's ridiculous to talk like this—the way we are—when nothing has happened and nothing *may* happen, with either Mr. Taplin or Mr. Carlisle."

"What would you *do*?" repeated Minta, not to be deterred.

"What would *you* do?" Aggie tossed back at her.

It was a fair question. Araminta's father was so oblivious, so contented, as long as he himself had a wife to look after him. His first two daughters Florence and Lily had married respectably, even if their husbands had done nothing to add to the family wealth. While some fathers might have demanded more for their daughters—fortunes, titles, grander names—William Ellsworth said nothing about any of these things. *Would* he speak up, if Araminta announced she wanted to marry a rakish spendthrift like Francis Taplin? Or would Papa go right on beaming amiably, wishing her well as she marched straight into disaster?

"My brothers-in-law and Flossie and Lily would likely have something to say about it, if I chose someone of whom they disapproved," Minta said at last. "And while I wouldn't mind crossing Florence or Lily, it would take some bravery on my part to cross Robert and Simon."

"Yes, I could see that," agreed Aggie. "Especially Mr. Kenner."

"Yes. Especially him." Lily's husband Simon Kenner had once been the curate of St. Eadburh's, their parish church, lending him an additional aura of authority.

"So you wouldn't marry Mr. Carlisle or whomever you wanted to marry if your family did not approve?"

They wouldn't disapprove of Mr. Carlisle, thought Minta. He was poor, yes, but after the passage of a few years, when he had his own practice, he wouldn't be significantly poorer than Robert Fairchild had been when he married Florence. And Minta was certain they would approve of his kindness and character.

But that wasn't Aggie's question—suppose Minta's heart were set upon a Francis Taplin? No, no—that wasn't the analogy, exactly. Suppose Minta chose a Mr.-Carlisle sort for herself, but the rest of her family thought of him as a Mr.-Taplin type? What would she do then? For, really, that was to put herself in Aggie's shoes. Aggie thought Mr. Taplin a paragon and seemed to believe it with as much sincerity as Minta believed it of Mr. Carlisle.

"I suppose I would elope with him and leave them to get over it," Minta murmured, more to herself than to Aggie. But Aggie seized on it.

"You would? You really would, Minta? Elope?" She rose up on her knees, tucking her heels under her and bouncing with eagerness.

Too late, Minta regretted her utterance. The whole point was that Mr. Taplin was *not* worthy, and Mr. Weeks was right to caution his daughters!

"On second thought," she said hastily, "knowing my family to be both wise and trustworthy, I would certainly listen very hard to what they were saying. Very hard. Very, very, very hard. They love me, after all, and want what is best for me."

"But if they were all mistaken, Minta—"

"That doesn't seem likely."

"But if they *were*—then you would elope?"

Minta threw up her hands. "Who can say? Like you said a minute ago, this is ridiculous to speak of at this point. For a thousand reasons, we are very far from having to consider such possibilities."

"I suppose." Aggie huffed out a disappointed breath, to have her daring friend prove so boringly prudent. She rocked back onto her bottom in the grass and leaned back on her hands. But the very next instant she was on her knees again. "Minta! Someone is coming up the drive! Who do you think it is?"

Turning, Minta squinted. Then she sprang up. "It's my aunt Jeanne! And she has a box—perhaps it's one of my new dresses." She waved and hollered, and then she and Aggie made a dash to meet the visitor.

"*Doucement, mes chères,*" laughed Jeanne Ellsworth, when the girls skidded to a halt beside her, Minta pelting her with questions about the box. "And your hair! The both of you." Clicking her tongue, she surveyed them. "Here, Minta—you may carry it yourself. It is not a dress. It is the more important thing for you. It is the bodice."

"Why should that be more important?" asked Aggie. "No one will see her bodice, Mrs. Ellsworth."

"They will see *this* bodice," answered Jeanne, her eyes twinkling. "Whether they realize it or not."

"Gracious," said Minta, some while later, as the three women and the maid Monk stood in her room studying her before the looking glass. For the first time in her life, Minta had a bosom worth the name. The little cotton corset, stiffened with cording, lifted and separated what little she had into two respectable globes, which were then amplified and undergirded by row after row of cunning, tiny ruffles. And the bodice of Minta's gown, which was pleated to soften her angular lines, now made full use of those pleats to contain the unaccustomed freight.

"*Voilà*," pronounced Aunt Jeanne with a theatrical gesture. "*Plantureuse.*"

"I need a tucker," gasped Minta, spreading her hands over her exposed flesh.

"It really is astonishing," Aggie said, shaking her head in incredulity.

"You look like a girl now, miss," added the unhelpful Monk. The maid grumbled under her breath as she brushed and twisted Minta's hair to restore it to order.

"But I don't want so many little ruffles," insisted Minta, digging two fingers into her bodice. "Can't we remove a few?"

"*Ne touche pas!*" cried Mrs. Ellsworth, smacking her hand away. "You must not damage the craftsmanship of Madame Blanchet."

"But it isn't *me*. This bosom. This—false front. Aunt Jeanne, with this thing on, I don't feel like me, and I don't look like me."

"*Tu vas t'y faire.*"

"But what if I don't want to get used to it?" Minta persisted. "And what if I don't want others to get used to me looking like I don't actually look?"

Her aunt did not reply in words. She merely raised one arched eyebrow and let her gaze flick over to Aggie and back to her niece. Then she raised her shoulders in a question.

It was enough. Minta understood. *Was she, or was she not, going to go through with her plan to save Aggie? And was it, or was it not, an essential part of that plan that she appear more buxom?*

She was, and it was.

"I suppose—all my new dresses were made for these measurements," she said slowly.

"Exactly."

"So it is either wear this thing or have all those dresses altered."

"Unthinkable."

"You do look well, Minta," spoke up Aggie. "Why, your bosom is as big as mine now. Or nearly."

"Is it?" asked Minta dully.

"Yes, and you'll see how much more difficult it is to engage in sport with such a burden. I only got a new corset myself, before the Domum Ball. Before that I used to try to smash 'em down, for convenience's sake."

There was a knock at the door and the chief housemaid Boots thrust her head in. "Miss Araminta, there's a caller, but your father is with Mr. Falk and Mrs. Ellsworth has gone into town with Miss Beatrice and Master William. And Mr. Tyrone is—"

"Mr. Tyrone is with my husband and his cousins today," finished Jeanne Ellsworth.

Araminta colored, half turning aside and hunching her shoulders in the hopes Boots would not notice her new figure (as if Monk wouldn't go straight downstairs and discuss it thoroughly with the entire staff of Hollowgate). "Who is it? Can you say no one is home?"

"It's Mr. Carlisle, the doctor's young man," answered Boots. "And he has flowers for you and Mrs. William Ellsworth."

Aggie gasped and clapped her hands to her mouth as Minta began shaking her head vigorously, her hand still splayed across her chest. "I'm not—tell him I'm not here. He can leave the flowers. But thank him for them."

"Wait!" Jeanne Ellsworth held up a peremptory hand. "I am very curious about this Mr. Carlisle, of whom I have heard a thing or two, and I am also very curious about if he will notice anything different about our Araminta."

"Me too! Me too! Oh, Minta, just go down and see," urged Aggie.

"No!"

"Yes," said her aunt.

"*Please!*" begged Aggie.

A few more rounds of this passed, and then Minta said with finality, "Only on one condition."

His work for the day at Beckford's completed, Carlisle was a hundred yards down the footpath from Weeke when an exuberant patch of pink lady's pincushion caught his eye.

I may as well call. The idea must be planted in everyone's mind—it cannot burst out fully formed at the next ball, like Athena from Zeus's forehead.

He had not seen Miss Ellsworth since their encounter at Drubbands' several days earlier, though he had thought about her from time to time as he compounded medicines or followed the doctor on his rounds or consulted Beckford's reference books. Would she still be game to enact their ruse?

There was some confusion at Hollowgate when he appeared. The footman showed him into one of the parlors before holding some conference outside the door with one of the maids, and then a lengthy silence followed. Carlisle wandered about, examining the trinkets and books (judging from the titles, many of them must belong to Mr. Tyrone) and the prospect from the window. After several minutes of this, he began to think he had been forgotten, but at last he detected returning steps—rather a lot of them—and the door opened again. In trotted the Ellsworths' old terrier, making a beeline for him to give him a sniff and a perfunctory growl. He was followed by Miss Ellsworth, Miss Agatha, and an older woman whom Carlisle could not immediately give his attention to, as Miss Ellsworth's appearance distracted him.

"Good afternoon, Miss Ellsworth, Miss Agatha," he bowed and held out the bouquet of lady's pincushion and yarrow. "I hope I find you well?"

"Perfectly well," returned Miss Ellsworth, as if being swathed neck-to-waist in a wrinkly shawl on a warm July day were nothing remarkable. Her own hands and arms being lost somewhere in the layers of her wrapper, she jerked her head at Miss Agatha, who lunged forward to take the flowers. "How pretty those are," Minta said. "My mama will love them. May I introduce you to my aunt Mrs. Charles Ellsworth?"

The dark-haired woman regarded him with her head cocked and then cried, "Ah, but we need no introduction! It is little Nicky, is it not? You were Orlando, when you were possibly ten or eleven years old? And your brother—*comment il s'appelait?*—he was Oliver."

Carlisle's face lit up in a most becoming manner. "*As You Like It*—yes! Madame Jeanne—if I might still address you thus—what a pleasure to see you again after so many years. You made our costumes and helped to paint our faces. What fun that was. I was sorry the experience was not repeated."

"*Moi aussi*. But now I see you again, and I find this very interesting."

Considering all Jeanne Ellsworth knew of Francis Taplin and Agatha Weeks and what Araminta intended to do about them with this young man's help, it interested her very much indeed.

Araminta was not sorry for her aunt's and Mr. Carlisle's prior acquaintance providing a diversion, but it was not long before perspiration broke out on her forehead and beneath her arms, and she wished with all her might he would take his leave before she smothered in this stupid shawl.

The stupid shawl served its purpose, however, for it was impossible for Carlisle to notice a thing about her bosom, even if he had been the sort of young man who made a point of doing so. He only puzzled briefly at her attire, venturing one more question—"Are you chilled, Miss Ellsworth?"—to which she replied, "Perfectly comfortable, thank you," as a drop of perspiration slid down her forehead. He could hardly gainsay her, so he dropped the matter.

What was clear to him was that Miss Ellsworth was indeed still game with their counterfeit courtship, and that she had laid some initial groundwork with Miss Agatha. For Miss Agatha smiled upon him and glanced back and forth between Miss Ellsworth and himself as if she were delighted to share their secret. How much Madame Jeanne knew (he still thought of her thus) or approved was less certain, but her liking for him was real, and when Carlisle did depart Hollowgate, it was with an overall feeling of satisfaction and a pleasant anticipation for what lay ahead.

Chapter Eleven

**Indeed, my first determination was to confine my cha-
grin totally to my own bosom.
— Fanny Burney, *Evelina* (1778)**

B ut the Bosom could not be hidden forever, of course.

Minta wished it could.

Because somehow the Bosom was worse than all the other strata-
gems combined. Worse than false timidity and assumed adoration
and intolerable titters. Certainly worse than having to pretend a
liking for the completely likeable Mr. Carlisle! The Bosom, once
strapped onto her, was something she could not control. Short of
going about the rest of the summer in the suffocating shawl, she
could not choose when it would or would not be part of her.

Immediately following Mr. Carlisle's departure from Hollowgate, Minta fled back to her room and threw off both shawl and

padded corset, but when her new wardrobe arrived a few days onward, she knew she must eventually either don the wretched thing or abandon that part of her plan altogether and beg for every one of her new gowns to be altered and Madame Blanchet's handiwork desecrated.

And of course that could not be done.

What could not be avoided must therefore be endured.

Mr. Taplin's absence proved a welcome reprieve in the ensuing days, however, though as his time away stretched, Minta was made to bear her friend's increasing sighs and listlessness, but these were nothing compared to Mr. Taplin's actual burdensome presence. In the meantime, Mr. Carlisle called once or twice more, always finding the girls out of doors, but without the Bosom strapped to her Minta received these visits tranquilly, and she would happily have gone on thus forever.

But all good things must come to an end, and with the turning of the month, Minta's first trial revealed itself. On that morning, Bobbins delivered a note at the breakfast table. Recognizing Mr. Carlisle's hand, Minta opened it to find one sentence: "He has returned and will attend the flower show."

There was no need to wonder at his meaning. The Annual Carnation Feast at the St. Cross was famous in Hampshire. Only members were invited to the florists' feast, but anyone might inspect the flowers at the inn afterward, and because Barney the head gardener at Hollowgate hoped to take the prized silver spoon, all Ellsworths were called upon to pay their sixpence and see the show. After which, the St. Cross, eager to make the most of a popular event, offered a tea reception for the public in their largest room.

Nor were the Ellsworths the only family with a contestant in their sphere. Nearly every large estate in the county supplied an entrant, a gardener or groundskeeper, if not the squire himself. These were joined by florists and amateurs without landed estates, who might have grown their submissions in moveable pots, rather than fixed flower-borders and beds. While Minta liked flowers well enough, she lacked the patience her sister Florence had for grubbing in the soil, and if pressed might have said that she preferred wildflowers to the cultivated varieties. Mr. Carlisle's offering of yarrow and lady's pin-cushion, for instance, had occupied a vase of honor in the drawing room beside the pianoforte as long as they lasted, and in admiring them Minta had even sat down at the instrument and practiced.

Upon reading Mr. Carlisle's note, Minta glanced down at her comfortable old dress and knew she must change into one of her new ones for the event. And if she must wear a new one, it would require the support of the Bosom. The day was bright and mildly oppressive, and Minta did not think she could venture even the lightest drapery about the neck and shoulders without melting in a puddle. No—the Bosom would have to be displayed in all its glory, for better or for worse. *This public outing will get it over with, at any rate,* she thought, steeling herself. And like a medieval knight donning his armor, with Monk's assistance Minta put on the cursed corset under a new dotted white muslin and had her hair curled and dressed as it had not been for nearly a fortnight.

"Heavens, how fine you look, Araminta," her stepmother told her, with only a few blinks at the Bosom before she hastily looked away. The remaining Ellsworths said nothing at all, and Minta did not know if her papa and Tyrone and Beatrice were avoiding looking at her, or if it was her imagination.

Only Willie acknowledged her new shape, but that was because when she went to pick him up, his little head crashed right into It.

"Ooh!" he yelped, rubbing his hair and turning astonished eyes on her. "The pillow got me."

"There's the carriage!" cried Mrs. Ellsworth, her cheeks pink. "Off we go. Willsie, you be a good boy for Monk and Boots."

A carriage was hardly necessary, it being less than a mile to the St. Cross, but on hot or inclement days Mr. Ellsworth insisted. Greaves the groom was obliged to let them down before the south gate because of the crowd gathered outside the inn, and as Minta rose to climb out, the first person she saw over the other heads was Mr. Francis Taplin, speaking to the dean's wife and Miss Wright.

This was getting it over with—with a vengeance.

"Ah, Mrs. Fellowes, good afternoon to you," said Mrs. Ellsworth. "Have you already seen the flowers, or are you headed within?"

"Headed within, Mrs. Ellsworth. I suspect you remember my granddaughter Miss Wright? Mr. Gilbert Wright's sister." Of course they all remembered her. Minta's sister Lily had been briefly engaged to Mr. Gilbert Wright some years before, and there had been an engagement dinner at Hollowgate on the occasion. The broken engagement was not a circumstance either party would willingly recall, however, so bows and curtsies were exchanged with nothing more said on the matter.

"Ellsworth," said Mr. Taplin, nodding at Tyrone.

"Taplin."

"Oh!" Mrs. Fellowes laughed shortly. "Forgive me. Mr. and Mrs. Ellsworth, have you met Mr. Francis Taplin of Beaumond? I see Mr. Tyrone Ellsworth already knows him from school days. Mr. Taplin, surely then you know of the other Ellsworths of Hollowgate? Mr. and Mrs. William Ellsworth, Miss Ellsworth, Miss Beatrice Ellsworth."

"It is always good to have the formal pleasure of an introduction," he answered with his most charming smile, acknowledging each in turn. "And, Miss Ellsworth, you and I had the good fortune to meet once at The Acres."

Once? Only the *one* time? Was he indeed trying to provoke her? As they stood beside the deep ditch marking the former city walls, Minta could gladly have pushed the man in headfirst. How many times had she met him now, and he *still* could scarcely be bothered to pick her out from her surroundings?

Nor was she better pleased to notice that his gaze, vague as it always was where she was concerned, sharpened abruptly when it drifted across the Bosom. Only by sheer force of will did Minta resist shrinking behind Beatrice. *Keep to the plan.*

"I hope you have been well, Miss Ellsworth, and your friend Miss Agatha."

"Perfectly well, thank you," she replied, so mildly and sweetly that her family regarded her with some surprise. "And you, Mr. Taplin? I hope you had a pleasant visit with your friend."

"Very pleasant," he answered blandly. "In fact, he has invited me to fish in Devon for a few weeks."

"What a delightful idea!" Minta exclaimed, instantly envisioning Mr. Taplin counties away, for a long enough spell that Aggie would come to her senses. "Fishing. As far away as Devon. You surely ought to go."

But a glimpse of Miss Wright's disappointed face alerted her that naked eagerness was probably the wrong note to strike, and she made haste to check her zeal. "Er—that is to say, a good friend's company is always pleasant."

She needn't have bothered. Mr. Taplin had already forgotten her, giving a vague nod as he turned to offer one arm to Mrs. Fellowes and one to Miss Wright, and the group began to make its way to the St. Cross. Rolling her eyes, Minta reached for Tyrone's arm and followed.

Barney's entry, a free-blown "Franklin's Tartar" carnation with two stripes of distinct colors, had not taken the silver table spoon, but the gardener was swelled with pride nevertheless to be awarded the fifteen-shilling second prize. The Ellsworths congratulated him at length and admired his entry up and down before moving on to inspect the other offerings.

Without being aware of it, Minta was frowning as she followed her family, automaton-like. So the new bosom was not enough? It had drawn his attention for a fraction of a second, but now he strolled beside Miss Wright and her grandmother as if bosoms did not exist. (Miss Wright's bosom was respectable, if not as generous as Aggie's.) Oh, dear, oh, dear. If being fair, buxom, and inane were not sufficient, what if Mr. Carlisle's scheme was not enough to turn the scale in her favor? Would she then have to hope that Miss Wright won the day? That seemed altogether too chanceful. Too much of a gamble. Unless she could somehow contribute to Miss Wright prevailing—she would have to ask Mr. Carlisle what he thought of that.

The carnations blurred together—solid, striped, whole-blown, bursters. White, pink, red.

At length, as if her fretting had conjured him into appearing, Mr. Carlisle materialized at her elbow. Minta went scarlet. For a dozen reasons. Chief among them—the surprise of it, the sudden irregularity of her pulse, the prominence of her new bosom, and the awareness that this would be their first attempt at fooling his brother. Because she was so occupied with her own discomfiture, she failed to notice his, only thinking that the heat of the day brought color to his normally pale countenance.

It was not the heat of the day alone. In fact, although Carlisle could not attribute any of his discomposure to surprise—he knew he would see her at the carnation show—the remaining causes were not altogether different from her own. He was glad to see her again, this young lady unlike any other of his acquaintance, and—was it that he had not seen her for several days, or was the coming into her presence always like stepping into a sunlit meadow? For she was sunshine and warmth and wildflowers and fragrant grasses, Miss

Araminta Ellsworth. He noticed the Bosom—being both an observant young man and, in so many words, a young *man,* of course he noticed the Bosom—but it was not the Bosom which allured him. If anything he experienced mild repulsion at the sight of it. Not toward Miss Ellsworth, to be sure, but toward the Foreignness of this new and prominent and artificially conspicuous feature. The Miss Ellsworth he first met was so thoroughly and charmingly natural that Carlisle automatically categorized the Bosom with her other recently adopted artifices: her new dress and manner and hair. That is, however attractive they might be considered by the world at large, he did not think of them as part of *her.* They were contrivances, and therefore distasteful.

These thoughts flitted through his mind in far less time than it takes to describe them, and then he too thought about how this would be their first attempt to draw Francis's attention.

When the greetings were accomplished, Carlisle offered an arm to Miss Ellsworth and to Miss Beatrice. "While your parents speak with their friends, shall we get some tea and refreshments?"

Beatrice glanced at her sister, who took a deep breath and squared her shoulders, nodding her agreement. Her jaw was set and lips pressed thin.

He couldn't help but chuckle. "Tea and refreshments, Miss Ellsworth. Not a gibbet and the hangman."

"That's what you think."

Garlands draped the St. Cross coffee room and the heavy oblong tables had been pushed against the walls so that the milling patrons could sit or stand as they chose.

"Would you and Miss Beatrice like to sit while I fetch you some tea?" Carlisle asked.

"But how would you carry the three cups?" countered Minta. "Here, Bea. Why don't you hold us some seats, while Mr. Carlisle and I fetch the tea."

They continued to the long counter, awkward with each other for the first time. Minta thought she could hardly meet his eyes, and he was little better.

"I suppose I ought to stand closer to you than is strictly necessary," murmured Carlisle, drumming his fingers on the smooth oak. "That is—if you have no objection."

"I have no objection," gulped Minta, though her person seemed to, for when he drew closer, her stomach took a leap within her. Flustered, she turned abruptly and only succeeded in banging the Bosom against the counter. "Dear me," she muttered, unused to any part of her projecting so far outward. As unobtrusively as she could, she tried to center the cursed corset again by pressing one of her arms against its side.

"Try to smile at me, Miss Ellsworth. My brother is approaching."

"Oh! Already?" She did her best, but her eyes were distressed.

"Shhh...." he soothed. "It will be all right."

His dark gaze was steady, reassuring, even faintly amused.

"Nick, Miss Ellsworth."

If Minta was surprised and alarmed Mr. Taplin should find them so soon, Carlisle was neither. "Francis."

Taplin's eyes flicked from one to the other, curious and calculating. Minta kept her expression as blank and vacant as possible and hoped he would interpret her blush as maidenly modesty, rather than the fear he would hear her pounding heart or notice her bosom was still slightly awry.

"Fetching Miss Wright and Mrs. Fellowes more biscuits, are you?" asked Carlisle mildly.

"That's right. They like the shortbread ones. What about you, Miss Ellsworth? Do you prefer ginger or chocolate or shortbread?"

She could hardly credit that he was showing an interest in her, so her hesitation was just long enough that Mr. Carlisle leapt in.

"Ginger," replied Carlisle and Minta in unison.

Taplin's eyebrow arched. "My—aren't you two good friends."

"No one could know Miss Ellsworth without admiring her and wanting to know her better," answered Carlisle, flashing Minta his crooked grin and tapping her on the back of her hand. "So, yes, I suppose she and I are good friends."

"Yes," managed Minta, as much undone by the grin as by Mr. Taplin's scrutiny.

"Well," drawled Taplin, as his brother dug out a few coins for the refreshments, "don't let my brother lead you astray, Miss Ellsworth. Nick tells me he isn't the marrying kind."

She felt her temper flare—as if Mr. Carlisle were not honest as the day was long!—but she stuffed this behind a vapid smile and said in her Cordelia voice, "Thank you then for your friendly warning, sir."

"At your service." Taplin bowed, shot a parting look at the Bosom, and stepped past them to the counter for more shortbread.

Minta's teacup rattled as she carried it back to the table, and her brow was thunderous.

"Careful," Carlisle told her, his voice barely above a rumble. "You have to appear delighted to be with me, remember?"

"It's not you," she hissed. But she smoothed her face. It would never do, in any case, to drip tea on her new dress, and it was going to require all the polish Mrs. Turcotte tried to stuff into her not to drop biscuit crumbs down her bodice.

"Good. Because you've already made great progress, Miss Ellsworth, if you only knew it, and we will make still more in the next few minutes. Just please do smile at me a lot and laugh at my jokes and such."

They set the offerings down in front of little Beatrice, taking a seat to either side of her. It so happened that Minta faced the end of the room where Mr. Taplin joined Mrs. Fellowes and Miss Wright, so it was fortunate she truly did like Mr. Carlisle, or it would have been arduous to manufacture constant smiles.

"Mr. Carlisle, do you think I should be encouraged that your brother pays these attentions to Miss Wright? I don't think Aggie would like to see it."

"I—er—don't think his attentions to Miss Wright would be so marked if Miss Agatha were indeed here."

"Does Aggie like Mr. Taplin?" spoke up Beatrice. "He's very handsome."

Minta scowled, forgetting herself momentarily, and then hastily pretended a miniature sneeze before emerging with the smile pinned back on. "Possibly. But you mustn't say a word to her about it."

"I wouldn't," protested her little sister. "I know better than that. And what is wrong with you, that you sneezed that way? Ordinarily your sneezes threaten to knock us all flat."

"All the better, if your sister sneezes with gusto," declared Mr. Carlisle cheerfully. "The whole point of a sneeze, Miss Beatrice, is to expel whatever is troubling one."

"Then I suppose that's why Minta blows it clear to Southampton, just to be safe."

"Just so. You really ought to emulate her, for your sister is the picture of health."

Beatrice looked skeptical, but after a moment she shrugged and returned to her refreshments.

"Speaking of health, Miss Ellsworth," he resumed, "how is your arm doing? Is the scar fading yet?"

She hesitated. But he raised questioning eyebrows and tilted his head a degree or two in the direction of where his brother sat. She knew what he was asking: was Mr. Taplin looking? Venturing a glance beneath her lashes, she saw he was.

"Yes," she said. "The scar is fading." Extending the forearm in question, she rotated it upward for his perusal.

But he did not merely look. He took it as he had before, in his gentle hands and ran two fingertips up and down the fading line. "Yes. That's healing nicely."

Minta's breath caught, and she snatched her arm back, a reaction she had to disguise with a giggle and a "that tickles!"

Beatrice paused, her ginger biscuit halfway to her mouth. First the miniature sneeze and now a *giggle* from her sister? What was happening here? Was Minta going to be *silly* about Mr. Carlisle? Not to mention, Minta did not look like Minta today. She looked far more grown up, to Beatrice's eyes. Practically a stranger.

After her two oldest sisters married, Beatrice had assumed her family would remain much as it then became for, oh, years and years. Tyrone would go to Oxford, and there was little Willie now, but surely Araminta would remain at Hollowgate, being Araminta, for the foreseeable future. And why should she not? Minta had never shown interest in either young men or in marriage.

Until now.

Chapter Twelve

His boding mind the future woe forestalls.
— Wm. Broome, Pope et al. translation of *The Odyssey*
(1726)

The return of Mr. Taplin meant Minta must resume haunting The Acres during the hours of morning calls. Only now she must wear her cursed corset and new dresses and traipse decorously from one estate to the other without running, stumbling, ripping her hem, or staining herself. It was a nuisance, but saving Aggie was worth it. And besides—Minta wanted Aggie to know about Mr. Taplin having tea with Miss Wright. "If Aggie could be made to give up Mr. Taplin on her own," Minta muttered, picking grass off her skirts and flicking it away, "Mr. Carlisle and I needn't try to deceive anyone."

"My word!" breathed Miss Weeks when Minta was announced and led into the morning room at The Acres. "How fine you look today, Araminta. I don't know that I've ever seen you so—so—" She trailed off into her *hm-hmm-hm*, her gaze sweeping from Minta's pile of curls to her blue-striped gown and neat slippers, with only the barest hitch at the Bosom.

"Thank you. Morning, Ags."

"Have you heard, Minta? Mr. Taplin has returned!"

"Uh-huh." Hitching up her skirts, Minta made a running leap for the sofa, causing it to slide sideways and the Bosom to go awry. "I saw him at the florists' feast."

"You did? I am eaten up with envy! How did he look? Did you...speak with him?"

Minta shrugged. "He looked like he always does. And yes, I spoke with him—a little. He spent most of his time talking to the dean's wife Mrs. Fellowes and their granddaughter Miss Wright."

Aggie's forehead puckered. "Oh, dear. I suppose she is very pretty."

"She looks just fine, as far as that goes," replied her friend, "but I didn't notice everyone falling over himself to speak with her, as the gentlemen used to with Lily."

Aggie did find some comfort in this, although, on reflection, no one ever fell over himself to speak with *her* either. She gave a huff of resignation. "Shall we play draughts?"

They were on their second game when Mr. Taplin finally appeared, the announcement of his name throwing Aggie into a fluster and Minta not much better.

"Ah," he said, entering the room and making his bow. "There you are."

"Where else would we be?" tittered Miss Weeks.

"It's always a comfort, finding people in the places you picture them," Mr. Taplin replied, not making matters any clearer. He smiled at his hostess. "Miss Weeks, a little bird told me that you are to be congratulated. Am I to wish you and Mr. Chester joy?"

Miss Weeks bridled and *hm-hmm-hm*ed. "It is so. I thank you. If you permit me, I will share your good wishes with Mr. Chester."

Their guest did his duty and canvassed this subject for some minutes before turning to Aggie and Minta, who had quietly carried on playing draughts because they didn't know what else to do.

"May I play the winner?" he asked.

In a passable imitation of her older sister, Aggie bridled. "This is our second game, sir. Minta won the first, and I am winning this one. So if it is a draw, whom would you play?"

"Perhaps I might play the winner of *this* game but offer a sop to the feelings of the vanquished," he suggested, drawing a chair closer to the pair of them.

"And what would that be?" pursued Aggie, uncertain whether she should try to lose the game at the eleventh hour.

"A trip to the theatre," Mr. Taplin announced. He directed his gaze to Araminta, who had not said a word this whole time. "They are performing *As You Like It,* followed by a farce called *Modern Antiques.* Do you like the theatre, Miss Ellsworth?"

She was thinking hard, even while trying to keep her countenance blank. Was he asking *her* and not Aggie? Or the both of them? It must be the both of them, or he would be treating Aggie as carelessly as he had treated herself, to this point.

"I do like the theatre," she admitted. "And that is why—that is why your brother Mr. Carlisle has offered to take my brother Tyrone and my sister Beatrice and me. And I have accepted."

She could hardly blame everyone for looking dumbfounded by this news, for indeed Mr. Carlisle himself would be dumbfounded were he there. Minta didn't suppose he had any plans to purchase four theatre tickets, but she would buy them herself and insist it was for the sake of the Plan.

It certainly worked as she hoped.

"You don't say," said Mr. Taplin, regaining his composure. "How—generous—of Nick. I was not aware you two—that is—Well, well, well. What say you, Miss Agatha, Miss Weeks? We cannot be left out of this delightful outing! Has Nick already bought a box, Miss Ellsworth?"

"Mm—oh, yes."

"Then I insist the three of us go as well," he said to the Miss Weekses. "And Mr. Chester, if he pleases." This declaration was met with claps and squeals, and Aggie hastened to resume her winning ways, her man leaping over two of Minta's and reaching the other side.

"Which night will you be attending, Miss Ellsworth?" pursued Mr. Taplin.

Minta crossed her fingers under the table and promised herself she would send a note directly to Mr. Carlisle at Mr. Beckford's, the second she returned home. "Tomorrow, possibly. I believe. Or—or the day after, if—er—if Beatrice isn't well. Or the day after that."

"Is Bea sick?" Aggie asked.

"Not right this moment, but the hot weather always does knock her up."

It took all Minta's self-control not to fidget or flee home during Mr. Taplin's and Aggie's draughts game, and, truth be told, it was not a very good match. Mr. Taplin seemed distracted, continually leaving his men vulnerable, and Aggie was in fits, not wanting to beat him hollow.

"How did you like the carnation show, Miss Ellsworth?"

"Very pleasant," she murmured. And then, unable to help herself: "Beware there, sir—you leave yourself open to a double jump."

"Oop. So I did."

Aggie scowled at Minta because then she was forced to avail herself of the opportunity. "I wish I had gone," she said. "I like carnations. Did you see—were there many other people there?"

"Many," he answered, sliding his piece into another inadvisable square. "Some new faces, some familiar. But even the familiar faces can surprise one." Here his regard traveled up Minta's person, slowing at the Bosom, and stopping at her face. A little bolt of fury shot through her, and her leg kicked out involuntarily. Fortunately her seat was far enough from his that her foot did not connect with him, and she forced an apologetic giggle.

"Dear me! Sitting still so long gives me pins and needles. I had better go home."

To her alarm, he half rose. "Will you require an escort, Miss Ellsworth? I should go soon as well."

"No! Please! That is—don't get up. Finish your game, sir. I have walked between Hollowgate and The Acres a thousand times before. We will all see each other at the theatre, will we not? I will see how Bea is doing. Good-bye. Good-bye!"

She did not need to remind herself to walk slowly on the way home; she was too deep in thought.

It was working.

Mr. Carlisle's plan.

Where Minta on her own had failed, where the Bosom had caused no more than a flicker of interest, one little cup of tea and a few biscuits in Mr. Carlisle's company had answered.

"He *is* competitive with his brother," she muttered, stooping to pick up a rock. Spinning in a quick circle to make sure she was not observed, she slung it as far as she could and admired its trajectory. "Mr. Carlisle's pretended interest in me was enough to awaken Mr. Taplin to my charms. But will it be enough to make him forget about Aggie? Or, just as good, will it annoy Aggie enough that she decides she wants no more of *him*?"

"We're going to the theatre tomorrow evening," announced Minta, bursting into the parlor where she found her siblings and stepmother gathered. "Or the day after, or the day after that. I mean, Tyrone and Bea and I are—not you, Willsie—you're too young. And Mama, you could and Papa could come if you like—"

"The theatre?" wondered her stepmother. "Where did this idea come from?"

"I'm inviting Mr. Carlisle. That is to say, Mr. Carlisle has invited us. Or will. In a few minutes." She skipped to the desk and whipped out a sheet of notepaper. "Ring the bell for Bobbins, would you, Bea? There's a good girl."

"Carlisle invited us?" frowned Tyrone. "Don't you mean that Taplin fellow?"

"No, I mean Mr. Carlisle his stepbrother. Who studies with the doctor Mr. Beckford."

"But Mr. Taplin called earlier and said he wanted to invite you and whoever else here would like to go to the theatre," said Beatrice, dutifully giving the bell rope a tug. She had been in the process of trying to affix little ribbons to the wiry hair on Snap the terrier's ears. "And we told him you were at Aggie's. Did you not see him there?"

Minta stared. "Mr. Taplin called here?" He called at Hollowgate *before* The Acres? Gracious! Was that only because the Ellsworths lived nearer the footpath from Weeke? But then, if he had ridden, which he probably did, he might just as easily have ignored footpaths altogether and gone across country straight from Beaumond to The Acres.

She shook this off. "In any event, I told him we were already going with Mr. Carlisle, so Mr. Taplin will take Aggie and Frederica. Now does anyone have a few guineas they could lend me? Oh, never mind. Here are some in the desk."

Rapidly she folded up the note around the coins and fiddled with the tinder lighter while Mrs. Ellsworth looked on with pursed lips. To her relief, not only did Araminta fail to set herself or the house on fire, but the wax blob she dripped onto the paper was of modest proportions.

"For Mr. Carlisle at Mr. Beckford's, please, Bobbins," she instructed, when the man responded to the summons. (Snap's half-hearted growls at the sight of his longtime archenemy were considerably undermined by the ridiculous bows on his ears.)

"Should Timmy wait for a reply, miss?" asked the footman.

She considered. "I suppose he could ask Mr. Carlisle if there will be one. I think I was straightforward enough."

The servant found Carlisle in Beckford's dispensary, preparing a strengthening compound for the fruitful Mrs. Purrock.

"I'm to wait and see if you have an answer," the boy explained, touching his cap and backing away a step. Which meant Carlisle had to clean his hands and open the note right off, with Timmy hovering. The doctor at least was out, seeing to someone's injured foot, and Carlisle was glad of it, for no sooner did he break the seal than the two guineas rolled out, chiming on the worktable, bouncing to the floor, and rolling away under the shelves. What on earth?

"Dear Mr. C," he read—one eyebrow lifting at the hurried, untidy hand that would have made Mrs. Turcotte question the futility of existence—"I hope you are free to go to the theatre tomorrow evening because I told F.T. that you had invited me and Tyrone and Beatrice, and now he is determined to go as well and invited Aggie and Miss W. If you cannot go tomorrow, I said it might be the day following. Please take these guineas for the tickets. I have no idea how much they cost. Could you get a box if possible? Let me know if there is a problem with tomorrow. Yours sincerely, A.E."

Carlisle could not say at first why vexation surged through him. He only saw that his vision was red, and his hand shook a little. Carefully, precisely, he turned his back to the servant, on pretense of wrapping up Mrs. Purrock's medicine. An act which might have been more convincing, had he not spilled some of it in his unsteadiness.

The boy coughed politely. "Will there be an answer, sir?"

Carlisle gave a jerk of a nod. Was it the tone of the note? Was it that Miss Ellsworth assumed he would be at her beck and call, and she could therefore make plans for them without consulting him? No—that might annoy him a touch but nothing more. And there was nothing peremptory in her words.

It was something else.

With an effort, Carlisle swallowed, forcing down his bitterness.

"Yes," he said to the messenger. "Say: 'Very well. Tomorrow.'"

When the boy was gone, Carlisle tried to slow his breathing. He discovered the corners of the worktable were digging into his palms. Come now. What was the matter with him? Was it that the sending of money shamed him in front of the servant? No—that wasn't it. The lad had given no indication, after all, that he thought it an unseemly business.

No. He was angry because—

Ah. He was angry because he was a fool.

And a greater fool for not realizing his foolishness until this moment, when the guineas rang out their particular note. For what business had he to play at being the gentleman suitor of Miss Ellsworth of Hollowgate? Even with the excuse that he did it to help her and to help Miss Agatha?

He, Nicholas Carlisle, was nothing and nobody. Even his connection to Beaumond was tenuous and at his stepfather's sufferance. Were anything to happen to John Taplin, Carlisle did not think for an instant Francis would be so willing to continue his brother's maintenance. There would remain his apprenticeship with Beckford, the hospitality of his apothecary uncle, and that was all.

So what had possessed him to suggest this scheme to Miss Ellsworth?

Even to maintain the pretense, she had to supply the means. Two guineas! Because she had no idea how much a theatre box might cost—and because she knew that whatever it cost, he would not have it—she enclosed the money. It was nothing to her. Pin money.

Well—what had he thought would happen? Courting a wealthy young lady—whether in earnest or not—involved more than conversations in bookshops and sixpence flower shows.

Carlisle swept Mrs. Purrock's spilled powder from the worktable onto a card and poured it into a packet. *This* was reality. This was his lot. And when he and Miss Ellsworth succeeded in luring Francis away from Miss Agatha—if they succeeded—she would continue along her primrose path of wealth and carelessness, and he would return to the way in life marked out for him. Or the way he had chosen for himself. A way which would rarely intersect with hers thereafter, much less run parallel.

Carlisle was not the only one discontented that afternoon. When he returned to Beaumond, Francis sprang out of nowhere and intercepted him before the house.

"Theatre, eh? You've got the grand ideas, I see."

"A promising production," rumbled Carlisle evasively. "It interested me, since we ourselves acted in our school production so many years ago."

His brother, however, knew as well as Carlisle did just where to slip the knife. "I know my father encouraged you to live like a gentleman, Nick, but gentlemen don't live on air. If you mean to pay attentions to this Miss Ellsworth, it will be an expensive venture."

Carlisle said nothing. He walked past him, but Taplin followed.

"Could it be my father inspired more than just me with his bracing counsel?" Taplin mused. "Perhaps you too now think of marrying for money. Medical ambition already waning, is it?"

At this Carlisle whirled on him. "Miss Ellsworth's money is the least among her many admirable qualities."

"Indeed? Do tell. I confess I hadn't noticed her much to this point, other than that she has a rather trying propensity to cling to Miss Agatha Weeks' side."

Carlisle's dark eyes flashed. "Yes. Her loyalty to her friend is one of the things I find winning about her."

Taplin clicked his tongue in mock chagrin. "Dear me. You speak as if I were in any way a threat to Miss Agatha's well-being. As if she needed protection from me."

"We both know that's not an unreasonable notion, and that her fortune is in danger, if not her person."

Taplin shrugged this off. "Really, Nick—her fortune is only in danger of being redistributed *in order that* her family's estate may be enlarged. If she marries me, she gets Beaumond."

"If she *doesn't* marry you," returned Carlisle through a tight jaw, "the Weekses own almost all of Beaumond already. They need only call in the deeds."

His brother laughed. "A fair point. How does the song go? 'Tis Wit for Wit, and Hit for Hit.' Very well, I freely admit—to *you*—that Miss Agatha's fortune is far from being the least of that young lady's 'admirable qualities.' What more do you claim for Miss Ellsworth, beyond her dogged loyalty and generous portion?"

Not being at all inclined to discuss Miss Ellsworth with his brother, Carlisle only muttered, "She's a pleasant enough creature. I'm going to wash before dinner."

But Taplin would not be got rid of so easily, and, now whistling the song which their conversation brought to mind, he idled after his brother up to his chamber. "She's rather on the big side," he remarked, leaning against the door jamb. "Strapping, I mean. Not overly tall, yet somehow Amazonian."

Carlisle poured water in the basin and repeated what he had said to Miss Beatrice. "She is the picture of health. And, yes, I consider her strength a good thing. She is no frail flower, no swooning miss."

"I suppose she's pretty enough," conceded Taplin. "You remember that Shakespeare sonnet—the one about how his sweetheart isn't like a summer's day because she's not quite so bold and brassy? Well, Miss Ellsworth strikes me as exactly that bold and brassy sort, when she isn't trying to behave herself. She ran into me once and fair knocked the wind out of me, and just earlier today nearly gave me a kick because she said her foot fell asleep."

Carlisle couldn't repress the grin this picture evoked, but he tried to hide it by toweling it away.

His brother was studying him. "You genuinely like her, don't you?"

Carlisle hesitated. There was only so much drying of his face he could do, and he hung the cloth again. "I—do, I suppose."

"And—you would think about marrying her even if she hadn't a penny!" Taplin further accused, his eyes narrowing.

Carlisle's grim response was unaffected and without forethought.

"I imagine I'd think about it a great deal more, if that were the case."

And when his brother was gone, Carlisle found himself wondering just how many truths were contained in that pack of lies he and Miss Ellsworth were foisting on Francis.

Chapter Thirteen

Wide Theater! where Tempests play at large.
— Edward Young, *A Poem on the Last Day* (1713)

The theatre in Jail Street was an unprepossessing building, small and not overly clean, and on ordinary occasions Minta's eye would be drawn to the other side of the street where the brick jail stood, housing debtors and felons and other manner of exciting people. But this evening even criminals could not distract her, and when she looked about, it was to see if Mr. Carlisle were approaching yet. The Ellsworths had arrived by carriage, naturally, Mr. Ellsworth not wanting them to walk past the gaol on foot, but Mr. Carlisle had refused the offer of a ride and proposed to meet them there.

"Here he is," said Tyrone. "He came over the bridge instead of along the High Street."

Minta's heart began inexplicably to thump and her stomach to flutter and her palms to dampen, and her clutch on her brother's arm tightened until he glanced over and said, "If you don't mind, I rather like having two working arms."

"He doesn't look very happy, does he, Minta?" whispered Beatrice.

Minta had to admit Mr. Carlisle did not. There was no crooked-perfect grin or gleam in his eye when he reached them. He was polite. That was all. "I hope you have not been waiting long. Shall we?"

"Do you have our tickets?" she asked, trying to sound bright, when in truth her spirits were sinking in the face of his mood.

He held them out. "Yes. Here are your tickets." With the faintest emphasis on *your*.

She snatched them from him and thrust one at Tyrone and another at Beatrice. "You go along. Mr. Carlisle and I will wait a minute for Aggie and her sister and Mr. Taplin."

Her siblings were hardly out of earshot before she plucked at his sleeve, trouble in her eyes. "Mr. Carlisle, you are angry with me. And I know why. After I sent you the note I thought I should have put an apology in there for being so—high-handed. I did not *ask* you if you would like to go to the theatre in the first place, and perhaps you had other plans for your evening, only you were too polite to refuse. It's just that your brother came to The Acres and invited me—or both Aggie and me—I'm not entirely certain—to come tonight, and I did not want to go without you there, because then we could not practice our stratagem, you know, but you and I have never defined explicitly what we would do or not do in various situations, and so I took matters in my own hands—"

He had both his own hands up by this point, and the hardness of his expression had given way to rueful amusement. "Miss Ellsworth—Miss Ellsworth, I beg of you. How is it that even your apologies are overpowering?"

His response to her contrition only made her feel worse. "Overpowering"? Could any girl like such a description being applied to her?

"But that *is* why you are not happy, is it not?" she persisted humbly. "Because I overpowered you?"

When he didn't answer immediately, she sighed. "I know you agreed to help me because you are a kind and helpful person, Mr. Carlisle. But I understand if you have since had regrets. If—you would prefer not to continue to deceive your brother, of course I would not hold you to it. Only say so, and I will release you at once from our agreement."

"Miss Ellsworth—" Her sorrowful face pained him, and he was quick to sacrifice his pride to comfort her. "Please don't misunderstand me. I didn't mind a bit you—er—making plans without consulting me. You were clear in your note that I could speak up if I needed to. If anything, I was unhappy with myself."

"But whatever for?"

"Because—I have told you my situation before. It happens that my comparatively modest means, while they do not trouble me for myself, trouble me when I think how—they will be a burden for *you*, in this enterprise."

"Oh!" Her countenance cleared at once, and she impulsively caught hold of his sleeve again to give his arm a playful swing. "Is that all? How relieved I am."

His mouth twisted derisively. "That is indeed 'all,' though I assure you, it is enough."

"Just money."

"Just money and my masculine pride."

"Oh, please, Mr. Carlisle," she pleaded, "don't take it as a blow to your pride that I sent the two guineas. They weren't mine either—I found them in the desk. I haven't a farthing more than you do and always have to beg any money I need off the rest of my family. It's simply a matter of blind luck that I was born to a rich father—it's not a *virtue*. It's nothing I earned or did myself. So please don't be strange about the money!"

Perhaps he wanted to be convinced. Perhaps it was her earnestness and the frankness of her clear gaze. Whatever it was, Carlisle felt his dissatisfaction and feeling of injury begin to dissipate, to be replaced by anticipation of the next few hours he would spend in her company.

They were smiling at each other—genuinely smiling—and she still had hold of his sleeve when they heard their names called and Taplin walking up with a Miss Weeks on either arm.

"Don't tell me you walked," said Carlisle dryly.

"All the way from the George Inn on the corner," his brother replied, "where I left the phaeton. Good evening, Miss Ellsworth. I'm looking forward to this."

With an inward sigh, she ducked her chin and favored him with a shy smile, tucking away her genuine self until it would be needed again. Then she took the arm Carlisle offered, and they entered the theatre.

"'O unhappy youth!'" declared Mr. Gill as Adam to Mr. Kelly's Orlando, "'Come not within these doors; within this roof the enemy of all your graces lives. Your brother—no, no brother; yet the son—yet not the son; I will not call him son of him I was about to call his father—Hath heard your praises; and this night he means to burn the lodging where you use to lie, and you within it.'"

Minta had, with some art, managed to be seated in the front row of the box, between Mr. Carlisle and her sister Beatrice, with Tyrone on the end. Tyrone and Beatrice were lost to the world, wholly absorbed in the action below, but the rest of them had much to distract them. For Aggie and Mr. Taplin were seated in the second row, directly behind Mr. Carlisle and Minta, and Minta could scarcely understand a word the actors spoke, so aware was she of how every word, every movement of her own and Mr. Carlisle's would be subject to observation and interpretation. And just as disturbingly, she was herself deeply conscious of Mr. Carlisle's nearness. His lounging form in the chair beside hers, the bulk of his shoulder and the lines of his arm.

"I am glad I have read this play," he murmured to her at one point, leaning so that his breath brushed her ear. "Or I would fear it did not end happily."

"I'm glad you can tell me it does," she whispered back, feeling her face warm, "because I know nothing about it. You would do better to sit by Tyrone if you wanted someone who knew his Shakespeare."

"Let me remain unenlightened, then," he replied. "For I am content where I am."

Minta gulped (not audibly, she hoped), clasping her gloved hands tightly in her lap. His face was turned toward the stage, away from her, but she saw the lift of his cheek and knew the crooked grin she liked so well was in evidence. She would have been content where she was, too, if not for Aggie and Mr. Taplin behind them. As it was, the tussle between the pleasant fluttering in her midsection and the unpleasant prickling at the back of her neck made her too confused to enjoy anything.

The unfolding plot of the play did not make her any easier. When Rosalind disguised herself as the page Ganymede and bid Orlando practice his wooing on her, the deception made Minta fidget.

She was not alone. Mr. Carlisle glanced at her, rueful awareness plain in his own eyes.

"'Come, woo me, woo me,'" teased Miss Kelly as Rosalind as Ganymede, "'for now I am in a holiday humour, and like enough to consent. What would you say to me now, an I were your very, very Rosalind?'"

Minta bit her lip. Then she leaned forward just a hair. "I think her disguise is not very convincing. She wears a doublet and the puffy hose, but if Orlando loves Rosalind, as he claims, you would think he would see right through that."

"I don't know," Mr. Carlisle murmured in reply. "What reason has Orlando to disbelieve what Ganymede tells him?"

"Here now. That's enough of your whispering," Mr. Taplin said crossly over their shoulders. He didn't trouble to lower his voice. "Some of us are trying to watch the play."

"Just so," answered Mr. Carlisle, with an expressive look for Minta. "Do pardon us. Although—I wish you might hold my hand, Francis," he threw back at him. "Because the scenes between the warring brothers make me anxious."

"And so they ought," muttered his brother.

Having succeeded in riling Mr. Taplin, Minta and Mr. Carlisle behaved themselves for some while afterward, even endeavoring to watch the show. But then, during the final act, Mr. Carlisle bent again to remark on some feature in the scenery.

"Do you mean *that*?" asked Minta, placing her hand on the wall of the box, so that she might point unobtrusively.

"No, not that."

His hand covered her own, and he repositioned hers so that she was pointing an inch farther to the left. "I mean *that*."

Minta's breath stuck in her as if a door had swung shut. Mr. Carlisle released her—he had touched her no longer than was necessary to move her hand—but that same hand suddenly felt—glove or no glove—as if she had thrust it in the fire, the sensation running up the length of her arm, until she was certain her entire person turned the shade of a sunburnt haymaker. Oh, heavens!

She did not catch another word of Shakespeare for the next twenty minutes. Oh dear, oh dear. *This* could not be right. Or advisable, whatever was happening to her. It was one thing to like Mr. Carlisle and enjoy his company, but another altogether to—

At any rate, there was no place for whatever *this* was, in her plans. She had meant only to foil Mr. Taplin's attack on Aggie—not to surrender any corner of her own heart to a hired knight. And that was all Mr. Carlisle meant to be—a hired knight riding to her and Aggie's rescue out of his native chivalry. How embarrassing it would be, all around, if Minta were now to make a fool of herself over Mr. Carlisle in earnest!

Keep to the plan, she urged herself. *Keep to the plan, as he does, and don't lose your head.*

She didn't know it, but she had whisked her hand back the instant he let go, clenching her fists in her lap, her head lowered and brow clouded as she railed inwardly.

Carlisle saw it all, however, from the corner of his eye, and he subjected himself to equally harsh words. He had overstepped—that was obvious. And Miss Ellsworth was dismayed and affronted. She was willing to accept his aid in separating Francis from Miss Agatha, but he, Carlisle, was not therefore to imagine there was anything deeper, anything more genuine, behind the ruse. Their courtship was a disguise, and the lines they spoke, the feelings they played at, were no more real than Rosalind donning doublet and hose to play Ganymede.

It had been their discussion about the money which had undone him, he realized. He had been cornered into baring his feelings—into admitting the blow the two guineas had been to his touchy pride—and she had responded as no other woman in all his acquaintance—nay, as no other woman in all the *kingdom*—would have responded. With freedom. With frankness. With generosity. With astonishing truth to the very depths of her clear eyes.

She didn't care about the money.

She didn't care about *money*.

And in return, some part of him had decided—there and then, without waiting for permission from the rest of him—that she was the girl he was going to marry.

It might take years before he could afford to offer for her with dignity, but she would be the one.

And now—with her recoiling from his touch—he thought the effort would require more than the saving of funds. He would have to win her to the idea as well. It was not that he had supposed she returned his feelings, but he had thought she bore him no dislike. He was not *Francis* to her, in any case. She was young. If she had never yet been keen on any particular person or had never yet given thought to marriage in general, all the better. He could be patient. He could make a virtue of necessity.

Let it be enough then for tonight, he thought. *Let me be her friend and her conspirator for now and trust the rest to time and perseverance.*

His love being newly discovered, he thought as many lovers do, that he could and would wait forever. He was hopeful and had his love for her to warm him. There was no need to frighten the girl.

But he could try to repair the damage.

Carlisle was forced to wait. When *As You Like It* concluded, all was bustle before the farce began. The younger Ellsworths were eager to discuss the merits of the play. Miss Weeks wanted sugar plums, and the orange-woman must be hailed so they might choose from her paper-lined basket. Francis seemed determined to shower attention on both Miss Agatha and Miss Ellsworth, and Miss Ellsworth must blink at him admiringly and titter at his jokes. In the meantime, various dances and songs and recitations continued onstage, to which only a fraction of the audience devoted their attention.

But at last the stage manager recovered enough of the theatregoers' notice to announce the beginning of the farce *Modern Antiques*, and all gradually returned to their seats. It was in this brief window, as Francis was untangling Miss Weeks' wrap from the leg of her chair with Miss Agatha's eager assistance, that Carlisle passed behind Miss Ellsworth and ventured *sotto voce*, "I hope I have not offended you, Miss Ellsworth. When I touched your hand, that is. I assure you, whatever has been said or done was all in the service of our cause and nothing more."

Her eyes flew to his, trying to read him, and she found only kindness and courtesy there. Instead of seeming relieved, she gave him back an uncertain smile. "I—thank you. I would never—ascribe—other motives to you, sir."

They sat. The farce began. The same company of actors appeared in new roles, tearing about in tricks and disguises, flirtations and conspiracies which made their audience roar and clap with as much enthusiasm as they had shown for the Bard.

But Minta paid as little heed to the farce as she had to the play because she was too occupied in turning over her own unhappy thoughts. She nearly forgot all about Aggie and Mr. Taplin behind her, and it took all her efforts to fix her eyes on the stage, rather than on Mr. Carlisle's shoulder and arm.

He did not turn to whisper to her anymore, nor did she dare whisper to him.

How could his apology so hurt her feelings?

It was right—only right—that she and Mr. Carlisle be playing parts, as surely as the actors on the stage. Heaven help her—had he somehow guessed she felt his pretenses too strongly? That she trembled in hope that true affection lay behind them? And therefore, from the kindness of his heart, he warned her by way of his apology.

Oh, dear. If that was so, how utterly mortifying.

And disheartening.

And crushing.

Minta moved mechanically through the remainder of the evening. She laughed when others laughed; she applauded when they applauded. She said, "Oh, yes," and "Yes, indeed," when opinions were shared afterward. She bid the rest of the party good-night and took her brother's arm for the short walk home.

And all the while there was a strain across her forehead and a tightness in her throat, and she thought, for someone who never used to cry at all, she was beginning to understand the temptation and the relief of tears.

CHAPTER FOURTEEN

Sin is the phaeton that sets the world on fire.
— Thomas Watson, *A Body of practical divinity*
(1692)

Minta may have successfully forestalled Mr. Taplin's attempt to invite her to the theatre, but he was determined to elbow his way to the forefront of her notice. The following day, while she was still eating her breakfast and had not yet thought of making her way to Aggie's side, the door to the breakfast room opened and Boots announced, "Mr. Francis Taplin."

"Gracious me. So early," murmured Mrs. Ellsworth, even as the terrier Snap hauled his aging body up from his cushion to meet this unprecedented challenge.

"When beauty calls," declared her husband, beaming upon Araminta. For her part, she was staring in dismay because she had bounced out of bed, eaten up with hunger and having put off Monk's ministrations for later. Her hair was twisted up, uncurled, a glorious rumpled mess, and—far more serious—she had not yet donned the Bosom!

"A shawl. I need a shawl," she muttered, looking all around in a panic, but neither Mrs. Ellsworth nor Beatrice wore one on this pleasant morning. What on earth was to be done?

Seizing her linen napkin, she hurriedly tucked it in the joining of her fichu. But one glance down showed her it did not provide nearly enough volume. She snatched up Willie's (which he never used in any case, preferring to wipe his mouth on the tablecloth) and layered that on top. Then Tyrone's, whisking it from his lap, though he threw her a bewildered look.

Fortunately the handsome Mr. Taplin was occupied immediately upon his entrance with fending off the hostile greetings of Snap, an effort in which he was only half-heartedly aided by the footman. By the time Mrs. Ellsworth scolded the terrier back to his cushion and Mr. Ellsworth formally bid Mr. Taplin welcome, Minta sat in demure, albeit flushed, stillness.

"Gracious me," said their visitor, in unconscious echo of his hostess. "What a tumultuous beginning! I beg your pardon for calling so early, but I could not contain my impatience. I am sure your daughter has told you what a marvelous theatre production we witnessed last night? Miss Ellsworth, if you would do me the kindness of taking a drive with me in my phaeton, it would allow me some relief of my feelings. How I wish my father had attended! As it was, I had no one to discuss it with."

"Why did you not then talk to your brother Mr. Carlisle?" Minta asked.

"Talk to Nick?" He gave a surprised laugh. "I'm afraid he is not terribly chatty at home, Miss Ellsworth, especially when he must march off to Beckford's bright and early."

"Oh, of course." She let fly a frightening up-and-down giggle that made Tyrone choke on his tea.

"But you did not answer my question," Mr. Taplin pressed.

"About the drive?" she temporized, folding her slice of toast in her nervousness and causing it to crumble and shoot crumbs. Was it that easy? Had Mr. Taplin so soon transferred his allegiance from Aggie to her? Simply to annoy his brother? If he had, Aggie must learn of it. She must see how fickle and unreliable he was.

"Could we pick up Aggie?" she asked.

"Miss Agatha? Er—I suppose so. It'll make for a squeeze in the phaeton."

"We could hardly go alone, sir," bridled Minta, flicking mock-reproving fingers at him and ignoring the stares of her family. Why, even her father's brow was creased, as if he were trying to determine what exactly was different about his third daughter this morning. "Besides, Mr. Taplin, the three of us have driven together before."

"We have," he conceded. "Very well."

"And perhaps Beatrice might ride with us over to The Acres," continued Minta, reluctant to be alone with the man even so short a distance.

"But—Minta, what would I do at The Acres?" gasped Bea.

"You can walk back home from there, funny little girl," Minta answered, wagging her finger at her younger sister.

Now Beatrice, when she was younger, had been the Ellsworth child most prone to tears, a tendency she had largely outgrown. Yet this morning, her older sister's odd (and repellent) behavior made her feel that familiar tightening in her throat again.

"But—I've never walked back from there by myself before," she said.

"Then let today be the day, my ten-year-old goosey goose!"

"And why do you keep calling me names?"

Minta had no idea why she kept spouting ridiculous epithets either, but they seemed to come easily to her adopted persona. "Tee hee! Little cabbage sprout, how can I help it?" Turning back to Mr. Taplin (carefully, so that none of her three napkins detached), she fluttered her fingertips again at him. "Thank you for your invitation, sir. Beatrice and I will be delighted to drive to The Acres with you, and, if Aggie doesn't want to come, I'm sure Bea would be happy to continue on."

"Splendid. Will you be ready soon? You both look charmingly."

Beatrice, as ever, was neat as a pin, but Minta choked at this and then made the mistake of thumping her chest, sending one of her three napkins sailing away.

"Mr. Taplin." Mrs. Ellsworth pushed back her chair, causing all the gentlemen to rise and little Willie to scramble to his feet in imitation. "While you wait, may little William and I show you the gardens?"

When he bowed in response to this, she reached to pick up her young son, leading the way from the room.

"Bless Mama," Minta exhaled, ripping the remaining two napkins from her fichu and springing to her feet. "And bless you too, Bea. I owe you one."

"What on earth ails you, Minta?" demanded her brother Tyrone. "You're acting like a perfect ninny."

But she only put out her tongue to him (something he found surprisingly reassuring). "Never you mind. Come with me, Bea. I have to get properly dressed."

More quickly than any genuinely frivolous young lady would have been able, Minta reappeared, her hair properly curled, the Bosom fastened on, and her person encased in one of her new dresses. Mr. Taplin paid her some ornate compliment, to which she responded with a demure titter which entirely hid her disgust and a light, "Of course I wore green to match my little flibbertigibbet of a Beatrice. Doesn't she look like a wee summer nymph?"

He made no response beyond a murmur of agreement, not even glancing toward the youngest Ellsworth daughter, and Minta plainly saw that poor Bea was going to suffer Mr. Taplin's indifference this drive, much as she herself had when he first took Aggie out.

The phaeton was brought 'round, and before Greaves could alight to assist anyone, Minta grabbed Bea's hand and gave her a push. "You first, Bea. Up you go."

But neither Bea nor Mr. Taplin were eager to have her play the wall between Pyramus and Thisbe, and just as Bea dug in her heels, Mr.

Taplin's own gloved hand pressed Minta's back. "Allow me, Miss Ellsworth. It will give your sister courage if you climb in first."

"But I—"

"It will give me courage," said Bea, a mulish set to her mouth. "And I want Greaves to help me."

Accepting her fate, Minta forced a smooth brow and let Mr. Taplin take her hand, and her smile of thanks was only slightly stiff and sarcastic. Her family would have noticed—and likely Carlisle—but Taplin accepted the simper as his due.

Once they were all seated, Araminta was hard put to hide her dismay, finding herself in contact with Mr. Taplin along nearly the entire length of her body. Had Aggie really sat so close to the man? As it was, Minta pulled one arm out to lay along the back of the seat behind Bea's shoulders, so that she might scoot that much closer to her sister and that much farther from their companion. For all the good it did. Mr. Taplin appeared to take that as an invitation to expand into the open space, and she had to fight an urge to force him back by kicking at his boot or elbowing him in the ribs.

"Ah, what a day!" cried he, when they were bowling down Hollowgate's graveled drive under the limes. "What do you think of my matched pair, Miss Ellsworth? Aren't they handsome? Fast as lightning when I ask, yet meek as lambs."

For heaven's sake, she'd already heard enough about his marvelous team, but she made an appropriate reply. But then, deciding it would be better if he did most of the talking, she followed up with a few questions to encourage him. Obligingly he launched into the horses' history and provenance, only to have Minta interrupt him when they passed the gate. "Mr. Taplin! You have turned the wrong way. This is the way toward town, and The Acres lies in the other direction, further along the Romsey Road."

"What? Why, so it does," he chuckled. "But what's done is done, so why don't we go up along the Weeke Road, and we can circle around Beaumond and come at The Acres from the other direction."

"I suppose," she muttered, her assumed pleasantness slipping a degree. Vexing man! But there was no use crying over spilt milk, she supposed. With another effort she pinned her smile back on. "You were saying about your horses...?"

"Right-o. Well, it was at Newmarket that an acquaintance of mine met a run of poor luck at the gaming tables. In one last desperate attempt to recoup the evening's losses, he ventured Silkie—that's the one on the left there—on his hand. And he might have carried it off, having strong cards, but—alas for him—his—er—opponent held a still stronger hand, and Silkie fell to him."

"Do you mean Silkie fell to you, Mr. Taplin?" asked Araminta, opening her eyes with wide innocence. "Were you gambling with this man?"

Taplin hesitated, but a quick glance revealed no condemnation in Miss Ellsworth's gaze, so he plunged in with full enjoyment. "You have caught me, Miss Ellsworth. I do indeed confess to being the victor of that game. In my younger, wilder days, I tried my luck once or twice at the card tables. All young men do, you know. But I've left all that behind now. After winning Silkie. All very long ago. Ancient history now."

"How remarkable that Silkie looks so young and healthy, then, for such an ancient horse," Minta said with wonderment. "And however did you find another to match him so perfectly?"

Taplin fidgeted, and his leg drew away from hers an inch. "Well—perhaps it was not all so *very* long ago. It seems long to me, now that I've settled to a quiet life at Beaumond."

"Did you win Silkie's match from the same unlucky gentleman?" persisted Minta.

"Silkie's match? Oh—not precisely. Once Silkie was mine, and before Corbett could run away and bury his woes in drunken oblivion—begging your pardon—I insisted he sell me Silkie's match Clarion. Corbett's pair had been the envy of Newmarket, you know."

"I'm sure they were," she agreed, thinking Corbett had likely got his revenge by naming an exorbitant price for Clarion, a price which Mr. Taplin had clearly paid. Doubtless Corbett had not been the only one drinking and muddled that evening. Honestly—it was a marvel any young gentleman of means escaped financial ruin, if this was how they spent their time! Mr. Carlisle might regret his own lack of fortune, but comparative poverty was not without some protective benefit.

The thought of Mr. Carlisle made Minta look past Bea in the direction of Mr. Beckford's house. If only Mr. Carlisle were the one taking her on this drive! Then there would be no need for pretense; there would be only genuine, genuine pleasure. They could talk of—oh—anything and everything. The play and sports and how exactly one compounded medicines and whether it was great fun or not to set bones and dress wounds. Musingly, she traced the scar along her forearm, now almost invisible.

Mr. Taplin's gaze followed the motion. "I admire your health and vivacity, Miss Ellsworth. And your fine color, as if you were kissed by the summer sunshine."

"Oh, you flatterer, you," shrilled Minta, edging nearer Bea, who frowned at her and pushed back.

"It makes one doubt all those paintings of shepherdesses," he went on. "They're all as pale as if they kept their sheep within doors, but you..."

Shepherdesses! Minta's mouth popped open—just—and she shut it again immediately, though her astonishment begged to be expressed. Why—she had done it. She was fair and buxom and put Mr. Francis Taplin in mind of shepherdesses. Unfashionably tanned shepherdesses, but shepherdesses all the same. Imagine!

In her amazement she failed to register the direction the phaeton took until they were passing Culver Close. "Mr. Taplin!" Araminta cried. "You have gone the wrong way again! Beaumond lies behind us. We will never arrive at The Acres at this rate."

Beatrice gave an anxious little moan, but Mr. Taplin only ho-ho-hoed at her. "All in good time, Miss Ellsworth. On such a day, do you not pine to see the River Itchen flowing through the city mill?"

"I—can't say it occurred to me," she replied, "but this drive begins to smack of a kidnapping." Seeing him straighten from the corner of her eye, she hastened to add a playful giggle, but she reached for Bea's hand all the same and gave it a reassuring press.

"I would like to go home, Minta," her sister whispered, leaning so close their bonnet brims crashed.

"A little longer," Araminta whispered back.

"What's this?" Mr. Taplin inclined toward her. "Secrets?"

"My little noodle mouse here is fretting over her neglected lessons," lied Araminta. "I'm afraid if I had known we would be taking a drive longer than the few minutes it takes to go from Hollowgate to The Acres, I would have suggested my brother Tyrone accompany us, rather than Beatrice. May we not turn around and fetch Aggie now?"

She held her breath, blinking at him brightly, and was unspeakably relieved when he nodded at last, touching the brim of his hat and sitting back to slow Silkie and Clarion. Minta was finding that being a fair, buxom shepherdess was a lot of work, and the sooner Aggie could witness for herself the capriciousness of her chosen one, the sooner she would be disenchanted (Minta prayed).

But her trials were just beginning.

Turning a carriage is no beginner's task, and Minta grudgingly admitted to herself that Mr. Taplin managed it well, though it could not be attempted until they reached the Swan Lane turnpike gate.

"Well done, sir! A handy maneuver," she blurted, when the last quarter circle was made, and perhaps it was the difference between her sincere admiration in this instance and her usual simpering silliness that made him give her a measured look.

"Thank you, Miss Ellsworth. The perfume of your praise tempts me to the performance of further exploits."

At once she shrunk back, taking refuge in a tinkling twitter. "Oh—you." If she'd had a fan in her hand, she would have rapped him with it because he was expanding into the slender gap between them again, his leg pinning her skirts. On pretense of pointing something out to Bea, she turned her face away from him. How could she keep this dreadful man occupied until they reached The Acres—if they ever reached the Acres!

"Speaking of exploits," she began again, "have you decided whether you will fish with your friend in Devon?"

"Would you miss me, Miss Ellsworth?"

"M-many people would." She could not help herself and added, "Your family, the Weekses, Miss Wright...among others."

A most disturbing gleam lit his eye, and this time he did lean closer. "You have been observing me, I see."

"I?" she tee-heed, ducking her head and smoothing and plucking at her skirts so she could free them from him. "I suppose you are the cynosure of many eyes, Mr. Taplin. But—about the fishing—?"

"It depends. On other circumstances. Perhaps *you* might be able to help me make up my mind." With that he clicked his tongue to Silkie and Clarion and directed them once more down the Weeke Road.

"Oh! But weren't we going to go past Beaumond to The Acres, sir?"

"The Acres, The Acres!" he chuckled. "What a single-minded young lady you are, Miss Ellsworth. On this beautiful morning, I find I would prefer the scenery and seclusion of the Weeke Road. It too will take us where we are going."

Where else it might take them Minta dreaded to think, and it did not reassure her that his leg pursued hers as if drawn by magnets, now pressing against her nearly from hip to knee. She might—and did—indulge in brief fantasies of dealing him a ferocious kick, but that would only undo all her hard work, just as she was on the brink of success. If only Bea were a little girl again—Minta might then have hauled her younger sister onto her lap, putting more space between herself and the unwanted suitor and reminding the latter that he was not alone with her. But alas, at only ten Bea was already nearly as tall as Araminta and would make for a gangling burden.

"Do—you know the Hamblys?" she floundered, scooting her leg away as she pointed through the trees to where the old spinsters, aunt and niece, lived in their cottage. "Dear, sweet old ladies. I-I imagine your brother Mr. Carlisle has made their acquaintance because Mrs. Hambly is not in the best of health."

But Mr. Taplin shrugged this off and fully lifted himself an inch off the phaeton seat to close on her again. "I'm afraid dear, sweet old ladies might interest my medically-minded brother, but I myself prefer to dwell on the dear, sweet *young* ladies. If I may be so bold, I find my mind full of one dear, sweet young lady in particular..."

"Miss Wright?" squeaked Minta, almost perspiring with distress by this point. Her arm which had lain behind Bea's shoulders thus far now removed to Bea herself.

"Not Miss Wright."

"Miss—Aggie, then?"

"My dear Miss Ellsworth, dare I say you have been *jealous*?"

And then Minta clutched Bea so hard that her little sister yelped. But it was either clutch Bea or knock Mr. Taplin over the head.

"You—are so popular one can't help but notice," Araminta managed. "Notice and wonder whether—whether any of your attentions are—more than idle flirtation. People are so different! With a person like your brother Mr. Carlisle, there would be no need to wonder. He is not the sort to pay meaningless attentions to anyone."

This helped. Mr. Taplin sat back in disgust. "His attentions may not be meaningless, Miss Ellsworth, but I assure you they are nevertheless *pointless*. If you have been setting your heart on my brother, you will find yourself frustrated there. Nick hasn't the means to marry, and he would be the last person to marry for means."

"You think so?" she asked, her disappointment not entirely feigned. Of course Minta didn't want anyone to marry her for her money, but she liked Mr. Carlisle so well that she almost wished the money would tempt him.

"I know so," answered her heartless companion. "Not only would he never marry for money, but he would view unequal fortunes as a positive drawback. Which is ridiculous," he added, more to himself. "For everyone knows that one's fortunes are as much a feature of oneself as blue or brown eyes or being short or tall. If one may prefer blue to brown and tall to short, why may not one prefer penny-ful to penniless?"

"When you put it like that..." murmured Araminta, thinking it wasn't such a bad argument, and—should the opportunity ever arise—she might make use of it herself with Mr. Carlisle.

Mr. Taplin was watching her again, with that same thoughtful look she had mistakenly engendered earlier. "Have I hit upon something, then, Miss Ellsworth? *Have* you set your heart on my brother?"

"That impoverished, funny-looking man? With his crooked nose and his fingers stained from—from compounding medicines?"

He gave a bark of a laugh, his humor restored (and one hand releasing the reins to *pat her knee*, at which her knee jerked as if struck by lightning). "Heh, heh—do you honestly think him 'funny-looking'?" he asked. "I do myself, but you never know about young ladies' tastes."

"*I* like his looks," spoke up Beatrice for the first time, having had just about enough of this nonsense. She leaned around her sister to frown at him.

"Ah! Miss Beatrice. I confess I forgot you were there. Well, well. I am glad you like Nick's looks because, by the time you are of an age for marriage, he might have saved enough to think of such things. You are—let me see—eight?"

This was not calculated to please Beatrice, and she did not deign to correct him, merely sitting back again and transferring her frowns to Araminta. *Why on earth are we spending our time with this person?* her countenance plainly said.

Even Minta was beginning to think Aggie was hardly worth this.

But things were about to grow worse.

When the phaeton entered an especially quiet and tree-shaded portion of the Weeke Road, Mr. Taplin unaccountably slowed his horses' pace.

"What is it?" asked Minta. "The scenery?"

"The scenery and the opportunity," he murmured, in what she supposed he thought was a killing voice. "If you do not love my brother after all…" Letting the reins go entirely, the man took hold of Araminta's shoulders instead, twisting her toward him. Before she could do more than stare in astonishment, he rammed his lips into hers so hard their teeth clacked.

Everything happened in an instant then.

Araminta gave a screech of outrage (which Mr. Taplin's bruising lips muffled, even as her boot came up to catch his shin. But she landed only a glancing blow because she was simultaneously trying to writhe away, the violence of her wriggling causing the Bosom to go askew in turn. Straightaway, fear of figurative and literal exposure made her forget everything else, as her more urgent concern became the repositioning of her corset. Undeterred by the fuss, Taplin persevered in his wooing, but what ultimately brought about Araminta's release—from both the blackguard's hands and his crushing mouth—was all down to Beatrice. The young girl no sooner saw her sister accosted than she took up the dropped reins and gave them a mighty flap, a flap that cracked like ten whips, a flap such as lamb-like Silkie and Clarion had never before been subjected to. The startled matched pair abandoned their tractability and calm on the spot, hurtling forward down the Weeke Road as if demons pursued them.

Lurch! Jerk! Rattle! Jolt! Bump! The runaway phaeton careered through the flanking trees. Taplin tried to call calming words but had to shout them, which only further alarmed the cosseted creatures. At the same time he grabbed for the reins, only to have them slip from the dash rail to drag between the horses, and it might have been how far he was compelled to lean over the rail, ever so precariously, that overset the balance of the vehicle. In any event, when Silkie and Clarion veered too sharply to take a curve, for one timeless moment the phaeton tilted up on its outer wheel.

And then they were flying.

Chapter Fifteen

Shall I lose my doctor? No, he gives me the motions
And the potions.
— Shakespeare, *The Merry Wives of Windsor*, III.i.94
(1602)

Her head ached as if a portcullis had been dropped on it, and there was a throbbing in her shoulder. No—there was a throbbing in several places, but it was worst in her shoulder. And somebody was crying.

Crying? *Beatrice!*

Everything returned to her in an instant: the kiss, the galloping horses, the overturning phaeton, flying—

Araminta snapped to a sitting position before she could think, but both her aching head and her throbbing everything were quick to follow. She was on a grassy sward—a bumpy one because the grass covered uneven tree roots, which must explain all the throbbing and aching—tree roots were no feather mattress, even if the grass was soft enough.

"Minta!" screamed Beatrice, clambering over and throwing skinny arms about her.

"Bea!" Minta screamed back, though it ended in a groan. "Are you hurt?"

"Just scratches and cuts—lots of them. I landed in the shrubbery, thank heavens, but you went farther. Can you move your fingers and toes? Is anything broken?"

"I think...nothing serious," she answered, tentatively moving and flexing. "My head feels like the carriage rolled over it, though, so I might have smacked it on something." A gasp stopped her. "But where is Mr.—Mr. Taplin? Bea—is he dead?"

"He's breathing but unconscious—I looked. And the horses stopped over there"—pointing— "further down the road. Oh, Minta! What should we do? We can't just leave him, I don't suppose?"

Araminta put fingers to her forehead, willing everything to stay in one place. "I don't know. I mean—of course we can't leave him. Just give me a second to think because my head—"

At this Beatrice wailed anew. "Oh, Minta! I might have killed us all! It's all my fault, you know. I didn't like how he was kissing you, and I grabbed the reins and set the horses galloping—"

"Well, it isn't as if I was enjoying the kissing either, so you'll get no blame from me. Only do stop caterwauling or my head will split open."

"But what if Mr. Taplin *dies*? What if—"

"Gracious me! What has happened here?"

Beatrice broke off, mid-sob, springing up, and Minta's eyes flew open once more. When her vision settled, she saw a frail, faded woman of middle age, her eyes wide behind her spectacles and hands clutched to her chest.

"Why, Miss Beatrice—can that be you? You're bleeding! And Miss Araminta?"

"Miss *Hambly*?" sniffled Beatrice.

It was indeed their longtime neighbor (and grateful object of Hollowgate charity), and the two Ellsworths could honestly say they had never been happier to see her. Every basket of garden bounty, every haunch of pork, every crock of preserves the Ellsworths ever bestowed on Miss Hambly and her ailing aunt Mrs. Hambly was here repaid richly, for no sooner did Beatrice explain the nature of the accident and the injuries sustained than Miss Hambly abandoned all thought of calling on the curate Mr. Hepple.

"I will fetch Mr. Beckford at once," she promised. "You'd better not go yourself, in your condition. We are not far, and I daresay he can return to you in a jiffy. Faster than I, at any rate."

"You shouldn't try to run, Miss Hambly," gasped Minta. "Take care."

"Nonsense," retorted the spinster. "From the looks of you both, I could crawl on my hands and knees to Southampton and back before you could drag yourselves so far as Cock Lane. Off I go."

"I will never complain about visiting her or bringing the Hamblys baskets again," vowed Beatrice.

"Nor I."

As wretched as she felt, Minta could not help but hope Mr. Beckford would return with Mr. Carlisle beside him, even as she dreaded it. What a disaster he would think her! And what if his brother was gravely injured? It was one thing for Mr. Carlisle to assist her in rescuing Aggie from Mr. Taplin's fortune hunting, and quite another for him to tolerate Minta nearly killing the man. But still, she wanted him to come.

The minutes passed.

Minta eased herself to a softer patch of the grass and gingerly lay back down, Beatrice plumping down next to her. Silence fell, apart from birdsong and Bea's sniffling.

Then came a low, broken moan.

"It's Mr. Taplin," hissed Bea, as if it could be anyone else.

"Mm," answered Araminta.

"Had I better go to him? I don't want to. Surely Mr. Beckford will be here any minute, and there's nothing I can do for him, is there, Minta?"

Another moan drifted to them.

"We can't just do nothing," Minta said with a grimace. "But you needn't do it. Help me up, Bea."

"Ought you to move, though?"

"Nothing is broken. Help me up."

Mr. Taplin lay fewer than five yards away, but it might as well have been five miles. As soon as Beatrice helped her stand, Araminta's head spun, and nausea washed over her. Her vision was funny, too.

"Let me lean on you," she mumbled, not so unsteady, however, that she did not remember to fiddle with her corset.

Slowly they made their way to the man, who lay with face half pressed to the ground and who muttered curses under his breath. Once there, Minta lowered herself laboriously to her knees, using Bea as a pillar to slide down.

"Mr. Taplin?" she ventured, bending over him to speak softly in his ear. "Mr. Taplin, there has been an accident. Do you know where you are?"

A grunt in response.

She leaned closer. "Mr. Taplin, can you hear me? It is Miss Ellsworth. May I—help you roll onto your back? It cannot be very comfortable to lie as you are."

Another grunt, but this one sounded vaguely affirmative. Very well. Chewing her lip and squinting at him (she felt less dizzy if she did not take in too much of the world at one time), Minta placed one hand on his shoulder and one—she did not know where to place the other one. It ought to be on his hip, surely, but she could not bring herself to clamp a hand there. His knee, then? His forehead?

Confound it. Steeling herself, she placed her second hand on his hip, ignoring the stab of pain in her shoulder, and gently, firmly *pushed.*

He gave a roar as he rolled, which made Beatrice scream and begin to cry in sympathy, and Araminta panic and whip her hands away. But her sudden motion made the surrounding trees and shrubs wheel like a merry-go-round, leaving her to scrabble dizzily for solid earth, her hands encountering first his waistcoat and then his arm before she lost her balance and toppled across his chest. The breath escaping both of them with a mutual, pained *oof!* Minta thought for a terrible moment she might throw up, and Taplin—poor Taplin was in too much agony to get out from beneath her, though one hand lifted to her waist to give a feeble push.

"Was this where they were thrown by the carriage?" It was the calm voice of Mr. Beckford, a little breathless, perhaps, from having hurried over. "Carlisle, why don't you tie up Taplin's team? We wouldn't want them to wander off while we see to the patients because we'll surely need that phaeton."

"Sir."

As soon as Araminta heard him, she knew she was not too injured that mortification could not add to it. Why must Mr. Carlisle find her sprawled over his brother, and his brother's hand at her waist?

"This is the place," answered Bea. "That is—that's where Mr. Taplin was thrown, and Minta and I landed a few feet back that way, but we came over to try to assist him when he woke."

"Are you badly hurt, Miss Beatrice?" Mr. Beckford asked, as Minta made a valiant effort to detach herself from Mr. Taplin and sit up again. She felt a light hand on her shoulder. "Better hold still."

When Little Beatrice reassured him of the superficiality of her injuries, the doctor said, "We will have Mr. Carlisle dress your cuts and scrapes, my dear. Can't have you go home looking like you were in the wars. It will cause enough of a panic when Miss Hambly reaches Hollowgate to report the accident."

"I—hope you have your Ball's—Bee's—Bar's Bensom with you," fumbled Araminta, trying to see Mr. Carlisle clearly. There seemed to be two of him, but they almost merged when she squinted and pinched her forehead. "Mr.—Beck—you had better check Mr. Taplin first. He is worse off, I think."

"Ah," replied the doctor. "On second thought, Carlisle, why don't you take a look at Miss Ellsworth? Miss Beatrice's cuts and scrapes will wait."

"Apply a little pressure here," Mr. Carlisle murmured to Bea. "And then use this dampened cloth to dab away some of the dirt." Then he rose to come and crouch beside Araminta. "Miss Ellsworth, how does your head feel?"

"Er. Achy. And something is wrong with my vision."

"If you would allow me..." He tugged on the ribbon of her bonnet which, while crushed and bent, was miraculously still on her head. Removing it, he placed it beside her on the ground. And then his gentle, gentle fingers were touching, probing, threading through her thick hair, brushing her temples and the nape of her neck.

Araminta shut her eyes and hardly breathed, cursing the pain and discomfort which prevented her from fully enjoying the moment. Nevertheless she thought, *I would be thrown from a dozen carriages, if it meant Mr. Carlisle would always be the one to examine me.*

"You have quite a lump here, Miss Ellsworth." A feather-light touch. A butterfly wing.

"I—landed near the base of a tree, and there were—roots—and I—suppose I struck one."

"That would suffice. You have a concussion, I'm afraid. You may be dizzy and nauseous for several days. And you had better stay at home quietly for that time."

"But—but—Aggie," she whispered. "I cannot sit home for days at a time. *Aggie*."

She couldn't see him clearly, but she could hear the smile in his voice. She could. "I think...judging from—the general conditions—Aggie will come to no harm while you are recovering." And then, louder: "How do you find Francis, Beckford?"

"A couple cracked ribs, I'll warrant," answered the doctor. "Concussion. Sprained arm. I'll strap him up." This announcement was met with groans and muted curses from his patient, and Mr. Beckford added wryly, "If Miss Ellsworth can be moved, it may be better for all to draw some distance away, Carlisle. That way your brother may give vent to his feelings with impunity."

"Just so. *Can* you rise and walk, Miss Ellsworth?"

"I—can."

"She can, if you don't mind her leaning her entire weight upon you," put in Beatrice. "I thought we would both pitch over when I tried to support her. But you're bigger than I am."

"So I am. In any event—" Before Minta could register what was happening, Mr. Carlisle passed one arm under her knees and the other behind her shoulders, scooping her up and carrying her slowly to where Silkie and Clarion cropped the grass placidly. She bit back a moan, though he was being so careful, and Carlisle would not have heard it except that she was pressed to him, for Taplin at the same time gave another roar of protest.

"You see," said Carlisle softly as he set her on the grass again, "judging by the fuss Francis makes, you will not be the only one housebound as a result of this day's happenings. I have some questions for you about those happenings, Miss Ellsworth, but first tell me—apart from your head, do you hurt anywhere else?"

"Not really. Not worth fussing about, that is. Only perhaps my shoulder..."

He edged to the side she indicated, and then there was his feather touch brushing along her arm and shoulder. "Does it hurt when I do this? What about this?"

"When you raise it there is a twinge," she confessed. "But honestly, it already begins to feel better." And then she blushed and was glad she could keep her eyes closed without arousing suspicion.

"A strain, I would call it. Tenderness. Bruising." He released her and sat back on his heels. "All in all, the three of you have had a miraculous escape, I believe. I'm—glad—and relieved—it was no worse. When Miss Hambly appeared on the doorstep, she was so collected and rational that I'm afraid neither the doctor nor I understood anything to be terribly amiss until she repeated herself. But we came as soon as we understood."

"Thank you."

"Our pleasure." And she heard the grin again. "Miss Beatrice, come here and let me finish cleaning you up. And I do plan to apply Blair's Balsam, as your sister requested. Marvelous stuff. I am going to see my uncle Blair, it so happens, at his request. I had a letter just this morning. I did not know when I might answer his summons conveniently, but now I think this would be the very time. I'll catch the morning Flyer tomorrow."

Minta could not fathom the man's sudden cheerfulness, but she felt a pang of disappointment that he would be going. Going, and he did not seem to care that she was concussed? Going in such a rush, with no mention made of his return?

"We wish you a pleasant journey," she muttered stiffly.

"Speaking of pleasant journeys—do please hold as still as you can, Miss Beatrice—thank you—I would never admit as much to my brother, but I consider him an excellent whip. In which case, how did you ever come to be thrown from the carriage? I see, from the plain fact that the horses are unharmed and still attached to the vehicle, that you did not roll over entirely, nor collide with anything, so I am at a loss to imagine what happened and how it happened."

The Ellsworth sisters were silent, Beatrice because she was panicking over her role in the accident, and Araminta because she was torn between wanting to tell him everything and wanting to protect Bea from blame.

Carlisle's gaze traveled from one to the other, and then he lowered them again, tucking the edges of Beatrice's bandage neatly. "Was Francis driving at the time?" he asked.

"Yes," said Minta. Her head hurt, and it made it worse to debate whether she should invent a lie. But she should—poor Bea! Of course she should invent a plausible story, cost what it might. Putting her hands to her temples and rubbing, she said in a rush, "I mean—no. He wasn't driving. I—asked to drive, and I'm afraid I was something too enthusiastic."

"That isn't so at all!" blurted Beatrice, her conscience smiting her. She liked Mr. Carlisle. He was kind. And—what was more—Mr. Taplin would be sure to say exactly what took place, if being thrown from the carriage hadn't knocked it clean out of his head. "*No one* was driving, Mr. Carlisle. I—grabbed the reins and—flapped them. Hard. And the horses began to run."

"'No one' was driving?" he repeated, one eyebrow arching in skepticism. "How did no one come to be driving?"

Minta inhaled sharply, and she would have shaken her head and pierced Bea with a Significant Look, had her concussion allowed her to make such movement or even to open her eyes, but she was reduced to thrusting out a groping hand to pinch her sister into silence.

"Ooh!" protested Mr. Carlisle. "There's gratitude for you."

"Mr. Carlisle!" gasped Minta. "Was that you? Do forgive me. I meant that for Beatrice."

"But why should you want to pinch poor Miss Beatrice? You would be sure to undo the bandages I've applied so carefully."

"Because—because—"

"Because she doesn't want me to tell you Mr. Taplin wasn't driving because he was *kissing* her!" cried Bea.

It was Carlisle's turn for the long silence.

Araminta could have kicked Beatrice for this awkward revelation, had she not been afraid of Mr. Carlisle's shin being the undeserving recipient. Shrinking in mortification, she cracked her eyelids. Everything whirled, a blur, but in that carousel she could see his face turned toward her and that he was not moving any more than the surrounding trees.

"Kissing Miss Ellsworth? Well—that *is* a compelling reason not to mind the road."

"I didn't ask for it," hissed Minta, indignantly. "He took me by surprise. And if Bea hadn't sent us careering into oblivion, the game would have been up in another second because I was on the point of making my displeasure known."

"You didn't...like it then?" he mused.

"Like it?" squeaked Minta.

"Shh—shh—do keep your voice down, Miss Ellsworth, or the game will indeed be up."

"What game?" asked Bea.

"No, I didn't like it," Minta retorted, though barely audibly. "I didn't like it, and I didn't invite it, and you should know that better than anyone!"

"Why should he?" from Beatrice. But her companions were too intent on each other to address her.

"Well, I knew you were an unusual young lady, and this confirms it." His cheerfulness had returned. "Most young ladies would love to kiss my brother, you know."

"They're welcome to him!"

A low chuckle. "Are they? But I thought that was the point of this whole farce: that one young woman in particular is *not* welcome to him."

"Oh, yes—you know what I mean. We can't argue, Mr. Carlisle—it makes my head ache!" Araminta said, almost with a wail. And then she felt his hand on her forearm, reassuring.

"You're right. I'm being quite the mischief and not a good doctor."

"No—no—that isn't so. You're a wonderful doctor or will be."

"Yes!" chimed Beatrice. "A wonderful doctor."

"Ah, you two just like me for my uncle's balsam," he teased.

A great groan and another volley of muffled swearing reached them then, and Carlisle dusted off his hands. "I had better assist Mr. Beckford in getting Francis into the phaeton, and then I must drive him back to Beaumond, where I suspect his injuries will keep him a good few weeks."

Araminta risked cracking her eyes open again, despite the general unpleasantness of it, so desperate was she to see him. "But—Mr. Carlisle—if you go off with your brother, how will Bea and I get home?"

"Hollowgate will send a carriage," he assured her. "That was Miss Hambly's mission. So now I will wish you good-bye."

"Thank you," cried Beatrice, giving him an impulsive hug. "Thank you so much."

"But—" sputtered Minta, "—yes, I do thank you also, Mr. Carlisle—but—if you go to London tomorrow—when will I—*we*, rather—when will we see you again?"

"Soon enough," he answered vaguely, rising to his feet. Before he went, however, he hesitated and turned back. "I appreciate your gratitude, Miss Ellsworth, Miss Beatrice. And your compliments to my doctoring. Do you suppose—you might still like me, were I to change professions?"

"Change professions?" breathed Minta, confused.

"Do you want to be a clergyman?" asked Bea. "I like clergymen as well. My brother Simon—Lily's husband—is a clergyman. And I like attorneys, too. My brother Robert who married Florence is an attorney."

"Thank you for your suggestions, Miss Beatrice." He bowed. "And you, Miss Ellsworth?"

He might drag the Thames for bodies, for all she cared, or go on the stage as a juggler. So long as he came back. But no words came to her lips, and she cursed her aching, whirling head.

And then, with another bow, he was gone.

Chapter Sixteen

I can now without fear let loose my heart, and give it a full range in the walks of love.
— Edward Ravenscroft, *The Wrangling Lovers* (1677)

"Easy, for the love of all that's holy," grumbled Francis Taplin, pale and grimacing as the phaeton bowled up the Weeke Road toward Beaumond.

"If you don't like it, you must blame the springs, for we are going as slowly as your fine pair can be held to," replied his brother.

"Some would-be doctor you are. Didn't you hear Beckford say I have cracked ribs and a concussion?"

"I did. But I suspect I am as good a doctor as you are a brother," Carlisle retorted, "for didn't you remember, before you asked her on a drive, that I have grown fond of Miss Ellsworth?"

Taplin's eyes were shut and his face drawn, but a grin split it nevertheless. "I *do* remember, in fact, and confess it was you who opened my eyes to her. For such a strapping girl, she can be surprisingly soft and feminine, wouldn't you say?"

Carlisle's only response was an indeterminate grunt.

"And since you admit you cannot afford to marry, Nick, and nor do you intend to remedy your lack by pursuing Miss Ellsworth's fortune, I do not see what you have to reproach me with. She is always free to refuse me, so you needn't be such a dog in the manger. And if she should happen to like me better than you, how can I help it?"

I am acting a role, Carlisle reminded himself. *A role.* And it was fortunate his role required him to be annoyed, for that was indeed the case. He was rather tempted to drive the phaeton over every bump and into every hole in the road, that Francis might be jarred and juddered and jerked for his smugness. But the budding doctor in him narrowly succeeded in resisting this petty urge. *Let him say what he likes. Have I not the ineradicable comfort of knowing that, whatever Francis feels or thinks, Miss Ellsworth does not share it?*

Yes. That was true enough. And doubtless if Francis ever wanted to force his embraces on Miss Ellsworth again, she would be better prepared.

"What of her friend Miss Agatha?" Carlisle prompted, after a pause. "I once thought your interests lay in that direction."

"Can a man ever have too many irons in the fire? You're as bad as my father. You both think I should choose one rich girl, kidnap her to the altar as soon as ever I might, and never thenceforth enjoy the freedom of flirtation and *free range* again."

"Forgive me," answered Carlisle dryly. "But I thought you had no idea of relinquishing those freedoms even after marriage."

"Ah!" Taplin gave a little scream. "I beg you—don't make me chuckle. It hurts."

"And as for your dragging the matter out," Carlisle went on, "you do run some dangers. Supposing I should somehow find the means to marry? I hope you would be content with the remaining irons in your fire, were I to pluck out Miss Ellsworth."

Taplin's eyes cracked open in suspicion, and Carlisle had to repress another impulse to jostle him. "You're bluffing, Nick."

"I might be."

"Admit it! You are." But a note of doubt was detectable.

"I might be," repeated Carlisle. "I honestly couldn't tell you. All I know is that I am headed up to town tomorrow to see my apothecary uncle again."

Taplin lost interest and gave a shrug, which only made him wince. "What of it? You need more drugs and elements to grind up in your mortar and pestle?"

"Mr. Beckford is well supplied," said Carlisle slowly. "No. It is that my uncle writes to tell me he has signed a contract with the navy for his balsam."

"With the navy!" Then Taplin did try to sit up in his astonishment, but this led to a most unmanly shriek and whimpered retreat. Sweat broke out upon his brow. "The navy!" he said again, hoarsely.

"Do you mean to say someone else has taken an interest in your uncle's oily little balsam?"

"Apparently."

"The Royal Navy! Blow me tight if he ever becomes a rich man!"

"He...just might. There's many a slip 'twixt cup and lip, of course. In the first place, my uncle's small lab has not the means of production on a scale to suit the navy." Carlisle sounded as if he were thinking aloud. "He will likely need a partner."

"And you propose to be that partner?"

Carlisle stared. "I? No—I mean my uncle Blair will require a larger medicine manufacturer for a partner."

"Then why do you intend to go running up there? No—I can guess it. Now that your uncle might be a wealthy man, you wisely want to remind him of your existence. Of his *heir's* existence."

Taplin's eyes were screwed shut again as they turned into Beaumond's drive, or he would have observed his brother's smothered wrath. "It may surprise you to hear this, Francis, but I am rather fond of my uncle Blair and am not wishing him a premature demise."

But Taplin wasn't interested in Carlisle's righteousness. He was tapping his fingers on the knee of his shredded and stained breeches. "Perhaps you might touch him for a loan. For Beaumond, you know. Father did shelter and raise you, after all. It would be appropriate for you to repay him in some form, with these new means. If your dear Blair uncle would vouchsafe us a few thousand pounds—not more than ten or fifteen, I'll warrant—Beaumond would be in the clear, and I wouldn't be called upon to save the day."

And then Carlisle could no longer check his temper. "If Beaumond is *not* in the clear, whose fault is that? And, no, I have no intention of touching my uncle for the loan of *ten shillings*, much less ten thousand pounds! I am grateful to my stepfather for his kindness to me, but I would not rob Peter to pay Paul. I would not ruin my uncle to save my stepfather's estate. Our neighbor and creditor Mr. Weeks is a deserving and capable man. If Beaumond goes to him, there are worse fates."

Taplin gave a pained shrug. "Suit yourself. Though it's not robbing Peter to pay Paul if Paul is already Peter's heir. But you're right: Mr. Weeks will do as a creditor, as well as any other. And maybe I wouldn't like you to hold the leases, now that you mention it. As it is, I could marry the Weeks girl and ask for the mortgages as part of the wedding settlement, or I could marry the Ellsworth girl instead and have the satisfaction of snatching Beaumond back from the Weeks' grasp."

"Admirable plans. I take it Miss Wright is no longer a contender for your favor, then?"

"Who says so? No, no. Lovely girl, Miss Wright," sighed Taplin. "Perhaps the prettiest of the three. A respectable fortune there. Not so great as the other two, but respectable. Thank you for reminding me of her. She would serve as well, I suppose. Though a fair few clergymen in that family." He gave a little shiver over the clergymen, followed by a pained peep. "Who knows, Nick? You might come back from London to find me an engaged man."

"That would be quite the feat, as I doubt I will be longer than a fortnight away, and you will be confined to Beaumond for nearly that amount of time, I imagine."

The note of satisfaction in his voice could not be entirely hidden, unfortunately, and it, as much as anything, spurred his brother's answer. "Confined to Beaumond? Nonsense. Where there's a will, there's a way."

They drove the rest of the way in silence, Taplin occupied with his physical discomfort and Carlisle with the mental variety. How easily Francis could needle him! At least there was a modicum of revenge when they drew up to the house, for Taplin required the assistance of two grooms to descend, and he cursed them both heartily. In the first instance because they greeted him too loudly for his aching head and in the second for their inadvertent clumsiness, bumping his injured ribs and eliciting from him that regrettable shriek.

I should not let him put me out, Carlisle reminded himself as he descended from the coach the following day at the Swan with Two Necks in Cheapside. *Suppose he does offer for Miss Ellsworth in my absence? She will not have him.* Though then Francis might turn to Miss Agatha, and Carlisle didn't doubt he would meet with a kindlier reception there. If that was the case, Miss Ellsworth would be greatly upset. *But she and I will simply have to put our heads together and devise another plan.*

The coachman tossed down Carlisle's bag, which he then hoisted over a shoulder before threading his way through the crowded inn-yard toward Milk Street. There had been a time when he thought he might live permanently in London, but it was gone now, even if he was never able to marry Miss Ellsworth. (The very thought of bringing Miss Ellsworth to London to live! One would as soon transplant wildflowers to the London docks. For she, like they, would lose her beautiful color and vigor in the narrow confines and pavement and smells and smoke of the city.)

Milk Street to Cheapside to Cornhill. The day was hot and dusty, the roads loud, noisome and thronging with wheeled and foot traffic. Carlisle was glad to reach the premises of "B. Blair, Chemist & Druggist," so designated by a modest plaque affixed to an equally modest brick front. Ducking within, he was momentarily blinded by the dimness, but a familiar voice wheezed, "Why, it's Mr. Carlisle! Have you come to stay again?"

"Jacobson." Setting his bag down, he shook the old man's hand. "Not to stay very long this time. I am settled for good in Winchester. Are you well, you and your brother? Yes? I am glad to hear it. Is my uncle Mr. Blair about?"

"Mr. Blair is at the laboratory, sir. Should I send Tribbet to fetch him?"

"No, I'll go myself, thank you, after I put my things upstairs." There was no place for his bag in the shop, certainly, for the shop of B. Blair was a tidy, dazzling display of medicines, preparations, elixirs, tinctures, unguents, and pills. Glass cases held botanical and chemical ingredients from across the globe, as well as salts, oils, plasters, and specimens. Rhubarb here, Peruvian bark there. Aloe, snakeroot, myrrh, camphor, mercury. Jacobson himself sat ringed by shelves and drawers, bottles, labels, wax, jars, display cases. One might look and look for hours and still not see everything the place held—and Carlisle had done just that, during the long vacations he spent there. But today he merely slipped through the door in the back which led to the staircases. Taking the steps two at a time, he dashed all the way up to the second floor and tossed his bag on the bed in the spartan spare room. Then he was off again in the direction of Lombard Street.

His uncle's laboratory was as jumbled as the shop was orderly. Here the space was choked with similar items, higgledy-piggledy, in addition to all manner of chemist's equipment, the whole miscellany arranged in a manner unknowable and unnavigable to anyone save Mr. Bertram Blair. The air was thick with pungent scents and hot and close as an oven. Carlisle waved smoke away from his face as he entered and was unable to stifle a cough, at which sound his uncle's round head popped up behind an assay table toward the back.

"Nicholas!" he cried, shoving up his goggles and pushing aside whatever he was working on. Carlisle winced when a little tin bowl slid off the surface, clattering to the floor and sending its contents rolling in every direction.

"Never mind, never mind," insisted his uncle, when Carlisle bent to retrieve them. "Tribbet can clean it up. I had no idea it was so late in the day! Come! Are you hungry? Let us go 'round the corner and have a chop. I daresay you haven't eaten since breakfast either. I have so much to tell you."

Some minutes later found uncle and nephew in a stall at Simpson's in Ball Court Alley, gladly tucking in. Carlisle knew better than to pepper his uncle with questions before the man had a chop in him, but once the first had gone down, followed by half a pint of ale, his uncle's pace began to slow, and it was Bertram Blair who began the talk, folding his arms over his sizeable girth.

"So you've come up to see me again. I knew better than to expect many letters from a young man your age, so I've not been disappointed."

Carlisle grinned. "To be sure. You have the advantage of me there. You've written me one letter, and I've written you none."

His uncle chuckled. "Too true. It's easier to say things face to face, is it not? And I do miss your face. I got to thinking, once you were back in Winchester at Beaumond, back with those Taplins—who have always thought the Blairs not half good enough to wipe their boots on—I've been thinking you might distance yourself from the...squalor of my business. For your own sake. Make a clean start."

"There's certainly no denying the squalor of your laboratory," Carlisle replied agreeably. "You'll blow yourself to high heaven one of these days, Uncle. Or burn down the city."

"I might. But it's my laboratory, and everything therein is just how I want it."

"Jacobson could get it in ship-shape in a few hours. Honestly, no one who stepped into 'B. Blair, Chemist & Druggist' would buy a thing from you again, if he saw the conditions from which his pristine medicaments emerge."

"I wouldn't let Jacobson near the laboratory for a hundred pounds," retorted his uncle. "That old fidget is worse than a spinster great-aunt, the way he tidies after me and puts things where I can't find them. If I set down any item in the shop and turn my back half an instant, he goes and puts it away as if it'll never be wanted again."

"I'm only saying the conditions of the laboratory are *dangerous*, sir. I wonder you can get fire insurance for the place."

"As a matter of fact, the fools refused to renew my policy," grumbled Blair. "But enough of all that. You didn't come to town to quiz me about my laboratory again, did you?"

"I did not," Carlisle conceded. "You know very well I came to congratulate you on your new naval contract. It's marvelous news. A vindication of your years of research and hard work in perfecting the formula. But how on earth will you be able to produce enough Blair's Balsam to supply the Royal Navy?"

"I need help, to be sure."

"You might partner with a larger company."

"I'll have to. I've already approached Plough Court and Corbyn & Company. Either one has the means and the equipment and the laboratory space and, I daresay, the labor to assist me in manufacturing."

"Exactly. And what did they say?"

"They were interested, naturally. They might have ignored me to this point, but no one ignores a navy contract."

"Then which will you go with?"

Bertram Blair waved a negligent hand at this and resumed his attentions to his second chop. "What does it matter? They both would like to swallow me up and spit out the bones. Absorb my shop, my laboratory, my recipe, my contract." He sighed gustily. "It's a young man's game, Nick, and I'm not a young man anymore."

This, too, was a familiar argument between them.

"I am...enjoying my studies with Mr. Beckford the doctor," Carlisle said carefully.

"Hear me out, Nicholas. You liked your long vacations spent here. You liked experimenting in the laboratory."

"I don't deny it. But I had my reasons for returning to Winchester—"

"I know them!" Blair struck the table between them. "I know the reasons. Gratitude to the Taplins. A wish not to saddle them with an unwanted connection. But I am telling you those are old ways of thinking, my lad. If I can accomplish this—if *we* can accomplish this—we will be rich men! Then the Taplins might go to the mischief, for all you would care! I warrant you they would be happy enough to admit such a 'disgraceful' connection, were you a rich man."

His uncle was working himself red in the face, and Carlisle covered the man's clenched fist with a placating hand. "But I don't wish the Taplins at the mischief—not all the time at least. And not my stepfather, in particular. Moreover, I find I prefer Winchester to town and the practice of medicine to the compounding of it. Uncle, you must therefore resign yourself to sole enjoyment of these theoretical riches."

"Sole enjoyment," muttered Blair. He took another gulp of his ale. "Listen to me, Nick," he said again. "What would you say to six months? Give me six months of your time. Put off your studies with the good doctor until the spring and stay to help me put the business in order. Six months."

"I cannot, I'm afraid."

"Not six months?"

"Not six weeks, Uncle."

"Why this rush?" Blair demanded. "You cannot spare me six weeks?"

Carlisle took a slow breath. "Uncle Bertram, the matter is this: Francis has spent a great deal of money, and my father has had to mortgage Beaumond. Now he tells Francis to marry money, to save the estate."

There was no denying a gleeful light flashed in Blair's eyes. "Oh? You don't say. Well, then, what has any of that to do with you?"

Another long breath. "...Francis has in mind a few young ladies whose fortunes will fit his purpose."

"Ah! Now we get to the root of the matter, Nicholas. I see. Indeed I do. One of these young ladies interests *you* as well. And therefore you fear to abandon her in Hampshire to the wiles and flirtations of Francis Taplin."

"Almost, but not exactly," answered Carlisle. "I do *not* fear the young lady I—favor—will give way to Francis' charms. Rather, it is her dearest friend who is in danger. And I have promised to assist—my—young lady—in keeping her dear friend's person and fortune from my brother. There is no denying Francis will need an heiress, but someone else must be the sacrificial lamb."

His uncle was silent some minutes, chewing, drinking, pondering. But then he passed a hand over his scalp and sat back against the high wooden stall. "You say your young lady is in no danger from your brother, but you wish to be on hand, lest he snatch up her friend and cause your young lady grief."

"In so many words. 'My' young lady and I are…cooperating in a fashion, to prevent the unwanted situation."

"Ah." Blair's brows drew together, like two furry caterpillars sharing a leaf. "You care for this young lady."

"I do."

"You think of marrying her."

It took a moment, but Carlisle gathered his courage. "I do hope to, Uncle. One day."

Blair gave one firm nod. "And how do you propose to afford this marriage? Here I thought you were flying to my assistance, or at least to rejoice with me. But now I find you have come only to beg for an allowance, now that I am to be rich. Confound it all. Or, worse, have you come to see how soon I'll drop dead and leave everything to you?"

Carlisle eyed him wryly and held up his table knife. "You have seen through me, sir. And if the papers are all signed with Plough Court or Corbyn & Company, I hope you won't mind if I run you through directly. I'm in something of a hurry."

Blair's round face crumpled in a laugh. "All right! Perhaps I put it too harshly. I know you mean me well, boy, but it is only natural you should think what is in it for you."

"I confess I built a castle or two in the air on the strength of your news. I would not be human if I did not. But I had already resigned myself to patience and am in no hurry to see you leave this world."

"What about the allowance, then? I wager you wouldn't raise insuperable objections to receiving one...?"

"I know of few people in my situation who would," confessed Carlisle ruefully. "Such a boon would shave years off my waiting, sir, but I insist in the same breath that you are under no obligation to make me one. Nor would I be comfortable accepting an allowance without having done anything to deserve it."

"Oh?" demanded his uncle, with a wave of his fork. "And if you will not remain in London even six weeks to help me settle my business dealings, what would you offer instead?"

Carlisle grinned. "I'm relieved to say I have prescribed your balsam several times and convinced Beckford of its efficacy. If it were available in greater quantities, the doctor might keep some on hand to sell."

"Mm. You suggest peddling my wares in return for an allowance?"

"I don't know about peddling, Uncle, but I would be glad to recommend your wares when the occasion arose. And I would be willing as well, in the fortnight I am here, to help you put your laboratory in order, so that if the gentlemen from Plough Court or Corbyn and Company want to inspect it, it will not be as much as their lives are worth to venture within."

"Fine. Agreed," said Blair, not needing much excuse to give what he already intended to give. "What would you say then to £50 per month? £600 per annum?"

His nephew's breath caught at the sum. Why, if that were the case—he might save enough in a year between his two allowances to offer for Miss Ellsworth! And then, if he could join Beckford's practice officially or begin his own—

With an effort he checked his careering thoughts. "It's all idle fantasy at this point, of course," Carlisle reminded both of them.

"It'll be real soon enough, Nick, if I have anything to say about it. Heh heh. No, my boy, my time has come at last. *Our* time has come at last." Mid-crow he began to slap his pockets absently. "Hm. Seem to have left my pocketbook somewhere."

"It would hardly matter if you had it, Uncle Bertram," laughed Carlisle, "for you wouldn't find much within. You had better let me pay for this meal."

"Well, if you insist. But I tell you, Nicholas, this will be the last time. Or nearly the last. When those contracts are signed—"

"I know. When those contracts are signed, I'll be as strong in the pocket as any man in England. Just you wait and see."

CHAPTER SEVENTEEN

**Did man…come wrangling into the world,
about no better matters?
— Thomas Dekker, *The guls horn-book* (1609)**

Mr. Beckford and Mr. Carlisle had prescribed quiet and stillness for Minta's aching head, without placing any great faith in their advice prevailing. But in this instance, the dizziness which swooped her up and spun her around whenever she moved faster than a snail's pace succeeded in confining her to one of Hollowgate's smaller parlors, one too dim for Tyrone's reading tastes and at the farthest reach from the clangor of kitchen pots, doors opening and closing, and ringing bells.

But lying immobile on a sofa alone was anathema to a girl like Araminta, and, like a spider waiting for the lightest vibration on the silken threads of her web, she would nevertheless call out if she heard anyone approaching or passing by without.

"This won't do," her stepmother told her in her low, soft voice, after she had forcibly removed from the room a protesting Willsie. (Mrs. Ellsworth had by nature precisely the sort of Cordelian voice which would have made her head girl at Mrs. Turcotte's.) "First I find Bobbins reading you the results of the horse races, and now you let Willie make a rumpus and toss his ball about. And it was all I could do this morning, to send your aunt and uncle and Flossie and little Peter away without disturbing you."

"What about Lily? Didn't Lily care that Beatrice and I were tossed like rag dolls?" asked Minta incorrigibly. Her eyes were shut, however, and she pressed her hands to her temples.

"Certainly she cared, even though I told Flossie not to tell her, lest it bring the baby early. Lily sent Simon to investigate, but I dispatched him as well."

This brought a sigh and a twitch. "And Aggie? What of Aggie?"

When Mrs. Ellsworth hesitated, Araminta cracked an eyelid. "What?" she demanded. "Where is she?"

"The Weeks family sent flowers."

"'The Weeks family!' What do you mean, 'the Weeks family'? Do you mean Aggie hasn't come?" In her agitation, Araminta bolted upright, only to subside again with a groan as the parlor wheeled.

"My dear Minta, you will only take longer to recover if you insist on doing expressly what you have been forbidden to do."

"But I must see Aggie. I cannot think why she has stayed away. Please, please, please, Mama, won't you send a note to The Acres and beg her to come? I promise we will sit here, still as statues. Please—it would comfort me so."

Mrs. Ellsworth yielded—of course she did—and agreed to write directly, though she didn't believe for a minute Minta and Aggie could sit still as statues if their lives (or Minta's recovery) depended on it.

As soon as her stepmother was gone, however, it was Beatrice who crept in.

"Minta—are you awake?"

"Don't be a goose. I'm in more danger of dying of boredom than of falling asleep."

Her younger sister dropped down on the carpet beside the sofa, and when she spoke again, her voice was uncharacteristically fierce. "If you do die of boredom, it would be just what you deserve!"

"What on earth—?" Once more Minta's eyes flew open, and once more she paid for it. But her double vision gradually resolved into one singular, scowling Beatrice. A Beatrice who, apart from a few plasters here and there, was again her tidy little self, neat as a pin. "Whatever can you mean, Bea?"

"I mean that I have given everything a good deal of thought, and I have decided everything is your fault."

"*My* fault? I presume you mean the carriage accident—and I do believe that was *your* fault, if it was anyone's, for flapping the reins and setting the horses off."

"I don't deny flapping the reins," Beatrice conceded, still frowning, "but I never would have had need to, if you hadn't got us in such a dire situation in the first place. I mean, if you hadn't been behaving like such a ninny and flirting with that dreadful Mr. Taplin and agreeing to go driving with him, when anyone with two eyes to her can see he's a rascal."

For a moment Araminta forgot all about her aches and pains in her astonishment. Could this be little Beatrice berating her? The most sensitive and timid of the Ellsworth Assortment?

"What has got into you?" cried Minta.

"What has got into *me*?" retorted Beatrice. "What has got into *you,* more like! I never knew you to be so silly as you have been these past several weeks. Having a new wardrobe made, curling your hair (much less brushing it), wearing a false bosom!"

"It's not a false bosom!" Minta defied her. "Not altogether. It's half ruffles and half me. It just pushes all of me into a smaller compass." But even as she said it, she knew Beatrice had reason to complain. The old Araminta—the usual Araminta—*Araminta* would never do any of these things, much less be caught defending a false bosom. Or half-false bosom.

But what could she do? She could not trust Beatrice with the truth—not when so much depended on the Plan to Save Aggie being carried out. And the Plan was about to succeed—if Minta could only lay hold of Aggie and tell her what Mr. Taplin had done in the carriage.

No—for a short while longer—perhaps even so little as another hour, she must continue to play her part, let Beatrice think what she might. Only when Aggie was safe could all be revealed.

Therefore, Minta once more gave the false little titter that made her family's hairs stand on end. "What a goose you are. When you are my age, you will understand all about dresses and hair and beaux. I don't remember you ever criticizing Lily for caring about such things."

"That's because Lily is *Lily*," answered her sister, which was undeniable and made perfect sense to all who knew Mrs. Simon Kenner, *née* Lily Ellsworth. "And she may have flirted with anyone in breeches, but she didn't *like* the rascally ones. Both her intended husbands were very nice, and I like Simon best of all, every bit if not more than Flossie's Robert. But you—! Mr. Taplin may be handsome, but how could you let him kiss you?"

It took every ounce of Minta's self-control not to blurt out that, *of course* she didn't like the rascally Mr. Taplin, and didn't everyone credit her with more sense than that? Not that she had been behaving sensibly of late, but how was it that, after being thoroughly sensible for eighteen long years, a few weeks of utter silliness and everyone believed this was the true Araminta Ellsworth? It was enough to make one scream.

One more hour, she told herself. *Just one more hour.* If Aggie would only come!

Although it nearly choked her, Minta held herself to a curt reply. "Mr. Taplin is handsome, as you say. Why shouldn't I let him kiss me? When you're older, it will make sense."

"It will never make sense, unless someone knocks every bit of brains out of my head when I'm your age," snapped Bea. "I would blame your concussion, except you've been like this for weeks. You can't marry him!"

"Who says I'm going to marry him?" cried Araminta, goaded beyond restraint. Then she slapped a palm to her forehead, which only made things worse. "Argh! I mean—I'd like to see you try to stop me. Mind your own business."

These taunts were not the sort to smooth any ruffled feathers, and little Beatrice took great umbrage to them. "See if I ever try to give you good counsel again!" she announced, springing to her feet.

"I wasn't aware you'd given me any to begin with!" Minta rapped back. "Why don't you go away, already?"

"I shall!"

Beatrice still being Beatrice, however, when she went to slam the parlor door in her dudgeon, she caught it at the last second and closed it quietly, only giving vent to her feelings with a loud sniff.

But Araminta's trials were not yet at an end.

Presently a step was heard in the passage which she recognized as Aggie's. But it was a tentative step. Uncertain.

"Aggie?" Minta called out. "Is that you?"

A silence, and then Aggie's step once more—determined. The door opened.

"Well—aren't you coming in?" Minta slowly rolled to one elbow to peer at her friend. Aggie looked pale and faded in the dim light, her skin as colorless as her white-blond hair.

"I'm—sorry you're unwell," said Aggie stiffly.

"Mr. Beckford and Mr. Carlisle say a week or two, and I'll be to rights again."

Aggie said nothing to this, but she entered the room and perched on the edge of a chair facing the sofa. Minta swallowed, her eagerness to expose Mr. Taplin's faithlessness dwindling in the face of her friend's coolness. But she must speak! Yes, Aggie would be angry, but it would pass.

"I thank your family for the flowers," she began.

Aggie gave the merest shrug. "Frederica sent them."

Minta swallowed again and balled her fists for courage. How much easier it would be to do this, if she could march around the room and stare and roar Aggie into sense, instead of lying there like a lump, hardly able to open her eyes for long spells.

Aggie must have lost patience with Minta's weakness because she clenched her own fists. "Why did you go driving with Mr. Taplin?"

"—Er—because he asked. And I said we should pick you up at The Acres."

"Then—why—" Aggie cleared her own throat. "Then why was the carriage accident on the Weeke Road and not the Romsey Road? Did you forget where I lived?"

Minta steeled herself. "Don't be ridiculous. I did point that out to him, but he said he wanted to take a different way because the day was so fine. I was...surprised, but it was true—it was a pleasant day, and he is pleasant company."

Aggie's head flashed up. "I am sorry you were hurt in the accident, Minta, but I did not want to come to Hollowgate today. Because I was vexed with you."

"I—don't see what cause you have to be vexed," said Minta faintly.

"Minta, you *knew* I liked Mr. Taplin! I told you so. From the very beginning! And I consider it the height of disloyalty that you would then try to win him yourself." Aggie's voice broke at the end of this speech, but Minta knew it was from equal parts rage and hurt.

"But he's so handsome! Handsomer than Mr. Carlisle," tittered Minta, wishing the last trumpet would sound, and she would be spared this farce.

"You didn't think that was such a weighty point in the beginning," Aggie rounded on her. "In fact, in the beginning, you said you couldn't think what was the least bit admirable or marvelous about him. In the beginning, you still bore a grudge against him for his youthful escapades."

"I got over it, as you advised," Minta replied lamely. "Because he really is, as you say, terribly, terribly handsome."

"And your purported liking for Mr. Carlisle?" Aggie persisted, her voice rising. "Is he so soon forgotten?"

Another uneasy laugh from Minta and a deprecating shrug. "Yes, well—a girl can change her mind."

Now Aggie really did burst into tears, and her fists thumped the upholstery of her seat until clouds of dust erupted from it. "What has happened to you, Araminta Ellsworth? The friend I knew could never be so completely indifferent to my feelings! Where is the girl who stood by me on my first day at Turcotte's, when those spiteful boarders called me a dandelion? Where is the girl who has been my dearest companion every day since?"

A colossal lump formed in Minta's throat, and she longed for nothing more than to wail alongside Aggie. Oh, that curses would rain down on Francis Taplin for causing this dissension between them!

"I—I don't see why you accuse me," gasped Minta, pinching herself so hard her eyes did indeed begin to water. "Can—I—help it if Mr. Taplin—prefers me to you?"

Then Aggie was on her feet, color flooding her and her eyes throwing sparks. "How dare you! How can you dare to say that, when you know as well as I do that Mr. Taplin never took a moment's notice of you until you started—started primping and prinking and—and putting yourself forward!"

"Why can't a girl look her best?" demanded Minta. She didn't dare stand, but she did drag herself to a sitting position. "Or are you the only one who is allowed to make herself fine?"

"At least it is *myself* I make fine!"

"What do you mean by that?"

"I mean, at least I still look like Aggie Weeks! I'm not wearing some—some fashionable *contrivance*." And here Aggie went so far as to poke Araminta in the Bosom. "How many yards of fabric did the modiste require to make this thing?"

For the second time that day, Minta felt herself called upon to defend the ridiculous undergarment which she would gladly have torn off and hurled out the parlor window. But this time she couldn't muster the will.

"You indeed have the better bosom," she agreed, hoping to redirect the conversation. "By far. But I think it pretty plain that, despite my—er—shortcomings in that department, Mr. Taplin does appear...fond of me. You are quick to blame me and accuse me of disloyalty, but what of him? Why should you want him, if he was inconstant to you?"

As quickly as she had fired up, Aggie faded again. She resumed her seat, as if her bones were too weak to support her longer. "He—never made me any promises. He was only kind and attentive and flattering." Biting her lip, she threw Minta a glance of pained uncertainty. "Has he—said anything to you?"

The dagger thrust, at last.

"He has not said anything...yet. But Aggie—on the drive, he—kissed me."

"I don't believe you!"

"You may ask Beatrice," said Minta with a sigh. "She was there."

Aggie panted as if Minta had literally pierced her.

"Then—that must mean—he really does—does prefer you."

Minta said nothing.

"And he must intend to offer for you," Aggie went on remorselessly. "Or he never would have done such a thing, no matter how hard you flirted with him."

"Flirted with him"! Were dressing herself to his taste and offering a few inane giggles considered flirting? Indignation ignited at this, and the game might have been up, had Aggie waited for an answer. As it was, she was on her feet again, pacing back and forth in the little parlor, and Minta had to screw her eyes shut against the motion.

"He will offer for you, I know it," Aggie repeated. "The Taplins are an old family, and the Ellsworths are an old family—"

"Not that old," Minta couldn't refrain from interrupting. "It was the Baldrics of Hollowgate who were an old family, and I haven't a drop of Baldric blood in me, you know."

"You know what I mean," insisted Aggie. "The Ellsworths may not be as old as the Baldrics, but they are certainly older than the Weekses. What is Papa but a silk manufacturer with a house he bought fifteen years ago? Of course Mr. Taplin would choose you over me."

"Oh, what a snobby delight he is," muttered Minta.

"What will you say to him, when he asks?"

"Heavens—how quickly your mind works. I haven't thought that far ahead."

"Well, think now. What will you say?"

"I—I wasn't thinking of marrying anytime soon, but—if I were to put him off, would you still want him?"

Aggie shut her own eyes, wincing. "I wish I could say I would spit on him, and that I wouldn't be anyone's second choice, and yet—"

"And yet," sighed Araminta, foreseeing that the day would not bring an end to her playacting. If tiresome Mr. Taplin proposed and Araminta refused, it was more than likely he would try his luck with Aggie.

Perhaps she could ask Mr. Carlisle to pretend an interest in Miss Wright? Then Mr. Taplin might transfer his shallow and mobile affections to *that* young lady. And then, if Miss Wright welcomed Mr. Taplin's attentions, he would propose, she would accept, and the problem would be solved. In fact, this might be the most satisfactory outcome of all, for perhaps Aggie would forgive Araminta in the face of a common enemy.

But Minta did not like the idea of Mr. Carlisle pretending an interest in anyone but herself. He was *her* partner, not Miss Wright's!

Suppose Mr. Carlisle agreed to feign an interest in Miss Wright, only to find his interest became all too genuine?

No. No, no, no. It was too great a risk. If Mr. Taplin made Minta an offer, she would simply have to feed his hopes until Aggie gave up. Oh, dear! But how long would that take? Aggie had as true a heart as ever beat in a young lady's body.

"Aggie, you'd better do your best to get over him because I—I think I'll have him after all. Eventually. When I'm good and ready." *Like in a hundred years*, Minta added inwardly. *Or when he is the last man on earth.*

Aggie tossed her head. "He hasn't proposed to you yet. And you're homebound for the present. Mrs. Ellsworth told me."

"What are you implying? Mr. Taplin won't be at any balls or plays or gallivanting about town either," Minta said. "For he's in worse condition than I am."

"That may be, but if the mountain will not come to Mahomet, Mahomet must go to the mountain."

"You wouldn't dare!"

"Wouldn't dare what?"

"Wouldn't dare try to steal him from me, Agatha Weeks!"

But Aggie was already going.

"He isn't yours yet, *Araminta Ellsworth*. You just got done saying so yourself. Good-bye."

And, unlike Beatrice, Minta's dearest friend gave the parlor door a resounding slam.

Chapter Eighteen

Things are thought, which never yet were wrought,
And castels buylt, above in lofty skies.
— George Gascoigne, *The steele glas: a satyre* (1576)

Tribbet found Carlisle knee-deep in laboratory paraphernalia, his neckcloth loosened and person disheveled.

"Mr. Nick—a letter has come for you."

After finding a place to set down the box of glass vessels he carried, Carlisle held out a hand to his uncle's whip-thin errand boy, his mind still on why Blair had so many vessels of one size and not enough of another. But his attention sharpened quickly enough when he saw the hand. He had only seen it once before, but he was not likely to forget it.

Hollowgate

10 August 1804

Dear Mr. Carlisle,
I hope you and your uncle are well and that you will
pardon me for chasing you to London with this letter. I
am deeply regretful that my few correspondences with
you should all be in the nature of peremptory requests,
but I am afraid everything is in danger of going terri-
bly amiss if we (you) do not take action.

In brief, I am house-bound, as you are well aware, and
Aggie did not come to see me until I wrote her and asked
her to come. She heard I was injured driving with Mr.
Taplin, and she was angry with me for trying to steal
him. Where I thought this revelation that he was court-
ing me as well as her would kindle a disgust for him
in her heart, I am afraid it did not. Therefore I was
obliged to increase the stakes and to tell her that he had
kissed me, thinking surely that would not be without
effect. But the only effect was that Aggie blamed me
and grew angrier still! She asked me if I intended to
accept your brother, if he offered, and I hedged and
turned the question on her: would she accept him if he
asked her second? Imagine my dismay when she said
she would! Aggie is determined to love him and to have

him, if she can, and she hinted before she left that she intended to re-engage his attentions while I am stuck at Hollowgate and unable to prevent it.

Oh, Mr. Carlisle! How I wish you were here to confer with me. As it is, I have been forced to cudgel my aching brains to devise a plan on my own, and this is it: what would you think of writing me a sham offer of marriage? One that I can wave about and brag about, so that your brother learns of it? I think it might have the salutary effect of prompting a proposal from him, that he might "keep up" with you. Once your brother is engaged to me, he cannot offer for Aggie, and it will allow more time for her to come to her senses.

I am certain a more shameless letter has never been written in the history of mankind, but I trust to your discretion and kindness not to make it known, however you might feel about it. I am ashamed to ask you to risk this little spell of notoriety but cannot think what might be done otherwise in the short time we have. You, who were so kind about the theatre ticket money! One day, when this is all past, I will show you what a friend I can be and how willingly I would do you a good turn, even as you have done for me.

Yours most sincerely,
Araminta Ellsworth

A sham offer of marriage?

Carlisle's first thought was not compliance with the unusual Miss Ellsworth's unusual request. No, his first thought was that he would return to Hampshire immediately. What he would do there was unclear. Lock Francis in his room? He could hardly imprison him there around the clock for the foreseeable future. Intercept Miss Agatha and warn her off? If Miss Agatha would not listen to her lifelong friend, why would she credit anything a jealous stepbrother might say? Perhaps Francis could be brought to propose to Miss Ellsworth, if he, Nicholas, walked in and announced his intention of doing so. But if that were the case, why would he not simply write, as Miss Ellsworth suggested?

Carlisle knew the answer to the last question soon enough. It was that, if Francis were going to be proposing to Miss Ellsworth and she were going to be "accepting" him in any sense, that was not something he wanted to be seventy miles away for. Not even if he knew it to be a sham engagement.

No.

Witness what already happened on Francis' drive with Miss Ellsworth, when he tried to take advantage of her! If he considered himself engaged to her or, at least, not outright refused, Francis would throw off restraint altogether.

His mind made up, Carlisle began to clear a space on the laboratory surface. He would write the letter, as she bid him, but he would follow it as quickly as he could with his own return. He had been already in London three days, and the laboratory was still all confusion, but it was a hair less higgledy-piggledy than it had been. His uncle Blair would be disappointed, but Carlisle would come again at a later date.

When the paper and ink and quill were collected (not the easiest nor speediest feat), he found himself perched on the wooden stool, absently scratching with his fingernail at gouges in the table. Because a proposal letter—even a counterfeit one—was not something that wrote itself. Miss Ellsworth had said she would wave it about and brag about it, but would anyone besides herself be allowed to read it? It was one thing to write a private proposal and quite another to write with an audience in mind. That question at least could be settled—clearly he must write as if everyone in Winchester would see the letter because they very well might. But more perplexing was how to write a sham proposal to a woman you seriously intended on marrying.

His first few attempts were disastrous, ending in crumpled wads at his feet. And then he thought of someone reading those crumpled wads and had to interrupt his composition to burn the pages over the spirit lamp.

But at last, after many starts and stops, the letter was finished, to be read yet once more before he folded and sealed it.

Cornhill
London

11 August 1804

Dear Miss Ellsworth,

Forgive me for writing without having first asked your leave to do so. I claim a would-be doctor's prerogative because, were I still in Winchester, I would have called at Hollowgate to assure myself of your continuing recovery. As my business in town prevents my return for at least another few days, I take up pen to satisfy both my curiosity and my heart.

Yes, Miss Ellsworth, my heart. For that day when I learned with horror of your carriage accident, it confirmed what I had already begun to suspect: that you have grown very dear to me. From the first moments of our acquaintance I was captured by your frankness and charm and high spirits, and my appreciation of these qualities in you only increased upon better acquaintance.

You will not wonder why I have said nothing up to now. The vast difference in our situations was enough to keep me silent, for I had neither fortune nor name nor even glittering promise of future success to offer. I picture you now, with your generous nature, saying, "Pah! What do I care for fortune or name or future success?" But I care, Miss Ellsworth. In my pride, I disdain to come empty-handed as a beggar to a woman I would make my bride.

But I write to you now, I speak now, because there has been a change in my circumstances. As you know, my uncle is the inventor and manufacturer of Blair's Balsam, the efficacy of which you yourself can vouch for. He has had the good fortune to secure a naval contract for his creation and now has only to determine how he will meet the contract's demands. As my uncle's sole remaining relation, he wishes me to share in his coming bounty and proposes to make me an allowance of £600 per annum. While this is no fortune, in combination with the allowance from my stepfather Mr. John Taplin and the eventual income I will earn when I have completed my apprenticeship with Mr. Beckford, I would feel myself well able then to support a wife and family in a year's time. Eighteen months at the uppermost.

Therefore, Miss Ellsworth—lovely, lively Miss Ellsworth—I beg you to tell me if there is any possibility you might come to return my feelings. If there is any possibility you might make me the most blessed and happy of men, for whose sake you would submit to a long engagement. I can offer you only this.

This and my entire heart.

Yours most faithfully,
Nicholas Carlisle

It was done. Carlisle feared it was done badly. That is, he feared Miss Ellsworth would recognize it at once as the genuine outpouring of his heart, and not a mere fictive proposal, a mere ruse.

Well, and if she did? In writing such a letter, he was only prematurely putting on paper what he fully hoped to say in the flesh, a few months hence, when the naval contract and its concomitant income had become actual fact.

But he was not a gambler by nature, and therefore the very thought of counting his chickens before they hatched made him feel physically ill.

"Post it and be done," he muttered. "Before you change your mind."

He did not know if it was good advice or bad, but he followed it. Putting on his hat, he emerged from the laboratory on Lombard Street and from there it was just a step to the General Post Office.

The deed done, Carlisle could not bring himself to return right away to work. His heart was drumming too insistently. Without any destination in mind, he began to walk. Down Walbrook to Thames Street and thence to the bridge. He crossed its crowded length, pausing over the Great Arch to observe the river traffic beneath, before wandering into St. Saviour's church at the southern end. Though the structure was in disrepair, he found himself consoled by its vastness and by the ancient tombs and monuments within. "'Many have died from time to time,'" he reminded himself, as he stood before the poet Gower's painted effigy, its head resting at a most uncomfortable elevation, "'and worms have eaten them, but not for love.'"

It was a full two hours before he returned to Lombard Street, calmed and even faintly optimistic, but the moment he opened the door, young Tribbet sprang up from behind one of the tables and flew at him.

"Mr. Nick! Mr. Carlisle! Where have you been?" the boy gasped and hiccoughed, and Carlisle could see the dried streaks of past tears on his cheeks.

"Walking. Good heavens. What is it, Tribbet?"

"It's your uncle, sir! It's Mr. Blair—"

The blood in Carlisle's veins turned to ice water. "Is he ill? Injured? Where is he?"

"Oh, sir—he's gone and *died!* Right in front of Mr. Jacobson. He came back from his luncheon and was hauling Mr. Jacobson over the coals for putting away some item Mr. Blair didn't want put away, and right there and then he gasped and turned colors and clutched at his heart and staggered around and knocked us fair over when we went to help him, and before he hit the floor, he were gone."

Carlisle swayed, and Tribbet thought Mr. Blair's nephew might hit the floor himself, if only there were room in the laboratory to do so. He caught the young man's elbow. "Will you come, sir?"

The premises of B. Blair, Chemist & Druggist were locked and the shades lowered, but Tribbet pulled out the key that hung on a leathern strap about his neck and let them in, calling, "I found him, Mr. Jacobson!"

Instantly the boy was hushed, by Jacobson himself and by an elderly woman holding a bundle of wool and wearing a mobcap that swallowed everything but her spectacles, sharp nose, and thin-lipped mouth.

"*Have* you no respect?" hissed the woman. She glared at Carlisle as if he too had been making noise, before turning on her heel and disappearing into the dead man's former office.

"It's the parish people from St. Michael's," whispered Jacobson. "We sent for Mr. Hilton the doctor, but he said there was nothing to be done except call the vicar, and the vicar sent first the sextons, who laid Mr. Blair out in the office upon his desk no less. And then this crew of harpies came, to—to—er—clean and prepare him."

"May I see him?" asked Carlisle, still green with shock.

"He's *your* uncle," replied Jacobson, "so the harpies can't refuse you."

The harpies did not refuse him. They ignored him, going about their work.

Bertram Blair, so very alive so recently, lay in unaccustomed stillness, his normally ruddy complexion pale and his normally irrepressible personality repressed for good. He was nearly unrecognizable to his nephew in this state, and Carlisle did not remain long.

When he stumbled back into the shop, Jacobson and Tribbet drew apart from each other, their whispers breaking off and their gazes turning to him expectantly. And why should they not? He was the heir.

The heir! Carlisle's mouth twisted in a bitter grimace. The heir of what, exactly?

The irony was too thick. That he should just have come from posting a letter to his beloved, boasting of his improved prospects, only to have those prospects turn to dust and blow away on the next breeze. It did not matter in the end that his letter had put the cart before the horse, for both cart and horse were no more. With his uncle's death, there would be no naval contract, no allowance, no possible eventual riches, no marriage, no Miss Ellsworth.

Nay, instead there would be debt and difficulty and—at the very end, when he had time to think about it—utter aloneness. He was now without a living blood relation in all the world.

"What do we do now, sir?" asked Jacobson.

Carlisle hardly knew. But he gave himself a shake.

"Well...I suppose we continue as we were for the time being. When—my uncle—has been laid to rest, you will man the shop, and I will finish arranging the laboratory."

"You mean you will take over the business, sir?" was Tribbet's question.

"No, I'm afraid not." Of that much Carlisle was sure. "It will have to be sold. Auctioned, I suppose." He turned to go up to his room, wanting suddenly to lie on his spartan bed and stare at the ceiling and contemplate the end of all things, but how could he, when there was so much to be done?

Slowly he turned back. The other two were still staring at him, hanging on his decisions as if he had metamorphosed into his uncle, with his uncle's authority over their lives.

"I am sorry. I know this is upsetting, not to know what will become of—everything," he said. "I, too, am upset. Let me see—Jacobson, when the vicar comes to talk about—arrangements—please call me down."

"But, sir—" Jacobson scurried nearer, keeping his voice low. "How will we pay for everything? Those harpies said they will sit up with the body, if we haven't anyone else, but they'll have to be paid. And the pallbearers and the refreshments and the vicar's fee and—"

"Yes, yes. I understand. Look, Jacobson, is there any money in the cash box there?"

"Maybe a few odd pounds and shillings."

"That must serve for the funeral purposes. But where did my uncle keep the rest of his money and important papers? Does he have an account with the bankers? Who are his lawyers?"

The old man was already shaking his head and wringing his hands. "I don't know of his account, but the lawyers were something starting with a T—Triple? Trimpi?"

"Truckle!" suggested the boy.

"No, no. Something else. It will come to me. You know him—he always kept such matters close. When bills came, he tucked them in his pocket. When it was time to pay Tribbet or myself, he would pull the exact amounts from that same pocket. Here is what the harpies found on him today." Jacobson tugged on Carlisle's sleeve and indicated a handful of coins and one small banknote.

"I think he hides things in his laboratory," volunteered Tribbet boldly. "It's such a humble-jumble in there, as you know, sir, that no one but Mr. Blair could find anything."

"Very well." Carlisle set his shoulders. "I will return there now. If the vicar comes, then, you may either send him to Lombard

Street or settle a time yourself for the burial. Any time at his earliest convenience will do. I do not know that there will be anyone besides ourselves who will care to attend." He frowned, thinking of the long vacations he had spent here—had his uncle had any friends to speak of? It seemed every person Carlisle ever remembered calling was a business associate, a supplier or customer or inspector or bill collector.

"Yes, sir. You're right, sir." Jacobson was wringing his hands by this point, and Carlisle understood for the first time his uncle's propensity to roar at the man. It only made him feel worse to see his anxiety reflected back at him. But Jacobson was a good man, an honest man, and he was losing his livelihood and future just as surely as Carlisle.

"Jacobson." Carlisle reached for him and gave a bracing squeeze to his shoulder. "We will get through this. And, if there's anything left over after the dust has settled, there will be something for you and Tribbet."

Relief washed over Jacobson's drawn face, quickly followed by doubt, as he considered how modestly the late Mr. Blair had lived and how the arrival of bills always threw the man into a ferment. But Jacobson, too, had heard of the naval contract, so a beam of hope lighted his countenance. "Thank you, sir. And I trust Mr. Blair shared his recipe for the balsam with you, his only nephew? Even if he cannot produce the balsam himself for the Royal Navy, perhaps the recipe could be sold to another firm?"

Carlisle blanched. "You do not have a copy of the balsam recipe?"

"I? Of course I don't! Mr. Nicholas, you think your uncle would trust his greatest secret to me?"

"Neither of you ever helped him concoct it?" demanded Carlisle, looking at each in turn.

"I mind the shop!" cried Jacobson, even as Tribbet shook his head violently and declared, "I'm naught but the errand boy!"

"Good heavens," muttered Carlisle, leaning over the nearest display case and heedless of his fingerprints on the glass. "I thought the same as you: that the recipe at least could be sold to cover any debts. But now you tell me no one but my uncle knew the recipe? No one but my uncle had any experience in its production?"

Glumly the three of them stared at each other. What a shame it would be, if B. Blair, Chemist & Druggist, died a bankrupt when all was said and done! He, who had been on the verge of wealth!

Carlisle took a deep breath. "All right. It is what it is. I will search for the recipe, too, as I clean the laboratory."

"Shall I come and help you too, Mr. Nick?" asked Tribbet.

"I suppose you better had," he answered. "Before this is ended we will all need all the help we can get."

Chapter Nineteen

Love is a monstrous telegraphe...
you cou'd read without spectacles,
that slighted passion is a piteous case.
— John O'Keefe, *The Irish mimic, or blunders at Brighton* (1794)

"You are improving nicely," Mr. Beckford told her, after looking into each of her eyes with his glass and testing her balance. "How quickly the young recover."

On this, the fifth day since her accident, Araminta had been allowed to leave her dim small parlor for the shade of the terrace, though she wore a veil to her bonnet, to protect her eyes from the glare of the summer sun. After her isolation, it felt as if all Winchester were there, her family, the doctor, even the curate Mr. Hepple and his wife. But missing from those gathered were three people who loomed large in Minta's world: Aggie had not reappeared since her one summons; Mr. Carlisle remained in London; and Mr. Taplin was, by Mr. Beckford's orders, still confined to Beaumond.

Minta was not called upon to say or do much, thank heavens, Mrs. Ellsworth having already told the visitors and reminded Willie (twice) that Araminta must be left in peace, and so uncharacteristically quiet was she that the others nearly forgot she was there. Her brother Tyrone, who ordinarily gave his noisy twin a wide berth, had taken the seat beside her on the bench, his book shut on his lap, and his elbow propped between them, his nearness comforting.

For Araminta was in need of comfort. It had taken all the strength and effort she could muster to compose her desperate letter to Mr. Carlisle, and she was on tenterhooks as to his response. What had she been thinking? A man who argued with her over spending her two guineas to buy theatre tickets was not simply going to go along with such a mad plan as she had devised. He would refuse. He would tell her she had gone beyond the pale. He would say all cooperation between them must end and that he deeply regretted having played any part in it. If he even wrote back.

And then, if he did any or all of those things, not only would she lose Aggie, but—nearly as painful to contemplate—she would lose her friendship with him! And, oh, how she treasured that friendship with him. How she wished it could go on and on. He need never love her or marry her, but if they could just continue enjoying each other's company—and, if at all possible, not loving or marrying anyone else!

So intent was Araminta in her ponderings that it was not until Tyrone nudged her with his elbow and inclined his head ever so slightly toward Mrs. Hepple that she returned to her surroundings.

"Pretend to be asleep," he whispered, hardly audible, and Araminta obeyed him without question, letting her head droop slowly toward her chest. He then opened his book, though she knew it was for show because he did not bother doing so where his ribbon marked the page.

"...In a towering rage, I'm afraid," the curate's wife was saying in low tones to Mrs. Ellsworth.

"But whyever should he be so?" asked Minta's stepmother.

"Miss Weeks tells me her father *intercepted* a note. From Miss Agatha to Mr. Taplin."

Minta twitched and got another elbow in the arm.

"Dear me!" From her stepmother's voice, Minta could tell Mrs. Ellsworth had turned to look in her direction. Then she resumed, much more softly, "Did Miss Weeks say if it was the contents of the note that angered her father, or the mere fact that Aggie was writing to a young man?"

"Both, apparently. Of course a young unmarried girl ought not to send notes to young unmarried men—" (another twitch from Minta) "—but had the note been but an innocent inquiry into Mr. Taplin's health, I doubt Mr. Weeks would have taken on so."

"Then—it was not?" prompted Mrs. Ellsworth, and both Tyrone and Minta could hear the ruefulness in her question, as she condemned herself for prying.

A pause. Minta guessed Mrs. Hepple must have been shaking her head—vehemently—because then she hissed, "It was *a declaration of her feelings!*"

Fortunately Mrs. Ellsworth's gasp masked Minta's own, but *un*fortunately little Willsie and his equally little nephew Peter chose that moment to get in a tussle over who would get to throw the ball next for Snap the terrier, and both Mrs. Ellsworth and Florence must perforce spring up and scold the two boys.

Araminta thought she would explode with the suspense of it and even considered pretending to wake up, that she might pump the curate's wife herself. But, reading her mind, Tyrone mouthed, "Wait."

His counsel was sound, for, as soon as she could resume her seat and satisfy herself that everyone was once more engaged in conversation, Mrs. Ellsworth said, "Pardon me, Mrs. Hepple. You were saying—?"

"I was saying that the note Mr. Weeks intercepted apparently contained a bald declaration of Miss Agatha's feelings for Mr. Taplin! All about how stricken she was to hear of his accident and how she wished she might call at Beaumond and how, ever since she met him, *she could think of no one else.*"

Another sharp breath from Mrs. Ellsworth, and then more that Araminta couldn't catch. Or it might have been that she couldn't hear because of the blood roaring in her ears. Her head came up without her realizing it, and Tyrone looked sidewise at her.

So Aggie had told the truth when she said she intended to pursue Mr. Taplin while Araminta was confined to Hollowgate. But if her note had been intercepted, would she then try to go to Beaumond in person?

"—Calling in the loans," Mrs. Hepple was saying. "He said, 'If it's Beaumond you want, it's Beaumond you'll get.'"

Mrs. Ellsworth made no reply to this, having noticed Minta was awake. She changed the subject abruptly, and the talk moved on.

"I have to see Aggie," Minta muttered to her brother. "I have to know what is happening. But I don't think I can walk all the way to The Acres."

"Why don't you send a note, then?"

Minta sighed. "She won't come. She's not happy with me right now."

One eyebrow lifted. "Not happy with you? This is a first. Can there be war between the two peas?"

She shut his book and clutched his arm. "Please, Tyrone—won't you go and fetch her? Tell her I *must* see her."

"Who says Aggie would listen to me?"

"Aggie won't say no to you because she wouldn't feel comfortable doing so. She doesn't really know you well enough. It's the only way. *Please*."

He made a wry face. "All right. But only because you've been knocked over the head. You mustn't expect this sort of cooperation in future."

"In future you'll be away at Oxford, so you ought to want to help me whilst you can."

When he was gone, Araminta cited her head as excuse to retreat to the smallest parlor once more, that she might speak to Aggie alone, God willing.

It was the maid Monk who popped her head in first. "Miss, Mrs. Chock walked this letter over because she said it fell on the floor yesterday and didn't get delivered. I said, why not wait until tomorrow, but I think it was that it came from London for *you* and not Mr. Ellsworth, and she wanted me to tell her what it was, as if I knew."

But Minta wasn't attending. There was only one person who would write to her from London. Thanking the maid (and frustrating her curiosity), she turned her back and went to the window, her hand trembling. It was impossible not to think that everything in her young life depended on what Mr. Carlisle's letter contained.

He had small, dense writing, however, and at first it simply blurred and blended before her weakened eyes.

"Oh, no, no, no." Minta held it closer. Then farther away. Then closer again. She squinted. She opened her eyes wider. She opened the window curtains as far as they would go. But the letter would only come into focus just long enough for her to make out a word here and there— "Ellsworth" "heart" (heart!) "business" "Balsam". She could not for the life of her grasp whole phrases, much less sentences. Tears of frustration filled her eyes, which did not help matters. What could she do? She could not ask anyone to read it aloud to her, when she had no idea what it contained! Suppose he wrote to say he would on no condition be a party to her scheme and that he furthermore never wished to hear from or speak with her again? But nor could she bear to put the letter away for when her vision was stronger—or strong enough to read his confoundedly small hand.

In desperation, she folded the letter just beneath the first paragraph. She must take a chance.

"Mama?" At the door, Minta bellowed into the passage. "Mama, could you come here a moment?" If anyone must know anything, it were better it were her kind, discreet stepmother.

Mrs. Ellsworth was with her in an instant, little Willie by the hand, but her younger brother was unlikely to understand anything Mr. Carlisle wrote, so Minta shrugged this off.

"Please, dear Mama—Mr. Carlisle has sent a letter, but my head is too feeble and my eyes too troubled to make out his dreadful small writing. Won't you please read this one paragraph to me, and I will tell you whether or not to go on?"

"Mr. Carlisle has written you?" Mrs. Ellsworth's eyes were wide—it was a day of surprises, after what Mrs. Hepple had told her. Releasing Willie, she plucked the paper from Araminta's hand and took it as Minta had, to the window. Even she had to hold it near to make out, her stepdaughter crowding by her shoulder and Willie embracing both their legs.

"'Dear Miss Ellsworth,'" she read, "'Forgive me for writing without having first asked your leave to do so. I claim a would-be doctor's prerogative because, were I still in Winchester, I would have called at Hollowgate to assure myself of your continuing recovery.'" She paused and looked up. "How kind of him, and what a good doctor he will make!"

Minta said nothing. Her stepmother went on. "'As my business in town prevents my return for at least another few days, I take up pen to satisfy both my curiosity and my—heart.' His heart!" Mrs. Ellsworth looked up, her lips parted in wonder. "Why—Araminta—could he mean—"

She was well to be concerned, for Minta had untangled herself from Willie's grasp to sag into the nearest chair. *He was doing it! He was doing as she asked, and sending her a mock proposal!*

"Shall I go on, Minta dear, or do you want to try to decipher it yourself? I believe your father keeps a magnifying glass in his desk for when he goes over the account books with Mr. Falk."

But Minta could not bear to wait. She had to hear it at once. "No—you go on, Mama. Please."

Mrs. Ellsworth nodded and, after another moment, unfolded the hidden part of the letter and read on. She could not help but be touched by the young man's praise of her stepdaughter and reached out a hand to lay upon Minta's shoulder. "Yes, that's well put. Your 'frankness and charm and high spirits.' He admires the Minta whom we all love."

"Go on," croaked the Minta whom they all loved, as Willie crawled onto her lap.

Mr. Carlisle's admission of why he had not spoken before drew a sigh from the compassionate Mrs. Ellsworth. "Ah, the worthy young man. How hard it must be for someone of his character and talent, not to be able to address himself to you, for lack of means. But something must have changed, for him to do so now."

"Go on," whispered Minta. She buried her face in her little brother's warm curls.

With increasing excitement and joy, Mrs. Ellsworth proceeded to the portion of Carlisle's letter describing his uncle's good fortune and its effect on his own situation. "A naval contract for the balsam! And an allowance for his nephew? Oh, Mr. Blair, I congratulate you and commend you for your generosity. You could not choose a more deserving object.—Yes, yes, Minta, I will go on.— 'While this is no fortune, in combination with the allowance from my stepfather Mr. John Taplin and the eventual income I will earn when I have completed my apprenticeship with Mr. Beckford, I would feel myself well able then to support a wife and family in a year's time. Eighteen months at the uppermost.' Minta!"

But still Minta said nothing. Her heart was pounding. Such a ring of truth his letter had! He could not have made the part up about the naval contract and the allowance, could he? Had such good fortune really befallen both uncle and nephew? If it had, she would be as glad for him as her stepmother was, even while it pierced her.

The last paragraph Mrs. Ellsworth read almost as breathlessly as Minta listened to it. "'Therefore, Miss Ellsworth—lovely, lively Miss Ellsworth—I beg you to tell me if there is any possibility you might come to return my feelings. If there is any possibility you might make me the most blessed and happy of men, for whose sake you would submit to a long engagement. I can offer you only this. This and my entire heart. Yours most faithfully, Nicholas Carlisle.'"

For a minute there was no sound but little Willie humming to himself and then scrambling from his sister's lap to chase a dust mote that floated past.

"What a letter," said Mrs. Ellsworth at last. She was sitting now. She did not remember taking the chair beside her stepdaughter, but there she was.

And Minta—Minta had never known such struggle. If she had not known she cared for Mr. Carlisle to this point, she would have known it now. Why else would she feel torn along her entire length between the wonder of hearing such words addressed to her and the agony of knowing they were all hollow? All meaningless. Put to paper merely at her behest.

Oh—what she wouldn't give for them to be genuine!

And then—and then she scarcely remembered in time—she was supposed to shrug this offer off! To use it as bait to capture another offer from Mr. Taplin.

She thanked the Lord she was supposed to be weakened by her concussion, for it allowed her to shut her eyes and rest her head against the back of the chair and frown as if in pain.

"Minta," Mrs. Ellsworth ventured, when it seemed the girl might never speak again, "what reply will you give him?"

Minta's hazel eyes flew open. "I—I—I will refuse him, of course. Probably. Almost—certainly."

"You don't like him at all, then?"

"What? Mr. Carlisle? I—never thought of him that way."

If Mrs. Ellsworth had not been somewhat distracted by her own thoughts, Araminta's performance would not have been very persuasive. But, no, Miranda Ellsworth was thinking wistfully that she had never in her life received a letter of this sort, not from anyone. Her own husband Mr. William Ellsworth had proposed to her only after he was left at the altar by the woman he intended to make his fourth wife. Finding himself abandoned, he looked about him and saw Miranda Gregory, faded spinster sister of the rector, and decided she would do instead. *Not* that William Ellsworth was unkind or even unaffectionate. And *not* that she was ungrateful for the pleasant pastures in which she found herself or for the unexpected gift of a son. She was indeed grateful. But there was no denying that Miranda Ellsworth had never felt, nor been the object of, a Grand Passion.

Repressing a sigh, she folded the letter again and, taking Araminta's limp hand, she returned it to her. "Well, if you cannot care for him, you cannot care for him. You are young and under no obligation to marry or even to think of marriage anytime soon. Mr. Carlisle is a good, kind man who will make a good, kind husband. I am sorry he will be disappointed, but despite his modest means, I cannot help but think he will meet with better luck the next time he tries."

"You mean you think he will try again with me?" Minta asked, unable to keep a humiliating quaver from her voice.

"What? Oh, no, I didn't mean he would propose again to you," Mrs. Ellsworth meant to reassure her. "He seems the sort to take a girl at her word and not to hound her into submission."

"Oh. I see."

"Poor Mr. Carlisle," sighed her stepmother again. She gave Minta a rueful smile. "It's courteous to give a gentleman your answer as soon as you know it. Would you like to try to write to him yourself, or would you like to dictate to me, and I can write it?"

"But—do I have to refuse him today?" gabbled Minta. "Can't I—think about it a little longer, just to be certain?" (And just to dangle it over Mr. Taplin as a possible threat, which had been, she reminded herself, the whole point of it.)

"Of course." Mrs. Ellsworth embraced her tenderly. "May I tell your father, my dear? I won't mention it to anyone else, and you know he will be content with whatever makes you content."

"Oh—er—yes." The more the merrier, Minta supposed. Though her papa was not much of a gossip, and what she needed was a gossip. If only Mrs. Hepple were still here!

The thought of the curate's wife revived her impatience to see Aggie. If Aggie was trying to send declarations of love to Mr. Taplin, Minta could not lose an instant in letting Mr. Taplin know quickly enough about his brother's proposal.

"Yes, please tell Papa," she urged her stepmother as they released each other. "And could I ask you to send Monk to me again with a cool washcloth?"

"Certainly. You stretch out here and rest a while, and I'll send her right away."

But when the maid entered a minute later, it was not to find her mistress prostrate on the sofa. Rather, Minta stood in the light of the window, fanning herself with the letter she had received.

"You needed a compress, miss?"

"Yes, if you please." Minta needed a gossip, and she knew no telegraph communicated news so swiftly as servants. "I'm all in a dither, you see, Monk, because that letter that came—it contained my very first marriage proposal."

"Marriage proposal!" cried the maid. "From town?"

"From Mr. Carlisle—you know—the brother of Mr. Taplin of Beaumond."

"Mr. Carlisle, the doctor's apprentice," marveled Monk. "Just look at him, behind his brother's back, when everyone knows it's the brother that took you driving and nearly got your head busted open."

"Oh, well." Minta shrugged and, taking a seat, laid the compress over her eyes. "I'm going to rest a little, Monk. Though, if Aggie comes, she can come in. And—about the letter—if you wouldn't say anything of it..."

"Never a word, miss," the maid promised solemnly as she retreated.

And it might have been Araminta's imagination, but it sounded as if Monk barely shut the door before dashing away with her news as if the house were afire.

CHAPTER TWENTY

**Now when Job's three friends heard of all
this evil that was come upon him,
they came every one from his own place.**
— Job 2:11, *The Authorized Version* (1611)

"I didn't see her." Tyrone slung himself across one of the chairs beside the sofa, tilting it on its back legs in a way that would have got him reprimanded by his stepmother or Florence.

"What do you mean?" Minta asked, removing the compress, which was no longer cool in any case. "You were gone long enough."

"I mean I was received by her father Mr. Weeks, who regarded me with most undeserved suspicion until I told him I was sent by you. To which he said (and I quote), 'You may tell that sister of yours that she and Aggie are no longer children, free to run wild about the county without any thought to the consequences. Miss

Ellsworth was lucky to escape her carriage ride with no worse than a bump on her head.' End quote." Seeing his sister receive this as she had received such lectures all her life, Tyrone shook his head, grinning. "But there's more: Weeks said he 'refused altogether' to let anything of his fall into the hands of 'a spendthrift reprobate like Francis Taplin,' and what was more, he was confining Aggie to The Acres until she could 'regain her senses.'"

"Aggie confined to The Acres!" echoed Araminta. "What can Mr. Weeks be thinking?"

Tyrone raised a questioning eyebrow. "You mean you think she might never regain enough sense to be set at liberty again?"

"No! I mean that Mr. Weeks hasn't any sense, if he thinks telling Aggie to stay at home will solve the problem. I must see her. Now more than ever."

"That's all very well, Minta," her brother replied, "but judging from Mr. Weeks' forbidding expression, I do not think he would let you see her anymore than me. If your dear accomplice really was attempting to send an indiscreet note to Taplin, as Mrs. Hepple claimed, I would give at least a week for his anger to cool."

"I can't, Tyrone. Don't you see? Though his anger might cool in a week, Aggie can't be trusted to behave that long. I must see her now. Tonight, I warrant."

"And how do you propose to do that?" he asked doubtfully. "Concussed and weakened and unwelcome there as you are?"

"You must help me. Oh, please, Tyrone! I know you already did me this one favor, but won't you do me one more?" She clasped her hands together, pleading.

"Why do I suspect this favor will be ten times more objectionable than the last?"

"I just need you to go with me after dark to The Acres."

"Are you afraid you'll faint?"

"That, though I think I am plenty strong enough now and hardly dizzy anymore, and I can see well enough if it isn't very small—" (she broke off for a moment, and her color came and went as she thought of Mr. Carlisle and his very small writing) "—but Aggie's bedchamber is on the first floor. And since I've never tried to climb up to her window from the outside, I don't know if I'll be able to do it alone. I might need a shove up or someone to hold a trellis steady or something of that nature. *Please*, Tyrone. I'll owe you one. I'll buy you ten books. Anything."

He grinned, shaking his head. "I guess I never fully appreciated Aggie's service to you before. Without her around, suddenly I am in great demand as a confederate."

"It's good for you," insisted Minta. "You will thank me. You cannot go away to university without having ever got up to any mischief, or what will your chums think?"

When utter darkness fell, however, their twosome increased to a threesome.

"Where are you going?" hissed Beatrice as her older sister tiptoed past her room.

"To see Aggie. Why is your door open?"

"Snap wanted to go and sleep downstairs." And then Bea was next to her, luminous in her nightgown. "I want to come."

"Nonsense. You're in your nightclothes. Go back to bed."

But then Tyrone emerged quietly from his own room, and Bea whispered, "Tyrone gets to go, too? I'm coming! I won't be a second." And then she slipped away before Araminta could protest.

Rolling her eyes, Minta beckoned her brother. If they could go quickly, Bea would just have to stay behind because heaven knew she wasn't brave enough to wander the grounds at night alone. The same thought evidently occurred to Beatrice because she caught up to them at the kitchen door.

Minta huffed out a disgusted breath. "Fine. But you have to be quiet as the grave. No squeaking or screaming."

She couldn't see her sister's annoyance in the gloom, but she heard it. "Fine. I'm not six anymore, Minta."

The three Ellsworths reached The Acres with no difficulties, apart from Bea slipping as she crossed the brook and Tyrone's hand flashing out to catch her. But, true to her word, there was no sound save the skid of her shoe and a tiny splash.

All lay quiet at The Acres in the moonlight, the house darkened except, suspiciously, a faint light slipping through the gap in Aggie's window curtains.

There was no convenient trellis. Nor was there any ledge, drainpipe, balcony, wall, windowsill, or so much as an uneven ridge of stone for a toehold.

Araminta tried calling Aggie's name in a whisper, but she dared not get very loud.

Then: "Look for pebbles we might toss at the glass." This was no easy task in the moonlight, and Minta reproved herself for not thinking of this at the brook, where they might easily have gathered a handful.

"This clod of dirt came loose," whispered Bea, holding it up.

"That's likely to break a pane," was Tyrone's opinion.

"Not if I toss it very, very gently," Minta decided. Taking the moist clump from her sister, she weighed it carefully and took a few practice swings before hurling it.

With a damp thud it struck the window softly, but still Aggie did not appear.

"Are you certain this is her room?"

"Of course I am."

"Maybe she isn't in it," suggested Bea. "Maybe she snuck out too and is over at Hollowgate, and we passed her in the darkness."

"Or she's asleep and didn't blow out her candle," said Tyrone.

Minta frowned. Each was possible, and it made her feel hopeful to think Aggie might be looking for her, in turn, but what if she was headed instead for Beaumond? "Well—before we go and look for her, we'd better make sure she isn't asleep in there. Give me a hand up, Tyrone. I think I could just barely reach and bang on the window."

"You've lost your mind. That's at least twelve feet up. I'd have to put you on my shoulders, and I'm a scholar, not a prizefighter."

"You could lift me," Bea offered. "I'm almost as tall as Minta now, but I don't weigh as much."

"That's true," agreed Minta eagerly. "I'll help brace you, Tyrone."

With a heave and a grunt and a few wobbles, Beatrice Ellsworth rose above the ground floor and stretched to her utmost to reach the glass. But before she could tap it, there was a flood of light as the window curtains were thrown aside and the sash rattled up. A heavy bundle of *something* flew out, hitting Bea square in the face and sending the entire trio tumbling to the grass.

Minta struggled to a sitting position, registering in utter astonishment that the bundle was a rope of sheets tied together, and even as she stared, Aggie climbed nimbly over the windowsill and was halfway down before she froze with a smothered shriek.

"What are you doing here?"

"Never mind us!" retorted Minta, as Aggie resumed wriggling her way down. "What are *you* doing, sneaking out of the house at this hour?"

"Says the girl who snuck out of her own house at this hour!" rapped back Aggie dropping the rest of the way to the ground.

"*I* did it in company with my brother and sister," insisted Araminta, pointing in their direction. "Tyrone—Bea—would you mind letting me talk to Aggie apart?" When her siblings backed away some distance and sat down to wait them out, she continued. "And I came—we came—to see *you*. Where are you going? Are you running away? Mrs. Hepple told Mama that Mr. Weeks ordered you confined to the house."

"Oh, so you know all about that, do you? If you know so much, why do you bother to come and ask me about it?"

"Because I was concerned for you! I wanted to ask you what was happening—what you were thinking."

"You already know what I'm thinking because we already talked about how there's nothing more to be said between us," seethed

Aggie, poking Araminta in her (Bosom-less) chest. "So why don't you go away and mind your own business?"

And then, without waiting for a response, Aggie whirled on her heel and marched away. Araminta flew after her, catching her elbow. "Are you sneaking away to Beaumond?"

Aggie shook her off, but Minta seized her skirts and held on. "Agatha Weeks, you answer me! Are you *eloping*?"

"Let go of me!"

"I won't, until you tell me!"

A silent wrestling match ensued which involved a good deal of grappling and running and gasping and kicking and a little tearing of fabric. Though the girls had never wrestled in their lives, Beatrice and Tyrone would have laid odds on their sister prevailing, but Araminta was hindered by the lingering effects of her concussion. Aggie, sportingly, did not take advantage of it by pressing the bump on Araminta's head, but it made itself felt all the same, and therefore the struggle ended in a draw, with both girls lying like felled trees, exhausted.

"I wasn't eloping, you blockhead," grumbled Aggie at last. "How could I elope with the man when he's been stuck at Beaumond with all his injuries? I was just going to deliver the note I tried to send earlier."

"But what do you say in your note? Is it what you said in the note your father found?"

"None of your business."

"If you tell me, I'll tell you something in return," bargained Minta. "No—I'll tell you first, to show my good faith. Mr. Carlisle wrote to me and asked me to marry him." (She forgot neither Beatrice nor Tyrone knew this until she heard their sharp intakes of breath.)

"He did?" Aggie sat up. "What are you going to say?"

With an effort, Minta also pulled herself to a sitting position. "I—don't know yet."

"He's a very pleasant young man," said Aggie. "Not as handsome nor as charming as Mr. Taplin, of course—"

"I don't think Mr. Taplin is charming at all," piped up Beatrice. She ended in a little squeak because her brother pinched her.

"—And Mr. Carlisle hasn't any family, really, or fortune," Aggie went on, "but you needn't mind that. *Your* papa is not so particular about such things."

"That's because Flossie and Lily chose well," blurted Beatrice again. "Therefore Papa didn't need to interfere." (At this point Tyrone forcibly dragged her further off, against her muffled protests.)

"I am not altogether surprised Mr. Carlisle proposed," said Aggie, resting her head on her knees. "I thought he liked you."

"You did?" Minta's voice lifted in hope.

"Well, of course. He invited you to the theatre."

"Oh. Yes. The theatre."

"You ought to consider him, at any rate," urged her friend. "Since you told me you hadn't decided what you would say to Mr. Taplin, were he to offer."

"Mm," grunted Minta. Then she remembered to add, "You just want me out of the way."

"Well, that too."

A little silence fell, but then Araminta nudged Aggie. "Go on, then. I told you something, now you tell me something."

Aggie sighed. "Very well. It isn't nearly as scandalous as you and Papa seem to think. The first note might have been, I admit, but I lost my nerve about declaring my feelings. *This* note simply says that I hope he we will recover quickly and that I would be glad to come and call as soon as ever he might feel like receiving visitors. It was still forward of me, I grant, but it wasn't like I begged him to elope with me."

"You're right," agreed Minta. "I don't think that sounds so very bad."

Perhaps it was this concession which wrung more from Aggie. "But now the damage is done because Papa has lost his mind and says something about the Taplins owing him money and calling loans or deeds or some such. I don't really understand, but I added a postscript about it, in case they would appreciate some warning."

Aggie was a first-rater, no doubt, Minta thought. If only her feelings were directed toward a more worthy object! What had Mr. Taplin done, to win so precious a prize as Agatha Weeks? Nothing but show off his handsomeness and scatter some of his meaningless attentions over the fertile ground of Aggie's heart.

Araminta shivered. She did not doubt Aggie would get her note delivered. Even if the Ellsworths spent the entire night guarding her, they could not do so every night.

So Mr. Taplin would know eventually he must have money, and sooner, rather than later. He would also learn, if he had not already, that his brother had proposed to her, Araminta. All of which meant that, however Mr. Taplin decided to respond, it would likely happen quickly. Perhaps as soon as his head and ribs allowed him to move about. Oh, heavens—would he act even before Mr. Carlisle returned? Suppose he chose to propose to her as his brother had? Could he possibly be put off with a vague answer? Or, if she was forced to agree to an engagement, how long could he be made to wait?

Minta seized her friend's hand and was sadly gratified when she did not snatch it away. "Aggie—if Mr. Taplin asked, would you marry him, even without your father's blessing?"

"I don't know," whispered Aggie. Then she did pull away. "But I—I might. Would you?"

"Never. I would want my father's blessing," Minta answered stoutly. Not because she had given any thought to it, but rather to sway Aggie.

"But Mr. Ellsworth probably wouldn't make any fuss about it," Aggie observed, "and not just because he liked Mr. Fairchild and Mr. Kenner, your sisters' husbands, as Bea said. No…Mr. Ellsworth doesn't seem the type to fuss if you married the *footman*."

Although Minta suspected this might indeed be true, she wasn't about to admit it. "Nonsense. Papa would mind very much if I wanted to marry Bobbins."

"He wouldn't lock you in your room, at any rate," persisted Aggie. "He wouldn't forbid you to leave the grounds of Hollowgate. I wish Papa were more like Mr. Ellsworth. My papa might go so far as to *disinherit* me, if he doesn't like my choice of husband, and I don't think Mr. Ellsworth would do that to you in a hundred years."

Aggie was no fool (except in the case of Mr. Taplin), and Minta had to agree that her father was not the sort to rouse himself to thunderous threats. He would likely just smile and leave it to his wife or sons-in-law to take her in hand.

"You have a point," she admitted.

In the moonlight Minta could see Aggie's shoulders sag. "I know it. If Mr. Taplin proposes to you and you accept, your portion would likely suffice to pay whatever the Taplins might owe Papa. But if Mr. Taplin proposes to *me*, Papa might keep his word and cut me off without a shilling, and then the Taplins will lose Beaumond to him and just have *me* on their hands."

Which is more than Mr. Taplin deserves, thought Minta angrily. Her hands were wound in her skirts, and she was twisting them in her struggle not to speak her mind. *Aggie is no fool*, she told herself again. *Given enough time, she will recognize for herself that it can never succeed, any union with* that man.

"Minta?" Bea's tentative voice floated across the lawn to her. "Can we go soon? It's chilly."

"I told you not to come in the first place," snapped her sister, redirecting her high feelings at the closest object. That Tyrone disapproved of this was evident when he then said, "As one here by invitation, then, Minta, I also vote that we wind this up."

With a huff, Minta scrambled up and extended a hand to Aggie. "Are you still going to Beaumond to deliver the note?"

"Yes. Does this mean you won't stay to stop me?"

"I won't stay to stop you. How can I? I'm facing a mutiny. But Aggie—" with a final wring of Aggie's fingers before she released her "—if Mr. Taplin were to choose you over me, no matter what happened, I would still be your friend."

"We aren't friends," said Aggie crossly. "Remember? You flirted with the man *I* chose and went driving with him and even kissed him."

Resentment surged through Araminta again, and she stomped her foot. "We see matters differently there," she rejoined through a clenched jaw, "but I am telling you I still consider myself your friend, whatever you might think. And if Mr. Taplin chose you, I hope you would be gracious enough to forgive my supposed wrongs, so we could be friends again."

"Possibly," was the maddening reply. "I don't know yet. It might take some time."

"Even if you won out?"

"Yes, even then. Besides, I don't know if I believe you. Because wouldn't you be the least bit angry if he chose me? The least bit jealous?"

"I would try very, very hard to overcome such things because we—were—friends for so very long beforehand." Not to mention, she wouldn't feel any such emotions. If all this wrangling had been over Mr. Nicholas Carlisle, however—that would be a horse of another color.

"Mm," Aggie considered.

"And—and—if Mr. Taplin were to choose me instead," persevered Minta, "I hope you might say the same. That you would try to forgive me, I mean."

"I make no promises."

"*Aggie!*"

But Aggie was already knotting her shawl tighter and marching away.

When she was several yards distant, however, she halted and marched back to the disheartened Araminta. "It's not the same, you know," said Aggie. "You're just amusing yourself with Mr. Taplin, for whatever reason. Dressing up, playing a role, having fun. I don't understand why you would do it, disloyal as it is to me, but I'm not just playing. I love him. Therefore I can't say so easily that I could forgive and forget. Because forgiveness is effortless only when it doesn't cost anything. Remember that, Araminta."

With a lift of her chin and a square of her shoulders, Agatha Weeks turned her back once more and hurried away in the direction of Beaumond, leaving Araminta to watch her until she disappeared through the hedge.

She was right, of course. If Araminta had told Aggie she loved Mr. Carlisle, and Aggie had then proceeded to mince and flirt and flaunt and go for a drive with the man—if Aggie had seemed to accept Mr. Carlisle's kisses—Araminta would not have been able even to pronounce the words "forgiveness" and "friend," much less live them out. It would have been a long and arduous road to overcome a betrayal like that.

Aggie was indeed no fool.

Chapter Twenty-One

Thus do the hopes we have in him touch ground
And dash themselves to pieces.
— Shakespeare, *Henry IV, Part II*, IV.i.2218 (c.1596)

"Shut those, blast you!" roared Francis Taplin when his impertinent valet opened the shutters to his chamber windows.

"Your father has asked to see you, sir," Dawkins explained, bland as porridge.

"Surely he knows where to find me,'" replied Taplin acidly, blocking out the light with a pillow.

"He requests that you *come down* because he is expecting Mr. West of Fairchild & West."

"What is that to me? I don't care about lawyers."

Not knowing the answer to that question, Dawkins knew he would have to tread carefully to coax his master into rising and dressing. It was not unheard of to have a book or pillow or even a candle hurled at his head when he did not go about things the right way.

"Perhaps it has to do with your stepbrother Mr. Nicholas Carlisle," Dawkins suggested, "now that his uncle has died."

That worked. Taplin removed the pillow. "I don't know what you can mean. My father can't do anything about Nick's situation."

"I'm sure you're right, sir."

"Did Nick send another letter?"

"Not that I know of, sir, but Blount did hear something interesting regarding Mr. Carlisle."

"Oh? Get over here and help me up." The valet was quick to obey, though the movement drew more curses and vituperation. "And what did she hear?"

Dawkins waited until he had helped Taplin from his nightshirt. "Blount heard from her cousin's husband, who heard from—"

"Spare me the details of the transmission, you fool, and tell me what Blount heard."

"That Mr. Carlisle had sent an offer of marriage to Miss Ellsworth of Hollowgate."

Taplin straightened abruptly, a hiss of pain escaping him. He said nothing, his lips pressed into a line. Dawkins held up two coats, and his master snapped his fingers and pointed at the one he wanted. Then he went to splash water on his face.

It was only some minutes later, when Taplin was dressed and his hair brushed that he took up the thread again. Pausing in the doorway, he said with elaborate indifference, "And did Blount hear of Miss Ellsworth's response?"

"Not that I know of, sir."

Taplin pulled a face, and the wily Dawkins waited until the door was nearly shut before adding, "It'd be quite the match for him."

"Good morning, sir," said Taplin, entering his father's library after a quiet knock. "Here I am, in answer to your summons."

His father gave a curt nod. "It is good to see you on your feet again. Would you be more comfortable sitting or standing?"

"Standing. It's the changing of positions and elevations that's the rub."

"Because of your ribs or your head?"

"Both. May I ask why you wished to see me?"

Mr. John Taplin gestured at the scattering of papers across his desk. "It's this. West will be here any minute to discuss it all."

"Then might you give me a hint as to what 'this' is? I'd prefer not to be surprised, sir."

"By 'this' I mean nothing more than the familiar wolf at our door."

"Yes, but we have discussed that, and you have given me my sailing orders: marry soon and marry money. Unless anything has changed...?"

"Something has changed," said his father grimly. "We will need that money sooner. Oh—and there's this." Reaching into his coat, he withdrew a sealed letter and held it out. "No one can tell me when this arrived, but one of the under-gardeners found it when he was sweeping the step. Please God it is from one of the inamoratas you have been cultivating."

Taplin regarded the careful, slightly uneven address, unable to guess which young lady might have favored him thus, though he doubted Miss Wright, granddaughter to a dean, made a habit of writing young men. Turning his back to his father, he slipped his finger under the seal and read it.

"Well?" prompted John Taplin.

"It is Miss Weeks. She hopes my recovery continues apace, and she would be pleased to call when I am able and willing to receive visitors, and do I like plums or blackberries."

"Miss Weeks. Hmm. Something tells me the left hand at The Acres does not know what the right hand is doing."

Before he could say more, the door opened to admit the footman. "Mr. West, sir."

In came the family attorney, whom Taplin had never paid much attention to, but he thought the man's manner less humble and pleasing than of yore, his smiles less ingratiating and his habit of nervously rubbing his hands together altogether abandoned.

"Let us have the worst of it," commanded Mr. John Taplin without ado, once he had waved West into the armchair facing the desk and pleasantries were exchanged. "Francis must stand because his ribs still give him grief."

"I was sorry to hear of your accident, sir," West said perfunctorily, and Taplin answered him with equal indifference. The lawyer adjusted his chair so that he might take them both in. "I don't know how much you have told your son, Mr. Taplin, but the matter is simply this: Mr. Weeks of The Acres holds the mortgages on a sizeable portion of Beaumond, as you are aware. Until now he was content merely to receive the interest payments on those mortgages, but now he has decided that, as he has come effectively to own the lion's share of the estate, he would like either to be repaid or to be given the deeds."

"The deeds!" protested Francis Taplin. "Would he like to remove here as well? Replace the furnishings? Sleep in my father's bed?"

John Taplin ignored this outburst, except to hold up a cautioning hand. "Would he accept a portion of the principal instead?" he asked. "In lieu of full repayment or the handing over of the deeds?"

West took a long breath. "The letter came, as I told you in my note, from Weeks himself, rather than from his attorney Simmons in London. Which makes me think it might be an impulsive demand. I, too, thought of offering some amount—a lump sum—greater than the interest payments, if it could be raised."

"Did you say as much, West?" his client pressed.

"I did take that liberty—for clarification's sake," the attorney admitted. "But it seems Weeks doubts a sum could be raised. He insists on full repayment or the deeds."

"These are hard lines," snapped Francis Taplin, impatient with the lawyer's hissy manner of speaking. "Weeks has money enough; I don't see his hurry."

The lawyer lifted deprecating palms. "The rich come by their riches through a combination of luck, cleverness, and keeping both themselves and others to what you call hard lines." He appealed to the elder Taplin. "If we treat his demand as an opening gambit, we might counter with your offer of a lump sum. The question is, sir, how much could you raise, and when?"

John Taplin stared at the papers on his desk, his brow dark. He shuffled the sheets, setting some aside and picking up others, only to set those down in turn.

West cleared his throat discreetly. "You might, perhaps, sell more of the remaining unmortgaged acreage. Or some of the house furnishings."

At this suggestion, Francis Taplin launched himself forward with a loud curse only partially attributable to his cracked ribs. "We won't sell another acre! Not another square yard! Nor one stick of furniture. There's money to be had, deuce take it! How much are we talking about?"

West's glance at the elder Taplin was answered with a nod, and the attorney said, "All told, it's nearly £100,000. So perhaps Weeks might be appeased if we were to come up with fifteen or twenty thousand."

Taplin blanched briefly at these numbers, but then he gathered himself again and waved the note he had received. "There's money to be had everywhere. Why, I have three heiresses whose company I have sought. I daresay any one of them could serve our purposes if I but say the word—one of them being old Weeks' own daughter Miss Agatha herself." He tossed the letter in the lawyer's lap. "Have a glance at that, West. It was delivered sometime last night or very early this morning."

West obediently read the missive, nodding thoughtfully. He folded it again and returned it. "It would solve the problem nicely. If Weeks could be brought to bless the match, the gift of Beaumond to his youngest daughter and her husband would return all to their starting marks. Then there might be no need to repay anything."

"Exactly."

For the first time that morning, the lawyer rubbed his hands together, the old deferential note sounding in his voice—sure signs the Taplin star was rising again. "If I might ask, young sir, of the 'three heiresses' you mentioned, do you yourself give the preference to Miss Agatha? And, if not, of the other two young ladies, which would you guess is the more—generously portioned?"

Pleased at how his news was received, Taplin drew himself up, hooking his thumbs in his coat. "Perhaps you can enlighten us, as to the latter question. God knows you lawyers know everyone's little secrets."

Mr. West absorbed this jab with a fixed smile, waiting him out.

"Very well. There's Miss Agatha, who might bring about a cancellation of the entire debt, if old Weeks will submit to it with good grace. And then there's Miss Wright of the Meadowsweep Wrights, outside Romsey."

But here Mr. West coughed into his fist.

"What?" father and son snapped in unison.

"Er—ah—I do believe I heard that Miss Wright has gone—at the behest of her family—on a very long visit to a relative in Kent."

"You mean someone in her family caught wind of my son's attentions and hastened her out of danger," said John Taplin bitterly.

"We may never know," said the lawyer tactfully. He was careful to keep his gaze lowered because it was obvious Miss Wright's defection caught Mr. Francis Taplin off guard, and West had no desire to pay the price for being the bearer of bad news.

But another unfortunate took this burden, as there were steps and the thumping of something heavy in the passage just then, and the younger Taplin stalked to the library door to fling it open and bellow his disapproval of this racket.

"Sorry, sir," came the footman's flustered voice. "We thought we'd carry Mr. Carlisle's trunk in this direction, as it's harder to manage on the front stairs with that turn they take."

"Stow your explanations—is Mr. Carlisle returned?"

"He would hardly send his trunk and not send himself," muttered the servant.

"Then call him to us, Bodkins—Borkins—whatever your name is."

"Bekins, sir. Yes, sir."

Taplin turned to regard the lawyer and his father. "Nick may as well be in on the conference because what I have to say will concern him."

His father sucked in his breath and rose to his feet. "Francis—I would rather—"

But what Mr. John Taplin would rather would have to wait, for Carlisle's quick step was soon heard, and he entered the room, his glance taking in the attorney's presence and the varying expressions of his stepfather and stepbrother.

"You're back," said John Taplin simply. "I had thought you intended to pay your uncle Blair a longer visit."

"I had."

"Well?" prompted his brother. "Has it happened? Is your uncle a made man, with his naval contract?"

West perked up considerably at these words. "Indeed?" He tried to catch his client's eye. "Here might be another possibility."

"My uncle has died," said Carlisle. Heedless of his road dust, he sank wearily into the window seat. There were questions, of course—he was peppered with them from every direction, but he held up a hand until they faded into silence. "How are your ribs, Francis? And your head?"

"Confound my ribs and head! Tell us what happened."

"Yes, tell us, Nicholas," seconded his stepfather. "You need not mind West being here. He is our confidential agent, after all."

Carlisle sighed and stretched out his booted legs. "I found my uncle well, I thought. He had indeed got his naval contract and was only wondering how he could meet it. He asked me to share in running the business, but I...refused, only agreeing to stay long enough to get his laboratory in order, that he might be better able to attract a manufacturing partner. Unfortunately—before anything could be accomplished—he suffered an apoplectic fit. I—left London as soon as he was buried. There are still odds and ends to be seen to, but I have left them in trust of his chief employee."

Each of his auditors burned with further questions, but they hesitated in voicing them. A man was dead, after all. Carlisle guessed at their impatience, however—having had the same questions himself—and after a minute he went on.

"You will want to know what will become of 'B. Blair, Chemist & Druggist,' I'm certain. My uncle's attorneys Trot and Trimble are looking into it all, to see if there will be anything left, once the debts are paid by the sale of the inventory and equipment. It seems people in my uncle's line of business depend a great deal on credit and tenuous supply lines, as so many of their drugs and simples—their ingredients—come from every place in the world."

"But—the recipe for the balsam must be worth something," his brother blurted. "If the navy placed an order for it, the recipe could still be sold."

"Yes. But Jacobson and Tribbet—who worked for him—they and I searched and searched. We could not find any recipe. Nor do Trot and Trimble have a copy. I fear it might only have been kept in my uncle Bertram's head." Carlisle tapped his own temple with a rueful grin.

"I am sorry for it," said his stepfather, stepping forward to rest his hand a moment on Carlisle's shoulder. "I confess I had hopes that, out of all the good fortune coming to him, Mr. Blair might share a little with you."

"He did offer," said Carlisle. "A generous allowance, once things came to fruition. I confess I had fleeting visions of independence and of—" He broke off. "Yes. Well. Anyway—"

"You thought of marriage, didn't you," declared his brother, a rising note of triumph audible.

"I might have," answered Carlisle tightly.

"You did. But you haven't any more freedom than I have, in that arena," Taplin pressed. "I must wed, to pay our debts, and you must refrain from wedding and devote yourself to Lady Poverty."

"Francis," his father rebuked him.

"What? Why can't I speak my mind?"

"Because your mind can be heedless. Cutting, it pains me to say."

"You mean my mind can be honest, and my lips can speak truth," retorted the son. "Why don't you just say what you think, Father?"

"What is it you think I am holding back?"

Taplin's face hardened. His nostrils flared. "We all know what you want to say. That Nick is your favorite. That we would never be in this quandary if he had been the son and I the stepson. That you wish he was your son, instead of me."

"It is a falsehood. I never wished that," said John Taplin quietly, sorrowfully. "I might have wished you shared some of Nicholas's seriousness, his diligence, for your own sake. I could not help it. And perhaps I spoke in anger to you, but Francis, I swear to you I have never wished you were not my son. You are my boy, my very own boy."

The younger Taplin's throat worked, and he struck the surface of the desk with a fist. "But—but you wished Nicholas was your son too, then. Your blood son."

John Taplin gave a slow sigh. He looked years older, and his shoulders bowed. "I—might have. No—I *have* wished that. Wished I had two sons, who loved me and...each other. But—hold, Francis—what you do not understand is that my love for Nicholas does not subtract from my love for you."

"How can it not?" demanded his son. "How can you tell me such a thing?"

"Because love does not subtract!" The father slammed his own palm down upon the stacks of papers, sending some fluttering to the carpet. "Love does not subtract, Francis. It only multiplies."

But his son was not listening anymore. He closed the distance to Carlisle in two strides. "I know you wrote to propose marriage to Miss Ellsworth."

Carlisle raised steady eyes to him.

"Do you deny it?" insisted Taplin.

"I do not deny it."

"My dear Nicholas," breathed his stepfather.

Taplin ignored this. "Has she given you an answer?"

"She has not."

"Good. Good." His brother bounced on the balls of his feet before his ribs reminded him to desist. "Because it so happens, as I was on the point of telling Mr. West here, *I* intend to make an offer for Miss Ellsworth." He turned in triumph to the lawyer, who was wisely keeping his mouth shut and his ears open. "I believe Miss Ellsworth as wealthy as Miss Agatha, if not wealthier. And the Ellsworths are *anciens nobles* to the Weeks' *nouveaux riches*. Certainly the Ellsworth family is more worthy of an alliance with the Taplins of Beaumond. What is Weeks, after all, but an uppish former silk manufacturer?" He gave a harsh laugh.

Here Mr. West tented his fingers together and gave an uneasy fidget. "Pardon me, but I feel called upon to remind all present at this juncture that my partner at Fairchild and West—that is, Mr. Robert

Fairchild—not only represents the Ellsworth family but is married to the oldest daughter."

Then Taplin was upon him. "Are you saying you will betray our trust and tell Fairchild our plans? If I'm not mistaken, that would lead to dire consequences for someone in your profession."

"I can keep my counsel, young sir," retorted West, bristling. "I know the duties of loyalty and confidentiality owed my clients as well as any lawyer in England, but I thought it worthwhile to remind *you* of my shared premises."

"Easy there," Taplin grinned. "Just testing you. If you can keep Fairchild out of what doesn't concern him, bravo. But how will it work to negotiate Miss Ellsworth's marriage settlement, with you on one side of the affair and your partner on the other?"

"We may each be trusted to do our duty by our clients and put their respective interests first. But you should be aware that Mr. Fairchild is no dimwit."

"Glad to hear it," said Taplin amiably. "Just think, West—if I succeed with Miss Ellsworth, Fairchild and I will become one happy family, and then you and he may talk all you like of Ellsworth matters."

"Sir."

Taplin clapped his hands together with finality. "So much for that. Now, before I speak to her, if I might only be assured of my brother's blessing...?"

Carlisle's face was unreadable. "I have the deepest respect for Miss Ellsworth's judgment," he answered at last. "And she is free to choose the man who pleases her best. My expectations were humble when I offered for her, and obviously now even what I hoped to lay claim to—is gone. But one thing I will say, Francis: my own lack of success by no means guarantees yours."

Taplin gave a mocking bow. "I understand, Nick, and thank you. However, I would point out in return, your own lack of success certainly doesn't hurt."

CHAPTER TWENTY-TWO

The fronts of dresses are generally cut to fit the form; and where the bust is finely turned, we know not of any fashion which can be more advantageous.
— *La Belle Assemblée*, October 226/1 (1807)

Francis Taplin was not the only one facing a father's summons. The following day, Araminta was trying to teach Willie and Beatrice how to play bowls on the lawn when Bobbins emerged, followed by the terrier Snap, who bent to gnaw at the footman's shoe buckles when he halted.

"Miss Ellsworth, your father requests you to attend him in his study." Bobbins' face was impassive, but he gave a sudden jerk of his foot that drew a growl from the dog. "As soon as you are able."

Minta had been expecting this ever since she gave her stepmother permission to share Mr. Carlisle's supposed offer, but her stomach did a flip all the same. "All right. I'm coming. Willie, you listen to Beatrice while I'm gone."

If not for missing Mr. Carlisle and fretting over what would become of Aggie or of their long friendship, Minta would have been quite happy this morning. It was fair and not oppressive; her head didn't hurt a bit; her vision was perfectly fine for anything but reading; she was wearing an old dress that didn't require her Least Favorite Undergarment; her unkempt hair was here, there, and everywhere; and there was unmistakably a fine sheen of perspiration on her face from running about with her brother and sister.

"Yes, Papa?" She fairly bounced into his study, smiling as she thought for just one bare instant what a joy it would be to announce that, yes, she would *love* to accept Mr. Carlisle's offer.

"My dear girl," he beamed, coming forward to kiss her on the forehead but thinking better of it when he saw the state she was in. Instead he grasped both her shoulders and gave her a fond shake. "My dear, dear girl. Who knew that all my girls would grow to be such belles? Two men wanted to marry Florence, a hundred men wanted to marry Lily, and now two more want to marry my Araminta."

"*Two?*" asked Minta, her eyes round.

"Yes. Your mama told me of the doctor's apprentice writing you, poor fellow, and—"

"Why 'poor fellow'?" she interrupted. "He said he would have two allowances and that he thought it would be sufficient after a while, and then there would be my money."

"Yes, well. Perhaps I should say 'relatively poor fellow.'"

"If I liked him, I would take him without a penny, Papa," declared Minta. "If I liked him."

Her father chuckled as if she had said something very charming. "Is that so? But I'm afraid he sounds the sort of person who would not take *you*, if he had not a penny. Some men are like that."

Araminta well knew that William Ellsworth had not been such a man, having been well content to marry Henrietta Baldric, though she brought to the match Hollowgate and a vast fortune, and he brought only his once-handsome person.

"But the second offer for you," he went on, "which I received this morning, is from the relatively poor fellow's own stepbrother, I believe."

"Mr. Taplin wrote you?" she yelped. "I had no idea he was even out of his bed, after the injuries from the carriage accident."

"He wrote and he says he will follow his letter with a visit." Ellsworth glanced at the clock on the mantel. "Very shortly. All done quite properly, I must s—" He trailed off at the sight of his third daughter gasping, slapping one hand upon her bodice and the other on her hair.

"Shortly? He comes shortly? I must go, Papa, if I am to receive him!"

"Does this mean you would like to accept him? Handsome young man. Good family. I like the nearness of the estate, if you must go from me—"

"No—I don't want him," cried Minta, bolting for the door, "but I may not tell him that yet."

"Oh. Very well, then," was his reply, but she hardly heard it, as she was already halfway down the passage.

"Monk! Monk!" she shouted as she thundered up the stairs and flew into her room. Splashing water into the basin (and over the table and floor), Araminta scrubbed at her face and neck, stopping every few seconds to yell for the maid.

Scurrying and sliding, poor Monk appeared. "Good heavens, what is it, miss?"

"Mr. Taplin is coming—now! We must fix *this*." Frantically Minta gestured at the entirety of herself, which, in addition to the disarray mentioned above, was now also water-stained.

The maid clapped a palm to her forehead. "Lor! Dear knows what I've done to deserve this." But she marched to the wardrobe like a soldier ordered into battle. "It had better be the dark blue, miss, or you might sweat right through it. And where has your corset got to?"

"What do you mean, where has it got to?"

"I mean it isn't here."

"But I've got to have that!" Minta protested. "None of my new dresses fit properly without it, and I can't wear any of my old dresses today—not when I've got to bring him to the point!"

"Did you leave it somewhere, miss?" Monk asked, still rummaging through every drawer and behind and under everything else. "I always brush it off and put it here."

"Can it be in the laundry?"

"The washer woman never comes today. You know that as well as I. When's the last you saw it?"

"I don't know. I haven't worn it since the carriage accident. There's been no need, with no one to see me. You had better ask Mrs. Ellsworth if she knows anything of it. Hurry! I will—I will brush my hair."

Somehow, brushing her hair made it expand into a frizzly, frowsy halo that made her want to throw her hairbrush at the mirror. Oh! What would happen if Mr. Taplin changed his mind when he saw her? If the fair, buxom shepherdess she had pretended to be all this time metamorphosed into a frizzled, flat-chested, perspiring Amazon?

When Monk returned an eternity later, her steps were slow, and she was accompanied by Mrs. Ellsworth.

"What is it?" breathed Minta, when she saw Monk's dread and her stepmother's chagrin. "What has happened?"

"Now, Araminta..." Mrs. Ellsworth braced herself. Then she drew from behind her a torn and mangled *something* of rags, trailing rag streamers like a cotton medusa.

Some horrors were too deep for words. Minta could only stare and point. If she wasn't sweating before, this would do it.

"Snap got a hold of it somehow," her stepmother explained.

"I can't think how," Monk spoke up. "Mrs. Ellsworth, I always take it from the chair or the floor where Miss Ellsworth flings it, and I brush it off and put it away carefully. There's no way that dog could have got the wardrobe door open, nor pulled on the drawer knob to get at that thing."

"He's coming," Minta uttered blankly. "He's coming, and I will have no bosom."

"You will have to drape a shawl over yourself," said Mrs. Ellsworth.

"Madam, she's sweating like a racehorse already," Monk pointed out, which did not help Minta stop sweating.

Mrs. Ellsworth threw up her hands. "Let's get her dressed, in any case."

The two women turned and pushed and bundled and prodded Minta into her darkest dress, swabbing her like a ship's deck. Then Mrs. Ellsworth pushed her into a chair while Monk tried to smooth and style Minta's unruly locks. Through it all, Minta only regarded the unfilled bodice of her gown with numb dismay. And when her stepmother swirled her Paisley shawl about her shoulders, Minta said, "I'm so hot I think I might faint."

"What did I tell you about the sweat, madam?" added Monk.

"Yes. All right," agreed Mrs. Ellsworth, removing the shawl. "What about handkerchiefs? We could wad the bodice with hand-kerchiefs."

"Or roll up her long gloves, madam, and stuff one on each side?"

A knock sounded, and the door opened.

"Mama! Minta! Mr. Carlisle just drove Mr. Taplin up to the house," announced Beatrice breathlessly.

"Mr. Carlisle is here too?" Minta asked. "He's back?"

"He's back, but he told Bobbins he only had a minute before he had to be at Mr. Beckford's. I think he wants to see how you're doing."

Minta's eyes met her stepmother's in the mirror. Did Mr. Carlisle wish to see how her concussion fared, or to receive an answer to his letter? The question didn't help with her feverishness.

But she was not the only one turning a bright, bright red. Beatrice was gaping at the collapsed bodice of her sister's dress.

"What?" demanded Minta with a scowl. "I know what it looks like, but it can't be helped. Snap ate my new corset."

"We can't think how he got to it," added Monk, still anxious not to be blamed. She jammed in one of the rolled-up gloves. "See, madam? That's not so bad."

"You're right," agreed Mrs. Ellsworth. "Give me the other."

"Snap—ate your corset?" Bea asked faintly.

"Surely you're not displeased?" snorted Minta. "You called it a 'false bosom,' if you recall."

"Well, I didn't mean it to be eaten by the dog, in any case."

As Mrs. Ellsworth and the maid busily disguised their handiwork with a lace tucker, Minta threw Beatrice a sharp look. "What do you mean by that? Do you know how Snap got hold of it?"

"...Yes. He must have found it."

"Of course he found it. But where?"

"Under my bed," whispered Beatrice. "Where I had—hid it."

"Beatrice!" gasped Mrs. Ellsworth.

Minta gave a roar, but there was no time for revenge because the gentlemen were waiting, and if she lunged at her younger sister, it was sure to dislodge the gloves and untidy her newly tidy hair. With a growl that boded ill for Beatrice later, Minta took three deep breaths and wrestled her countenance into smoothness. Then, donning again the false persona so gladly laid aside since the carriage accident, she swept from her bedchamber.

Bobbins, as aware as every servant in the house that Miss Ellsworth had already received a proposal of marriage from one of the gentlemen callers and was on the brink of receiving another from the other, bowed Mr. Carlisle and Mr. Taplin into the main drawing room, large and formal as it was. When Minta entered, head lowered modestly and pace measured, she found the former gazing out the window and the latter beside the pianoforte.

She looked first at Mr. Carlisle—she could not seem to help it, and she was so very glad to see him again and so grateful for his cooperation in her plan—and he stepped toward her even before making his bow, an answering light in his dark eyes which flustered her so much she muttered something unintelligible and turned hastily to curtsey to his brother. His brother, who had not missed this tiny interchange between the two.

"Miss Ellsworth—" said both men together.

Araminta gave an uneasy titter which had more genuineness in it than her usual attempts. "How nice to see you—both—again."

"I wanted to make sure—" began Carlisle, before his brother cut him off.

"Miss Ellsworth, you know why I am here, I daresay," Taplin chuckled. He lounged against the instrument beside him. "Therefore you will be as amazed as I that my dear brother inserts himself into so ticklish a moment."

"I don't intend on remaining long," Carlisle said brusquely. "Beckford expects me. I merely wanted to make certain you were continuing to recover satisfactorily, Miss Ellsworth."

"Thank you, Mr. Carlisle. Mr. Taplin, I am not amazed at all that he should come. Your brother is very conscientious." With that, she turned her back on the man. "I won't keep you, then, Mr. Carlisle. I am happy to say my head doesn't hurt any longer, and my vision isn't double. But—but I haven't attempted much reading. Any reading, really. Especially smaller print." Her eyes sought his. "When—the print is very small, I have to ask my stepmother to read it to me. But I do—love to be read to. When the reading material is...something I've been waiting to hear."

The corner of his mouth lifted the smallest degree in answer. "I rejoice to hear it. All of it."

"Then you'll be going, Nick?" drawled Taplin behind her.

"Yes. But first—I do like to validate a patient's testimony with evidence I gather myself. If you'll permit me, Miss Ellsworth..." And then, to Araminta's utter astonishment, Mr. Carlisle placed one hand along her jaw, from the side of her neck to her cheek, while his other ran lightly up the back of her neck, his fingers threading their way through her thick hair to probe and touch and press, as he had once before when the injury was fresh. But this time she was not so dizzy with pain that she could not register it. No, this time she held her breath, her eyes wide and alarmed as a cornered doe, and thought for one mortifying instant she would collapse at his feet. He was—what—two feet from her? Twenty inches at the least? Then why did it feel as if she were standing in a fire? And how could he expect her to listen to his brother's offer of marriage with anything like a level head, if he was going to upset her so?

Too late and too soon he released her, and Araminta stumbled, catching hold of the nearest chair to stay upright. The spell broken, she could hardly look at him, and neither did he look at her.

"Yes," Carlisle muttered. "It is as you say. Better. That is—just as it should be. I will leave you now."

There was a thick silence when he was gone. Minta sank into the chair, but she did not dare raise her head to look at Mr. Taplin because she *knew* everything would be written all over her face.

But of course Francis Taplin had never been particularly interested in what might be written on Miss Ellsworth's face; he was far more intrigued by what he had seen in his brother's. And suddenly it did not seem so indifferent a matter, whether he married Miss Ellsworth or Miss Agatha or the escaped Miss Wright, for Nick's own preference made the choice clear.

Taplin almost laughed aloud. It was too wonderful! He would marry Miss Ellsworth, possibly clear the debts on Beaumond (and thus tell Mr. Weeks to go to the devil), and take from his brother the one thing his brother most wanted. Nicholas might have usurped Francis' place in his father's heart, but usurping Nick's place in the heart of his beloved would more than make up for this. What the girl felt Taplin couldn't be certain—her back had been to him—but what girl in her right mind dreamed of marrying a poor country doctor of lowly origins?

In his elation, Taplin glided across the drawing room and gracefully sank to one knee beside Araminta. With his cracked ribs, he wouldn't be able to give the girl a good kissing, but he would do what he could.

"Miss Ellsworth," he murmured, his eyelids heavy and his voice a purr. "Lovely Miss Ellsworth."

Minta hardly heard him. She was thinking too hard. What had her papa said? That, even if she chose to marry a "relatively poor man," Mr. Ellsworth did not think that relatively poor man would be able to set aside his pride and take a rich wife. It was true—only see how angry Mr. Carlisle had been over the theatre money.

The offer he had written her was merely *pro forma*, at her request, but could she possibly convince him that it was, in fact, a very good idea? That she would love and love him and be the very best wife she could possibly be to him, and, if he didn't like anyone else better, he might come to love her in return? Was it truly so terrible to be rich because you married a rich wife? They need not live like rich people—Araminta didn't care a straw about that.

Taplin had caught hold of her hand sometime while she was working things out, and he pressed it to his breast. "Ah, Miss Ellsworth, since I first saw you, I have only had eyes for you."

But it was too irksome to be troubled by him when she had so much on her mind. This tiresome man who had caused the quarrels and estrangement between her and Aggie! Therefore Minta was not as careful as she would have liked to be.

"When?"

He blinked. "When what?"

"When did you first see me, Mr. Taplin?"

"Why—it was at The Acres, was it not? When I called the day after the Domum Ball?"

Despite all the time that had passed, Minta still felt vexation stir.

"The first time was *not* at The Acres," she said tartly. "It was at the Domum Ball, when I was fifteen." At his blank expression, she added, "Some three years ago."

"Oh—heh heh. Is that so? I am deeply gratified that I made such an impression on you then, Miss Ellsworth. But you must let me finish. Ever since I saw you in the *full flowering* of your beauty, I have had eyes only for you. Everything about you enchants—"

"Is that so?" Though her head was still lowered, she screwed her eyelids shut. "What color are my eyes?"

"What?" This second interruption seemed to addle him, as if he were reading from notes and had lost his place.

"I am all a-flutter to think you have been so—captivated by me," she giggled (it had a maniacal trill at the end, but Minta hoped he mistook that for nervousness). "So do you think my eyes are more like a summer sky or like forget-me-nots?"

"They are blue like—like a robin's egg!" he declared triumphantly, only to have her burst into tears and bury her face in her hands.

"They are *hazel*," howled Araminta. "It's Aggie's eyes which are blue! Are you sure you don't mean to be saying all this to Aggie?"

"I knew I ran the risk of making you jealous," said the infuriating man, recovering quickly, "with my attentions to your friend. But how else could I strike at the fortress of your heart? You are such a-a strong-minded, independent young lady—not that I mind—indeed, I *admire* such qualities. But I confess I stooped so low as to pretend an interest in Miss Agatha, that I might awaken something in *you.*"

Araminta persisted in weeping silently into her hands, mostly because she was doing her best to force a few tears out for form's sake. If the man would only hurry up and propose, so she could tell Aggie he had done so!

She was about to get her fervent wish, but, to her horror, she felt Mr. Taplin's arm snake around her shoulders and squeeze. "There, there, my dear girl," he soothed, trying with the other hand to press her head down against his shoulder. "Dry your tears. I am asking you to be my wife, you know." Squeeze. *Squeeze.*

If it had just been the shoulder squeeze, Araminta might simply have wriggled out of his grasp with no harm done, but it was that, in all the squeezing, she felt—oh, dear—the insidious, unstoppable, unmistakable disarrangement of the rolled-up gloves. She felt—oh, dear, oh, dear!—one of them migrating inchmeal toward the other, coming to rest mortifyingly above her sternum. And it was this displacement that sent her into blind panic. In a frantic spasm, she elbowed Mr. Taplin with all her might, effectively using him as a spring-board with which to vault away.

Mr. Taplin gave a bloodcurdling shriek, crumpling to the floor, and it must be admitted that Araminta tended to her own rearrange-ments before she spared him a thought. His cry drew a stampede of footsteps, however, and the drawing room door flew open to admit Mr. and Mrs. Ellsworth, Tyrone and Beatrice, with Bobbins and Monk peering over and around them and Willie thrusting his head between his siblings' legs.

"What did you do to him, Minta?" marveled Bea, the first to collect herself. "We thought he was murdering you, at the very least."

Mr. Taplin was crawling and panting and wincing in the struggle to clamber up again, and when Mr. Ellsworth strode forward to offer a hand, it was pointedly refused.

"I—had a-a twitch," said Minta, "and I'm afraid Mr. Taplin was—er—seated so near me that he got the worst of it. His cracked ribs, you know."

Beatrice, guessing what might have brought on her sister's twitch, favored Mr. Taplin with a disapproving frown, suddenly not sorry at all she had overset his phaeton.

"Dear me," said Mrs. Ellsworth. "I do apologize for Araminta, Mr. Taplin. She doesn't realize her own strength. Shall we call Mr. Beckford for you?"

"I—will be—fine," wheezed Minta's suitor.

None of the Ellsworths knew quite what to do. Should the couple be congratulated? Or had Mr. Taplin not yet had a moment to speak, and they ought all to withdraw again and continue waiting in the neighboring parlor? The servants at least could think of no further excuse to hover about, so they reluctantly withdrew.

Mr. Ellsworth shrugged and raised his hands in preparation of benediction, but when Minta jerked her chin—*no*—he abruptly lowered them. "No? Oh—well, then. Off we go."

Awkwardly Minta's family retreated, and just as awkwardly she crossed to Mr. Taplin's side of the room again, pretending interest in the music on the pianoforte, that she might scoot away if he came too close.

She need not have worried. Taplin had had quite enough for one day.

"You are indeed a strong young lady," he said, his handsome face still rather white and a muscle in his cheek jumping.

"Yes. I am. But—if you don't mind, I would rather save embraces for when I am engaged."

"Do you mean when *we* are engaged?"

"But we aren't engaged," Minta replied apprehensively.

"Then are you saying you refuse me, or that you have not yet decided?"

She swallowed. Rubbed her perspiring palms down her skirt. "I—uh—I would like some time to think about it."

"Not too much time, I hope. You would not keep me in painful suspense?"

Painful suspense, indeed! She would like to show him painful suspense.

"Can it be, Miss Ellsworth, that you are considering accepting my brother's offer?"

It was her turn to fidget and grow pale. "Mr. Carlisle's?"

"He says neither have you given him an answer," said Taplin. "But you should know—he will of course tell you himself, when he has an opportunity—that is, when he is not obliged to work for his bread—that his circumstances have changed since he made his proposal to you."

Minta would have loved to tell Mr. Taplin to let Mr. Carlisle tell his own story, but she was too overcome with curiosity to do so. Had Mr. Carlisle met someone in London he preferred? She felt her insides tighten in dread at the idea. Or had he decided he would rather return to London after all?

"What has changed?" she managed.

Taplin shook his head in pretended regret. "Nick hoped—we *all* hoped, rather—his Blair uncle might be able to provide something for him in the way of income, so Nick wouldn't be so very poor. But I'm afraid Mr. Blair has died, most abruptly and inconveniently, leaving Nick nothing but his business debts and effects to clean up."

"I am sorry for Mr. Carlisle," said Araminta softly.

"So that dashes Nick's hope for marriage," sighed his brother. "Therefore, if you were weighing his offer in the balance against mine..."

"I wasn't," she said, her chin lifting. "They were two entirely separate things. But I still would like to think longer about what you have said. And talk to my parents and such."

"Your father has already told me he approves the match, if it's to your liking."

"Oh. Has he?" With a magnificent effort, she managed another idiotic titter. "Still, if you would be so gallant as to wait, sir."

He bowed gingerly, as if he were hinged at the waist and uncertain whether the motion would not break him in two. "If only it were permissible to hurry a lady because, my darling Miss Ellsworth, my ardor grows from minute to minute. Please say you allow me to hope. Please say I might know by—say—tomorrow?"

Tomorrow? Good heavens! She ducked her head and hunched her shoulders (moving as gingerly as he did, lest she dislodge anything).

"I—*tee hee*—I will answer you as soon as I am able. I promise. Now, if you will excuse me..."

Without waiting for his response, Araminta fled the drawing room, nearly colliding with Bobbins and Monk, who were still hovering in the passage, and ignoring her family's presence in the parlor. It could all, all be dealt with later, please God, if only now Aggie might finally be persuaded to give Francis Taplin up.

Chapter Twenty-Three

**Behold, how good and how pleasant it is for brethren
to dwell together in unity!
— Psalm 133:1, *The Authorized Version* (1611)**

Though she was dying to seek Mr. Carlisle and talk to him at very great length, Araminta knew she could not lose an instant in trying to see Aggie. She wished she had known he lost his uncle, however, in the brief moment she was with him, so she might have told him how sorry she was. And she was also conscious of a heavy weight settling in her now-deflated chest. For if Mr. Carlisle would have needed convincing to marry her, with only the savings from his small allowances to satisfy his pride, hoping for him to do so without financial expectations of any kind struck Minta as all but impossible.

"I'm here to see Mr. Weeks, if you please," she told the Weeks' butler Orton, a vast, imposing man who nevertheless had an equally large soft spot for Araminta. "That is, if you won't let me see Aggie first."

"Now, miss," Orton wheedled, "it sounds like you know Miss Aggie isn't to receive visitors, even the likes of old friends like you."

"You know I'll find a way to see her anyway, Orton," whispered Minta.

"I do know, sure as I'm alive. But if you do, it won't be my neck, miss. So if you'll pardon me, I'll show you to the parlor and let Mr. Weeks know you're here."

Minta was glad to see no sign of Aggie's older sister Miss Weeks, at least, given the sensitive nature of all that must be disclosed. As game as Aggie always was, Minta thought her two older sisters humdrum sorts of girls. And of course Mrs. Weeks had not been about all summer, being still in Bognor with the aged aunt.

"Miss Ellsworth." The bald and bearded Mr. Weeks entered. He made her a polite bow, but Araminta was on him in a flash, taking hold of his hand beseechingly between her own.

"Mr. Weeks! Why do you call me Miss Ellsworth, when you have called me Minta since I was eight?"

"Time passes, I'm afraid, and you girls have grown up," he replied, adding ominously, "for better or for worse."

"Oh, Mr. Weeks, I know you think it's been for worse, but I beg you will let me see Aggie. I *know* you will let me see her, when you hear all I have to tell you."

He made a grumbling sound and withdrew his hand but gestured for her to take a seat. "You have ever been a good friend to my daughter, despite your harum-scarum ways, and it is with deep regret that I see you two so silly over such a—such a young man. I credited you both with a great deal more sense and have been sadly disappointed."

"But that's just it, Mr. Weeks," insisted Minta, taking her chair obediently but leaning over the arm of it as far as she could go in his direction without pitching over. "I too have been deeply regretful and sadly disappointed ever since Mr. Taplin appeared on the scene! I don't think him the least bit deserving of Aggie's affection, and if I could launch him from a cannon, never to be seen again in Hampshire, I would run over to the Barracks directly."

"Do you mean to say *you* have not lost your head over the man?" Mr. Weeks demanded. "Aggie tells me you and she are at odds because you've tried to steal him from her. And though I dislike Taplin heartily, I thought it a rotten thing to do on your part. Rotten and disloyal."

At this, Minta nearly gave way to tears. For Mr. Weeks to say such things and believe such things of her—he who had always been so fond and avuncular!

"I *have* tried to steal him from her, Mr. Weeks," confessed Minta, "but not because I wanted him. I tried to steal him because I wanted to steer him away from Aggie. A—a little bird told me that Mr. Taplin might be more interested in her money than her love, and

I couldn't bear for Aggie to be *thrown away* on someone like that! Moreover, he's a flirt and not as gentlemanly as he could be. Don't you see, Mr. Weeks? I am on your side. And Aggie's side, though she doesn't know it. I am trying to make Aggie see Mr. Taplin for who he is, and that was why I tried to steal him—to reveal him for a faithless, capricious man."

Mr. Weeks crossed his arms over his chest, frowning fearfully. Did he not believe her? Did no one but Mr. Carlisle believe her, that she had intended good, and not evil?

But at last he grunted, "And how have you fared?"

"Wondrously!" she declared, lighting up with relief. "Marvelously! Because Mr. Taplin has just come from making me an offer of marriage."

"Minta—" (and she was delighted to hear him use her Christian name again) "—I hope you have not accepted him."

"Mr. Weeks, have I not just got done telling you that I don't want him and don't think much of him? I have told him to wait for an answer."

"Because his character leaves much to be desired. Much."

"Have I not just said so?" she asked again, with a touch of impatience.

"And the family owes me a fair amount," Mr. Weeks went on, as if she were as much in need of persuasion as his youngest daughter. "And it is largely that son's doing."

"Yes, I understand. I do. May I see Aggie now?"

He shook his head and gave her a rueful tap under the chin. "It's a good thing you and I are in agreement because you listen no better than Agatha. Go, then, my girl. And may you fare better than her family has."

She did not need to be told twice. Flying up the grand staircase in the entrance hall, she turned the key to Aggie's room and burst in. And not a moment too soon! For Aggie's window was wide open and the rope made of sheets pulled taut from where it looped around the bed-post.

"Aggie!" Araminta thrust her head out the window in time to see her dear friend making her way down.

Aggie looked up, her eyes red and her flaxen hair coming loose from its braid. "Minta? What are you doing here? Why won't you leave me alone?"

"Because I've come to make a full confession and to grovel at your feet!"

"Then you've wasted your time," said Aggie, descending another few inches. "I can't wait any longer. Not even until dark. I need to see Mr. Taplin for myself. I have things to say. Even if he received my note, and even if he replied, no one will tell me, and I can't ask because no one knows about it."

"He hasn't replied, I could swear it," vowed Minta. "Please, Aggie! Either you come up, or I will come down and chase you all the way to Beaumond, and you know I run faster than you. So you had better climb back up."

Aggie threw her a mutinous glare. "I don't want to talk to you. I'm still angry at you."

"I know it."

"And I'll have you know, I wasn't going to Beaumond to beg him to run away with me or anything. I simply need to know the truth."

"I understand," said Minta, her heart leaping as she felt a glimmer of hope. "But maybe I can help. And I want to tell you why I've been such a terrible friend to you."

"You admit it, then?"

"I do. I've been terrible. Dishonest. Villainous. Monstrous."

"You have," agreed Aggie. She sighed and looked down at the ground below her and then up again. "Oh, fine, you wretch. I'll hear you out. I can't just hang here all day. My arms are getting tired." With a grimace she began hauling herself back up. "What are you doing in my room, by the by? Does Papa know you're here?"

"He does, and I've just got done begging and pleading with him, too." With a grunt and a foot braced on the wall, Minta took hold of Aggie's hand and helped heave her over the sill, sending them both tumbling to the carpet.

"That's done it," said Aggie. "I think you've dislocated my shoulder now, too."

"Then I won't need to tie you to a chair," returned Minta unrepentantly.

"You wouldn't need to in any event. I said I would listen to you."

Araminta rolled over onto her stomach and propped herself on her elbows. "All right, then. Here it is: you were right to be angry with me for trying to steal Mr. Taplin from you because I was."

"I know."

"I know you know, but just let me say it all. That's what all my silliness and new clothes and false bosom was about. I was trying to attract him. But not because I wanted him for myself. I don't. I want Mr. Carlisle, as a matter of fact."

"Mr. Carlisle?" Aggie sat up. "You've decided you do prefer him, then?"

"No, I've preferred him all along."

"Then it was even worse of you to try for my beau, when you didn't want him yourself and when you preferred another. I could begin to forgive you if I thought you, too, loved Mr. Taplin terribly, but you don't, and I *knew* you didn't."

"You were right. I admit it." Minta rolled up and hugged her knees. "I didn't love him and don't love him and have scarcely even liked him since the day he grabbed my bottom at the first Domum Ball. I know you told me people grow and change and improve—and you're not the only one to say this to me—but does a young man who is caught embracing a serving maid and grabbing people's bottoms improve to the same extent as a young man who doesn't do such things in the first place?"

"Oh, Minta, don't nag me." Aggie pressed her eyes with her palms. "I know he isn't perfect. Papa told me—that Mr. Taplin—kept a mistress in London." This last emerged in a whisper.

"Did he really?" marveled Minta. "How exciting. And reprehensible, of course. But exciting. However did Mr. Weeks learn such a thing?"

"His lawyer Mr. Simmons. It's humiliating to tell you, but Papa enlisted him to spy out what he could, and Papa tells me Mr. Simmons discovered Mr. Taplin ran up a great deal of debt, between the mistress and some gambling and other affairs young men do seem to get into."

Not all *young men*, Minta thought to herself. But she was determined to win Aggie back and succeeded in biting her tongue.

"I told Papa that spying on people wasn't honorable, but he said what I call 'spying' others would call 'due diligence.' And that only a fool would let his daughter marry a fortune hunter and watch all his hard work be made to line a rascal's pockets."

For a moment Araminta was silent. After all, though Mr. Weeks put it so baldly, would not most men in his position agree? It was certainly no tribute to her own father's sense that he would so blithely give his daughter's person and fortune to Mr. Taplin. But then, how could William Ellsworth object to Mr. Taplin's methods, when he had won his own wealthy (first) bride in the same fashion?

"Aggie," said Minta suddenly, "I have my papa's approval to marry Mr. Taplin. And I have Mr. Taplin's offer, as well."

It was Aggie's turn for painful silence. Her reddened eyes searched Minta's but found only pity and truth there.

"I'm going to refuse him, of course," Minta rushed on, "because I only want to marry Mr. Carlisle, if I ever marry anyone, but I wanted to tell you Mr. Taplin proposed, so you would think there wasn't any hope."

"Ah," said Aggie. She traced the design in the Wilton carpet with her finger. As with everything at The Acres, it was the newest and finest to be had. "Mr. Taplin loves you, then."

"But he doesn't!" protested Minta. "He doesn't love me at all. Why, if I hadn't any money, and if he didn't think his brother might like me, he might never have spared me a thought. It certainly was hard enough to get his attention! But don't you see, Aggie? That makes it worse. Because I think he did like you better—as much as a person like him can like another person—but he was willing to lay that aside because I gave him better odds."

"He must not have liked me very much, then." But she sounded a little soothed by this.

"I think you could find someone else who will like you better," Minta answered carefully. "Someone, in fact, who will love you like mad and therefore deserve you more."

But Aggie shrugged at this. "What would it matter? I wouldn't want this someone else."

"Well, you might not want someone else straight away, of course. I meant later."

"I don't know. I mean, I recognize that Mr. Taplin has his flaws. It's not that I don't believe Papa or you. I'm not so stubborn as that. And I recognize Mr. Taplin probably would not want me, even after you refuse him—not if Papa won't give him a penny. In fact, Papa tells me that, if I promise not to marry Mr. Taplin, he will not call in the loans as he has threatened. He says he will reconsider and give them more time. That makes two very good reasons for Mr. Taplin not to marry me."

Araminta grabbed for her friend's hand and gave it a crushing squeeze. "The more fool him," she declared. "But if you weren't going to defy your papa and elope with Mr. Taplin, what *were* you going to say to the man when you found him?"

Aggie's eyes brimmed, and she dashed the tears away with a ruthless swipe. "I only wanted to see for myself that he was all better—I haven't seen him since before the carriage accident, you know. And to tell him—to tell him what was in Papa's mind, so he wouldn't be discouraged."

"You were going to tell Mr. Taplin *not* to marry you?"

"How could I do that, when he hasn't offered for me?" sniffed Aggie, provoked. "But I was going to tell him that, if he could give my father assurances that he was in no way interested in me, my father would relent about the mortgages." She gave her eyes another pitiless rub. "It was going to be humiliating, but I was going to do it, for his sake."

"'Was'?" repeated Araminta. "Are you no longer going to do it?"

"I don't know. I suppose *you* could tell him about the mortgages, when you refuse him. Or he could simply find it out for himself, if he tried to propose to me after he proposed to you. Do you think he would—propose to me?"

Minta pondered. "I think he probably would."

Aggie gave a deep sigh. "Oh. That would be lovely. I would have to say no, but it would be lovely all the same, up until that moment."

"What if you're tempted, in all that loveliness, to say yes?"

"What would it matter?" Aggie scoffed. "Even if I did say yes, I suspect he would beg off after meeting with Papa. After learning it wouldn't get him what he wanted or needed. But maybe—before he met with Papa—he might try to kiss me."

"He would almost certainly try to kiss you," Minta agreed grimly.

"Ooh," breathed Aggie, hugging herself. "Then hurry up and refuse him, Minta, so that he will come and kiss me."

Laughing, Minta gave Aggie a shove. "Fine. I will send a note refusing him the moment I return home. But you had better not go back on your word. If I find you've eloped with him, to live in penury in some hovel until your father relents, I will be very, very angry with you."

"You don't know Papa, if you think he would relent," replied Aggie. "He would forgive me, but he would also make sure the lawyers tied up every penny of my portion so Mr. Taplin could never touch it. And then he would probably remove to Beaumond and sleep in Mr. Taplin's bedchamber just to spite him. And then Mr. Taplin would cease to care for me, if he ever cared for me to begin with."

For a girl so blinded by Mr. Taplin's charms, this evidence that Aggie's good sense had not wholly abandoned her reassured Minta. She threw an arm about Aggie and rested her head on her shoulder. "Oh, Aggie, promise me you won't die of heartbreak."

"Of course I won't. That's just silly. But I don't think I'll find anyone else to marry, either. It will be lonely, though, when Frederica is married to Mr. Chester and you are married to Mr. Carlisle."

"Well, since I am going to marry Mr. Carlisle or nobody," said Minta, "and since Mr. Carlisle will not marry for money like his brother, it will be ten years at least before I can convince the man to take me. So you and I will keep each other company as we always have."

Aggie pressed her own head atop Minta's, and a few more tears ran down and fell in Minta's hair, but at last she gave a great sniff and struggled up from the floor.

"You'd better go and write your note," she said.

"Say you forgive me first, Aggie."

"Don't ask me yet. I will, I'm sure, but I'm too bruised right now. Imagine if I had done everything I could to make Mr. Carlisle propose to me, instead of you! Even if I had very good reasons, you would still be resentful."

"Fair enough," conceded Minta, rising and shaking out her dress.

"It will help me forgive you sooner, though, if you promise me you're done stuffing your bodice and cocking your head and all that nonsense."

"I never will again. I promise. That's why I'm wearing this old gown. Snap ate my new corset, in any case, and I refuse to get another like it, so poor Monk has to take in the bodices of all my new dresses, which means I will have to duck Madame Blanchet whenever I'm in town. I'm just going to be plain old me from now on. Take me or leave me."

"What if Mr. Carlisle preferred your false bosom?" asked Aggie slyly.

Minta pulled a face. "Then we would have to negotiate. I wear the Bosom, and he agrees to marry me within five years."

Her friend gave the beginnings of a smile. "But in all seriousness, how do you intend to get him to marry you? You can't propose to him, you know."

"I haven't worked that bit out," admitted Minta. "The good news is, he's so poor he can't go proposing to anyone else, so I have all the time in the world to capture him with my lures."

"Hm," Aggie said. "This should be interesting."

Chapter Twenty-Four

A litle hope I caught: That for a whyle my life did stay.

But in effect, all was for naught.

— Earl of Surrey, *Songes and Sonnettes* (1577)

Araminta returned to an empty house.

Empty of family, that is. But the household servants were gathered in the kitchen, partaking of a hearty dinner.

"Oh, miss," said Wilcomb the cook, as, with a clatter and scrape of chairs, they all rose.

"What's happening?" asked Minta, surveying the spread of soup and ham and salad and fish in surprise.

"Mrs. Kenner's time has come," explained Boots breathlessly, "and they all went to the house in the close to see about it."

"Mrs. Ellsworth told us to eat the dinner," added Bobbins.

"Lily having her baby!" cried Minta. "But you mean to say even Papa and Tyrone and Willsie went along?"

"I think they were going to keep Mr. Kenner company," Monk spoke up. "Occupy his mind, like. That was the idea."

"Well—I'm going too! I don't want to miss out."

"I'll tell Greaves to drive you," said Bobbins. "That way he can bring back anyone who wants."

"And I'll make you a sandwich," said Wilcomb.

In a fever of impatience Minta waited for the word to be passed and the horses hitched and a basket filled. Only as she was about to run out did she remember she had promised Aggie she would refuse Mr. Taplin directly, but there would be paper and pen at the Kenners'.

The cathedral close was but a short drive away, and Minta could have walked there in almost the same amount of time, but with no one to accompany her that would have been out of the question. Once there, she leapt down without waiting for Greaves' assistance and dashed for the door, giving only the quietest, most perfunctory knock before letting herself in.

"Minta, dear!" It was Florence, descending the stairs with an armful of bed linens. "What good fortune you've come."

"Is the baby born?" she asked eagerly, setting down the basket."

"Not yet. It will be a while. Mama is with Lily, and Papa took everyone else to the coffee house in St. John's House, but I imagine Peter and Willie are making a ruckus there. Now that you've come, you can wait for Mr. Beckford to return, can't you, while I take the little boys home to Kingsgate Street?"

"Of course," said Minta, her heart beating faster at the mention of the doctor. Would Mr. Carlisle be with him?

The linens and the basket were passed to one of the maids, the sisters kissed each other good-bye, and then Minta blew out her breath and went to wait in the parlor.

Minta and Beatrice had agreed that, while Florence's home in Kingsgate Street was larger and newer, Lily's was the more charming, tucked behind the cloister in the shadow of the cathedral where her husband served as a prebendary. The parlor was papered in glossy and matt ivory stripes with a scrolled border and furnished with soft chairs, a sofa, tables, and a dainty desk. It was at this desk that Minta stationed herself, taking up a sheet of Lily's notepaper and spending the first fifteen minutes mending the pen. Apart from the maid bringing her a cup of tea and poking at the fire, she was alone. Her eyes wandered to the pictures hanging on the walls (mostly landscapes), and her ears listened for sounds from upstairs (all muffled), but eventually there was nothing to do but write.

It was not a long note, but writing did not always come easily to Araminta, and she had no experience whatsoever in writing refusals to proposals of marriage. When the door opened again, she held up a finger without glancing up. "Just put the sandwich on the table, please."

"And if I haven't any sandwich?"

"Oh!" she exclaimed, her pen skidding across the page and leaving an expanding blot as she stared at the newcomer. "Oh, Mr. Carlisle. How—how do you do? How very—pleasant—to see you again."

"And you, Miss Ellsworth. But I see I am interrupting."

"Not at all." She rose belatedly and gave a jerk of a curtsey. "Please do come in—unless you must proceed upstairs directly. I can't think why the footman didn't announce you."

"No one came in answer to my knock. I suspect the occasion is something of a holiday for the servants, with Mr. and Mrs. Kenner so preoccupied."

"Yes."

"Beckford told me to wait here for him to return from his rounds," Carlisle went on. "Don't let me disturb your writing. I can work on the notes from the patients I saw this morning."

Thoughtlessly she crumpled the paper beneath her hand and then looked down in dismay to see what she'd done. "Dear me. I will have to write it all out again, and it took me so very long." Swallowing, she gave herself a mental kick. *You told Aggie you wanted to cast your lures at him—well, here he is!* But she had never felt less alluring. Here she sat, the old Minta once again, with unkempt hair and modest bosom and old gown. Even inkblots on her fingers. (And a smudge on her cheek, but she didn't realize that.)

"It's my—refusal, you see," she added.

Carlisle chose one of the soft chairs. "Of my proposal or my brother's?" he asked mildly. "You never did give me an answer, you know."

And then Minta sprang up from the desk, coming to sit opposite him on the sofa. But that was too far away for the urgency which drove her, and she abandoned it in turn for the chair nearest him. He had, in courtesy, popped up each time she did, so that when he settled back once more, he was grinning. That lovely, crooked grin which did funny things to her.

"Mr. Carlisle," she began, with embarrassing breathlessness, "I have not until now had the opportunity to thank you for sending your—sham offer. It was quite accommodating of you. And effective. You have been, all along, more obliging than I can express."

His grin faded, and he said quietly, "No need to thank me. It has been a pleasure to help you. In fact, I can't remember when I've enjoyed deceiving and undermining my own family more."

"Yes," was her sober reply, "that is exactly what I asked you to do, and I ought to be sorry for it, but it's hard to be, when we have succeeded. Your brother proposed to me and, when Aggie learned of it, the combination of his defection and her own father's stern counsel persuaded her to give him up. Not that Mr. Taplin was hers to give up, but you know what I mean. She decided she wouldn't marry him, even if he asks."

"Has she indeed? That's very good news for you, Miss Ellsworth. Exactly what you hoped."

It was. Yet why did she feel so confused?

"Would you have helped me, Mr. Carlisle, if your brother had been a different sort of person?" she asked after a pause.

He studied her. "What do you mean?"

"I mean, if he had been sincere and kind—still poor, but genuinely in love with Aggie. Would you have helped me then?"

She watched him rub his knuckles along his trouser leg as he considered this.

"Are you feeling guilty, Miss Ellsworth?"

"Yes. For causing trouble for you. I mean, you were teasing me, saying you deceived and undermined your family, and yet there's more than a grain of truth in it, isn't there? And that's my fault. I am the one who asked you to do that."

"I made my own choices, and you are not responsible for them. You are thinking that you would never have served any of your brothers or sisters so, I imagine."

Stricken eyes met his. "That's precisely what I'm thinking, and yet I asked you to do just that."

"But Miss Ellsworth, I do believe if my brother had been a different sort of person—if he genuinely loved Miss Agatha, as you say, and had no interest in her money and would not have absorbed her marriage portion for no better reason than to save his own skin—I would have refused you. I promise. But that was not the case."

She felt that dreaded heat behind her eyes again. Why, if she wasn't careful, she would become a veritable watering pot. "Oh, Mr. Carlisle. Thank you for saying so. It's just that I was selfish for having asked you at all. And how easy it is to beg your pardon now, instead of thinking what it might cost you beforehand."

He touched the back of her hand with the lightest of fingertips. "What has brought all this remorse on, if I may ask? Should you not be rejoicing?"

With an audible gulp, she whipped her hand away and scooted to the farther end of her chair. She *had* to, in self-defense, or she would make a dreadful fool of herself. Clutching her hands safely in her lap and keeping her gaze lowered, Araminta prayed he wouldn't notice that her face was on fire. Or felt like it was on fire. And her hand still felt as if he had held it to the fire.

He didn't notice. He was too mortified by her reaction and by his own stupidness in touching her. He had only meant it in compassion, hadn't he? In a desire to give comfort. *Hadn't he?*

"I suspect I feel this way because Aggie told me I did her a rotten turn, even if I did it for laudable reasons," Minta explained in a rush. "And she said she would never have done so to me—made such a pretense or-or-or tried to steal away someone I—cared for. If I cared for someone. Not that I told her I cared for someone. This is all hypothetical, you understand. Anyway, now I see I put you in that same position. Made you into a deceiver and a liar, and-and I just want to say I'm sorry for that and for my blindness and selfishness. I suppose I want everyone to forgive me but maybe that's selfish too."

"You were selfish for good reasons," he answered. But his voice was cool and hard. "Please don't trouble yourself about me. As I said, I made my choices. It's done."

Then Minta really did think she might cry. Casting lures? How had she ever supposed she might make Mr. Carlisle love her? Marry her? She didn't know the least way to go about it. If only it were possible to turn the tables and ask Mr. Taplin how his brother might best be won.

A silence fell, save for the tick of the brass-and-china clock Beatrice had given the Kenners for a wedding gift. There was a terrier among the figures frolicking at the base, and Bea thought it would remind Lily of Snap.

Araminta rose and returned to the desk like a sleepwalker. "I'd better rewrite my note to Mr. Taplin."

Carlisle took the hint. Seizing a book from the nearest table, he opened it at random. But the words would not arrange themselves so that he could make sense of them, and in another minute he closed the volume.

It seemed he must be stupid.

"Miss Ellsworth, if you have groveled and begged forgiveness to your satisfaction, perhaps you might indulge me."

She brightened immediately, to be addressed again. "Anything."

"Then tell me—how did my brother's proposal compare to mine?"

"Far inferior," declared Minta, straight off. "His was insincere from start to finish, beginning all in flattery—that is..." She trailed off, remembering Mr. Carlisle, too, had flattered in his letter, calling her "lovely" and "lively" and praising her "charm."

Another blot appeared on her note to Mr. Taplin, and she set the pen down. "That is—I know the kind things you said in your pretended proposal were also—invented—for the purposes, but when you said such things, they didn't sound so—so—" Again she faltered, aware that she was only making matters worse.

"I meant every word."

The unwilling confession, dragged from him, stopped Minta in her admittedly halting tracks. She went three different shades of crimson. He thought her lovely, lively, charming, frank, and high-spirited, then? (Yes, she remembered every word of his letter because, once her eyes could bear it, she read it a dozen times through with her father's magnifying glass.) Really truly? Or—even more dumbfounding—could he possibly be saying he meant every word of his *entire* letter?

No.

Of course not.

Don't be silly, Minta. You told *him to send you a proposal, and he did.* Though he said gratifying things in his letter, the proposal part of it was not real. It would be wicked to use it against him. To ensnare him with his written words.

Carlisle ran a finger under his neckcloth, which felt suddenly noose-like. What was he doing? Was he about to make a declaration to her? The young lady whom he could not afford to marry for ten years, if ever? What sort of man exacted a promise from a woman, to waste her youth in waiting? What sort of man helped rescue Agatha Weeks from a fortune hunter, only to lay a trap for Araminta Ellsworth?

He wouldn't do it. He would not.

He would keep his mouth shut if it killed him.

And it just might kill him.

Don't be such a dramatic ass, Carlisle reproved himself.

Slowly, he pulled out the little notebook and pencil with which he recorded patient notes. Minta, seeing this, bowed her head over her letter again, unconsciously gripping the quill until it bent and willing herself not to do or say anything embarrassing.

"'*While I am grateful for your offer, I am afraid I cannot* except *accept,*'" she wrote, curving her words around the blot of ink because she hardly cared how it looked now. "'*I wish you every happi—*'"

There was a crack. Minta looked up.

"I must have been too emphatic in enumerating Mr. Harvey's symptoms," Mr. Carlisle said, frowning at his pencil, the lead of which had broken off.

Determined to put their awkwardness behind them, she favored him with a bright smile. "Do you have a knife to point your pencil again, or would you like me to do it?"

In answer he rose and crossed the room to her. "If you give me the knife, I can do it myself. I don't want to be dressing another one of your injuries when Beckford arrives."

Minta might have answered Carlisle's jest with one of her own, had she been more at ease. But instead she mutely turned to offer the pen knife to him just as he extended a hand for it, and the blade sliced straight across the side of his forefinger.

"Great guns!" she cried as the blood welled up. "Who knew Simon kept his knife so sharp?"

"Well, you never know when you might want to murder someone with it," said Carlisle, retrieving his handkerchief to press against the cut.

"I am so sorry! Did I hurt you dreadfully?"

"You'll have to bandage this one, Araminta—that is—Miss Ellsworth. If you've the stomach for it." He nodded toward his bag. "Over there."

She was glad to fetch the bag, so he wouldn't see the shiver of delight it gave her to hear him say her name. But her happiness was forgotten when she pulled out the bandages and saw the little stoneware pot. "Blair's Balsam! I expect you will want this too. And it reminds me: Mr. Carlisle, I'm afraid I have to beg your pardon again."

"What for this time?"

"For not condoling you earlier on the death of your uncle. But I didn't know. It was—Mr. Taplin who told me of your loss."

"I'm sure he did," he muttered dryly. But then, louder: "Thank you, Miss Ellsworth."

"…He was your only blood relation, was he not?" she asked, after another hesitation.

"He was."

"And it was so sudden," she said softly, "which must have been a shock. I *am* sorry."

"Yes. Thank you." His answers were brief, but she could see he was not angry with her for speaking her sympathy.

Carlisle lifted the handkerchief and inspected his wound. "It wasn't very deep, the slash you gave me. The bleeding is already stopping. I can apply the balsam, but you will have to wind the bandage."

She watched him smooth the ointment over the edge of the cut and had the appalling thought that, if she'd only managed to jab *herself* with the pen knife, she might even this moment be enjoying the gentle stroke of that fingertip. Pinking up again, she fumbled with the roll of bandage.

"Mr. Carlisle—if I might ask you a question—?"

His eyes flicked up from his work, and he said what she had said to him earlier: "Anything."

"In your—letter—you said that your uncle planned on making you an allowance. Was that really so, or just something you made up to make your—offer—sound plausible?"

A muscle in his jaw tightened. He took the roll of bandage from her hand because she was picking at it absently. "It was really so. But if Francis told you about my uncle's death, I'll warrant he also told you that my...expectations, such as they were, have vanished into air. The allowance, the naval contract, the balsam recipe. All buried with my uncle Blair in the churchyard of St. Michael Cornhill."

"Dear me. I'm sorry for it," she murmured again.

"No need," he said shortly. Decisively. "I always intended on making my own way, and now I shall. However long it takes."

She meant to comfort him, to show him she was sorry not about the money but about his aloneness. That was why her tentative hand came to rest on his forearm.

He stared at it, as if a web of gossamer had drifted through the summer air to light on his sleeve. She did not mind touching him, then?

The moment stretched. She saw the rise and fall of his chest. She heard the ticking once more of Bea's clock over the thunder in her ears.

He moved first.

Or perhaps it was Minta.

But either way, they were suddenly in each other's arms, hers about his neck and his pulling her against him. His lips sought hers, and she closed her eyes. Only to have them fly open again a moment later. *This* was kissing? *This*? Why, kissing was glorious! She would gladly do this *forever*. And she shut her eyes again, prepared to do just that.

But the door opened, with a clatter of porcelain and silver rattling against each other, and the two sprang apart. The maid who was entering with the sandwiches saw nothing, however, because she was backing in with her tray. Setting it down on one of the tables with a curtsey and a mumbled greeting, she was gone again the next instant.

Minta turned rapturously back to her lover, eager to continue their embrace, but for him the spell had been broken. He had regained control of himself and was already winding the bandage about his hand, brisk and business-like. He could not quite meet her eyes right off, but he nodded at her. "I've gone and bled on your dress."

"Never mind that. My family is used to seeing me with blood on me—my own or someone else's." She took a hesitant step toward him, but stopped when she saw him draw back, correspondingly. "Mr.—Carlisle?"

"It is my turn to beg *your* pardon, Miss Ellsworth. For what just happened."

"But—I *liked* what just happened!"

"It should not have happened, in any event."

"But don't you—didn't you—did you not like kissing me?"

With his teeth he tore off the end of the bandage and began to tuck the edges in.

"I could have helped you with that," said Minta, subdued. "In fact, I thought you had told me I would have to bandage you."

"There was nothing wrong with your kissing," he said shortly, unable to bear her disappointment. "It was—pleasant."

"Oh," replied Minta in a very small voice. He called it "pleasant"? Then what she had felt, the thrill and wonder and delectableness—the world opening up and herself soaring above it—all that had only been her own experience? For Mr. Carlisle the kiss had been only, merely "pleasant," a word Minta applied to good weather or listening to Tyrone read aloud to the family.

"Oh," she said again.

But that was too much for Carlisle. He could see he had hurt her feelings, and he cursed himself even as he forged ahead. Because he must disappoint and hurt her. There was no other way. If he had learned anything about Miss Araminta Ellsworth, it was that she was a steadfast girl and loyal to a fault. If he told her he loved her and asked her to wait ten years for him, she would accept at once and think nothing of it.

But he would think of it. He would think of how she had everything to live for and everything to offer, and he had nothing but himself—family-less, penniless, possibly soon to be homeless, once Weeks took back Beaumond. Carlisle knew she wouldn't care about any of this, but because he loved her—*he loved her!*—he had to think of it for her.

Therefore he was business-like. Practical.

Cold, even.

He replaced the rest of the bandage roll and the pot of Blair's Balsam in his bag and buckled it. Then he deliberately took up the pencil and the knife and applied himself to the task of shaving the pencil to a point. All while she stood helplessly and watched.

"Did you...kiss me for no reason, then?" she ventured, when he still said nothing.

"Not for no reason." Taking the pencil, he resumed his seat and took up his notebook again. "I wanted to kiss you, so I did. Or did you think my brother was the only one to give in to such impulses?"

"I'm glad you had such an impulse," Minta replied stoutly. "I very much liked your kiss. If you—ever think it might be—pleasant—to kiss me again, I am perfectly willing."

Despite all—despite the tension that held him stiff and miserable—he felt a chuckle burst from him. "Whatever is to be done with you, Miss Ellsworth?"

She stalked across the room to take the chair beside him again. "I know I'm behaving shockingly, and I can only say in my defense that, if you were a different sort of person, I wouldn't say what I am about to say."

"Heavens. What are you about to say?"

"Just this: the whole time I was playing at liking your brother, I didn't like him at all. But, at that same time, when I pretended to like you, I found it required no effort, and that I liked you very much. I even told Aggie that—I liked you."

"Thank you." He was barely audible.

"And—I know you're poor and everything. And that you aren't thinking of marrying anyone, much less me, but I thought your proposal was—lovely. And, since you liked me in return well enough to kiss me, I—hope that when you do think of marrying—one day—you will take me into consideration."

"Miss Ellsworth, you sound like a candidate making a speech." But the jest was bitter on his lips, and he threw down the notebook. "What do you want me to say, then? That I love you? Very well. I love you."

Minta gasped, clapping her hands together. "You do? Oh!" She would have thrown her arms around him, only he looked furious and she didn't dare.

"Of course I do. Love your beauty and your naturalness and your artless frankness. I already told you I meant every word of that letter."

"How glad I am to hear you say it again! Then why do you look so unhappy about it?"

"Because there's nothing to be done. We can't marry on your fortune alone—"

"But we could, Mr. Carlisle!" cried Minta, bouncing on her chair in her excitement. "I've already thought of the solution. I was going to ask my brother Robert Fairchild how it might be arranged. You see, we could live on your little allowance and what you make as a doctor, when your apprenticeship is over, and whatever money Papa gives me we could just put aside, for the children, you know. We would live so modestly! I don't care a bit about big houses or wallpaper or furnishings or clothing or jewels, and I don't suspect you do either. So why would we let Papa's money prevent us being together?"

Carlisle was silent, struggling.

"I have your letter," she added threateningly. "If you won't see reason, I could use it. I could tell Robert I want to sue you for breach of promise."

"What would you take?" he scoffed. "My pocket watch? My medical bag?"

"Both, if I had to."

"You really are shameless."

"I have to be, now," she retorted. "Now that I know you love me, and you're just being obstinate and prideful and silly."

"Even if—your idea worked," he began, "you don't know what you're talking about. Even for just me and you to live on my meager earnings—I would have to save for years. It might be ten. I couldn't ask you to wait ten years."

"Five."

"What?"

"Ask me to wait five years, then."

"No!"

"I'm not as old as you, you know. I'm only eighteen. Ask me to wait five years."

"I will not."

"Four?"

"Araminta—"

"Nicholas—" She slipped her hand into his and rejoiced when his grip closed on it.

"Blast you," he grumbled, sighing and carrying her hand to his lips.

"And won't you kiss me again?" she asked. "I assure you I will get better with practice, so that it might become even better than pleasant."

He shook his head. "I hope not *much* more pleasant, or waiting so many years to marry you might be the sheerest kind of torture."

At that confession, she only smiled up at him, glowing with joy.

"You don't seem to understand. We will be very poor," he told her sternly. "Even in four years. Very, very, *very* poor."

"Hurrah!" shouted Minta. And then she wriggled her way onto his lap.

CHAPTER TWENTY-FIVE

Many a Doubt, many a Qualm,
overspread his clouded Imagination.
— John Arbuthnot, *An appendix to John Bull still in*
***his senses* (1712)**

Mrs. Simon Kenner was safely delivered of a little boy, later christened Edward John, after his grandfather and father, and there was much joy, though Beatrice remarked that, after so many years of so many girls in the family, there were now as many boys as girls.

"There are more boys," pointed out Tyrone, "if you count our cousins Benjamin and Austin."

But newsworthy as an addition to the family was, in the larger circles of Winchester gossip, little Edward Kenner's arrival was wholly eclipsed by other developments, namely Miss Araminta Ellsworth's engagement to impoverished almost-nobody Mr. Nicholas Carlisle, and the disappearance of Mr. Carlisle's brother Francis Taplin.

In chronological order, the announcement of Minta's engagement came first, coming some days after Edward's birth. She asked Mr. Carlisle if she might do it alone, that any Ellsworth expressions of surprise might be got through without his witness, and he agreed, if only she would tell him later their honest responses. "They will all be delighted after a minute," Minta declared.

However, to her chagrin, reactions were decidedly mixed.

Mr. Ellsworth beamed and blessed, as was his wont, but his wife said, "We like Mr. Carlisle very well, Minta, but such a long engagement—! Would it not be better to delay such a commitment on both your parts for a couple years?"

A couple years? How blithely older people could talk of *years*, when Araminta had lived so few of them. "But I won't change my mind, and neither will Nicholas, so why should we not be engaged? And I thought you approved of him, when he wrote his letter offering for me."

Mrs. Ellsworth shook her head helplessly. "When he wrote his letter, Minta, he spoke of a modest allowance from his uncle, which would just have made marriage possible, and even then he would have had to save for two years, but now—"

"Why don't you just get married in the spring?" asked Beatrice. "Papa will give you money enough."

"Indeed!" cried Mr. Ellsworth, holding up his hands as if he might call a shower of guineas down. "And you are both always welcome to live at Hollowgate. In fact, I would prefer it."

"Nicholas wants to support us himself, as much as he is able," she explained, shuddering to think how her intended would respond to being entirely supported and housed by his father-in-law.

"If that's so," spoke up her brother, "even after four years, he might only afford a tent on the Hollowgate lawn."

She rewarded him with a furious look. "I am most disappointed," she announced, "to find my family so mercenary—except you, Papa—and so lacking in faith toward such a good, hardworking, honest, kind man as Mr. Carlisle."

It was worse when Florence and her husband came for dinner.

"I understand Mr. Carlisle's reluctance in wanting to get engaged in the first place," said Florence, laying a fond hand over her husband's. "Robert felt very strongly that he did not want to come empty-handed to the match."

"And my prospects were admittedly more sound than Carlisle's," said her husband. He gave his wife's hand a squeeze. "No, Flossie, I don't think I would have dared speak up, had I only a precarious allowance from a father in financial difficulties and an apprenticeship to my name."

Minta could have shouted in frustration. "He himself is good as a gold mine," she insisted. "And Robert, I thought my money could be put in trust for any children we might have, and we would just get along with whatever he manages. That way there is no blow to his pride."

Fairchild considered as he took another sip of his wine. Then he shrugged. "That may be. For him. And I can certainly arrange it for you. I just know that I myself would still have balked. Heaven knows, if difficulties came, it would be all too easy to draw on that money. And then, if it was done once, each successive time would be easier, until at last you might as well have taken it for your own from the outset."

Yes, Minta could have shouted in frustration.

And even with the recent practice she had had, in pretending to be otherwise than she truly was, Carlisle was not fooled.

"I knew it," he said darkly, after she attempted to paint a picture of her family's joy in the event. They were walking together in the grounds in the late afternoon, his work done for the day. "I knew they would not approve. That they would think you were throwing yourself away."

"Not *throwing myself away*, Nicholas!" Minta protested, leaning on his arm. "They like you very well. It's the long engagement they mind—the precariousness of it all. But I prevailed."

But he drew away to pace up and down. "I talked to Beckford about compounding medicines not only for his patients, but for sale to other Hampshire doctors. Many of them send all the way to London now. I gained experience working for my uncle during the vacations. It would not be much, but it would be something."

"What a splendid idea! I'm sure Mr. Beckford thought so too." Though it was a sunny day, Minta swung her bonnet by its ribbons, and her gloves she had peeled off some time ago.

"Beckford observed that it would require considerable outlay at the beginning: the purchase of drugs and elements, equipment, jars, pots, bottles, labels, and such."

She yearned to tell him she would be glad to ask her father for this outlay, but she pressed her lips together, fidgeting with the effort this required.

"And therefore I have decided I will go to London again," Carlisle continued. "Not only to see my uncle's lawyers—there are matters to be settled, and I may as well do it in person as through correspondence—but also to see if there is anything left after the debts have been paid. Heaven knows my uncle's laboratory was bursting with everything I just enumerated. Anything still left would be useful."

"Yes," said Araminta, aware of a sensation of lowness. She let her bonnet drop to the grass. "That makes sense. How long might you be gone, Nicholas?"

"I can't say." He looked at her then, ruefully. She was trying so hard to be approving and enthusiastic, the beautiful, darling girl. It would not be a bad thing—a little distance between them. It had only been six days since they were engaged, and it was just as he suspected: how could he possibly endure this for four years? But, he thought, with a curl of his lip, if he was going to leave her for an indeterminate time, what was one more golden afternoon?

"You will write to me, I hope," he said, "when I know where I will be staying. Your charming, demanding letters."

At that, she closed the distance between them. "Oh, Nicholas, you don't mean to say you'll be gone that long! So long that I will have to write?"

"The post is rather speedy nowadays. Did you think I might only be away a few hours?"

"You know what I mean."

He pressed a kiss to her hair, but that didn't satisfy her, and she turned her face up toward him.

"You'll miss me a little, won't you?" she asked after a minute, pulling away, that they might catch their breath.

"A little."

"Very well. I won't miss you either."

"Come, then. Let's kiss on it."

But this was getting them nowhere, and after another interval and one last kiss, and then one more last kiss, and then a final, final last kiss, he took her by the shoulders and held her gently away. "I have to look for Francis, too, while I'm there."

"You think he might be in London?"

"Unless he's been pressed into the navy, I can't imagine he's gone anywhere else. Between Francis' disappearance and the mortgages looming over Beaumond, my stepfather is sleepless with anxiety. I must do what I can to relieve him."

"But Mr. Weeks won't press for the deeds to Beaumond, now that there is no danger of Aggie marrying your brother."

"The debts remain, however, and my stepfather fears that, wherever Francis has gone, he is adding to them."

"Oh, dear."

"Yes."

There seemed nothing more to be said on the matter, but Araminta heard herself blurt, "Nicholas—tell me—are you happy? Are you regretting engaging yourself to me?"

He didn't answer at once, and her heart sank somewhere about her ankles.

"I...wish you hadn't a penny," he said at last.

"I don't need to have a penny," Araminta insisted. "I will tell Papa and Mr. Fairchild to take my pennies and give them to everyone else."

"And what will that accomplish besides being another reason for me to think I have wronged you? It's nothing to do with *you*, Araminta, not you in yourself. You're everything I might have wished for, once I was standing on my own two feet." That rueful smile again. "But you—I seem unable to say no to you."

"Thank heaven for that," she returned roundly, relief flooding her. "For, if you didn't listen to me, you would make the terribly stupid decision to sacrifice our happiness to your pride."

"I know. If I could only be a little more like Francis, you are thinking. A little more comfortable taking what I want, where and when and from whom I want it."

"The only quality of your brother's I wish you shared was his tendency to seize any and all opportunities for kissing, be the young lady ever so unwilling. And this one is willing!" She threw her arms around him and turned a radiant countenance to his. "If you're going away, hadn't you better kiss me again?"

"Araminta, I believe if we do much more kissing, our lips might fall off."

"Who needs lips?"

"Or I might go further than I intended."

"That sounds thrilling!"

"My dear innocent." Reaching behind him, he unwound her arms, but he softened this withdrawal with a kiss to her forehead. And then one more.

"Write to me," he murmured.

And then he left her.

As for Mr. Francis Taplin, as Minta had foreseen, hardly had she sent her note rejecting him than he called upon Aggie at The Acres.

"I was determined to give him his opportunity," Aggie related, the day after the adventure took place. They were in Florence's walled garden, where they would not be disturbed. "And Papa relented, after I swore, hand on heart, that I would not give way or do anything foolish. So he let me out of my room and said I might be at liberty, within the bounds of the estate."

"That was risky of him," said Minta. She plucked one of the plums and hurled it at the brick wall, where it hit with a satisfying smack. "I know you swore, but suppose you succumbed, despite all, to Mr. Taplin's charms—or that he threw you over his shoulder and kidnapped you?"

"He could hardly do the latter, with his cracked ribs," Aggie replied practically. She picked her own plum and flung it, hitting directly below Minta's pulpy mark. "And, to be very honest, I did not know if I could trust myself. But Minta—maybe it helped to see that he bounced so quickly from you to me...He found me sitting on the broken wall of the abbey ruins where you and I used to play at the siege of Kenilworth Castle. He came up to me at once and took hold of my hand." She shut her eyes, remembering, and a sad smile played over her lips. "Then he said, 'Miss Agatha, since I first saw you, I have only had eyes for you.'"

With a start, Minta stared. Did Mr. Taplin have only one proposal he delivered to whoever could be made to listen? For that was how he had begun with her. She held her peace, however, picking more fruits and letting Aggie tell on.

"I'm not a fool, Minta. I took my hand away and asked him, if that was so, why had he just come from offering for you? And he told me it was done because he tried to please his family. He knew it was my papa who held the mortgages to Beaumond, and there would be no love lost if he offered for me, so he decided to—sacrifice himself to the family interests and propose to you."

A snort escaped Araminta here, but she masked it with a throat-clearing, followed by a sneeze.

"He said he was so relieved when you refused, since his heart was not in it. And he was overjoyed, too, because once he had failed in his attempt to marry you, he was free to follow his own wishes. He was free to ask me."

"I see," said Minta.

Aggie heaved a sigh. "I know you prefer Mr. Carlisle, but if you could have seen him, Minta, you might have changed your mind. Mr. Taplin is so dreadfully handsome. And he took my hand again—" she stood, acting the moment out "—and pressed it to his bosom and said, "I am asking you to be my wife, Miss Agatha, and I hope you will not keep me long in suspense, for my ardor grows from minute to minute.'"

At the same rate in which his creativity diminished, Minta thought wryly.

"Oh, Minta, for just an instant I wavered. It was so lovely to hear him say such things, even if he didn't mean them—or wouldn't mean them, if I weren't rich."

"Did he try to kiss you?" asked Minta.

"He didn't just try—he *did* kiss me." Aggie grinned wickedly. "And for just a second I kissed him back, and I liked it very much."

Minta turned her head so her skepticism wouldn't show. But maybe that was all it took to make a kiss agreeable: a liking for the person and a willingness to be kissed.

"And then I told him I would not keep him in suspense," Aggie concluded. "I said, 'Just as you tried to please your family, I want to please mine. And my Papa has told me that, if I were to marry you, he would not be well pleased and might even—disinherit me.'"

"What did Mr. Taplin say to that?"

"He asked if I thought Papa was in earnest, and I told him that, in matters of money, Papa is *always* in earnest, or how did he suppose Papa had got so wealthy?" She sighed again, and the fleeting delight the remembered kiss had given her faded. "So Mr. Taplin told me he understood and that he would never wish to alienate any girl he loved from her family; therefore we had better part as friends. And he kissed my hand and then—me—one more time and walked away. Oh, Minta! I watched him until I couldn't see him anymore. Tell me I didn't make a mistake. Even if he didn't truly love me, he might have come to love me in time."

Minta put an arm around her dearest friend and sat down with her on the stone bench. "If I believed Mr. Taplin the sort to feel deeply and to be won by worthiness and loyalty and affection, he could not have helped learning to love you. The fault never lay with you, Aggie."

"Didn't it?" asked Aggie, downcast. "Look at you: you decided you liked Mr. Carlisle, and lo and behold, he likes you back, and now you are engaged."

That is because Nicholas has a heart, Minta wanted to say. There being no answer she could say aloud, she merely hugged her friend.

They lingered in the garden, Minta trying to distract and cheer Aggie with games and races and talk of Lily's new baby, and she thought she succeeded a little. But when the sun sank in the western half of the sky, and Aggie decided she should be going, she said, "It will be awkward to see him again. At balls and in town and such. Especially when he begins to court someone else. Which he will. I don't know if I can do it, Minta—get over my affection for him, if I must see him constantly."

But that was a trial Aggie was to be spared. Because shortly after Mr. Taplin's ill-fated proposal to her, he vanished.

The news traveled like lightning, passed by the servants. How his valet Dawkins entered Taplin's chamber the following day to find the coverlet smooth and the wardrobe empty. No money was missing from the room because Taplin hadn't any to miss, but it was known soon enough at Beaumond that the family lockbox was nowhere to be found, and the master did not even trouble himself to line up the servants for questioning or the chance to fingerpoint.

Theories abounded. The dean's wife Mrs. Fellowes told her daughter Mrs. Wright that Mr. Francis Taplin must have gone into hiding from creditors. Mr. Weeks thought Mr. John Taplin must have instructed his son to absent himself for a time, in hopes "out of sight, out of mind" might apply to mortgagers. One of the Hollowgate tenant farmers claimed he saw the missing young man walking down Cock Lane one evening in his cups and peering into the Barracks, "thoughtful-like, as if he hankered after being a soldier and doing somewhat useful." Those not personally acquainted with any of the parties whispered that perhaps the impoverished stepbrother Mr. Nicholas Carlisle had murdered the favored son in a fit of jealousy and buried the body on the Beaumond grounds.

But the nine days' wonder passed, with no additional information surfacing and no sightings reported, so that, by the time Carlisle left for London, when those still interested declared that murder would out, and young Carlisle's conscience must have driven him to flee, most auditors met the pronouncement with little more than a shrug.

CHAPTER TWENTY-SIX

And the Lorde was with Joseph,
and he was a luckie felowe.
— **Genesis 39:21,** *Bible (Tyndale)* **(1530)**

Carlisle walked right past the former premises of B. Blair, Chemist & Druggist and was nearly to Birchin Lane before he realized his mistake. Stopping short, he turned on his heel and marched back. Well, no wonder. The plaque bearing its name was removed, the door locked and the shades drawn. He knocked and, when no one answered, rapped firmly on the windows.

Nothing.

The lawyers would have the key, of course, but Carlisle had hoped he might still set his bag down and save himself the cost of the hotel.

Setting his shoulders, he made his way to Lombard Street, imagining he would find the laboratory twimilarly locked and shuttered, but to his surprise, it was the scene of great bustle, the door open wide and burly men entering and exiting, arms full of exactly the equipment and furnishings and surplus materia medica Carlisle had hoped to claim.

No one challenged him when he made his way within, and he turned in a slow, dismayed circle, taking in the bareness of the space he had last seen crammed and overflowing.

A man carrying one end of his uncle's worktable backed into him, and Carlisle begged his pardon automatically.

"Mr. Carlisle?" From a far corner where he had been on his knees filling a box, Tribbet the errand boy leapt up. "Have you come back, then?"

"I have. What is happening here?"

"Packing up," said Tribbet.

"But where is everything being taken?"

"Just down the street and 'round the corner to Plough Court, sir."

"Plough Court!"

"That's right. Because it's all theirs now, as you know. And Jacobson and me, too, sir. Part and parcel." The boy stuck out his chest proudly, and Carlisle could hardly blame him, for, as chemists and druggists went, Plough Court was a much bigger affair than B. Blair had ever been.

"I—congratulate you, Tribbet," he said. "How glad I am to hear you and Jacobson have lighted on your legs."

Tribbet grinned. "That's right, sir. Like cats. And I'll be congratulating you, too."

Carlisle held very still, his dark eyes searching the boy's. Could he possibly know about his engagement to Araminta Ellsworth? Not wanting to say her name aloud with so many strangers about, he gave a bow of acknowledgement. "Thank you, Tribbet. I'm off to see my uncle's lawyers now. Give my regards to Jacobson."

"Very good, sir." Tribbet lifted his cap and made a comical little bow, leaving a bemused Carlisle to emerge into Lombard Street again and set his steps for Holborn.

Trot and Trimble occupied the first floor of a narrow building in a narrow corner of a dusty court, reached by a narrow staircase with little light. This second visit to the premises reminded Carlisle of the bustle and tumult of the days following his uncle's death, and he felt the depression of that period fall like a cloak once more upon his shoulders. Had Plough Court swooped in to buy the remains of B. Blair at a bargain price? Carlisle had given Trot and Trimble permission to settle the debts as they could, but he was bitterly disappointed all the same to find nothing would be left upon which to start his own small business in Winchester.

The withered clerk, whom Carlisle imagined had shriveled from being tucked away from sunlight for decades, raised a slow head when he entered, but the movement ended in a jerk.

"Mr. Carlisle! How is it that you are here? I thought surely you would not be able to attend the meeting because Dundas & Fulbright gave us little warning, and of course Mr. Osborne said nothing to us at all. I dispatched the letter to you at once, nonetheless."

"I'm afraid I have not the pleasure of understanding you," he replied, unable to append the clerk's name because he could not remember it. "What letter?"

"About the partnership!" cried the clerk, with a glance at the wall clock. "If you go now, sir, you will be only a few minutes late. Dundas & Fulbright are extremely punctual."

"But where on earth is Dundas & Fulbright?" demanded Carlisle, skipping over *who* on earth Dundas or Fulbright or Mr. Osborne might be.

The clerk was already reaching for his hat. "Come with me, sir. And leave your bag. It will be easier to show you than to tell you."

Therefore Carlisle found himself in the London streets again, actually having to lengthen his strides to keep up with the unexpectedly agile clerk. At such a speed, and with the clerk's knowledge of short cuts, they soon arrived at an imposing edifice with "Dundas & Fulbright" in large letters on the gleaming brass name plate. The Trot and Trimble clerk deemed his task complete, and he vanished after a quick bow, leaving Carlisle to ascend the steps alone.

An entire roomful of clerks looked up when he opened the door.

"Ah," he said. "I am here for the meeting between Trot and Trimble, Mr. Osborne, and Dundas & Fulbright."

"And you would be…?" asked the stiffest of the bunch, as if Carlisle had entered in rags, clutching a chimneysweep's brush.

"Nicholas Carlisle," he answered promptly. "Nephew of the late Bertram Blair."

"Oh!" The clerk's pomposity fled away, to be replaced (to Carlisle's amazement) with its groveling opposite. "Mr. Carlisle. We are honored to meet you. Do forgive us—we were told not to expect you. Will you kindly follow me, sir?"

He led Carlisle down the wide passage and, after giving a discreet knock at the door on the end, ushered him in with a dramatic, "Mr. Nicholas Carlisle."

Seven men rose from their seats around the large mahogany table, and of them Carlisle recognized only Mr. Trot and Mr. Trimble, looking like elderly children invited at the last minute to a royal birthday party. The others, who regarded him measuringly as they made their bows and spoke their names, were quietly dressed, but Carlisle did not miss their superb tailoring or the fineness of the few pocket watches which had been laid upon the table.

"Another chair, Brinsley," ordered the man who had introduced himself as Simon Dundas, sending the clerk scuttling away. When he returned, the chair was placed between Mr. Trot and the man called Osborne, and Carlisle took his seat.

"Messieurs Trot and Trimble told us not to expect you," Mr. Dundas said.

"Yes," answered Carlisle. "I understand a letter was posted to summon me, which must have crossed while I was already en route to town. Therefore, if I might have a brief summary of the business...?"

Mr. Dundas tented his fingers, nodding. Carlisle realized now that the gentlemen of Dundas & Fulbright were arrayed all along one side of the table. Did that mean they were in opposition to his interests? And where did Osborne fall, seated on the Trot and Trimble side?

"If you will allow me," spoke up Osborne, a tall and distinguished man in perhaps his early forties, and such was his importance that Dundas yielded the floor immediately. Osborne turned in his chair to address Carlisle. "We have not met before, Mr. Carlisle, but I had the pleasure of representing your uncle Bertram Blair in his dealings with Plough Court, who are represented in turn by the firm of Dundas & Fulbright."

"He—never told me of you," said Carlisle, "though I will be the first to say I was not privy to all aspects of his business. I knew of Messieurs Trot and Trimble, of course—"

"My esteemed colleagues Trot and Trimble," Osborne said with a nod that caused the latter to shrink in their seats like naughty schoolboys, "were entrusted with Mr. Blair's ordinary law needs—his will, contracts with petty suppliers, contracts with creditors, and so forth. But for his more ambitious endeavors, he retained me."

"Unbeknownst to us," squeaked Trimble, apologetically.

"That is," went on Osborne, not deigning to acknowledge the interruption, "when the Royal Navy approached Mr. Blair regarding his Blair's Balsam, he in turn approached me, entrusting my firm with negotiations of the all-important contract and any subsequent partnerships Mr. Blair would require in order to meet the terms of said contract. Furthermore, Mr. Blair thought it fit to deposit the recipe for the balsam with Osborne and Osborne."

Carlisle stared. "*You* have the recipe?"

"Osborne and Osborne received the recipe into our safekeeping, yes."

The chair in which he sat had no arms, and Carlisle was forced to grip his kneecaps as he absorbed this news. The recipe was not lost. The naval contract could yet be fulfilled.

"On the day of your uncle's death, he had just come from this very office, where we executed a partnership contract with Plough Court, a much larger druggist and chemist firm—"

"I know of Plough Court," said Carlisle in a low voice. His pulse sped, and he felt his color rising. Then *this* was the reason for Tribbet's congratulations, and not Carlisle's engagement to Miss Araminta Ellsworth. And yet—and yet one of them would lead—please God—inexorably to the early fulfillment of the other.

"Good," rejoined Osborne. "I need not explain then that Plough Court has both the laboratory facilities and the supplier system to manufacture the balsam in quantities the navy demands. And Mr. Blair—or should I say, Mr. Blair's *heir*—holds the exclusive right to the recipe."

"We were going to present Mr. Osborne with two possibilities," Dundas said, with an apologetic nod for interjecting when the great man might not yet be done speaking, "which he in turn would present to *you*, Mr. Carlisle, regarding how to proceed. You are presently a partner of Plough Court, which entitles you to half of the profits of the five-year contract as they are received, to be paid out quarterly. This also entitles you to sit on the company's board, with one vote on general business matters and votes equal to half the board on matters pertaining to the specific product's manufacture, distribution, advertisement, and possible expansion of markets. To remain in this position of partnership is the first option."

Carlisle's head was spinning. Such a sudden elevation alarmed him as much as it exhilarated. What did he know of "business matters," to hold such power? Suppose he were to make the wrong decisions, bringing not only his uncle's legacy but Plough Court as well down about his ears? Moreover, if he were to try to make wise decisions, he must necessarily deepen and extend his knowledge of the business, an undertaking that would surely entail his frequent presence in London, if not his outright residence. *That,* he knew already, could not be.

"The second possibility," Dundas continued, "would be for Plough Court to buy you out of your partnership, Mr. Carlisle. This would require a significant amount of capital, as Mr. Osborne has calculated, and Plough Court would not be able to do it in one blow. Rather, the contract would begin with one larger payment, and then the remainder of your share would be re-purchased in quarterly installments over the five-year life of the contract, with the possibility of extension if the naval contract is in turn extended. In return, you would relinquish all rights immediately to the balsam recipe and the balsam's manufacture, distribution, advertisement, and possible expansion of markets, to Plough Court. In addition, the name 'Blair's Balsam' would belong to Plough Court. Mr. Osborne can give you the exact figures, but this is the essence."

Let it be £600 per annum to buy me out, prayed Carlisle. If it were so, he could marry Araminta in two years, as he had originally proposed in his letter. Possibly sooner, depending on the size of the "larger" first payment.

Aloud he said, "I understand."

Osborne consulted a paper in the portfolio before him, but Carlisle suspected it was a theatrical gesture, for he too soon replaced it and folded his hands together. "The amounts of the second option would be slightly greater because Plough Court pays you not only your percentage of the naval contract, but also to stay out of their business, as it were. In the second option, however, you give up that power to direct the present and future of your uncle's balsam, and, if the navy contract is not extended or renewed, all payments from Plough Court end at that contract's termination."

"I understand," said Carlisle again.

Osborne cleared his throat. "Very well. I will write these up for you, but in brief, the first option would be half of the five-year naval contract, paid out quarterly. The total contract being for £10,000, half that then being £5000 over five years, or £1000 per annum, or £250 per quarter. The sharing of any additional revenues brought in by the balsam from other markets and contracts would be negotiated separately."

To this Carlisle said nothing, inwardly marveling at the size of the figures named.

"In the second option," Osborne resumed, "Plough Court offers to pay you £8000 over five years, with an initial larger payment of £3000 when the recipe is turned over to them, followed by quarterly installments of £250, ending with the termination of the naval contract and being re-negotiated if that contract is extended or renewed."

Three thousand pounds.

There would be lawyers' fees, but say £2900 was left. He might marry Araminta as soon as they had somewhere to repair to. If Mr. Weeks insisted on foreclosing on Beaumond, his stepfather could be housed somewhere as well, but if Mr. Weeks did not, perhaps a downpayment on what was owed would put him off. And then five years of £250 per quarter! At the end of five years there might be children, but there would also be his own medical practice and possibly the making of medicines, as he had proposed. Carlisle could not believe his luck. He shut his eyes briefly, thanking heaven and his uncle Bertram for this unforeseen bounty. Then he said to Osborne: "Thank you. If you will give me that in writing, I can advise all of my decision shortly."

But Osborne was no Trot and Trimble. He opened his portfolio again and slid a paper to Carlisle.

"Thank you." Carlisle folded it without a glance and tucked it away in his coat.

"Where can you be reached, Mr. Carlisle?" asked Trot.

Carlisle shrugged. If he had been his brother Francis, he would have named the most expensive hotel in London. But he was not. "Better say the Swan with Two Necks. I won't be long in town."

He did allow himself one indulgence, however, one outlet for his soaring spirits. Hiring a hackney coach to take him to the West End, he alighted at Sackville Street in Piccadilly, there to visit the premises of the famed Thomas Gray, jeweller to the royal family and seller of "Fancy Articles in Diamonds, precious Stones, Pearls, Gold, Silver, Steel, &c." While Carlisle knew his bride was not one to deck herself with jewels, and while he suspected bracelets and necklaces and chatelaines and tiaras would sit admired and unworn in her jewel box (if she even had a jewel box), he could not resist the urge to buy her a wedding gift worthy of his love for her. Let Osborne think he was extravagant when he saw the bill, but Carlisle had never in his life had the means to make such a gesture. He chose an old-fashioned jasperware brooch, an allusion to their first meeting, a female archer in relief against the meadow-green stoneware—and directed the clerk to send the bill to the attorney.

Satisfied with his purchase and with the world entire, he was on the point of leaving the glittering shop when he paused to let a couple enter. The woman caught his eye first. She was queenly and beautiful, though her flawless features knew the benefit of paint, he suspected, and there was a hardness to her bright blue eyes, which swept past him with indifference. But when his own gaze moved to her companion, he found the man gaping at him, astonishment even then metamorphosing into laughter.

"Nick!" cried his brother Francis. "Whatever can you be doing here?"

"What am *I* doing here?" retorted Carlisle, finding his hand grasped and shaken heartily. "You disappear without a word, and you ask me what I am doing in London?"

"Ah," Taplin waved this concern away with a lazy hand. "What was there to be said? I could not bear to be buried in the country any longer, made by my father to chase after each and every purse which crossed my path. Not when my mind and heart were elsewhere." With a grin, he drew his lovely companion forward. "This may not be how things are done, Nick, but may I introduce you to Betsy? Betsy, this is my brother Nicholas Carlisle."

"How do you do, Miss—" Carlisle made his bow.

"Clarke. But not like the Miss Clarkes you've known, most likely," she shrugged.

Taplin gave her a little push. "You run along, Bets, and have a look around. See what you think the most honorable the marquess would like to be invoiced for next. My brother and I will have a little chat."

"I don't understand," said Carlisle, watching the departing Betsy.

"Don't you? I've gone back to Betsy, is all."

"Your former—lady love?"

"That's it. She adores me, you know, and sent a number of ill-spelt letters attesting to the fact while I was away."

"But Francis—how are you living? Do you intend your father to support you in this?"

Taplin gave a chuckle. "I dug the old man in deep enough already, wouldn't you say? With me gone he has a chance of unburying himself, if Weeks will let him."

"Then how—"

"It's simple, dear boy. I live off Betsy, and Betsy lives off the marquess. She is his kept woman, and I am her kept man. Though that last bit must be a secret a few months longer."

Nonplussed, it took Carlisle a minute to understand this. "But—supposing the marquess finds out and objects? Or that he grows tired of her?"

Taplin gestured at their surroundings. "You see us planning for that very eventuality. We are making hay whilst the sun shines, brother. And there will always be a little sunshine because Betsy is with child and his lordship's man of business has already arranged an allowance to begin when the babe is born and to continue until the child reaches his majority."

"Francis."

"Now, now, don't shake your head at me. You may spare me any sermons."

"It won't be a sermon, but—is this the life you want to live?"

Taplin's handsome face distorted in derision. "Is it so very different from the life my father proposed? Here at least I have money enough, entertainment enough, but I need not play the hypocrite. Betsy and I suit each other—for the present. Let tomorrow take care of itself."

"Oh, Francis." But Carlisle gave one nod. "May I at least tell your father where you are?"

"If you like."

"I wish I might tell the whole world. There is a school of thought in Winchester, I'll have you know, that whispers I have done away with you in a paroxysm of uncontrolled jealousy."

"Why, that's delightful!" exclaimed Taplin, genuinely amused. "Better even than the truth. But now you must tell me what brings *you* to town and to such a place as Gray's."

Carlisle gave him a brief summary and was not surprised to see his brother's eyes light up. "You will take the partnership, of course. It will pay longer and better, and then you might live in town and abandon that nonsense about becoming a country doctor. You might even make me a loan or a gift, from time to time, out of your abundant and increasing wealth."

"I'm sorry to disappoint you, but I plan on letting them buy me out. Miss Ellsworth has accepted my proposal, you see, and neither one of us would like to live in London."

"Ah, the strapping Miss Ellsworth. Better you than me, Nick. That girl would be the death of me—too strong and clumsy. And her dreadful tittering!"

"Did you not like it?" asked Carlisle, a grin tugging at his mouth. "It's music to my ears."

"Well, good-bye for now, Nick. I may still ask a loan of you, in future, but I will reduce my proposed amount to suit your reduced circumstances. Best of luck to you."

"Where can I reach you?"

"You can always write to me care of the Bedford Coffee House, if need arise."

"All right, then. And, Francis, I'll keep an eye on your father."

Something flitted across his brother's face and was gone the next moment. But he grasped Carlisle's shoulder for a second.

"Don't you mean *our* father?"

And then he turned away.

Chapter
Twenty-Seven

He will in Mercy yet return, Tho' now he hides his Face.
— S. Harrison, *Songs in Night* (1780)

"He is not going to marry me," Araminta told her reflection calmly. She lay her brush down upon the table and absently braided her thick and waving hair into a messy plait, from which whole strands were left out. Then she climbed into her bed and blew out the candle.

What else could explain his long silence? His long absence could be excused: he was still searching for his brother Mr. Taplin. But his long silence? He had asked her to write to him in London, but how could she, when he did not write to her first? He had not even told her where he might be staying, and it was too humiliating to think of dragging herself to Beaumond to ask his stepfather where her intended husband might be found. Too humiliating and perhaps too painful a question, considering Mr. John Taplin's other son was truly missing.

"He did not find what he hoped to find in London," she told the ceiling in the darkness, "and therefore he will not be able to pursue his idea of making medicines. Which means he sees no way of marrying me before so many years have passed, which means in turn that he wishes I had not forced his hand."

But she *had* forced his hand, and now he felt trapped. Doomed.

"I'll let him go," she announced, rolling onto her side and burying her face in the pillow so that no telltale tear would trickle down her cheek. "I'll tell him I release him. I can't bear to watch him be miserable. And I'll tell him we are both free, so that he will not feel guilty. And then I'll just wait for him. We won't be engaged anymore—not officially—but I will wait for him all the same. It's no terrible hardship. If he had not come along, I would likely not even be thinking of marrying for *ages*. That's what I keep trying to tell him. What do I care about waiting four years? I'm only eighteen. Well—almost nineteen, but not old enough to worry about marrying. Flossie and Lily weren't married at my age."

When she woke up it was still dark. "It's too bad you can't kiss gentlemen you aren't engaged to," she said then, as if sleep had not interrupted her thoughts. "Perhaps I can inveigle him under some mistletoe every Christmas season, so that he has to kiss me once a year." That was a comforting idea. Not nearly as pleasant as kissing him every day, several times each day, but better than never kissing him again for years and years.

The next time she woke, light leaked in through the shutters, and Monk was bustling in, humming. Seeing Minta's hair, the maid sighed heavily. "Come on, then." At least she had finished the alterations to the girl's new dresses, and they had not had time to accumulate holes and tears and stains. But no sooner did Monk congratulate herself on this than Minta said, "I think I'll see if Aggie feels like shooting today."

"Guns or arrows?" asked the maid resignedly.

"Arrows, to be sure. It's been forever since Aggie and I shot anything. We could set up a row of apples on the garden wall."

"And kill poor Mr. Barney while you're at it."

But the gardener was not destined to lose his life that day, even if he had not learned over the many years to give Miss Araminta and her chosen targets a wide berth. For while she listlessly stirred more sugar into her porridge at breakfast, Bobbins entered and said the words she had, after ten long days, given up hope of hearing: "Letter for you, miss."

Tearing it open at the table with such vigor that she then had to hold the two torn pieces together to read it, she found only a few words: "My dear Araminta, the coach from London is due to arrive in Winchester by noon. I will call as soon as I walk in from the George. Yours, Nicholas."

"Hurrah!" she shouted, sending Snap into a frenzy of barking and her younger brother into bouncing and hallooing in his chair.

"Mr. Carlisle returning?" asked Tyrone mildly, while Mrs. Ellsworth tried to restore order.

"Yes! How do I look Bea?"

"Like your usual self," said her sister with approval.

"Mr. Carlisle will be here a little after noon, perhaps. I was going to invite Aggie to shoot with me, but I don't want to be all sweaty when I see him."

"Good thinking," said Tyrone, propping his book up again.

"I'll read, too," she decided.

But she was much too excited to read and ended in popping up every minute or so to peer from the window or even to walk a ways up the drive toward the Romsey Road. At last her stepmother advised her to take Snap on his lead if she could not sit still, and Araminta was glad of the excuse. But even Snap made her impatient. He was not as young and spry as he used to be, so he walked more slowly, and he had grown more obstinate when he wanted to sniff at something.

"Fine, then," she told him, letting his lead drop. "You walk yourself, and serve you right if one of the under-gardeners knocks you over the head with a rake."

But as soon as the words left her mouth, Snap lifted his head contrarily and dashed away, barking. And when Minta looked after him, she saw Mr. Carlisle approaching.

"Nicholas!"

She was flying, and Carlisle dropped his bag and began to run, and then they were in each other's arms, and he picked her up and swung her around as if she weighed no more than a feather, giving her a sound kiss when he put her down.

"Oh, Nicholas—I didn't hear from you, and I thought you didn't want to be engaged to me anymore."

"I didn't."

"Why, you cruel man!" she scolded, before he silenced her again with a longer kiss, a gentler one.

"I didn't want to be engaged to you anymore," he began again, "and certainly not for four endless years. I wanted to be married to you."

"Oh...that's all right, then. But why didn't you write to me?"

"Because what I had to say I wanted to say in person, and I couldn't get away any sooner. There were meetings and papers to be signed. So many meetings and papers."

"All that for some leftover laboratory equipment?"

"It was a bit more than that."

"Oh, good. Then your new business will be well supplied," she said with satisfaction. "And did you have any luck finding your brother?"

"I did. He's in London, as I thought, and has no intention of coming back to Winchester. He has taken up with his former mistress, and the two of them seem to be hoodwinking some lord into supporting them. Not that you may say a word of that to anyone."

"Oh! But Nicholas, what will you tell people?"

Carlisle grinned. "That he's a gambler. It's true enough. Nor do I imagine I've seen the last of him. He even said he would come to me for a loan at some point."

"A loan," laughed Minta, poking him. "Of what? Your pocket watch? Your medical bag?" It was a joy to tease him, and she was fairly dancing in a circle around him.

He caught hold of her hand and pulled her back to him. "I hope you didn't want to marry me for my lack of money, Miss Ellsworth."

She was suddenly still. "Why would you hope that?"

"And I hope you weren't counting on having four long years to learn to sew, that you might make your trousseau."

"My sewing is very bad, you know," she whispered. "Mrs. Turcotte said everything I stitched would only be wanted by the rag-collector. Therefore I had better have the four years, Nicholas."

He was shaking his head slowly but still smiling. "Then I am sorry to disappoint you. On both counts."

"What do you mean? No more mystery! Tell me at once!"

"I'm asking you to marry me again, Araminta. But this time I want to do it my way, on my own terms." He dropped carefully to one knee in the grass bordering the gravel drive. "Miss Araminta Ellsworth, I haven't much family to offer you or an ancient name to give you—"

"Yes—I say yes. I already said yes. You know I don't care about any of that—"

"Shhhh." He reached up and lay a finger to her lips. "But I do have a draft for more than £2800 in my pocket and at least five years' worth of quarterly payments of £250 pounds to look forward to, if you will have me, but I'm afraid I must insist on you having me very soon."

Her eyes grew round with wonder, and her mouth fell open when he named the sums. Not a sound emerged.

Chuckling, he pushed up her chin to close her mouth. "What would Mrs. Turcotte say, if she saw you?"

"Confound old Turcotte!" Minta replied, but without any vehemence. "Where does this money come from, Nicholas? Did you rob the Bank of England?"

"I won't tell you until you answer me."

"Yes! *Yes!* Yes, I will still marry you, and soon, Nicholas. I am just amazed."

"Then seal your promise with a kiss," he commanded, rising.

She did so, but it was nothing more than a short peck. "Tell me."

When he leaned in to reclaim her lips, she darted away. "Kissing is all well and good, but I will burst with curiosity if you do not tell me what happened."

"Fine. I will explain. But only if you come back." He pointed peremptorily at a spot in the gravel, and she hastened to it. And then he did tell her everything, though she did not catch every word at first for his lips persisted in traveling along her jaw to the tender spot below her ear and on down her neck as he spoke, and it thus took much longer to be understood than it needed to. But at last the story was told, the questions asked and answered, and the sight of several under-gardeners emerging around the side of the house served to make them more circumspect.

An hour later found them hand in hand, still walking together through the Hollowgate grounds and building their castles in the air, his bag forgotten, the dog forgotten. And the late summer sun shone down upon the lovers in benediction, as if the season and, indeed, all creation shared their joy.

The adventures of the Ellsworth Assortment continue with Tyrone's story in *A Scholarly Pursuit.*

THE HAPGOODS OF BRAMLEIGH

The Naturalist
A Very Plain Young Man
School for Love
Matchless Margaret
The Purloined Portrait
A Fickle Fortune

THE ELLSWORTH ASSORTMENT

Tempted by Folly
The Belle of Winchester
Minta in Spite of Herself
A Scholarly Pursuit
Miranda at Heart
A Capital Arrangement

PRIDE AND PRESTON LIN

www.christinadudley.com

9 781963 408089